GLADYS MITCHELL

Gladys Maude Winifred Mitchell – or 'The Great Gladys' as Philip Larkin described her – was born in 1901, in Cowley in Oxfordshire. She graduated in history from University College London and in 1921 began her long career as a teacher. She studied the works of Sigmund Freud and attributed her interest in witchcraft to the influence of her friend, the detective novelist Helen Simpson.

Her first novel, *Speedy Death*, was published in 1929 and introduced readers to Beatrice Adela Lestrange Bradley, the heroine of a further sixty-six crime novels. She wrote at least one novel a year throughout her career and was an early member of the Detection Club along with G. K. Chesterton, Agatha Christie and Dorothy Sayers. In 1961 she retired from teaching and, from her home in Dorset, continued to write, receiving the Crime Writers' Association Silver Dagger Award in 1976. Gladys Mitchell died in 1983.

VINTAGE MURDER MYSTERIES

With the sign of a human skull upon its back and a melancholy shriek emitted when disturbed, the Death's Head Hawkmoth has for centuries been a bringer of doom and an omen of death – which is why we chose it as the emblem for our Vintage Murder Mysteries.

Some say that its appearance in King George III's bedchamber pushed him into madness. Others believe that should its wings extinguish a candle by night, those nearby will be cursed with blindness. Indeed its very name, *Acherontia atropos*, delves into the most sinister realms of Greek mythology: Acheron, the River of Pain in the underworld, and Atropos, the Fate charged with severing the thread of life.

The perfect companion, then, for our Vintage Murder Mysteries sleuths, for whom sinister occurrences are never far away and murder is always just around the corner . . .

GLADYS MITCHELL

Death Comes at Christmas

VINTAGE

3 5 7 9 10 8 6 4 2

Vintage
20 Vauxhall Bridge Road,
London SW1V 2SA

Vintage is part of the Penguin Random House group of companies
whose addresses can be found at global.penguinrandomhouse.com

Penguin
Random House
UK

This edition published in Vintage in 2019
First published in Vintage in 2014 with the title *Dead Men's Morris*
First published in hardback by Michael Joseph Ltd in 1936 with the
title *Dead Men's Morris*

penguin.co.uk/vintage

A CIP catalogue record for this book is available from the British Library

ISBN 9781529110920

Printed and bound in Great Britain by Clays Ltd, Elcograf S.p.A.

Penguin Random House is committed to a sustainable future
for our business, our readers and our planet. This book is made
from Forest Stewardship Council® certified paper.

First Figure

FOSSDER'S FOLLY

He is going to call on his lawyer.
Va a ver su abogado.
I advise you not to say anything about it.
Le aconsejo a Vd. que no diga nada de ello.

HUGO'S 'SPANISH CONVERSATION SIMPLIFIED'

CHAPTER 1

Once to Yourself at Stanton St John

'Gently, my man, gently,' said Sir Selby Villiers.

'Ease your end a bit, George,' said Mrs Bradley.

'Arf a mo, mate,' said the vanman.

'Another couple of inches, buddy,' said George. The boar's head, carefully packed, came to rest on the luggage grid of Mrs Bradley's car and was strapped into place. George and the vanman tested the straps and Sir Selby handed Mrs Bradley in.

'A Happy Christmas,' he said.

'A Happy Christmas,' said Mrs Bradley.

'A Happy Christmas, George,' said Sir Selby, giving him ten shillings.

'Thank you very much, sir. The same to you,' said George, saluting before he took his place at the wheel.

'That's it, then, mam,' said the vanman.

'A Happy Christmas,' said Mrs Bradley, tipping him; and in an aura of general goodwill she drove off in the direction of the Great West Road.

The car, not new, but of impeccable behaviour, slid through Hammersmith and Chiswick, took a right incline on to the Great West Road at Gunnersbury, and was soon leaving it again for the Bath Road at Hounslow. George went slowly through Colnbrook and Maidenhead, crawled through Henley, then struck a modest and respectable twenty-eight miles an hour for the greater part of the remainder of the journey. By Headington Quarry he found a secondary road and a right-hand branch to the northern end of the village of Stanton St John. The time was half past three. It was daylight still, but hinting of dusk to come.

George stopped the car at the first public house, went up to the door and hammered for the innkeeper. Evoking no response, for it was during closing hours, he found the way round to the back to discover the innkeeper, his wife and son plucking and trussing fowls.

'Good day,' said George. 'Where's Mr Lestrange's farm, if you'll oblige?'

'You're welcome,' said the innkeeper. He put his reeking hands into a bucket of rainwater, and dried them on the apron he was wearing.

'Pretty cold job?' said George, as they walked out on to the road. The innkeeper laughed.

'Ah. Not so bad this Christmas as some I could tell ee of. We got no runnen water endoors round this part, you see. Now, Mr Lestrange? That ud be the party as keeps pigs and paints them pictures. The Old Farm, that's what ee wants to ask for. You'll need to turn the car. Bear left when you comes to the church, and then get down at the post office and ask 'em to guide ee from there. I'll back I'll only mizzle ee if I tries to direct ee from 'ere.' He smiled at Mrs Bradley. 'Good day to ee, mam. Nice weather we be haven, but onseasonable.'

George turned the car and took the narrow opening by the long grey churchyard wall. The car crept down the road and bore to the left past a very small farmyard and then beside cottages. The post office was a small brick house, lettered unmistakably above its plain sash window, and appearing uncouth and ugly in that land of benign grey stone.

The post mistress came out on to the road to direct them.

'Straight on past where the brook babbles – hear et all night, ee well, tell ee gets used to et, mam, I say – and then ee'll be see-en that there old cart-road on the right. Egypt Lane we calls 'er – I dunno for why. Turn up there, and you be right beside the 'ouse.'

4

They proceeded fairly slowly down the long and gradual gradient for about two miles and a half, and came at length upon a narrow track, grass-grown and wheel-rutted, which diverged to an angle of about forty degrees from the road. It appeared to run past a house (which they could see behind elm trees), and into a tiny wood.

George stopped the car and got down.

'I'm very sorry, madam, but I'm of opinion that I overlooked the turning coming along. I think we've come too far.'

'Too bad,' said Mrs Bradley sympathetically. She lowered the window further and put out her head. George moved aside politely. 'It doesn't seem to tally with the description we were given, certainly,' she said, 'and – George, there's a fight going on! Let's go and join in!'

'I really wouldn't advise it, madam,' said George, alarmed. 'You remember in Spain that time –'

'Nonsense!' said Mrs Bradley. She opened the door for herself, since the chauffeur seemed indisposed to assist her, and set out at a brisk, short-striding run across the fields. George tossed his cap inside the car, and, sadly incommoded by his leggings, trotted, like a faithful hound, a respectful couple of paces in the rear.

It was getting dark, but Mrs Bradley's old, long-sighted eyes had not misled her. Outside a pigsty, in the field adjoining the house, an old man and a young one were fighting furiously. The old man had a walking-stick, a heavy ugly blackthorn. The younger man had a pig-bucket in his hand. He was using it as a shield against the blackthorn, and at the same time he remonstrated with the old man loudly and angrily. It was obvious which was the aggressor, and Mrs Bradley, standing ten yards off, could not sufficiently admire the scientific defence which the pig-bucket was putting up against the heavy stick. Blow after blow clanged harshly on the bucket as the young man side-stepped, with considerable adroitness, every murderous advance. Suddenly the old man perceived Mrs Bradley and George, and swung round viciously towards them.

'You be trapesing yere!' he announced, as he lowered the black-thorn. 'What do ee warnt on my land?'

'Peace, peace,' said Mrs Bradley sonorously.

'Then you be crazy,' said the old man, raising the stick again. 'Be off, before I catch ee one or two!'

George stepped in front of his employer, but Mrs Bradley pushed him out of the way.

'I also want my nephew, Carey Lestrange,' she added, gazing with the impersonal interest of a replete and basking alligator at the fermenting little old man. His knuckles were white with the grip he had of the stick.

'Carey Lestrange?' said the young man, coming forward, and now standing unconcernedly within easy reach of the blackthorn. He put down the pail, and jerked his thumb westwards. 'He lives at Old Farm, not here. This place is called Roman Ending.'

He was a strongly-built, uncouth and brutal-looking youth, and in his appearance there was something which seemed familiar to Mrs Bradley.

'But I've certainly never seen him before,' she thought, as she looked him over. 'George –' she said.

'The Holbein portrait of his grace King Henry the Eighth, madam,' George responded politely.

'Good heavens, George!' said Mrs Bradley, impressed. Enlightened, she resumed her scrutiny. Certainly in the heavy jowl and little pig-cyes before her there was more than a suggestion of the portrait.

The old man was like a crab-apple. He took a step forward, returned Mrs Bradley's gaze with a stare of hatred, and said,

'You've come past the turning. Didn't ee 'ave enough sense to ask the way?'

'Sure,' said George, planting his gaitered legs apart and eyeing the old man coldly.

'Be ee a fool, then?' demanded the crab-apple, shaking the blackthorn at him.

'Yes,' said George, 'but I can keep my language civil, which is more than you can do. And,' he added, 'if this here chap wants any help in rolling you into a ditch, he can count on me for a start. How's that, you old gooseflesh, you!'

'Now, now,' said Mrs Bradley, with a cackle. 'Don't be belligerent, George. It doesn't become those leggings. Direct us, please,' she said to the younger man.

'Back on to the road again, go down hill a bit until you come to a forked road just this side of where the brook turns off –'

'Ah, yes, the babbling brook,' said Mrs Bradley reminiscently, thinking of the woman in the post office.

'Then up the hill,' the young man added, 'and from this side you'll see the house. It stands out grey on the other side of that little wood over there. I shouldn't think you could miss it. Lestrange is a friend of ours. Get him to bring you over. Glad to see you again.'

To Mrs Bradley's surprise the old man seconded this invitation, although in curmudgeonly fashion.

'Ah, come again. Do ee good, perhaps, to see pigs reared up proper. Him with his new-fangled notions! Scandinavian nonsense! Give me some honest British bacon, that's what I be always saying to him. But come again! Oh, ah! Ee may as well.' He turned to the younger man. 'This 'ere's my nevvy. Not much to look at, and the gals don't like him neether, but he'll have my money when I'm gone, and the right to do as he likes with what'll be all his own. Good day to ee. Ah, and a Merry Christmas, I suppose I did ought to wish ee, and so I do, and good reddance, too and all!' he added suddenly, with a squeal of rage at the end.

'Thank you. The same to you,' said Mrs Bradley. 'I shall look forward to our better acquaintance, Mr –'

'Simith. This is Tombley. George William Tombley.' He shot a sour smile at his nephew.

'Geraint Wilfred Tombley,' said the young man, in a very surly tone. 'Christened so in Cowley church twenty-six years ago this coming February.'

Mrs Bradley and George walked slowly back to the car.

'It's cold, George,' said Mrs Bradley. George looked up at the sky.

'Preparing for snow, I should fancy, madam,' said he, 'and coming on very dark.' He assisted her over a stile. 'And the countryside pleasant, but *old*, madam, if you kind of know what I mean.'

'Perfectly, George,' said Mrs Bradley calmly. 'Thor and Odin, and the sleeping Charlemagne.'

'Well, no, madam; older than that; gentler, if I may express it so, and rather more subtle, madam, it seems to me; but, of course, I'm London born, and shall never get used to the country. And yet it's a pleasant landscape. Very pleasant indeed. But the hills, madam, like the leviathans of Creation. Rounded and, somehow, squamous, madam, I feel.'

'Squamous, omnipotent and kind,' said Mrs Bradley absently. 'You want a drink, George. You deserve one. You shall have one when we arrive.'

'Thank you, madam,' said George.

Carey Lestrange, Mrs Bradley's first husband's nephew, was a grey-eyed young man in flannel trousers so thick as to give the impression at first sight that he was wearing bearskin leggings. He also sported a bright blue pullover and a very old tweed jacket with sagging pockets and a disreputable air of having been slept in. He had long, well-shaped, nicotine-stained fingers, and the becoming affection of an elf-lock, which had been trained, Mrs Bradley suspected, to fall artistically into his eye. At any rate, his habit of removing it with a picturesque motion of the hand came, she felt certain, under the general heading of Learned Behaviour; no impatience was betrayed, rather a sense of the value of significant gesture, as the young man with his paint-stained, grubby hand negligently shifted the elf-lock an inch to the side each time it fell out of place.

'Dear Carey,' said Mrs Bradley, squeezing his arm. She had the extreme felicity to be fond of all her relatives. Some of them, it is true, amused, and others irritated her, but she liked to be stimulated, and had the enviable faculties of impersonal observation and objective thought, so that she was seldom inconvenienced by having to dislike people or over-excited by feeling angry with them. For Carey she felt both personal regard and respect. He had nearly all the qualities which had endeared her first husband to her, and was, like his uncle, very hardworking, and, in spite of his lackadaisical appearance and habits, an excellent man of business. He not only ran an experimental piggery but painted posters, and, occasionally, pictures. He might, in fact, have made a name for himself as a portrait painter, but that he was fastidious on the subject of sitters. He would rarely paint women, for example. He said he did not like women's faces. He had painted Mrs Bradley, however, and at his own request, not hers. The repulsive-looking result gave them both considerable pleasure.

He gave his aunt an armchair near the fire in the parlour, and, seating himself on the settle, drew her attention to his furniture. There was a sixteenth-century Bible chest, a Jacobean sideboard and a Charles II chair.

'I stand in front of each of them in turn whenever I have visitors,' he said. 'I feel like a mother guarding her daughters from Vandals. Do you know, Aunt Adela, women come here who would *sit* on that chair if I let them.'

Mrs Bradley cackled.

'Oh, by the way,' he added, getting up, 'what do you want us to do with the hundredweight of coal, or whatever it is, that we took from the back of the car? It's in the hall at present, awaiting instructions, as they say.'

'Oh, yes, the boar's head,' said Mrs Bradley. 'By the way, where's your friend Hugh? I thought he would be here again for Christmas.'

'He is, and so is young Denis. They've gone to the market in

Oxford. And by the way, Aunt Adela, I'm sorry but we can't put George up in the house. I'm afraid we'll be rather crowded. Girls of sorts, and a fearful tick called Pratt – engaged to Fay – you remember Fay and Jenny? – are coming over for Christmas, so we're rather short of room. I expect they'll stay a day or two. Do you mind?'

'Girls of sorts!' said Mrs Bradley. 'And I thought I was being invited for myself alone, not to chaperone a gaggle of hussies who will probably refer to me in private conversation as "that old scream" if they like me, and "the Cenci" if they don't.' She got up, fixed her nephew with the eye of a good-humoured snake, and poked him in the ribs exuberantly. Then she gave a harsh cackle and suddenly made for the door.

'Come and help me drag the boar's head to the kitchen, child, and then come and show me my room.'

'Your room? Yes, of course,' said Carey. 'The washing arrangements are rather primitive here, but we've indoor sanitation – of a kind! But Mrs Ditch'll show you. A most valuable woman. She housekeeps, and her husband and her youngest son are my pigmen. She has other children – a girl of eighteen or so, who works at Simith's place, and three more boys, aged twenty upwards, I think. Nice people. Came from Headington originally. Mrs Ditch is quite a mother to me. I'll summon her.'

He lifted his head and yodelled. The sound, invented to carry over mountain valleys, rang through the quiet house like the call of a bugle, and Mrs Ditch came hastening. She was a shrewd-eyed, pleasant-faced woman, grey-haired and bold-featured, of a type to be seen all over the county. She was wrinkled and roughened from being out in all weathers, had the coarse, red skin of the middle-aged peasant, and square-palmed, masculine hands, the fingers scarred with potato-peeling, the cuts deepened by hot soda water. Her manner was like her appearance – countrified – not that of a servant, and yet respectful and courteous.

She carried the parlour lamp, which she trimmed and lighted. She looked at the yodeller affectionately.

'Oh, I say, Mrs Ditch, you might show my aunt her room. I don't know which one you're giving her, but I suppose it's all ready, and so forth?' Carey said.

'Mrs Bradley's hav-en the room over this one, mam,' said Mrs Ditch, dividing the sentence politely between her listeners. 'Tes a very good room, and them younger ladies have softer bones than at our age, mam, I thenk. Well you come this way, mam? I'll light ee with a candle, else praps ee might mess your step.'

She held her candle so that Mrs Bradley could see the way out of the parlour and up the stone staircase. Carefully she illumined every stair, and then led the way along a narrow stone passage to Mrs Bradley's room.

'There ee be,' she said, with great goodwill, as she set down the candle on an ancient chest of drawers. 'Shall I draw the curtains, or well ee leave 'em open? Nobody can't see ee, as I knows on, but I'll draw 'em ef you like.'

'Don't draw them,' said Mrs Bradley.

'Dinner's at seven, along of Mr Denis,' said Mrs Ditch, withdrawing. She closed the door quietly behind her, and Mrs Bradley could hear her dignified retreat along the passage.

The bedroom was bare and clean. Brightly-coloured, very thick rugs covered the cold stone floor, the bed was modern and there was an adequate wardrobe. The bedside table was also a revolving bookcase. The fire was burning red, and the room was warm.

'Carey plus Mrs Ditch, and a pleasant combination it makes,' thought Mrs Bradley. She went to the window and looked out. Before her, dim in the dusk, was a field of rough pasture; beyond it, the road to the village led up to the church. She could just make out the squat tower, she thought, in the distance. Behind the house lay Stanton Great Wood, but nothing at all of its great blue mass could be seen from her bedroom window. Somewhere at hand she could hear the winter singing of the brook in the stillness of the desolate countryside. The gurgle of fast-flowing water pleased her ears. It reminded her of a honeymoon spent in the

11

south of France in the days when she was young and had been in love.

Immediately under her window was the gravelled front yard of the farm, under Carey's tenancy free from manure heaps, refuse, sodden half-hayricks and scavenging, squawking fowls. It even boasted a narrow flower bed under the wall of the house.

There came a rhythmic tapping at the door. Mrs Bradley walked towards the fire whilst the visitor concluded the first few bars of Handel's Largo in G, and then invited him in. It was Carey who had knocked. He was not alone. Hugh Kingston, whom she had met at Carey's mother's house at one time, entered just behind him. Hugh was taller than Carey, a thin-mouthed, good-looking man in a greenish suit of plus fours.

'How are you, Mrs Bradley?' he said. 'We're fellow-sufferers over Christmas, I take it. I've done nothing but work since I came. This man –' he indicated Carey, who had shut the door and was standing with his back to it, 'has saved up all his odd jobs for the year, and pulled me in to help him out with them.'

'But what have you done with Denis?' asked Mrs Bradley, whose grandnephew, at that time twelve years of age, afforded her almost endless entertainment, and of whom she was very fond.

'I expect he's practising carols on his oboe,' Hugh replied. 'Musical instrument, so-called,' he explained in response to Carey's look of alarm. 'Makes noises like a modern poet in pain.'

'Modern poets are never in pain,' said Mrs Bradley, reprovingly. 'They have no inhibitions. But who taught Denis to oboe?'

'Priest, Simith's pigman, I believe.'

'Can Priest oboe?' asked Carey. 'Good Lord! I'd sack him if I were Simith, I think! Still, I rather hope he won't, because at the moment I can't do without him very easily. He's posing to me for a set of London Passenger posters to advertise country outings.'

'He looks like an inmate of a thieves' kitchen to me,' said Hugh. 'But if he's a musician, as you say, perhaps he'd give you tips on yodelling. But, look here, now! What about tea for Mrs Bradley?'

'Ready, I expect, by now,' said Carey. 'I warned Mrs Ditch to stand by. I'll yodel for her to come up.'

He had seated himself on the bed, pulled Mrs Bradley down beside him, and was talking amicably to Hugh Kingston over the top of her head. He inflated his lungs and yodelled long and loud, and Mrs Ditch came up with a loaded tray.

'Well done, Mrs Ditch!' said Hugh, who had stayed in the house before. 'You think of everything!'

'And so does Mr Carey, too and all,' said Mrs Ditch, with a comical air of giving the devil his due. 'It were him who warned me to have the pot ready to wet.'

'Ah, but you've trained me, Mrs Ditch,' said Carey. 'I regard you as the angel of my better nature. But what have you done with young Scab?'

'Mr Denis a-ben playen just lovely for the dancen and now he's chasen about playen smugglen. I don't know what he gets up to half his time, but there! He's a dear lettle chap,' said Mrs Ditch, 'and plays for the dancen just beautiful.'

'On his oboe?' said Mrs Bradley, determined to sift Hugh's statements about this mythical instrument.

'You don't mean his lettle drum,' said Mrs Ditch, 'and his lettle whestle?'

'I shouldn't think so,' Mrs Bradley replied. 'What is an oboe?' she asked, sotto voce, of Carey. Carey shrugged and grinned. Hugh said,

'He plays the violin. Not too badly, either, for a kid.'

'I should thenk he don't! But they'm worried about Mr Tombley. Says he's gev up the dancen. Can't thenk for why. A beautiful dancer he is, and capers lovely. He says his uncle don't like et, but all my eye and all, that is, I reckon.'

'Well, now, these people', said Hugh, when Mrs Ditch had retired. Mrs Bradley drank tea and ate thin bread and butter. Her nephew munched biscuits. Hugh leaned against the door.

'I think we'd better cut it down to Fay, Jenny and that wart

Pratt,' said Carey. 'We *must* have him, I suppose, since Fay has really decided to put up the banns.'

'Has she? Already?' asked Hugh. 'I thought she had a crush on Tombley, your pig-farming neighbour.'

'He who has given up dancing?' asked Mrs Bradley.

'That's Morris dancing, you know. Yes, the same chap. Perhaps we ought to have him as well. No. Can't very well, with Pratt. Although how any spouse of yours could have a sister who'd be such a mutt as to team herself up with that strip of bacon-rind, I can't imagine,' he added to Hugh. Hugh grinned.

'Not so much sisters, really, you know. Jenny is illegitimate,' he said. He turned to Mrs Bradley, 'I'm afraid the marriage will be very much in the future. I've got to make some money somehow, first.'

'I hope you'll like Jenny, Aunt Adela,' said Carey anxiously.

Mrs Bradley smiled, and pinched his knee. 'Anyhow,' Hugh continued, speaking to Carey, 'you can't fetch that lot in the side-car.'

'I know I can't. Anyway, I'm not going. *You're* the man to transport the lovelier fair. Borrow Aunt Adela's car. It's old, but it goes all right, or she wouldn't have got here in it.'

'A good idea. But George is to drive, not Hugh', said Mrs Bradley firmly. 'When are these children coming?'

'Christmas Eve. The day after tomorrow,' said Carey. 'But Hugh isn't going over to fetch them until after dinner. And, talking of dinner, Hugh, do we or don't we dress? Aunt, what are you going to do?'

'We've got to dress,' said Hugh, before Mrs Bradley could answer. 'Mrs Ditch has given orders. Said she to me, when she knew that your aunt was coming: "How nice for you, sir. You can wear your nice black and white. I always think gentlemen look so nice in their Dress!" Sinister, don't you think?'

'Talking of sinister,' said Carey, 'old Fossder, your father-in-law to be –'

'Uncle-in-law,' said Hugh.

'Sorry. Your uncle-in-law to be, has received a Rummy Communication, and also two hundred pounds.'

'Oh, Lord. Anonymous stink of some kind, do you mean?'

'Not exactly, no. It's anonymous, all right, but it takes the form of a couple of shields sketched in pencil. One's got a cross on it and the other a criss-cross. They came by post in an envelope postmarked Reading. I heard all about it from Pratt, when I went over there on Sunday to fix up this Christmas weekend. The two hundred pounds impressed Pratt less than the drawings.'

'Oh, Pratt *would* be impressed. Doesn't he make a sort of hobby of that kind of thing? It used to be crossword puzzles, but now it's odd bits of archæology and folk-lore and what-not. He doesn't really know anything, but he browses about and collects odd bits of information which he insists on retailing,' said Hugh. 'Not to me; to the girls. He knows I won't put up with it!'

'No. You might be able to put him right,' said Carey, grinning, 'surrounded, as you are, by slabs of learning.'

Mrs Ditch knocked at the door.

'Hullo?' said Carey.

'Just to inform ee, mam, the water's got hot for the bath, ef so be ee warnts one, after your ride en the motor.'

'Thank you,' said Mrs Bradley, dismissing her squires by standing up and pointing towards the door. When they had gone she prepared for her wash, and followed Mrs Ditch along the stone landing. Suddenly Mrs Ditch halted.

'Come out o'that, Mr Denis! What next, with all them clean cloes!'

Mrs Bradley's grandnephew crawled from a large old cupboard built into the wall. He looked crumpled but full of purpose. He was a grave child, earnest and intelligent, whether in goodness or sin.

'I've proved it doesn't come out into that, at any rate,' he said. 'Oh, hallo, Aunt Bradley! How's George?' He came up and shook hands gravely.

Mrs Bradley cackled, and poked him in the ribs. 'Hallo! How's Christmas?' she said.

'Been on a diet,' said Denis, 'to make enough room to stodge.'

The conversation at dinner was of crime.

'You can't possibly know what crime is, really, in these parts,' Hugh said, when the discussion had passed its zenith. 'After all, the villagers can always kill a pig. It must make a good deal of difference.'

'Aunt Bradley,' said Denis, tilting his glass and peering at the ginger wine it contained, 'do murders seem to follow you about?'

'I hope not,' said Mrs Bradley. She cackled harshly and accepted from Mrs Ditch a second helping of hot boiled bacon and winter greens. The meal had begun with bacon pudding. It was to continue with fried blackpudding and potatoes.

'Everybody for miles around breeds pig, eats pig and talks pig,' Carey said. When she had come downstairs he had broken to her, gently, the menu for dinner that evening and for breakfast on the following morning. 'But on Christmas Day there will be turkey, and even fish, if you want it,' he now added. 'We thought of taking the sidecar to Oxford market to-morrow and securing a whole halibut or something, and some prawns. With prawns and olives and a sardine or two, we could pretend we were having hors d'œuvres.'

'You can use the turkey's liver,' said Denis, helpfully. He drank some ginger wine. 'At any rate, Aunt Bradley, you do believe that murders follow certain people about don't you? *I* think they do. In fact, I've nearly proved it.'

'There's something in that theory, you know,' said Carey, yodelling for Mrs Ditch to substitute the third course and remove what remained of the hot boiled bacon and greens. 'Now, what about a jolly good ghost story, Aunt Adela?'

'Or a nice little monologue about dangerous lunatics you've met, Mrs Bradley?' said Hugh, with a grin.

'Or both,' said Denis, with his mouth full. He swallowed and then wiped grease from his lips. 'But I'd much sooner have a jolly good murder in the village. A jolly good murder,' he continued with enthusiasm, 'would make Christmas jolly well worth while. What do you say, Mrs Ditch?'

'Well, I dunno as I should enjoy my fowl and plum pudden any the better for a murder, Mr Denis,' said Mrs Ditch, entering the dark doorway bearing blackpuddings cut in halves and a dish of creamed potatoes.

'But think how exciting it would be,' Denis went on, 'to have detectives and the inquest, and everybody afraid to go to bed in case the murderer was lurking all over the place. I bet you'd be scared, Mrs Ditch. I bet you'd hide in the pantry.'

'Yes, Mr Denis, I daresay,' replied Mrs Ditch, unperturbed by the aspersion cast upon her courage. She served him some creamed potato and took away his empty wineglass.

'Here,' said Denis, 'I want some more ginger wine.'

'Not until Christmas Day,' said Mrs Ditch, quietly and firmly. She gave him a third half of hog-pudding, and then retired with the tray-load of empty dishes. Denis caught Mrs Bradley's eye and grinned as he poured some water into a tumbler.

'You don't really think, then,' he said, a little wistfully, 'that murders *do* follow people about? I mean, there's you, for instance. You wouldn't consider yourself a kind of low-pressure area – *you* know –'

Carey laughed, and Hugh, after a startled pause, joined in. Mrs Bradley grinned.

'I don't know about a low-pressure area, but I shouldn't like to imagine that just because I once –'

'You don't mean,' said Denis, round-eyed, 'that *you've* ever murdered anyone?'

'This is uncanny,' said Mrs Bradley to Hugh. She drank some wine, and attacked the blackpudding resolutely. Denis drank water, and eyed her reverently over the rim of the glass.

'Could you – would it be bothering you too much –' he blurted out, after a moment.

'I don't think I will. It wasn't pleasant,' said Mrs Bradley briskly.

'Sorry,' said Denis. 'Have some ginger wine.'

Further yodelling from Carey brought Mrs Ditch with tipsy-cake, some cheese and a dish of jam tarts.

'Why not mince pies?' asked Denis, taking a tart.

'Because it's not Christmas yet, Mr Denis,' said Mrs Ditch, heaping his plate with tipsy cake and producing, apparently by magic, a bottle of mushroom ketchup. She placed this on the table beside the cheese. Then she went back to the kitchen and brought in a bottle of brandy.

'Smuggled, accorden to Ditch, by way of that there old pack-horse road over Shotover 'Ell,' she observed. ''Er's dirty enough, in conscience, to be as old as Boney.' She dumped the grimy bottle on the table.

'She is as old as Boney,' said Carey, gazing enraptured at the filthy-looking receptacle. 'Napoleon brandy, Hugh. Mrs Ditch, get two more glasses, and bring Ditch back with you. Though we ought to save it for Christmas, I suppose.'

Ditch, a good-looking, middle-aged fellow with the easy yet upright stance of a Morris-man, a large moustache, and tolerant, grey-blue eyes, came in and smiled at their plaudits.

'I *found* 'er,' was all he would say in response to Carey's questions. 'Overlooked when the folks left this house in '74, I'll back, and never thought on again.'Er was well 'id, but I come upon 'er one mornen, and here 'er be. And here's to your health, my lady and masters all, and ef ee be thinken of goen through Sandford on Christmas Eve, look t'other way ef that there old Sandford coach come along.' He chuckled, and gulped his brandy.

'And what is the Sandford coach?' asked Mrs Bradley.

'It's a local legend – a ghost story,' Carey replied. He crossed his legs and leaned back in his seat, a comfortably-upholstered armchair of modern conception. Dinner over, they had grouped themselves round the fire. 'I've heard that in the reign of Queen Elizabeth a certain Catholic priest named George Napier, of the Sandford family of Napier, was executed at Oxford. His body was hacked into four pieces and a limb was placed on each of the four Oxford gateways. His head was on view in the city somewhere – outside Christchurch, I believe. Anyway, his relatives came secretly and possessed themselves of the body, but couldn't get the head, so they brought him, headless, back to Sandford, where they buried him. Since that time, George Napier drives in a coach every Christmas Eve round Temple Farm, at Sandford, in search of his missing head. To see the coach means death within the year, or so they say. I know some better ghost stories if you'd like to hear them. Incidentally, the two hundred pounds we're all so thrilled about! – I notice nobody's mentioned it during dinner! – is a freak bet made with old Fossder to go and look for the ghost.'

'Lousy,' said Denis. 'I could do you a better story myself. Of course there won't be any ghost.'

'I know the story, of course, but why the coach, I wonder?' put in Hugh. 'I should have thought a *walking* headless ghost would have been more natural. Old Fossder's going to take up the challenge, by the way. You know – the anonymous letter from Reading.'

'Query,' said Mrs Bradley. 'Is a headless ghost *in* a coach more or less horrible than a headless ghost *not* in a coach?'

'As a matter of fact,' said Carey, 'last Christmas I thought I'd have a shot at seeing the ghost for myself. But it was so wet that I gave up the idea, and went to bed instead. Perhaps old Fossder will be lucky. He gets two hundred pounds if he sees it, anyway.'

'Really,' said Mrs Bradley, 'I should like to have an eye-witness' account of the matter.'

'Well, you wouldn't have got it from Carey, anyway, would you?' observed Denis. 'I mean that Carey would have been dead by now, if he'd seen it.'

'Possibly not. The year isn't up until tomorrow night,' said Hugh. He arranged some chestnuts on the bars of the grate. 'Which reminds me; at what time of day did you say you'd call for those girls? I know it was after dinner, but when, exactly?' he asked.

'I said about half-past ten, so that you need not hurry. It's a nuisance they've got to come the night before, but we shouldn't want to fetch them on Christmas morning, and Mr Fossder doesn't keep a car. Can't think why not! The man's got plenty of money. Will George expect to have his beauty-sleep broken?' he added suddenly, turning to Mrs Bradley. 'We must give him the word in the morning, I suppose.'

'George won't mind,' said Mrs Bradley, 'as long as the roads are good.'

'They're not bad. It's all main road from Thornhill Farm, you know. Better go into the city through Headington and out again along the Iffley Road. That's better than going across country in the dark.'

'Aunt Bradley,' said Denis, breaking into the silence which had followed the conclusion of the arrangements, 'would you like to hear me play the pipe and tabor?'

'What?' said Mrs Bradley. 'But they told me it was the oboe!'

'Well, what's the difference?' said Carey, appealing to Hugh.

'I don't know. But I'll bet you he tried them both, and decided upon the more hideous,' said Hugh, adroitly dodging the cushion that Denis threw.

'The pipe and tabor,' said Denis, 'is not one instrument, you fathead. It happens to be two. I'll get them, shall I?' he asked, looking at Mrs Bradley. 'Of course, I'm not much good. I generally keep the tabor going, but I forget to play the pipe. Or, if the tune's a bit twiddly, then I have to concentrate on the pipe and let the tabor go.'

'All right. Get 'em out,' said Carey.

'You'll all have to look the other way, or shut your eyes or something, then,' said Denis. 'I don't want anyone to know where I keep them, you see, at present.'

Something in his voice made Carey glance sharply at him.

'A secret hiding place in *my* house?' he asked mockingly. Denis grinned.

'I ought to show you, I suppose, but I found it myself,' he said. 'Nobody told me about it. I didn't even know there was one. I went over all the panelling one night when everybody was in bed. I was jolly well scared, I can tell you, being down here all alone at dead of night. It was jolly eerie, and no end weird and creepy. Funny noises – not rats – just noises that you couldn't account for, and me with just a candle, and all the shadows everywhere, and a beastly wind in the chimney. But I found the right panel, and then I was jolly glad, but I didn't explore behind it until the morning. It's a priest's hole, I expect. Look here! I'll show you,' he concluded generously. 'After all, it *is* your house.'

It might possibly have been a priest's hole. It was certainly a secret room. Even its air-vent was concealed from outside by a thick growth of ivy, they discovered.

'I'll have that cut away,' said Carey, pleased to find that the house had a secret hiding place. 'I'm much obliged to you, Scab. In times of stress, I can hide from Mrs Ditch and her motherly ways. Yes! Good for you. I call that a handsome hole, and quite up to the recognised standard for such places.'

'I believe it ought to have another exit. I've been searching for one,' said Denis. He took up the pipe and tabor, and, after a few preliminary skirmishings, began to play a saucy little tune.

'You'll bring Ditch up,' said Carey. 'He'll offer to do a Morris dance. You'd better be nice about it,' he added to Mrs Bradley. 'Ditch is a Headington man, and knows all the dances backwards. They won't have a six, because Tombley and Bob Ditch aren't here to oblige, but he's taught me a bit, and Hugh can walk it. Here he comes! I thought so.'

But it was Mrs Ditch who came into the room. She carried a very large milk jug filled with mulled ale.

'A loven-cup, mam,' she said. Mrs Bradley took the jug and

drank, and it went the round. 'And now, ef ee pleases, Detch'll dance,' she said, 'ef Mr Denis well oblige 'em with the toon.'

'I'll bring my violin. I'm better on that,' said Denis. He went out with Mrs Ditch, and as they reached the door Carey suddenly asked,

'What *is* that tune that Denis was playing just now?'

'Er? Er's *Constant Billy*, Mr Carey. Ull I seng et for ee? Though my sengen days be over, I do thenk.'

'Do sing it,' said Mrs Bradley. So Mrs Ditch, her hand on Denis' shoulder, sang in a thin, untrained, but tuneful voice, the Headington words of the song:

> 'O Constant Billy,
> Shall I go with ee?
> O when shall I see
> My Billy again?'

'*Beggar's Opera*,' said Hugh. 'But different words, of course. I knew I'd heard it somewhere. Sing it again, Mrs Ditch.'

The Morris men were not in their Whitsun costume.

'Our whites be all put away by mother 'ere,' said Ditch. They were wearing belts round their trousers, and cricket boots on their feet. On their legs, between knee and ankle, were fastened pads of bells. The pads were made of soft leather cut up and down to within an inch of the top and bottom of the pad, to give the bells more play. The men carried handkerchiefs and Morris sticks. Denis took up his position near the door. The men put down their handkerchiefs and sticks, and helped to clear the centre of the room. Carey and Hugh took the middle positions, opposite one another, and Young Walt whispered to Hugh,

'You follow Dad. I'll push ee through the hey. Never mind the steps. Ee can walk, so be ee doesn't throw us all out. Tell ee what, our dad! Let us do *Blue-Eyed Stranger*,' he added, raising his voice. So they all caught up their large handkerchiefs, holding all the four corners in proper Headington fashion, and Denis played over the tune.

'Ee shudn't 'ear the beat o' the feet, like, not really ee shudn't,' whispered Mrs Ditch to Mrs Bradley. ''Tes done on grass or the road, you see, at Whitsun; and always remember, mam, when ee sees the dancen, as ee don't know who 'tes that does et! Onderstand, do ee, I wonder?'

'I think so,' said Mrs Bradley, who had seen ritual dances before.

'Us onpacked the boar's head, like ee told us, mam,' said Ditch, when the dance was over and the dancers were taking refreshment. 'Very well er looked, too, didn't er, young Our Walt?'

'Ah, our dad, er ded,' said Walt, with a nod.

'A case of carrying coals to Newcastle, all the same, I'm afraid,' said Mrs Bradley, remembering with a shudder the blackpuddings.

CHAPTER 2

Foot up at Old Farm

'Are you keen on pigs, Aunt Adela?' Carey enquired next morning. 'What I mean to say – you have told Hugh some revolting stories of your medical student days; listened to young Scab's performances on various musical instruments; you have seen Ditch dance, and heard Mrs Ditch sing. Where do I come in?'

'Show her Sabrina,' said Hugh. 'Sabrina is my favourite,' he added to Mrs Bradley. 'She is the only one of her race who has ever known me by sight after the second meeting. She gave a bellow of rage and nearly pushed the side of her sty out in her frantic efforts to savage me. I can't think why she finds me offensive, but she does. The only other female who ever took a dislike to me was the late Countess of Serren. I was sick on her shoe at a school prizegiving. Sheer nervousness on my part, but not well received, none the less.'

He accompanied Mrs Bradley to the pig-houses. Carey stayed behind for a word with Ditch, who had come to ask for instructions.

'Let's do the fattening house first,' suggested Hugh, as they crossed the yard. 'We can pretend we are at the Zoo, if that makes it any easier. I expect Carey will be wounded if you don't make your inspection pretty thorough.'

The fattening house, as Hugh had indicated, was not unlike the cattle sheds at the Zoological Gardens. It was warm inside, and consisted of a large centre passage or gangway between numbers of adjoining sties, in which white pigs, alert to the welcome sound of footsteps – for it was almost feeding time – came nosing, snuffling and squealing up to the front boards.

Behind the sties ran manure passages to facilitate the work of clearing out the house. There were plenty of windows in the two long walls. The lower half of each window was fixed, but the upper half opened on an elbow-shaped iron ventilating rod, so that air, without the danger of draught, was admitted.

'You have to admire this fully,' said Hugh, conducting her slowly along the centre gangway, and waiting politely while she stopped to look at the pigs. 'I had to, and I'm not going to let you off.'

'But I *do* admire it,' Mrs Bradley protested. 'Carey enjoys keeping pigs, and there are too few people in this world who really enjoy what they're doing.' She stopped and gazed with benign and earnest interest at several halfgrown porkers who thought she was going to feed them. Carey joined her, and Hugh slowly sauntered away, to make a bee-line back to the house as soon as he left the pig-house. Carey laughed.

'Old Hugh does hate these pigs. He's off to sweat at a book about tunny fishing. For a public librarian he's got queer hobbies. He loves to kill things, you know. Come along here and have a look at Buttercup. She's not my best gilt. She has only ten teats, confound her, but to look at she's a rather pleasing specimen of the result of mating a pure bred Large White boar with an Essex sow. She forages well, and seems a good-tempered young woman. She ought to make a good mother, in spite of her shortcomings. If she has a big litter I expect I shall rear the runt and one or two others by hand. It's fun feeding little pigs. They're very much jollier than puppies. Greedy little devils, too, and full of fight. Simith, my neighbour, crossed a Large White with a Berkshire, and got quite good results. Have to be careful in your choice of breeding pigs. Black pigs ain't popular for table. I'd like you to see Simith's place. He runs it on the open-air system, but his nephew, a chap named Tombley, is always trying to get him to alter to a

Scandinavian stunt like this one. They fight over it like fiends. You'd have to laugh.' He led the way out, and they strolled to the larger pig-house.

'I've met them,' said Mrs Bradley. She described her first evening's adventure. 'Do take me over again, child. I should love to see them again – and their pig-farm, too, of course,' she added hastily. Carey looked at her sideways.

'Don't bother to apologise,' he said. 'Is Simith going to be one of your specimens, love?'

'No, Tombley, I think,' said Mrs Bradley, laughing.

'Bit of an oaf, that fellow,' said Carey, frowning. 'I don't mind old Simith. He's a countryman to the marrow, for all his money. But Tombley's a bit of a mixture. Simith came from Bampton, you know, on the other side of the county, and hasn't been here very long. The local people don't like him. I think it's only prejudice, although I *have* heard that the old chap likes to exercise a sort of Droit de Seigneur with the daughters of his tenants, and that don't go down very well. We're moral coves, you know, in Stanton St John. I've often wondered what makes Mrs Ditch let Linda go on working there, but, of course, she comes home when she likes, and Mrs Ditch is a bit of a terror as a mother, although you might not think so. Got 'em all under her thumb, and held pretty tight, you know. Here's Buttercup.' He leaned over and smacked the gilt. Mrs Bradley stood by in what she hoped would pass for an admiring attitude. 'And here's my favourite, Clytie.' He stopped by a very large sow and called to her. She squealed with pleasure, lumbered up and planted her forefeet against the wood of her run. She opened her jaws and seemed to grin at him. Carey caressed her chops and tickled her snout. He pulled her large ears gently, and talked to her all the time.

'But how can you bear to kill them?' asked Mrs Bradley. Slavers of dripping saliva, the product of almost uncontrollable love, were coming from the jaws of the sow. It was pathetic and disgusting, fascinating and abhorrent, to see her attachment to Carey, and to hear her squeals of reproach when he went away.

'I don't kill my sows,' said Carey, 'unless they are ill. They die in their pampered old age. Sentimentality, that is, and very bad for business. My bacon pigs and porkers I take care never to make friends with. Now come along and see Tom.'

'I always thought boars and sows – in fact, pedigree animals in general, including dogs and cats – had resounding important names such as "Blue China Charles the Second of Bloomsbury",' said Mrs Bradley, following her nephew to the place where the boar was stied.

'They do. But in private life we shorten 'em up a bit. This, for instance, is Christchurch Tom of Stanton, and the sow you've just seen in Brockenhurst Clytemnestra the Fourth.'

'And is Tom savage?' asked Mrs Bradley, looking down on the boar.

'Oh, no, not a bit, except with strangers. Look.' He opened the gate and walked in. Tom backed away, stood with his back to the fencing, and scratched the ground with his feet. 'Come on, you old stupid,' said Carey. Slowly the boar advanced, as delicately as though he were treading a minuet, but when he was less than four feet away from Carey he made a frenzied rush. Carey leapt aside like a Spanish bull-fighter, slapped the boar on the hams and faced him again. This happened three times, and then the boar turned quiet and walked away. Carey went after him, held his head, and showed Mrs Bradley his tusks. Then he walked calmly out of the run, and fastened the door behind him, wiping his hands down his trousers.

'I shouldn't like to say he wasn't savage,' was Mrs Bradley's comment.

'He's only playing. He likes it. But, of course, he's a bit of a rough-neck. I always go into his sty for ten minutes' exercise each day when I want to train for a fight. Gets your eye in, and makes you pretty nippy on your pins, both very encouraging attributes in the ring. But Hereward's the one you want to see. He's in a separate sty. We'll pass him on our way to the house,

27

and I'll show him to you. He's more like a dog than a boar. Anyone could handle *him*, I should think. He's young, and I've brought him up myself, from babyhood. He's a lovely chap. Only two years old.'

'Come on, you two. It's a quarter to one,' said Hugh, who had come to the pig-house to find them.

So they went indoors without stopping at Hereward's sty. Mrs Ditch appeared with a joint of beef.

'Great heavens, Mrs Ditch! This is heresy!' Hugh observed, regarding the beef with rapturous surprise.

'Ah, so et es, too and all,' said Mrs Ditch. 'Hearsay is right, though how ee knowed et es more than I can fathom. However, be ee enformed that Mester Dellock kelled for Chrestmas, and I says to Ditch to go over there with the dung cart and bring back a nice piece for dinner. And here er be. Though 'ow ee could 'ave knowed aught about et beats me, that et do.'

'He's also among the prophets, like Saul, Mrs Ditch,' said Carey, handing the carving knife to Hugh. 'Here you are. Professionals forward, please.' He addressed Mrs Ditch again. 'Where's Scab, by the way? Fallen into the New College tenants' well at last?'

'Mr Denis 'as got some notion of see-en old Napier's ghost tomorrow night,' said Mrs Ditch, a little anxiously. She looked at Mrs Bradley. 'I aren't a one to be fanciful, mam, I'm sure, but I really don't like the idea, and him so young a child. Ef I was mother to him, he wouldn't be go-en to see no ghost at Sandford, and so I tell ee.' She sounded breathless, and looked defiant. 'Two hundred is a lot of money, mam.'

'You surely don't believe in the Sandford legend, Mrs Ditch?' said Hugh, surprised. Mrs Ditch began twisting her apron between her fingers, and did not meet his eye.

'I don't believe nothen, Mr Hugh,' she said, half-angrily. 'But ef nobody else don't keep that child at home, I'll do it myself, be blowed to me ef I won't! It isn't safe, I tell ee, for anybody down that way to see that there old coach. I don't believe nothen, but et isn't for lettle children, as haven't their mothers with 'em, to go to Sandford on Christmas Eve, tomorrow night as is.'

'Very well, Mrs Ditch. He shan't go,' said Mrs Bradley.

'Why, thankee, mam,' said Mrs Ditch, surprised. She appeared to be going to say more, but changed her mind, and went out.

'You know,' said Carey, when Mrs Ditch had gone, 'it strikes me that the retainer is just a bit high-hat. Why did you give in to her like that, Aunt Adela? Bad policy, I should have thought. There can't be anything really. Besides, if Scab has made up his mind, he's a difficult kid to argue with, you know.'

'The woman is fond of Denis, and she is very much afraid,' said Mrs Bradley, eyeing the beef with favour and helping herself to potato. 'And Denis will do as he's told, you'll find, without a silly fuss. Disobedience is not a characteristic of children of his type.'

Hugh laughed, and Denis came in.

'I say,' he said, sitting down, 'I've just met Mrs Ditch, and she says I'm not to go to Sandford tomorrow night to have a look for the ghost. I jolly well told her I should! Somebody seems to have sloshed some bright red paint in the form of a fancy-shaped cross on Mr Fossder's gate, and it seems to have made her windy. At least, that's what she said. Tombley, the chap at Roman Ending, told her, I expect. I know Mrs Ditch is afraid of the ghost. She said so. But that's no reason why I should be!' He glanced at Mrs Bradley, scenting opposition, and prepared to fight for his rights.

'It's a very good reason why we all should be,' said Mrs Bradley, calmly. She looked at Denis, and Denis looked back at her. Her bright black eyes were as sharp and unwinking as a bird's.

'Well, who *is* going to Sandford?' asked Denis, dropping his gaze.

'No one. But Hugh is going to Iffley,' said Carey, 'and you and I are jolly well staying at home.'

Denis raised his eyebrows, but said no more, except to remark, as he looked at the joint from which Hugh was carving his portion,

'Beef? Good. Bloody? Cheers!'

When lunch was over, Carey and Mrs Bradley set off along the cart-track, and, by way of footpaths, very muddy in places, came up the slope of a field already half-ploughed and looked down on Simith's farm.

'He does mixed farming as well as the pigs,' said Carey. 'If you use the open-air system you've got to grow your own feed. There are his wheeled shelters. A very handy idea. Of course, the pigs have to be fenced away from the arable on this kind of farm, unless you actually want a crop cleaned up.'

He led the way down the ridge towards Simith's house.

'You get the pigs to manure your land, you see – that's one of Simith's big points – he's always harping on it – but to do that properly, that is, to obtain your uniform distribution of manure, you must move the huts and feeding troughs every day. I prefer my own methods, much, but this is interesting, and, of course, is a better life for your breeding stock. In fact, I find, in practice, that for sows it's a necessity.'

'The pigs feed themselves, I take it?' said Mrs Bradley. 'That is, I imagine, the main argument in favour of this system?'

'Oh, yes. This winter, for instance, Simith's getting his pigs to clean out a field of potatoes. Of course, pigs out of doors, getting all this exercise and foraging for themselves, eat a good deal more than they do the way I rear them. This seems to me an expensive and troublesome way of rearing the stock that's going to make pork and bacon. My pigs, for instance, are kept warm in the fattening houses; his have to keep themselves warm, and they do it, of course, by consuming extra food. But Simith's a clever old fellow, and his interests lie pretty wide – his business interests, I mean – although they are all connected with pork and bacon. But here we are. Step clear of the mud if you can!'

They entered a yard gate, and picked their way through muck to the front of the house. A servant of about twenty opened the door. She was a good-looking girl, with wide-open, impudent eyes, a deep bosom and a short, very clean frock and apron. She smiled at Carey.

'Hullo, Linda,' said Carey. 'This is our Mrs Ditch's only daughter, Aunt Adela. Mr Simith in, Linda? If he's busy, we'll go away and call some other time.'

'He's in, sir, and Mr Tombley, too. Did you want to see 'em? They be only arguen, as usual.'

'Well, I said I'd come over and see that new fencing he's ordered.'

'Ah, he haven't ordered it yet. He was awaiten your good word on it afore he ordered, he says. He'll be glad to see ee. So well Mr Tombley. Come this way. I don't know as *I* be sorry to see ee, neether,' she added, cryptically, as she led the way to the big, dark, stone-flagged kitchen.

The uncle and nephew were seated on either side of the hearth. For a rich man, Mr Simith appeared to have particularly simple tastes. He was dressed, as before, in corduroys and gaiters, the latter thickly encrusted with dried mud. The only sign of affluence about him was a gold hunter which he was comparing with the kitchen clock at the moment that Carey and Mrs Bradley were shown in. The kitchen was a big, bare, ugly room, ornamented by a dresser full of crockery, and furnished with a large kitchen table, some Windsor chairs and an old armchair stuffed with horsehair. The latter indicated its presence in no uncertain fashion by appearing at the front of the seat of the chair through a hole in the black leather covering.

The old man rose and put the gold hunter into his pocket. His greeting, to Mrs Bradley's great surprise, was very hearty and cheerful, but the young man scowled at them both, and muttered a greeting which might have been an oath. If he was pleased to see them, his manner did not suggest it. Carey introduced his aunt with grave formality.

'Come to see the pigs? Why, for sure ee shall see the pigs. Tombley too,' said old Simith, his cheerfulness changing abruptly to a

31

scowl as he looked at his nephew's lowering countenance. 'What'll ee look at first?'

'Boars,' said Mrs Bradley.

'Ah. We can show ee two, a good un and a bad un, can't us, nevvy?'

'Nero's all right,' said Tombley. 'A boar's all the better for being a bit bad-tempered.'

'Is er, indeed?' said Simith. He gave a glance of contempt at the slouching young man on the opposite side of the fireplace. 'Well, you ought to know, I suppose.'

'Who are you calling bad-tempered?' his nephew growled. 'Come on, Mrs Bradley,' he added. 'I'll take you along.'

The two of them walked on in front. Carey and Simith followed, but, stopping to look at the new fencing, a short length of which had been sent for Simith's inspection and had the specification still attached, they were soon left well behind.

'The boar, then, doesn't run loose?' said Mrs Bradley, wading through and over pigs, as she and her younger host traversed the yard and cut across the corner of a mucky, trampled field.

'Oh, no. We sty the boars. Otherwise, you see, we couldn't regulate the breeding of the pigs.' He led the way to a fairly large, stone-floored sty. 'There's Nero, a very fine fellow, getting old, but not yet past doing his bit. There's only one man in the world dare enter that sty, and that's my pigman, Priest.'

'Oh, yes, the musician,' said Mrs Bradley absently. She was gazing entranced at the boar. 'He looks very savage to me,' she said, as the boar crashed against the fence of the sty with a screaming bellow of temper. 'And I thought one extracted their tusks.'

'Oh, no. When there's no one about, and we've fenced all the pigs and the sows, Priest lets this chap out for a run, and he roots about and snorts and carries on like a young bull-elephant. He couldn't do that without tusks.'

'And do you let the other boar out as well?' asked Mrs Bradley.

'Oh, Bill Sykes! Yes, but not at the same time as Nero. They'd fight to the death, I should think. What else would you like to see?'

'Bill Sykes,' said Mrs Bradley.

'It'll be a messy walk. He's over by the orchard. But come along. I suppose you don't clean your own shoes.'

He looked down at his gaiters and laughed, but the laugh was not pleasant.

'He doesn't like it here,' thought Mrs Bradley. Aloud she said,

'I wish you'd explain your system. It seems quite different from Carey's.'

'Well, yes, it is different, of course. The rough idea is that the pigs lead an out-door life and grub up their food for themselves. Naturally we add to the diet where necessary. It's a messy, wasteful system, I always feel, but uncle's keen on it, and at present it happens to be to my advantage to stay on here and help him. But I'm not much good with these pigs. You've got to be keen, you know, tremendously keen, to make a success of pigs. I like them all right, but I'd rather adopt Carey's system. I wish I could go to Denmark and Sweden, and see how they do their stuff there. Uncle and I don't get on at all, unfortunately. Quarrelling stimulates him, but it bores me stiff. I want a little money, and a wife, and some peace and quiet.'

'To be sure,' said Mrs Bradley. They had reached the orchard wall, and another sty. 'So this is Bill Sykes,' she added. 'Not as savage as Nero.'

'Not nearly.' Bill Sykes was young, and seemed interested, rather than offended, to hear them approach.

'I'm afraid of boars, as a matter of fact,' confessed Tombley. 'I wouldn't go into that sty for a hundred pounds.'

'But if he's not savage –'

'I know. But a boar will always want to be king of his castle. They hate to have people come into their sties and start cleaning 'em out, for instance. As for feeding, we shove it in here or fork it over the fence. When we clean, we have to entice the boar into the hut, and let down the door. Then we undo the door, and make a bolt for the fence. It's quite exciting, but it makes me sweat. Hullo, here's Priest. That means I'd better be off. Got some potatoes for the boars in the copper. I must hop off and see how they're doing.'

Mrs Bradley went with him, and as they passed the pigman, who grunted a greeting in much the same voice as his charges might have employed in similar circumstances, she looked at him shrewdly.

'I suppose he's the ugliest man in the county,' said Tombley, smiling. 'A more murderous-looking visage I've never beheld.'

'Oh, I have,' said Mrs Bradley. 'My profession brings me within sight of a good many murderous visages, one way and another, I'm pleased to say.'

'Pleased?' said Tombley, looking at her in surprise.

'I always think murder is interesting,' Mrs Bradley replied. 'It's the applied mathematics of morbid psychology, isn't it?'

'Well, so are suicide and rape and incest, and all the other perversions, don't you think?' said Tombley, amused.

'I do,' said Mrs Bradley. She regarded him encouragingly out of her sharp black eyes, but Tombley appeared to consider the subject sufficiently dealt with, for all he said was,

'Aren't you *the* Mrs Bradley, the psychoanalyst?'

'I *am* a psychoanalyst, or used to be, when Sigmund Freud was popular. They call me an alienist now.'

'And can you minister to minds diseased?'

'I think so, child. It depends on the willingness of the mind to be ministered unto, you know.'

'I'm not talking of myself, but of my uncle. He's begun having curious lapses.'

'Lapses?' said Mrs Bradley.

'Yes. Takes a pig out on a lead as though it were a dog, and calls it Fido. All that kind of thing.'

'Bless you, that isn't a lapse, child. That's an idiosyncracy,' said Mrs Bradley, grinning.

'Yes, well, perhaps that isn't the best example of what he does.

Last night, for instance, he declared he had seen a ghost with its head tucked underneath its arm. Oh, I've heard the comic song,' he added hastily, catching Mrs Bradley's ironic eye. 'Neither was the old man tight, I declare. He came in all of a sweat, and said he'd seen it.'

'Did he say where, dear child?'

'Yes, coming out of our little wood over there. It lies between Carey's house and ours. I reckon, if he really saw anything, it was one of the Ditch boys in his Morris whites.'

'Our Mrs Ditch has put them all away,' said Mrs Bradley.

'Yes, I see,' said Tombley. 'What do you make of the letter Mr Fossder got, inviting him and me to go to Sandford to see the ghost of Napier?'

'You as well?' said Mrs Bradley.

'Yes. I get half the two hundred pounds if I go.'

Denis next day again raised the question of seeing the ghost at Sandford.

'Hugh is going to Iffley tonight,' said Carey impatiently. 'There won't be any question of ghosts at Sandford. A lot of rubbish, anyway.'

'And *aren't* you going with him?' Denis enquired.

'I? No. I told you I wasn't. There wouldn't be room in the car.'

'And I'm leaving Iffley not later than eleven-fifteen,' said Hugh. 'So the ghost couldn't possibly function before I get home. Cheer up, Scab, you aren't really missing any fun.'

'And you and Carey and I will be alone in this house,' said Denis to Mrs Bradley, 'because Ditch is going to Oxford, and Mrs Ditch –'

'And the sinister *Mrs* Ditch is staying at home,' said Mrs Bradley, with relish.

That night, at just after ten, Mrs Ditch stopped Hugh on his way to the cottage where George, the chauffeur, was lodging.

'I know Mr Carey would only laugh, Mr Hugh. But do ee

get away before midnight, won't ee, now? Don't ee be chancy about et.'

'Look here, Mrs Ditch! What *is* all this!' said Hugh. 'I thought you had more sense than to think about such tomfoolery, or believe such a pack of rot as that Sandford ghost! And I don't go through Sandford, anyway, tonight.' His tone was sharp with annoyance.

Mrs Ditch looked wretched.

'I'm sure I beg pardon of ee ef I be talken too much. I mean et well, be ee certain.'

'Oh, yes, I'm certain,' said Hugh. 'But we're sure to be leaving Iffley well before midnight, Mrs Ditch, and Sandford doesn't come into it, as I say.'

'But the ghost got to *get* to Sandford, haven't he?' Mrs Ditch said slowly. 'And I *wish* ee needn't go, to be sure I do! I'd a sight sooner 'ave ee stop yur. I don't like the talk there is about that anonerous letter. Ef Tombley's mexed up en that, et bodes no good. And I be afraid, with all this talk about money for see-en a ghost.'

'Look here, Mrs Ditch, I do wish you'd say what you mean. What is it? You're *not* afraid of a ghost. There's something else,' said Hugh. 'What about the letter? It's only a bet for a joke.'

'Assepten that there pigman of Mester Semeth's declared he'd seen et walken the woods last night.'

She opened the door – they were standing near the back entrance – and went inside. At the same moment Carey came out of the front door, and, hearing Hugh's footsteps going across the yard, called out to him. Hugh halted, and Carey came up.

'I'll walk with you as far as the cottage,' he said. They set off, side by side, came out at the gate, and on to the cart-track, and walked along it to the road.

'I wish,' said Carey, as they walked briskly uphill in the darkness, 'we needn't have Pratt and Fay. Blisters, both of them. Why not just bring Jenny back with you? Pratt and Fay have got each other, anyway. They won't want us. They're engaged.'

'Under protest from Fay,' said Hugh. 'Naturally, Fay and Jenny are as thick as thieves, and tell each other everything the way girls do, you know, and I'm given to understand that the engagement was engineered by Fossder. The choice of sons-in-law lay between Pratt and Tombley, and Fossder can't stick Tombley, for some reason.'

'Still, Tombley will be quite well off one day, when Uncle Simith kicks in. The pig-farm ain't the only iron in the fire. Simith's got big pork interests in Norfolk and Leicestershire, and he's more or less of a sausage king besides. You see his stuff everywhere now. Fay might do worse for herself, financially speaking. But I don't know how she'd like young Tombley for a husband. Bit of a brute, I should think, when he gets a bit older.'

'Well, you can't blame people for fighting shy of Simith. Unsavoury old devil,' said Hugh, as they left the lane and were walking past the church.

'Tombley's mother was Simith's sister, and I believe *old* Tombley was in Parliament or something,' Carey continued carelessly. 'Landowner of sorts. Cambridge man, I heard. Got into Parliament on agriculture. Dead now, of course; so's the mother; Simith adopted the boy. I took Aunt Adela over there this afternoon while you went into Oxford for the grub. I think she enjoyed it quite well. Of course, it's not the time of the year to see an open-air place at its best.'

They reached the cottage, and Hugh knocked for George, the chauffeur.

'Very good, sir. Just coming,' said George.

'Bored down here?' asked Carey. George grinned. He had a little boy on his shoulder. Another child was clutching his trousers to help it to stand on its feet.

'No, sir. It's interesting to study conditions at first hand.'

'What conditions?' asked Hugh.

'The conditions obtaining in a small village community, sir,' said George. 'The evidences that ghosts are still firmly believed in, and that the water problem really is as acute as is indicated in the London press.'

'Ghosts?' said Carey. 'Don't tell me they've been serving you that old stuff as well!'

'I have been solemnly warned, sir, not to show my face in Sandford after half-past eleven tonight. I've also been told that a ghost has been seen on the farm called Roman Ending.'

'Who warned you?' asked Carey sharply.

'Your Mrs Ditch, sir, twice, and each time most emphatically.'

'Look here,' said Carey, after Hugh had laughed and assured George that they would be home by midnight or earlier, 'I'm going to bounce the truth out of Mrs Ditch. She's scared of something, and that something is *not* the ghost of George Napier. That name does persist,' he added.

'What name?'

'George.'

'Well, it only means a farmer.'

'Gosh!' said Carey, punching him gently in the ribs. 'What a thing it is to have had a classical education and to live one's life in a library!'

Mrs Ditch, approached upon his return, was not to be bounced into anything. She persisted that it was the ghost and the foolish bet that she feared. He gave it up, and joined Mrs Bradley in the parlour.

'Going to leave right away,' said Hugh, putting his head in, 'and I hope you'll see me back safely.'

'Why, that's all right,' said Carey. 'It takes place within the year, you know, if you see the ghost, not tonight.'

There came a knock at the door. They admitted George. 'Very sorry, sir,' said George, to Hugh, 'but we're in for a bit of trouble, I'm afraid. Could you wait half an hour, do you think? I'll hope to have her ready for you by then.'

'Why, what's the matter?' said Hugh.

'Someone been interfering, sir, I imagine. But I'll soon have her right, sir. Ditch or Walt will come and give you the word in half an hour, or as soon as we get her fixed.'

'Yes, but, man, what's the trouble?' said Hugh.

'Leak en the tank. Ben done a-purpose,' said Ditch, who had followed George in. 'Garage job really, but George here thinks we should manage. Ef she don't blow up,' he added, after a pause.

'Blow up or not, I'm going to Iffley tonight. None of them yokels are going to play games with my car,' said George, annoyed, 'and stop me getting where I like.'

Mrs Bradley nodded solemn approval.

'But it's not a bit like the people round here,' said Carey.

'Some lout's trick, sir,' grunted George. 'I'll learn him if I lay my hands on him.'

'I can't understand it,' said Carey. He walked into the kitchen where Mrs Ditch was rubbing bread on a grater and making a big pile of crumbs. Hams and onions were hanging up, and a line of Ditch underclothing was airing on a string across the vast, dim room.

'Look here, Mrs Ditch,' said Carey, very sternly, 'what *is* going on round here! Somebody's put Mrs Bradley's car out of action. And there's you with all this nonsense about ghosts! What's the idea? Come on!'

'I dunno no more than you, Mr Carey,' Mrs Ditch replied. 'I only know what I've told ee, and *that* I had from my darter, that at last 'as come home out of et, and time enough, too, I say, and from our Bob, that see et with his eyes. And all that money. Onnatural.'

Carey gave it up, and went back to the parlour.

'Hullo! Not gone?' said Denis, coming down in his pyjamas, and taking some biscuits from the sideboard.

'The car's been held up for a once-over by the conscientious George,' said Carey lightly, before Hugh could make any reply. He glanced at Hugh, who nodded, and filled a pipe. But Denis was not so easily deceived. He waved the piece of biscuit and capered joyously. His eyes were alight, and shone with excitement and pleasure.

'Then there *is* dirty work at the cross roads! I knew there would be! I *told* you there would be!' he said. 'Oh, dash it, I say, *do* take me to Iffley tonight!'

'Oh, get back to bed!' said Carey. 'I thought you'd got a book.'

'Read it. Couldn't wait,' said Denis sadly. He took a few more biscuits. Mrs Bradley gave him a slab of nut-milk chocolate.

'He'll ruin his teeth,' said Hugh. 'I bet he won't sweat to clean 'em when he's got through all that muck.'

Mrs Bradley gave Denis an apple.

'That will do just as much good as brushing them,' she said.

CHAPTER 3

Corners – the Challenge – at Sandford

Twice Hugh went out to the cart-shed to see how the breakdown gang were getting on with the repairs, and the second time their report was optimistic.

'I'll be able to go, after all,' he said, returning to find Carey in a hopeless position at the chess board, and Mrs Bradley grinning like a fiend above the pieces.

'Good,' she said. Carey grunted, and, abandoning the game, fished out a pipe and tobacco.

'Lucky if you don't get Jenny turned out of house and home and bidden never to darken the Fossder door again,' he said, reaching up for the matches.

'You mean Mrs Fossder won't let her come? Oh, dash it, too bad,' said Hugh. 'Still, the old lady likes me, you know.'

'Yes,' said Carey. 'And doesn't Tombley still have her warm good wishes? She can't stick Pratt, at any price, I believe.'

'And old Fossder can't stick Tombley. But I don't believe it's Fossder's fault exactly. You see, Simith once clumped him over the head with an empty bottle. Simith was jugged for that, and has had it in for Fossder ever since. He also thinks that Fossder mucked a law-suit for him over a bridge or something.'

'Interesting,' said Mrs Bradley, who was lazily partial to gossip. She was about to request her nephews to continue their instructive remarks when the jangling bell at the hall door startled all the house. It startled Mrs Ditch in the kitchen, and her immediate reaction was to sit back on one of the Windsor chairs, clutch the table with a hand dark-stained from the giblets she was in the act of removing from a capon, and observe:

'Our Walt, ee aren't to let 'em in, tes not en reason.'

To this, Our Walt, Mrs Ditch's youngest son, replied pacifically,

'Now then, our mam, 'ow do ee know oo be there? Wait, won't ee, tell I tells ee.'

Then he went and opened the door.

'Oo be there?' he asked, peering out suspiciously.

The noise of the bell had also startled Carey.

'Good Lord, who's that?' he demanded, swinging his feet to the floor from the end of the settee. Hugh walked across to the door.

'Who's that, Walt?' he called.

Upstairs in his bedroom Denis sat up and listened. Then he slid out of bed, and put on his dressing gown and slippers. Reconnoitring with the skill born of years of experience in descending to the dining room at home to pilfer biscuits, he descended the stairs halfway, and, having located Hugh because of the light of the parlour lamp which silhouetted him against the open doorway, he squatted in an angle of the stairs and awaited possible developments.

Even Mrs Bradley experienced a sudden tightening of the nerves at the sound of that jangling discordance so late on Christmas Eve.

'Who's there?' said Hugh again. Walt came along the hall.

'Tes a gentleman named Pratt, warnts to be knowen whether ee're goen to Effley or not,' he said.

'Pratt? Ask him in,' said Carey. A tall, thin, slightly stooping young man emerged into the lamplight.

'One rather thought that one was misinformed,' he said. 'One understands from one's fiancée, as it were, that we were to expect one of you at half-past ten this evening.'

'One understood correctly,' said Carey coldly. 'Unfortunately the car has conked. I expect Hugh will have to postpone his visit until the morning.'

'One regrets the mishap,' said Pratt. He blinked at Mrs Bradley. Carey introduced them.

'Well,' said Mrs Bradley, with the loving smile of a boa-constrictor which succeeds in engulfing its prey with the minimum of hazard, 'and so this is Mr Pratt! How do you do, dear child?'

'One finds oneself well,' said Pratt. He looked vaguely about him. 'One had been under the impression –'

'Yes, that's all right,' said Carey, 'and we're really awfully sorry, but something really has gone wrong with the car. They're on the job now, as a matter of fact. And I mean it when I say I don't know whether Hugh will be able to make it or not. You can stay and see, if you like, and go back with him if he goes.'

'One had intended to return forthwith. One had come on a bicycle belonging to Jenny,' said Pratt, edging apologetically towards the door.

'Righto. See you later,' said Hugh off-handedly. 'I can't say I admire Fay's taste,' he added, when Pratt had gone. They all settled down again and the room was quiet once more, when there came a sudden cry, and a heavy body crashed against the door.

'Good Lord!' said Hugh. 'What's that?' He sat up stiffly, staring towards the door. Carey went and opened it.

'All right,' said a sulky voice which Mrs Bradley recognised. 'I came in by the back entrance. Sorry to trouble you at this time of night. Slipped in the passage. Wouldn't wait for Mrs Ditch to bring a light.'

'Oh, come in, Tombley,' said Carey, not too cordially. 'What's the matter, man? Nothing happened, I hope?'

'Nothing, probably,' said Tombley. 'All here at home, I suppose?'

'We are,' said Hugh. 'Why, is anything serious the matter?'

'No, I suppose not. Certainly not, if you've got my uncle here, but if you haven't, I'm half afraid – his heart's bit funny, you know, and he's had a drinking fit –'

43

'I'm sorry to say Mr Simith's not here,' said Carey. 'What's the trouble exactly, do you think?'

'Well, I don't know. There may be none,' said Tombley. He had entered the room by this time, and stood within the rays of the parlour lamp.

'Well, my dear Claudius!' said Mrs Bradley, loudly. She was standing in the shadow, and at the sound of her deep, mellifluous voice, the young man took a step forward in its direction.

'I beg your pardon?' he said. Mrs Bradley appeared with startling suddenness inside the circle of light, her knitting still in her hand. The young man started. He could have been certain that she had been farther off. He did not expect her to leap so suddenly near.

'I classify people,' she said, with a wave of her claw. In the glow of the lamp her skin, on both face and hands, was a dirty, incredible yellow. Her black eyes gleamed like those of a witch or a wolf, and she leered as she smiled and spoke. 'Haven't you read Aldous Huxley's remarkable Mr Scogan on the vastly intriguing subject of the Cæsars? Types. Types. We are all of us types, dear child. There is no such thing as an individual, you know. Did you think there was, and that you were he? Never mind.'

Carey began to laugh.

'Don't mind my aunt,' he said. 'She's an alienist with a lot of foreign degrees. None of us can help it. We don't attempt to cope with it, that is all!'

'Sit down,' said Hugh, 'and tell us what's the matter.'

'Well, it sounds a trifle silly,' Tombley said. 'It's this way. My uncle went off to Oxford, leaving our place at nine o'clock this morning. I expected him home by teatime, and he hasn't got there yet. I can't think what has happened, unless he's met some friends. The trouble is, his heart is none too good. That's why I always worry a bit if he doesn't get back at about his usual time. And just this time, in any case, it happens –'

'Yes. A very proper spirit,' said Mrs Bradley, popping out of the blackness again after the nerve-trying manner of the cuckoo in a cuckoo clock. 'It does you credit, young man!' She popped back, leaving a startled silence behind her. Then Tombley completed his sentence.

'The thing is, I had a date with my lawyer, Fossder, at Iffley, and shan't be able to keep it, I'm afraid. I wondered, if any of you were going over – I'd rather understood that you might be going that way – whether you'd leave a message to say I can't be there. That silly bet, you know.'

'My car is out of action,' said Mrs Bradley, before the young men could speak. This was so palpable a lead for them to follow that neither could ignore it. Hugh took the visitor to the door. Carey walked over to the parlour door and shut it. He grinned at Mrs Bradley, whose saurian smile was again illumined by the lamplight, and sat down again with his book.

'You don't like Sir Geraint of the Swine-Farm,' he observed.

Mrs Bradley did not reply to that. 'I wonder how George and the Ditches are getting on with the car?' she said, as she gazed at Carey, who was laughing.

By eleven o'clock the car was ready for use, and George drove off with Hugh beside him and some extra rugs in the back. The car swung carefully out of the farmyard on to the track, and negotiated the opening to the road. There was nobody about. Lights were out in the cottages, the shouting of the brook was lost in the sound of the engine, and very soon they had climbed past the church, rushed past the inn and eaten the mile or two that brought them to the Headington–Oxford Road.

They soon reached the outskirts of Oxford, swung across the end of Cowley Road at the Plain and ran in top gear towards Iffley.

A little beyond the church Hugh indicated to George that they had almost reached their destination, and the car crawled into the next narrow, sandy opening and stopped by a thick hedge of laurels. Hugh got out.

'Wait here for a bit, George, will you? I expect they've given us up. I may have to rouse the household.'

'Very good, sir,' said George.

'I may be at least half an hour, so have a smoke or anything you like. Got cigarettes and matches?'

'Yes, sir, thank you.'

'All right, then. Get me out that parcel for Mrs Fossder.' Armed with the parcel he walked past laurels, then between lawns and rang the front-door bell. A small, grey-whiskered man admitted him. It was the lawyer, Fossder. His jacket was over his arm, and he carried his shoes in his hand.

'Confound it, we had given you up!' he said. 'Come in and have a drink. They've gone to bed! Weren't you to come at a quarter to ten, young fellow! But it's midnight! It's midnight!'

'Very nearly, sir, I'm afraid,' said Hugh in his meekest tones. 'You really must forgive me. We had a spot of bother with the car, but it's all right now. Only, it rather delayed us.'

'I should think so! I should think so! Well, come along! Come along! Although I don't for one moment, not for one moment, anticipate that my wife will allow the girls to go!'

'Oh, come, sir! It's all arranged!' protested Hugh. He followed his host to the dining room.

'Very great nuisance! Very great nuisance!' said Mr Fossder, angrily. 'I think you had better go home! Yes, really, really! I'm busy. Extremely busy. I really must be about my business. I'm sorry for you, my boy!'

Hugh looked grieved, and said 'when' to the whisky too soon.

'But, look here, sir –' he said. He stood there, glass in one hand, brown-paper parcel in the other, irresolute, angry and disappointed, whilst Mr Fossder put on his jacket and shoes. Then he went outside for an overcoat which he took from a peg in the hall and came back carrying a grey felt hat in his hand.

'Now drink up that milk and water, and get along home,' said Mr Fossder. Before Hugh realised what had happened, he and his host were both outside the front door, and the door was shut. 'Got to keep that appointment, you know.'

'Well, I'm damned!' said Hugh. He gazed after the stiff little figure, and heard the click of the gate. The footsteps on the sandy road went forward, firm and regular, although not particularly fast. Hugh listened until he could hear no more of them. Irresolute, he turned to look back at the house. In two of the first-floor windows lights were burning. He walked down the road to meet George.

'George,' he said, 'did a gentleman go by?'

'Yes, sir, but not particularly fast. He looked at his watch by the beam of our headlights, sir.'

Hugh looked back at the house. The lights were still burning. He turned to the chauffeur, and said,

'Well, I must get back again, George. I may be longer than I thought. Stand by to get away quick. I'm going to abduct one of the ladies.'

'Very good, sir,' said George. 'I'll keep the engine running.'

'I'm just going to follow the old gentleman up,' Hugh added, 'to make sure that the coast is clear. I'll let him get a good start in any case. If, after I come back again, you hear him coming this way, you might give one toot on the horn. By Jove! Now I remember, I've got a message to give him from Mr Tombley! Good thing I remembered it! I'll have to try and catch him.'

'Very good, sir. I shall be fully alert,' said George. He let Hugh go by, and then he turned the car. When Hugh returned, and was coming towards the car, George suddenly tooted on the horn. Hugh stopped, with a startled exclamation. 'Now then! Now then!' he said, sharply. Then he pushed the gate open for the second time, and walked up the gravelled drive between the two shadowy lawns. The house was larger than its modest approach suggested. There were still no lights downstairs, but a third window on the first floor was now illumined. The window opened, and a girl's voice said, in a startled overtone not far short of panic,

'Who's that?'

Hugh, elated by the sound of the voice, which was that of Jenny, explained himself hoarsely and softly.

'We expected you at a quarter to ten,' said the girl. She leaned further out of the window. 'And now it's a quarter past twelve! Wherever have you been, you lunatic?'

'Mess-up with the car,' said Hugh. 'Push a few clothes on, wench, and let's be getting!'

'What!' said the girl, with a squeak. 'But I've been in bed for *hours*! I can't come back with you now! Besides, what will aunt and uncle say? I can't possibly come with you now!'

'Why ever not? Be reasonable. Where's Fay?'

'Asleep, I expect, you idiot. Go away! We shall have to come over tomorrow.'

'But listen here!' said Hugh.

'Well, what do you want? Be quick. I'm getting cold!'

'Come down, and I'll tell you,' said Hugh, whose buccaneering conduct would have amazed and delighted Carey.

'Oh, *sure*!' said Jenny. She laughed, then suddenly relented. 'Hold on, then! I'm coming!'

At this moment another of the lighted windows was opened, and the voice of an older woman said sharply and clearly,

'Really, young man! And what do you think you're doing at this hour of night? You should have come before!'

'I'm sorry, Mrs Fossder,' said Hugh. 'But we had a spot of bother with the car. I'm really *frightfully* sorry, but I came as soon as I could.'

'I suppose you didn't pass my husband on your way?'

'Well, yes, in a manner of speaking,' said Hugh, with caution.

'Did he have his overcoat on? No matter. Either way it can't be helped. Yes, well, you'd better be off. The girls will come over in the morning. I hope Mr Lestrange's aunt has come to stay with you as he promised me faithfully she would. The whole affair, in my opinion, has nothing to recommend it. It savours of –'

'Yes, she's come. But, look here, Mrs Fossder –'

'Go away. Goodnight. A Merry Christmas. Come over first thing in the morning,' said Mrs Fossder irrevocably. She shut the window with a bang and the next moment her light was put out. There was a long silence. Hugh stepped back into the bushes and hid himself. After about three minutes the bright beam of an electric torch began to search the laurels among which he was in hiding. He had put his gloves on and had taken the precaution of holding his cap in front of his face. After a patient and exhaustive search, the torch was switched off. Hugh waited another two minutes and then ran on tiptoe across the lawn and up to the front door, where he took shelter in the porch. He knew that Jenny would manage to come down and speak to him.

At the end of another five minutes the front door softly opened and Jenny came out.

'Hugh,' said Jenny softly. Somewhere a clock chimed twelve.

'Here I am,' said Hugh; he stepped out and kissed her. Jenny hugged him, kissed his ear, and pulled herself away.

'I really must go now,' she said. 'A Merry Christmas, darling! See you first thing in the morning. We can get old Bidster from the village to drive us over. Don't you bother to come. Is Carey's aunt really there – Mrs Bradley? I'm longing to meet her! We all are – especially Maurice! Good night, sweet!' They kissed again. Jenny stifled a little chuckle, and murmured, 'You ought to go back by way of Sandford, and see whether you can spot uncle and the ghost!'

'Uncle and the ghost?' said Hugh. 'What do you mean? Has he really gone to see it?'

'As you say. Uncle and that Geraint Tombley are hunting the Sanford ghost.'

'Good Lord!' said Hugh, beginning to chuckle softly. 'Of course! The date that Tombley couldn't keep.'

'Couldn't keep? What do you mean? Isn't Tombley going to be there? I say, it's a dirty trick to get uncle to go over there on a fool's errand, Hugh! What a shame! Poor old uncle! He's money mad! And Tombley gets half the two hundred if he's there at Sandford as a witness.'

'Come down and sit in the car, and tell me about it,' said Hugh. 'It sounds a bit dotty to me!'

'Of course it's dotty,' said Jenny. They crept to the gate like cats and walked to the car. 'You never in all your life heard anything half so daft.'

Hugh helped her into the car, sat beside her, and wrapped the rug round her. He held it in place, and Jenny wriggled closer.

'The letter came last Tuesday or Wednesday morning. It was all done up in a parcel, with two hundred pounds in Treasury notes, not registered or anything. It said in the letter that the money was a bet, and that Tombley and uncle could have half each if they would go to Sandford to see the ghost. And then those little shields –'

'But I went after him, and told him that Tombley wasn't coming. He took not a scrap of notice, and yet he must have understood me. Fancy his bunking off into Sanford tonight like that! It seems a bit odd, bet or no bet.'

All Mrs Ditch's warnings came flooding back into his mind. Out there, in the quiet and the dark, a ghost seemed germane to the landscape, not alien – a possibility, not an old wives' tale. He shivered, and tucked his hand under Jenny's arm. She squeezed it comfortingly.

'Of course, it's all rot – but he's gone,' she said. She put back the rug. 'And, Hugh, I'd better go too.' There was a pause, and, in it, Hugh kissed her.

'I'm afraid poor uncle will get so cold. And his heart's in a terrible state, and the cold affects people's hearts or something,' said Jenny.

'But they're sure to meet in a house or somewhere,' said Hugh. He held Jenny tight, wrapped the rug round her again and kissed her chin. 'You're coming along,' he said. 'Mrs Ditch can lend you a night-dress. Right away, George!' The car roared into the darkness and swung upslope at Iffley Turn for Rose Hill. 'Look here. Perhaps you're right. It's a rather cold night. We'll go and look for him if you like,' he said suddenly.

'I say, do let's,' said Jenny. 'May I speak to your chauffeur through the tube?' She picked up the tube and told George to stop the car as soon as they had rounded the bend.

'It might be best,' said Hugh.

'We could drop down towards the river, leave the car, and follow him up. He'd walk along the towing path. It's much the quickest, you know. He's sure to have crossed the lock and walked to Sandford that way,' said Jenny.

'Oh, yes. All right,' said Hugh. He gave the necessary instructions. George turned the car, and they dropped back into Iffley and crawled towards the lock.

There was a toll-gate at Iffley, where once was Iffley Mill, but after eleven at night no tolls were taken and the way was left open for travellers to cross the lock.

'Someone was drowned – a woman, I think,' said Jenny, 'trying to get across when the way was closed. So now they leave it open all night long. Uncle is certain to have come this way, and his heart is so weak that he's bound to walk quite slowly. I shouldn't be surprised if we caught him up this side of Kennington Island.'

They crossed the lock, first by the wooden-planked bridge which spanned the noisy waters that once drove the mill-wheel round, and then where the main stream ran quietly. Hugh was ahead, and when they reached the opposite bank he waited for Jenny. They walked side by side after that, half-running, in their haste, by the great fields, wide and unfenced, which bordered the narrow path. On the opposite bank the trees came down to the water's edge and vaguely loomed against the flat night sky.

'It's rather strange in the dark,' said Jenny, softly. 'I'll tell you what! We'd better go straight to the lock and cross the river, if we don't catch him up before then. We must hide if we see uncle coming, and follow wherever he goes. If he goes to a house –'

'I don't know Sandford by night,' said Hugh, 'but I'm sure we're doing the best thing.'

'Of course, I'm not even sure that he's got to cross the river,' Jenny said.

'The road goes off on the other side across a little bridge where the river makes a loop below Sandford Pool. There it joins a bigger road by Radley Large Wood,' said Hugh. 'He may go off that way.'

'I thought you didn't know Sandford in the dark!'

'I don't believe I know which is Temple Farm, and that's where the ghost rides, isn't it?'

As he was speaking Jenny stumbled, and fell. She gave a little cry.

'I'm falling! Oh, Hugh!' She began to pick herself up. With an oath, Hugh also fell forward. He got up and took an electric torch from his pocket. The obstacle over which he and Jenny had fallen was the body of Mr Fossder.

'Good heavens! What's this?' said Hugh.

'Oh, Hugh! Poor uncle! His heart!' said Jenny, beginning to wail.

'Hold up, Jenny. It's quite all right! It's quite all right,' said Hugh, as he knelt on the ground and felt for Fossder's heart. But Mr Fossder was dead. Hugh had not the slightest doubt of it. He raised his voice a little and spoke with curt authority.

'Jenny, go back to the car and get George here!'

Jenny sat in front going home, while Hugh, who had carried the body, held it, and tried to prevent it jolting, on the back seat of the car.

George helped Hugh to lift the body out, and they bore it up to the door between the lawns and the laurels. A frightened servant came to the door and called through the letter-box to them:

'Who be there, this hour of the night? Go away!' But the servant was very soon followed by Mrs Fossder, who had been lying awake to hear her husband come in.

'I'm terribly sorry. An accident,' said Hugh.

'Bring him in here!' she said. 'Tell me what's happened! His heart?' She seemed extraordinarily calm.

Hugh and George laid the body on a couch in the drawing room.

'I'm terribly sorry,' said Hugh. 'I'm afraid his heart's given it up. He must have been running, I think.'

'He's been murdered,' said Mrs Fossder.

He looked at her, then put his arm round her waist and lowered her into a chair.

'Brandy, George. In the sideboard of the room next to this.' He had seen the bottle when Mr Fossder had got out the whisky less than two hours before.

'Well?' said Mrs Bradley when Christmas breakfast was over, and Carey had gone off with Ditch and Denis to see to the feeding of the pigs. 'Tell me all about it from the beginning.'

Her black eyes were brilliant. The yellow topaz in the ring on her right hand blinked like the eye of a lazy cat as she laid her yellow hand on the carved arm of her chair, and let the firelight sparkle on the stone.

Hugh nodded, and pushed a log with his shoe. 'The more you think the thing over, the worse it looks, I should say; Fossder's weak heart wasn't a secret, by any means. I ascertained that from Mrs Fossder last night. There was a bit of a fuss about the girls, you know, and old Fossder went off in the middle of it to keep this date with the ghost. It seems that Fossder had been betted a good deal of money – two hundred pounds, in fact – that he wouldn't go out and have a look at the ghost. He could take a witness with him, and chose Tombley, I can't think why. Well, Fossder went off, and I tore after him to give him Tombley's message, then I went back to the house and dug out Jenny and we thought we would go through Iffley to Sandford and have a chase after Fossder, who, she thought, would get terribly cold. Well, we were walking along, gassing, when Jenny, poor kid, tumbled right over Fossder's body which was lying facing Iffley. All I can see is that somebody must have chased Fossder along the towing path, and Fossder fell dead. That's all. It looks pretty fishy to me. I mean, why should Fossder run and bust his heart, unless he was being followed?'

Mrs Ditch came in.

'Mester Semeth got home all right,' she said. 'Mester Tombley's just come and left the message for ee, and says would ee care to go over.'

'Any idea what had happened to him?' asked Hugh.

'Nothing, Mester Tombley said,' replied Mrs Ditch. 'He'd ben to see a man about –'

'A dog?' said Hugh with a chuckle.

'No, Mr Hugh. A boar.'

'But they've got a boar. In fact, now I come to think of it, they've got a couple. One's a savage old tusker nearly nine years of age and not much good for anything, and the other is a sprightly young blood of two. Do they want another boar in place of old Nero, then?'

'I couldn't say,' said Mrs Ditch. 'He just said to give ee the message, and tell ee' a Merry Christmas!'

'Interesting,' said Mrs Bradley absently. She rose and began to collect her things – a book, some knitting, and a fountain pen. 'Tell me about the two hundred pounds,' she said, when Mrs Ditch had gone.

'The tale of that two hundred pounds is almost incredible as I understand it at present. But, look here,' said Hugh, 'I'll find out what I can this afternoon from Mrs Fossder herself.'

'Yes, do.' Mrs Bradley picked up the handbell that she used to summon Mrs Ditch, and rang it vigorously. Walt appeared in his shirt-sleeves, grinning shyly.

'Our mam be putten the capon en the oven, and her says well I do ee for once?'

'You will,' said Mrs Bradley. 'What time was it when Mr Simith came home?'

'Last night, mam, do ee mean? Mester Tombley said it were half-past two 'en the mornen, ef ever ee 'eard such a theng! Him and some friends had ben out Wetney way, a-thinken of buyen a boar, ef ee ever 'eard anythen so onlikely, on Christmas Eve, of all times, too an' all!'

Young Walt seemed amused. Mrs Bradley eyed him. He looked an intelligent youth.

'Walt,' she said, 'do you think Mr Simith went to Witney?'

'I couldn't say, I'm sure. Her's purty nigh to Bampton, edden her? And he be a Bampton man.'

'Do you know whether he was acquainted with Mr Fossder, who lives just out of Iffley?'

'What, Fossder, the lawyer? Ah, too an' all he was! Dedn't old Fossder send to him to know ef he'd wetness his well? Or so our Lender was sayen.'

'And how did they get on together, Fossder and Mr Simith?'

'They never got on at all.' Walt began to laugh. 'Though I only knows what our Lender says about 'em. Hate each other and trust each other. Ee *do* find old fellers like that, like, now and again.'

'Oh? Thank you, Walt. What time is dinner, do you know?'

'Our mam said a quarter after one.'

'Then I think I'll go for a walk,' said Mrs Bradley. She left Hugh lying on the settee. He had a book – a Christmas present – on his chest, and his eyelids were gently closing. Mrs Bradley went to look for Denis. She found him staring at Hereward, who, chewing thoughtfully, stared back pugnaciously.

'Do you believe that people turn into animals when they die?' he asked, as she came up beside him.

'No, my dear,' said Mrs Bradley, gazing benignly on Hereward. 'I certainly don't believe anything of the kind. Do you care to come for a walk before dinner, Denis?'

'Rather,' said Denis. The morning, though rainless, was cloudy. Mrs Bradley looked at the sky, and then said,

'Go and put on a coat or something, dear child. It's cold and it's going to snow.'

Denis ran in, and soon reappeared, struggling into his overcoat. On his head was his cap. Mrs Bradley eyed him approvingly, and off they went, up the cart-track and on to the road.

'Where are we going?' asked Denis.

'This way,' said Mrs Bradley. They turned away from the village, and tramped downhill towards Stanton Great Wood. The road ran to within a hundred yards of the wood, and from there a footpath skirted Simith's land. They crossed a stile, and the footpath led up to the edge of the wood and along the western side of it.

'Have a good look at Mr Simith's farm,' said Mrs Bradley, 'and if you see anybody, wave. Your eyes are younger than mine.'

They were not sharper than hers, however, for as Denis began to lift his hand uncertainly, Mrs Bradley waved.

'Was it them? I wasn't quite sure,' said Denis. A figure straightened up and waved in reply.

'Come along,' said Mrs Bradley. 'It's Mr Tombley.' They left the path and set out across the next field. Tombley came towards them.

'A Merry Christmas!' he said. 'Did Lestrange get my message about my uncle, do you know?'

'Oh, yes. Or, rather, Hugh and I did. I'm glad your uncle returned quite safely,' Mrs Bradley said. 'Have you heard about the death of Mr Fossder? I think you knew him, didn't you?'

'Fossder? Dead? But – how on earth did it happen? I had a letter from him only the other day.'

'About the Sandford ghost?'

'Why, yes! How did you know?'

'Hugh told me about the bet. You mentioned it, too.'

'Oh, did we? Yes. Rather mysterious, don't you think?'

'Very mysterious indeed,' said Mrs Bradley. She paused. 'Last night Mr Fossder went towards Sandford by himself, and was chased by some person or persons, and had to run, with the result that he collapsed and died.'

'Good heavens! What a terrible thing! But where did this happen? He didn't get to Sandford, you say? You don't think – I say! What a terrible thing!' Tombley seemed genuinely agitated. 'A terrible thing!' he repeated.

'It is, indeed,' Mrs Bradley replied. 'The "ghost" will have to be traced.'

'I should think so, indeed. But it all seems quite extraordinary. Did Hugh, then, go over after all? But, if he did, that means he gave Fossder my message! I sent a message to say I could not go, because of uncle, you remember. But I thought Hugh said the car was out of action –'

'They got it right in the end, and Hugh went over rather late. He said he went after Mr Fossder with your message, but apparently it didn't make any difference. Mr Fossder would not return with him to the house. What were the arrangements, child, exactly, between you and Mr Fossder?'

'We were to meet at Iffley Mill, and cross the lock, and walk along the towing path to Sandford.'

'Are you certain those were the arrangements?'

'Perfectly certain. Ten to twelve was the time.'

'Ah,' said Mrs Bradley, as though satisfied. 'Was Fossder a nervous man, Mr Tombley?'

'Lawyers aren't usually nervous. Excuse me! Promised the vicar I'd go to church.'

'Have you got your Christmas dinner on to cook?' asked Denis, suddenly.

'Oh, yes. Mrs Parsons came in. We shall do very well. A nuisance, of course, about Linda. Times are not what they were!' said Tombley, quite good-humouredly.

As no adequate reply to this – at least, no reply that she wanted Denis to hear – occurred to Mrs Bradley at the moment, she turned and walked back to the footpath, the boy beside her. They retraced their steps to regain the road and were back in good time for Christmas dinner. Hugh came in shortly afterwards.

'Finished your nap?' Mrs Bradley enquired, with her usual mirthless smile. Hugh dropped his eyes and then laughed.

'Nap? Oh, yes, thanks. Thought better of it, and went for a stroll instead. I think I'd better go over to Iffley this afternoon,' he added. 'After all, the old chap would have been a relation of mine, if he'd lived until after my marriage.'

Mrs Bradley looked interested. 'Do you mind if I come as well?' she asked, before anyone else could speak. 'Not to the house, of course, but into Iffley? I think I should like the drive.'

'May I come too?' asked Denis. Carey caught his aunt's eye.

'I was depending on Scab for table tennis,' he said; so Denis, always good natured, remained behind, whilst Mrs Bradley and Hugh went off in the car together. Mrs Bradley drove. She had brought out an ordnance map, and, whilst Hugh was with Mrs Fossder, she cruised about in the car. The route she took branched off at Littlemore, crossed the main road below Cowley, went out of its way to Garsington, and then, by Coombe Wood, into Wheatley. It met the main road at Wheatley, then followed it past Hill House, through Forest Hill, and so a mile or two northwards back to Stanton St John. Then she returned across country direct to Headington Quarry and back to Iffley. There she left the car outside the public house, and went for a very short stroll along the towing path. There was nothing to show where the body of Fossder had lain. She spent some moments, on her return to the house, studying the cross on the gate.

CHAPTER 4

Corners – the Fight – at Iffley

Hugh was waiting for her.

'Would you mind coming into the house and having a talk with Mrs Fossder?' he said. 'She's cut up, of course, but it – she's being jolly good about it. Quite composed. As a matter of fact, she's intensely angry. She puts the whole thing on to Simith. Well, it *is* a bit odd, you know.'

'I know,' said Mrs Bradley.

'Where does this go when it passes the house?' she asked as they stopped for a moment at the gate. She waved her hand onwards to indicate the little lane in which the house was set.

'It's a cut through to the river,' Hugh replied. 'Flooded at its lower end in spring, and fearfully boggy now. I don't think Fossder went – in fact, of course he didn't. He passed the car, and must have crossed by the mill – or where the mill used to be. That was the way that Jenny and I went after him later on.'

They went up the path to the house, and Jenny, who had seen them from a window, came herself to the door before they rang.

Mrs Fossder was white, and looked very ill. But her voice was as full and purposeful as it had been when she had ordered Hugh away on the previous night.

'My husband's been murdered,' she said.

'Manslaughter, anyway,' said Mrs Bradley briskly. 'What have you got against Mr Simith, my nephew Carey's neighbour.'

'They never got on. Edmund lost a case for him, and Simith never forgave it. He knew Edmund had a weak heart – everyone knew it – he's had it for years, and always had to be careful. He wouldn't drive a car in case of having a seizure when at the wheel.'

'Do you know what made your husband so anxious to keep the tryst with Mr Tombley?'

'Yes. It was some ridiculous wager in conection with the Sandford ghost. He was to meet Geraint Tombley at Sandford. They were to share two hundred pounds if they would go. Poor Geraint Tombley! Poor boy! He has a bad time with that wicked old man.'

'Your feelings for Tombley, then, are not the same as your feelings for Simith?' Mrs Bradley said. Mrs Fossder opened her eyes.

'Good gracious, no! Quite different. Simith is a nasty, common person. Tombley is a gentleman. But, of course, as Simith's nephew, my husband would not consent to his engagement to Fay, even although she desired it.'

'It seems to me much more likely,' said Mrs Bradley bluntly, 'that a young man of Tombley's age should have chased your husband along the towing path – that is, if anyone did – than that a man of Simith's age should have done it.'

'You don't know Simith,' said Mrs Fossder. 'That's plain. He's tried to murder his nephew more than once. He's a terribly vindictive old man, and has a very bad reputation in other ways.'

Mrs Bradley remembered the fight between uncle and nephew which she and George had witnessed upon their arrival in the neighbourhood of Stanton St John. It had been obvious then that the aggressor was Simith. Tombley, with his pig-bucket, had been doing little more than defending himself.

She nodded.

'May I see the letter which your husband received from Reading? I heard it was anonymous,' she said. Mrs Fossder went out of the room. 'I can't believe it was Simith,' Mrs Bradley whispered. Hugh grimaced.

'I can't make head or tail of it,' he said. 'I'll tell you another thing –'

But before he could do so, Mrs Fossder came back.

Mrs Bradley read the letter. It contained nothing beyond a statement of the terms of the wager and a proposal that Fossder and Tombley should meet at Sandford Church. Mrs Bradley consulted her map. The church was off the main road, and lay on the northern side of the little road that led to the weir and the paper mill.

'There was another anonymous communication – the one with the little shields,' said Mrs Fossder. 'You noticed the cross in paint on the gate?' She held out another envelope. Of the pencilled shields – there were two on the same piece of paper – one bore a cross, the other what looked rather like a sketch of some diamond-shaped trellis.

'One is a cross, and the other a criss-cross,' said Mrs Fossder. 'Only, the cross isn't Christian!'

'Oh, yes, I think it is,' said Mrs Bradley. 'It's an heraldic one, and is known, I believe, as the Cross Patée or Formée. But about Mr Simith –'

'Hugh told us he was out last night,' said Mrs Fossder, catching her teeth in her bottom lip, and frowning. 'Mrs Bradley, I *know* he had something to do with poor dear Edmund's death. I feel *certain* that he was there. Hugh said he did not get home until half-past two o'clock. Isn't that proof positive for us?'

'Well, no, I'm afraid it isn't,' said Mrs Bradley. 'But I want to check up some times. Now, Jenny, you begin.'

Jenny stirred uneasily, and, looking at Mrs Bradley, and then away, said doubtfully,

'It was striking twelve when I went to meet Hugh in the garden.'

'Go on,' said Mrs Bradley.

'We talked a little, and then we got into the car. The chauffeur drove off, and we stopped for a minute or two, just this side of Rose Hill – well, just on the slope as you turn up out of the village going towards Littlemore.'

'I say!' said Hugh. 'Not a lunatic's joke, by any chance? Some poor unhinged blighter thinking he himself was the Sandford ghost?'

'The most unlikely thing in the world,' said Mrs Fossder. 'Lunatics never think of themselves as obscure sort of people like that George Napier, a gentle, inoffensive Catholic priest. They imagine themselves to be someone everybody knows – world-builders – more often, world destroyers – but always people of power and influence. They are often martyrs, but not the kind of martyrs who only figure in local legends afterwards. Still, no doubt the authorities will tell us whether all their charges were accounted for last night. My husband was interested in lunatics, and really rather afraid of them,' she added. 'I believe his interest was really somewhat morbid. He used to visit the asylum occasionally. We got to know one of the doctors there. He used to come here to tea. Poor man! He died last year. He was really very nice, and most interesting on the subject of his work.'

Mrs Bradley looked at Jenny.

'Then your man George turned the car, and we went to the lock. We crossed the river and walked towards Sandford. We had not gone very far before I – before I stumbled over him.'

'Which way was he facing?' Mrs Bradley enquired. It was Hugh who had to reply, for Jenny was overcome.

'He was face downwards, and the head was towards Folly Bridge.'

'But that looks as though he was coming *away* from Sandford, not going *towards* it!' Mrs Fossder exclaimed.

'We ought to be able to trace the ghost, if there *was* one,' said Mrs Bradley.

'Mrs Bradley,' said Mrs Fossder, looking her full in the face, 'I have heard that you are a very clever woman. You came to this hateful affair with an open mind. Will you answer me one question?'

'Willingly,' said Mrs Bradley gravely. 'I do believe that your husband was deliberately murdered. I'm not trying to get away from that.'

'How did you know what it was my aunt wanted to ask you?' asked Jenny, when they reached the front door.

'It was obvious, child. I can't tell you how I knew.'

'Then ought we to call in the police?'

'I cannot advise you, child, with regard to calling in the police. What has your doctor said?'

'He signed the certificate. Said uncle was liable to fall dead of any kind of over-exertion or even sudden shock, so there won't have to be an inquest.'

'I'm afraid there's hardly a case for the police, then, at this juncture, child, you know. Dangerous practical joking would be the most you could hope to make out of it, even if you could discover the practical joker. And if I understand your aunt aright, what she wants is someone hanged. Like poor George Napier,' she added.

'I think he was only drawn and quartered,' said Hugh. Mrs Bradley looked at him and shuddered.

'By the way,' she said, 'was Mr Fossder deaf?'

'Deaf? Not a bit,' replied Jenny. 'His hearing was rather acute. I believe,' she added later to Hugh, as they took their leave before Hugh got into the car beside Mrs Bradley, 'Carey's aunt is more angry at the foolishness of the crime than at its wickedness.'

'It doesn't sound to me foolish, you know,' said Hugh. 'I should call it rather a brainy effort myself. Incidentally, Mrs Fossder's taking it pretty well. I'm really rather surprised.'

'Hugh, who do *you* think it was?' asked Jenny, after a pause.

'I'd plump for Tombley without a thought,' said Hugh, 'if I could prove he wasn't at Roman Ending between half-past ten and one o'clock last night. But, you see, to prove *that* –'

'You would have to interview separately Tombley and Simith, and perhaps the pigman, Priest,' said Mrs Bradley, poking her head out and grinning like the sea-serpent at them. 'Go in, child. You'll get a cold,' she said to Jenny. Jenny obeyed, and waved to them before the laurels hid her. 'Your point about Tombley, I suppose,' added Mrs Bradley, 'is that, in spite of the message he asked you to deliver, Tombley *did* keep the appointment, although not, from poor Mr Fossder's point of view, in an entirely acceptable manner.'

'Exactly,' Hugh replied gravely. 'Poor little Fay!'

'I like your fiancée,' said Mrs Bradley smoothly. 'Some time I must meet that little sister.'

'Well, not her sister, actually,' said Hugh, 'but the Fossders treat them alike. The person I really want you to meet is Pratt.'

'But I've met him,' said Mrs Bradley. Hugh nodded and laughed.

'But not in his fullest beauty,' he remarked.

'Well, it's been a very odd Christmas Day,' said Carey, as they sat down to tea at six. Denis took a stick of celery.

'All I want,' he said, and bit off a piece with great solemnity. 'I'm not very keen on tea, today, for some reason.'

'Saving up for supper, Scab?' asked Hugh.

'Been eating all the afternoon,' said Carey. 'Kids are disgusting, really!' He punched Denis lightly in the ribs. Denis wriggled, and took another bite from the celery.

'What have you two been doing?' he asked, pausing in his mastication to stare at them.

'Been over to see Mrs Fossder,' Hugh replied.

'I told old Simith about that this afternoon. He *was* surprised. Said he'd never believed in ghosts, and said I was pulling his leg. So I said, "Well, *you* ought to know! Where were *you* last night, Mr Simith? That's what we'd like to find out." It didn't go awfully well. He went most frightfully red, and his eye went frightfully blue, and he took the most frightful whack at me with his stick, and called me what they call you in these parts when they mean –' he glanced at Mrs Bradley and paraphrased swiftly – 'that you're rather interfering, and then, of course, I legged it, and there was Tombley standing by and laughing like the silly jackass he is. Oh, and I've seen three grey horses for you, in case the ghost was in its coach, you know.'

He pulled out a piece of paper (laying down the celery to do so) and spread it out on the table. The flattering interest and breathless attention with which his remarks were received he found peculiarly gratifying. His relatives very seldom took him seriously. First Hugh and then Mrs Bradley bent over the paper. On a rough but remarkably well-sketched map of the neighbourhood, the three grey horses were indicated in the form of elaborate question marks. One was on Simith's farm.

'Amazing!' said Mrs Bradley.

'Three of them!' said Hugh.

'And you'd have nothing on earth to do,' said Denis eagerly, 'but lead them out through a gate.'

'But surely they're stabled at night?'

'I expect the ghost would have got one out in the daytime, wouldn't he, Aunt Bradley? I asked Priest what he thought, and he said he would.'

Mrs Bradley caught Hugh's eye over the top of the child's bent head. Hugh raised his eyebrows. Mrs Bradley nodded.

'He's done very well,' said Hugh.

'Is it really any good?' asked Denis.

'Unspeakably helpful,' Mrs Bradley replied. 'Please may I keep that piece of paper?'

She impounded it forthwith. Denis returned to his celery. Later he managed two pieces of Christmas cake and half a dozen chocolate biscuits.

'That's better, Scab,' said Carey. 'I don't want to send you home thin.' Denis smiled politely and went off with Carey after tea to play darts in the gallery upstairs. Hugh lit a cigar, and said to Mrs Bradley, when Mrs Ditch had come in and cleared away,

'Not exactly helpful, I suppose? But the little devil's got brains.'

'Yes,' said Mrs Bradley. 'That's interesting about Simith owning a grey. Simith was certainly doing something unusual, if not

65

unlawful, last night, and Priest bears neither of his employers much goodwill, I should say.'

'Still, Scab's proved one thing. There doesn't seem much shortage of greys, and – of course the coach is absurd, but if the fellow was on *horseback* –'

'True.' Mrs Bradley looked thoughtful. 'What did you make of the Fossder household today?'

'Nothing in particular. Mrs Fossder's a very brave woman, I think.'

'Or a very vindictive one,' said Mrs Bradley. 'And, by the way, there's something you can do.'

'Me personally?'

'None other. I want you to find out from Jenny the terms of Fossder's will as soon as it is proved.'

'Oh! Motive for the crime, if any, you mean?'

'That is what I mean. Although –' she frowned a little.

'Say on,' said Hugh. 'By the way, I can tell you the terms of the will, unless they've been altered recently.'

'I suppose Fossder *was* meant to die?' said Mrs Bradley musingly, half to herself.

'You mean perhaps it wasn't murder at all, but simply a joke with a very unforeseen ending? It's much the more likely, you know, in which case, you can't necessarily implicate any of the people who knew how bad his heart was. Probably they would lay off any practical jokes.'

'I wish,' said Mrs Bradley, beginning her knitting, 'I had any pretext whatever for examining Fossder's heart.'

'It would mean a post-mortem, and the doctor has written the certificate.'

'Yes, I know. What a bit of luck for the murderer –'

'If any!'

'Yes. Suppose that someone saw it done.'

'Couldn't. It was pitch dark.'

'Heard something, then.'

'Could you prove anything from that?'

'Of course you could. Why not?' She grinned at him evilly. 'Men have been hanged on very much slighter evidence.'

'Yes, I suppose so. What we want to do, I should say, is to sort out the people at Roman Ending, and see what they have to say about last night. Simith and Tombley were both away from home at some time during the night. That's clear enough. Tombley even came here, as though to see how the land lay regarding my going to Iffley. I expect, if we knew all, it was Tombley who damaged the car. Now, I propose that we all go over there as though to pay them a visit. Get your chauffeur to take on the pigman for a bit; then Carey and I could separate uncle and nevvy, and you could go the rounds and ask the questions.'

'It will have to be done tomorrow. There is no excuse we could offer for disturbing them again on Christmas Day. Denis and I walked over their land this morning; Denis has been there again this afternoon. We really must leave it until tomorrow, I think.'

'Very well,' said Hugh. 'I agree entirely. You know, I did wonder at one point whether Mrs Fossder killed her husband, but one hardly likes to think so, without something definite to go on.'

Mrs Bradley shrugged.

'Wives do kill husbands,' she said, 'and husbands wives. But I do want to know about that will.'

'In a nutshell, Pratt gets the practice – he was Fossder's partner, you know – and the three females get the money – in equal shares, I believe. I don't know how much it amounts to – precious little, I should think.'

'I see,' said Mrs Bradley. 'That's very interesting. So that if Geraint Tombley were short of a few hundreds, all he would need to do, having frightened Mr Fossder to death, would be to marry Fay immediately, and hope she would be willing to hand him over the money.'

'But I don't think the money can amount to enough for that,' objected Hugh. 'A country lawyer couldn't have much to leave, and old Fossder used to dabble in speculations a bit, you know. Soon lose a packet that way.'

He turned to his book. Mrs. Bradley continued her knitting and read modern verse, frowning slightly.

Denis and Carey came down.

'Let's have some drinks. Scab, you shall have a cocktail if you swear not to tell your mother. What do you say?' said Carey. 'Oh, by the way, Hugh, a note for you from Roman Ending. Tombley just brought it over. Said he wouldn't stop, as his uncle was left with the whisky.'

Hugh read the note.

'An offer to lend us their gramophone all day tomorrow,' he said. 'I told them we'd got some new records. When we return it, we'd better lend them the records.'

At supper the boar's head was the centre piece at table. Hugh saluted it and murmured something about a 'little tidy Bartholomew boar-pig.'

''Tis handsome, that's what *I* say,' observed Mrs Ditch.

'Carve some of it for yourself,' said Mrs Bradley. 'How many of you are there?'

'Five, counting Lender, mam,' replied Mrs Ditch.

'Oh, by the way, have you got a bed for Linda?' Carey enquired.

'Thanken you, Mr Carey, she can have a nice shakedown with us. We've got two mattresses on our bed, and a couple of feather beds on top of they, so Lender can have a mattress, and do very well.'

She carried away the slices of boar's head, and a bottle of port which Carey took out of the sideboard.

Denis was sent to bed at midnight, and Mrs Bradley, who never cared much for late hours, decided to go to bed at half-past twelve. Carey and Hugh soon followed her example.

Except for Carey, they slept late on Boxing Day morning, and it was ten o'clock before Mrs Bradley and Denis, the latest risers, had finished a leisurely breakfast. Mrs Bradley propped up a book of verse and drank two cups of coffee, and Denis sat, elbows on table, devouring a detective story. At eleven Mrs Ditch came in and cleared away.

'Well,' said Mrs Bradley, 'what shall we do?'

'I'm going on reading,' said Denis. He lifted up his book to allow Mrs Ditch to take the cloth off, and then sank back with a sigh, on to the trail of the murderer. Carey came in just then.

'Hallo, you lazy things,' he said, coming forward to the fire. 'Even old Hugh has beaten you both this morning! He's gone over to Roman Ending to borrow Tombley's gramophone. I brought a lot of records back from Oxford the other week.'

'Haven't you a wireless set?' asked Denis.

'Oh, yes. It's a portable. It's usually in the kitchen being taken to bits and rebuilt, with the latest improvements, by the Ditch boys. I thought the gram would be a change. We can stick on the Sword Dance records – "Kirkby Malzeard" and "Flamborough" – I love those tunes – I could hear them all day long. He's taken the bike and sidecar. He can load the gram on to that. I expect old Simith's giving him a drink or something. Tombley ain't there. He's gone over to Iffley this morning to visit Mrs Fossder and Fay.'

'Oh, yes. Mrs Fossder would rather have *him* for son-in-law than Pratt,' remarked Mrs Bradley.

By lunch time Denis had finished his book. They had the gramophone on during most of the afternoon. Tombley and Simith came over, but both went back before dusk to help Priest get in the pigs. The sky was grey and heavy. It looked like snow.

'Tell ee what, Mr Carey,' said Mrs Ditch, when the uncle and nephew had gone, 'I wish, when the weather gets better, ee'd plead with that there Priest to come and dance this year.'

'Priest! I didn't know he was a dancer,' said Carey.

'He ent,' Ditch assured him solemnly. 'But ef Mester Tombley have made up his mind not to dance, us *must* get another, Mester Carey.'

Carey rubbed his jaw.

'I'll see to it,' he said. 'It's a long time yet until Easter. We can safely leave it until then.'

'Easter us starts re'earsen, Mester Carey. Ee ent forgotten that?'

'No, that's right. Oh, I'll get him. We'll have him here, and teach him. Don't worry, Ditch. We'll get together a side!'

By ten o'clock Hugh said he was sleepy, and bade them all goodnight. At eleven, Denis, struggling with drowsiness, went to bed. Mrs Bradley went upstairs with him, and Carey followed almost immediately after them.

Before she began to undress, Mrs Bradley walked to the window and gazed out into the darkness. There was no moon, and the stars were hidden by cloud. As she stood there, the first flakes of the snow, which had threatened all day, began to fall fairly thickly. She stood there, in the unlighted west-windowed chamber, and watched the fall of the snow. In less than a quarter of an hour the ground was glimmering white. The snow had settled.

She came away from the window, undressed very slowly, splashed some icy water over her face and hands, and then got into bed. The hot-water bottle was comforting. The bed was thoroughly warm. The room was warm, although the fire had gone down and only showed a dull red wink of life when she peeped at it with one eye.

Suddenly a pig began to squeal, and other pigs followed suit. The noises soon died down. Mrs Bradley turned on her side and slept. In the next bedroom, however, Carey was wakeful and alert. He too, had heard the pigs. He got out of bed and went to his window, which looked out on to the pig-rearing houses, but it was too dark to see anything. He put on his dressing-gown and went downstairs. Here he exchanged his dressing-gown for an overcoat, his slippers for shoes, took a good thick stick from the stand and sallied out towards the pig-house. The snow fell thick on his hair and soaked into his shoulders. The toes of his shoes were covered and his sleeves were soon thick with snow. He shook it off as he walked, but it came again, with soft, unhurrying persistence, wetting his face and dropping with hideous precision down the front of his collar.

He went first to Hereward's sty, because it was nearest. The boar was not stirring, although Carey stood for a moment listening beside the run. Hereward's was the only separate sty on the pig-farm, for Tom was kept in the larger of the pig-houses, next door to the farrowing pen. Carey went to this pig-house next, and, when he got inside, took a lantern from its nail and lighted it. He then walked down the centre passage between the two rows of sties and made a thorough inspection. The young pigs in the pig-rearing pens seemed to have quietened down, but two of the sows were restive. Tom, too, was awake, and ambled up to the feeding trough in a fairly hopeful manner, and yawned and blinked at his owner and scratched the floor with his natty little front feet.

'Nothing doing,' said Carey. The farrowing pen, an enclosure twice the size of the usual sty, was empty, but next door was a weaning pen which had several attractive pinkish occupants. Carey looked reproachfully at them.

'Now, which of you squealed?' said he. 'And what for, anyway, fat-heads?' The little pigs, wide awake, began tumbling over each other at the sound of his voice. Their pen came next to the outside wall of the pig-house, except for a narrow passage-way. Another weaning pen was opposite, but this was empty, and next door again was Sabrina, the savage old sow. She seemed more disturbed than Buttercup, her next-door neighbour, and grunted at Carey, and rubbed her great side along the edge of the sty, and snorted at him complainingly.

'What is it, then?' said Carey. 'Didn't you like the noise? But why did they squeal, Sabrina? It's a shame! You're all upset!' He reached over and smacked her sympathetically. He went to the smaller pig-house, built on similar lines to the other, but twenty feet shorter. This building was further away from the farmhouse, and in it the pigs seemed undisturbed except by the sound of

Carey's footsteps, which woke the weaners, nervous, hungry little pigs, as he went past their sties.

Carey walked into the snowfall again and flashed the lantern about, but nothing was to be seen except the snow, now lying sufficiently thickly on the ground to have covered his own tracks from the house to the sty of the boar, and to begin to obliterate his fresh tracks as soon as he made them. He bent his head and hastened back to the house, and then discovered that he had shut the front door and had no latch-key with him. He knocked, and Ditch, who had stopped to pull on his trousers, came down and let him in.

'All right, Ditch,' said Carey. 'It's only me. One of the pigs must have had a bad dream or something.'

'Ah. A dog came prowlen, I should thenk. Soon start off they pegs, a dog well. Wonder who he belonged to? Nobody nearer than Welliam Smart have a dog.'

'Doesn't seem to be anything wrong,' said Carey, stamping to shake off the snow. 'Beast of a night out there.'

'Ah. Soon start up they pegs, a dog well,' Ditch repeated. 'Never woke that gal of ourn, though, not our Lender. Her never stirred a finger. Mother woke up, and me. But not our Lender. Sleep like a milestone, that gal do. Always ded. No thought for nothen but herself.'

'That's true, too and all, our dad,' said Mrs Ditch, looking over the banisters, candle in hand. 'Nothen at all but a bolster in the bed, laid lengthways down the meddle. Ef we had 'lectrec light enstead of these 'ere old candles, we'd a-seen when we come up to bed!'

'But where can she be?' asked Carey.

'Ee needn't ask that,' said Ditch, in bitter tones. 'Her's over at Roman Enden, betch that her be.'

'Hush ee, our dad,' said Mrs Ditch peremptorily.

'Would you like me to go over?' Carey enquired.

'Nay, us'll just let her be. Her can make her a bed where

she well. 'Tis her 'aves to lie on it later,' said Ditch, with heavy philosophy.

'Can't understand it,' said Carey to Mrs Bradley, whom the various sounds had wakened again. She had come out on to the landing, a bizzare coat embroidered with dragons covering her thin upright person. 'I thought Linda Ditch had hopped it from Roman Ending because she couldn't stand the attentions of old Simith. I shall have to go over in the morning. Curse these good-looking wenches! They're always in trouble of some sort. I don't in the least want to have a dust-up with Simith, but he can't seduce Mrs Ditch's only daughter. Pity Linda's not more like the boys. They're all as mild as milk. Think of nothing but the wireless and Morris dancing. I believe one's got a motor bike. But you know what I mean. I shouldn't think they've ever given their parents the slightest bit of worry in the world. Young Walt lives here, and is almost too good to be true, except as a pigman. Don't know the first thing about pigs. Wish I could tempt that bloke Priest from his allegiance. But I think he's hanging on to get the chance of murdering Simith. Hates him like poison, I know. Oh, well, come and have a spot of whisky, because I'm cold.'

He led the way into the parlour, and lighted the lamp. The door of the priest's hole was open. A slight draught blew from it into the empty room.

'Oh, lor,' said Carey. 'What's this?'

They went and explored the hole. It was innocently square and bare. Carey shut the panelling again and put his back against it.

'Odd, don't you think?' asked Mrs Bradley. Carey shook his head.

'One of Scab's jokes. Nipped down and did it while I was out there at the piggeries, I expect.'

CHAPTER 5

Cross Over at Old Farm

'Scab,' said Carey, collaring him before breakfast, 'why did you leave the priest-hole open last night?'

'But I didn't!' said Denis, surprised into what he afterwards regarded as a depressingly juvenile squeak.

'Honest?' said Hugh, who was lounging on the window seat, looking out at the snow and longing for rashers and eggs, and sniffing the smell of the coffee which Mrs Ditch had brought in.

'Of course I didn't, Hugh! I wouldn't give away my secret to Mrs Ditch, or whoever it is that comes in here first in the morning!'

'Queer, then,' said Carey. 'I know it was shut when I went to bed at half-past ten or so.'

'We can't be sure of that. It's possible it was ajar, you know,' said Hugh. 'Still, I went up before you, and I didn't notice anything.'

'Well, it ain't ajar now,' said Carey. 'I shut it up pretty tight when we went to bed for the second time last night, and shoved a chair against it.'

He took the heavy chair away, then suddenly pulled it open. 'Good Lord!' he said. 'What's this!'

Linda Ditch, in a fainting condition, tumbled into the room. The two young men and Denis gathered round her.

'Get back a bit, you two. Give her room,' said Hugh, kneeling down. At almost the same time Linda Ditch sat up.

'Don't tell our mam,' she said.

'But how did you get in there?' asked Hugh. 'Here, just drink this!' He signed to Carey to bring her some coffee. Linda waved it away, and struggled to her feet, white-faced. She was dressed in what appeared to be her party frock, a tawdry affair of cheap blue lace which reached to the ground and was cut fairly low in the front. Over it she had on her outdoor coat. On her feet were silver shoes slightly wearing over at the heels, and her head, untidy now, had been not too becomingly waved. In all, she looked a slightly bedraggled object, but it did not look as though she had been out in the snow.

'Let me be. I don't want to tell ee nothen. I was let down,' she said.

'Shut up, Linda,' said Carey, with a very slight nod towards Denis.

'Oh, that! I don't mean that! Can't ee tell? That happened weeks ago. I mean I was just left flat. So I come back and slept en that there hole.'

'Be sensible, Linda,' said Carey. 'There's no sense in making a mystery. Where have you been, and how did you get in there?'

Hugh stepped over, closed the aperture, and stood with his back against the panelling.

'I'd better clear out,' said Denis helpfully, and in his most grown-up tones. He went out into the snow, now sparkling in sunshine.

'You let me go,' said Linda. 'I'm goen into service at Littlemore. At the Asylum,' she added, as though in defiance of something.

'You won't like it there,' said Carey. 'Aren't you really going to tell us about all this?'

'Not I. So you leave me be. Got my own business to mind, so do you mind yours!'

'But it is his business, you silly girl!' said Mrs Bradley, appearing like the Devil to Doctor Faustus. 'It's his house, and he has a perfect right to ask you questions if he finds you in a part of it where you certainly ought not to be. Go upstairs and change that frock and those shoes, and then send your mother to me.'

At this Linda fell on her knees.

'You won't tell our mam! You won't tell our mam!' she sobbed.

'Not a word,' said Mrs Bradley, 'except that you got shut in by mistake. Were you wearing that frock last night in this house for the family Boxing Day party?'

'Ah, that I were! And our Walt tore it, too!'

'Then that's all right. Now, be a sensible girl. I won't defend you unless you tell me the truth. And make no mistake! I know the truth when I hear it! Several strange things appear to have happened last night!'

She leered at Linda, who shrank back, and then, still spirited, gave a little giggle.

'That's better,' said Mrs Bradley.

'And will she tell you?' asked Carey, when Linda had gone.

'Oh, yes, a *part* of the truth!' said Mrs Bradley. 'She's quite a bad lot, that girl.' She shook her head at Linda Ditch's short-comings. 'Of course, she's been to see someone over at Roman Ending.'

'You think, then, that that was the row that frightened the pigs last night? Linda hopping it over to Roman Ending?'

'I don't know, child, but I doubt it. When did the snow begin to fall?'

'Before I went out to the pigs. It was coming down fast just then.'

'Then Linda went earlier than that, and came back earlier, too, unless she went under cover, or changed her dress and her shoes.'

'By way of the priest's hole, you mean? By Jove –' He went to the panelling and opened the door again. At that moment Mrs Ditch came in with the eggs and bacon, and stared with some curiosity at the opening in the wall. Mrs Bradley waved a skinny claw.

'Linda got shut in there. We've just let her out,' she said. 'She's gone upstairs to change. She still had her party frock on. I shouldn't worry her at present. She's had rather a shock, I expect.'

'But we made sure as she went up to bed at just afore ten.'

'She couldn't have done. But it means there's another entrance to this hole,' said Carey suddenly.

'If she went to Roman Ending the ordinary way, she'd have had to be out in the snow. She couldn't do that without marking those silver shoes. Take my advice. Let it go. Mention it in joke, as you would have done if young Walt had been shut in there instead of Linda. But don't plague the girl, Mrs Ditch,' said Carey, in whose chivalrous opinion Linda was never quite fairly treated by her mother.

The circumstantial evidence of the shoes convinced Mrs Ditch. She took the first opportunity of examining them for herself, and, finding that it was obvious that they had not been worn out of doors, she gave in to the extent of remarking sardonically,

'Get herself locked up one way or another, chance what, our Lender well.' She left it at that for the time.

'By the way,' said Carey, when Mrs Ditch had gone, 'I heard from Tombley, who heard it in some way from Fay, that Fossder's will was all right.'

'What do you mean, child?'

'Well, there was some idea at one time that he was going to leave a funny will or something, cutting out Jenny and perhaps Mrs Fossder, or something. But he seems to have changed his mind and left 'em all in.'

'Oh, really? So much more satisfactory.' She nodded, as though in congratulation of all the legatees, and took her seat at the table opposite a dish of fried bacon and the apparently inevitable hog-puddings. After breakfast she covered herself with a good deal of unnecessary glory by knocking six bottles off the kitchen garden wall with six successive snowballs, and, having paid this amount of tribute to the seasonable downfall, she felt that she had earned the right to return to the parlour and drink the Bovril which Linda Ditch brought in on a small silver tray.

'I say,' said Denis, following her into the room, 'have you ever tried shying at coconuts, Aunt Bradley? I should think you'd be rather good.'

'I have been warned off the coconut shies at no fewer than three fairs in the Home Counties alone,' replied his great-aunt, with becoming modesty. Denis whistled.

'You *do* look rather like a witch, in some respects,' he commented.

'That's rude of ee, Mr Denis,' said Linda Ditch. 'Do ee drink up that there Bovril, no more nonsense!'

Denis was so much incensed that he did not reply, and, having drunk the Bovril, he took a couple of biscuits and went off to find Hugh and Carey, who were helping Ditch and Young Walt to sweep the various paths.

'Now, mam,' said Linda, briskly.

'Now, Linda,' said Mrs Bradley.

'Well, mam, no denyen I went out to meet my bo.'

'Your what?' said Mrs Bradley. 'Oh, yes, of course. Go on.'

'Him be-en that there Priest, over to Roman Ending.'

'Come now. Don't be so silly!' said Mrs Bradley. 'A man with a face like that! What on earth would the children be like?'

Linda stared, then laughed.

'You do be a one,' she said. 'Well, here, then. I went to see Tombley – Jerry I calls him – because we had to get talken about this here.'

She sketched a sufficient gesture.

'Ah, yes. The illegitimate child,' said Mrs Bradley offensively. Linda eyed her coldly.

'Not all that bad, it ent! He'll marry me, see ef he don't!' she replied with spirit.

'He can't, if he's hanged,' said Mrs Bradley calmly. 'Where was he on Christmas Eve?'

The girl, although sullen, looked frightened.

'I don't know what you be talken about,' she said.

'Oh, Linda!' said Mrs Bradley.

'I don't, I tell ee! Can't you believe what I says?'

'Not very much of it. Why did you leave Roman Ending in such a hurry?'

'Because Jem Priest, he heared a row and went off.'

Mrs Bradley began to hum a tune. Linda scowled, and then her sullenness vanished. Once again she laughed.

'He's a Constant Billy, all right! He makes me laugh. Always jealous! Always hangen about when a gal don't want him no longer!' She, too, began to hum. 'Ah! And I wish them there fishes might *never* fly over no mountains,' she added, in mysterious parenthesis.

'What's that!' said Mrs Bradley.

'What's what?' said Linda, entirely innocently this time.

'Fishes and mountains, child. I don't think I place the reference.'

'Oh? Tes that there song they Morris dancers sengs. Our Dad, he knows et. Young Walt, too and all.' Her voice was more tuneful than her mother's; her sense of rhythm less strong.

> 'O my Billy, my constant Billy,
> When shall I see my Billy again?
> When the fishes fly over the mountains,
> Then you will see your Billy again!'

'Thank you, child. That's very interesting,' said Mrs Bradley, and packed into the back of her mind (subsequently to be transferred to her notebook) the variation on the words she had heard Linda's mother sing not so long before. 'Go on with your night adventures. My nephews will be coming in soon.'

'Well, Jerry Tombley and me, we arranged to meet in that there old barn beyond the garden wall. Cellars of this here house goes underground, and comes up in that there old barn, as everybody round here knows. Was an older house than this built a bet to the north, and that's the reason for why.

'Well, Walt and me, playen as children, found that there lettle room there, behind the wood wall.' She pointed to the panelling to make her meaning clearer. 'And we found it went down to the cellar, so I thought I'd purtend like to slep up to bed a bet early, and then put the bolster en the bed, and go down this way to the cellar, case our dad come down for some beer. Come right into the corner of the cellar, that passage leaden from that little room behind.

'Well, they kept playen tiddly-winks, and haven the wireless on, and then the gramophone, and wanten me to keep dancen, tell I felt quite fet to go to bed, even without pertenden, so after supper – half-past ten that were – I sleps upstairs like I said, and down I comes, not through here, but another way we found. Shan't tell ee where. Ee can find et, like ee found this un.

'But what does I find when I gets down into the cellar, but our dad and our Walt, between em, have shefted all the coal and coke and that, tell the passage be quite blocked up. I tell ee I didn't know what to do for roaren. I sat there en my big coat, on one of the hogs' 'eads, and I'll back I roared like some poor lettle child. I daren't sheft the coal and coke away, even ef I hadn't had my best dress on, for fear our dad should be hearen, so when I'd 'ad enough of roaren, I thought I better go back to bed, and forget Jerry Tombley was waiten on me en the woodshed.'

'But that isn't all. You couldn't have gone back to bed,' said Mrs Bradley, 'because we found you in here. Why couldn't you return the way you went?'

'Comes of goen and putten emprovements en all these 'ere old 'ouses,' was all that Linda vouchsafed by way of reply; and Mrs Bradley perceived that the girl had said all that she intended saying at that time.

When Linda had gone back to her mother in the kitchen, Mrs Bradley went in search of Denis.

'Go down into the cellar, dear child,' she said, 'and tell me, when you come back, exactly where the coal and coke are placed.'

'Oh, I know that,' said Denis. 'I went down there with Ditch two days before you came, and it's all piled up in a corner, blocking up a rather decent little passage which goes along to the old barn over there.'

Mrs Bradley was somewhat mystified. Linda had spoken as though she thought the heap had been shifted only a very short time before she had gone to meet Tombley. Surely she would have gone down into the cellar to see that the way was clear, thought Mrs Bradley. Perhaps she had trusted to luck. People of her temperament always did trust to luck, only to find, on nearly every occasion, that luck had betrayed their trust. She sighed.

'Linda been lying? She always does, young Walt says,' Denis observed.

'I don't know, I'm sure,' Mrs Bradley replied. 'Denis, what would it mean, to put improvements in an old house?'

'Is that a riddle?'

'If you like.'

'Do you know the answer?'

'Well,' said Mrs Bradley cautiously, 'I think I might recognise it if I heard it.'

'Well, I suppose it means sticking in some bathrooms. *You* know –'

But his great-aunt did not wait to hear more.

'Come with me quickly,' she said. 'You wanted to find another entrance to the priest-hole, Denis, didn't you? Well, I expect you have found one, dear child.'

They went up the stone stairs together and entered the larger of the bathrooms. There was no fixed bath. A large zinc bungalow bath stood almost touching the wall behind the door, and below the window stood the repellent type of washing stand which has a tip-up basin capable of decanting its load of soapy water into a movable earthenware receptacle at the bottom. The rest of the furniture comprised a rush-bottomed chair, a bath mat, a towel rail and a small enamel bathroom cabinet bought to fit an angle of the wall.

'Now, where?' said Mrs Bradley. They searched, most diligently, every square inch of the room. Denis went flat on his stomach, an electric torch in his hand, to peer at all the floorboards and in the corners. He got up at last and sighed.

'Let's try the other one,' he said. The second bathroom, Mrs Bradley thought, was the likelier of the two, as the Ditch family had the use of it when they felt they wanted a bath. It had been screened off from one of the bedrooms with a wooden partition which did not reach quite to the ceiling, and what remained of the bedroom was now devoted to lumber.

'We might search that, as well, if the bathroom yields no results,' Mrs Bradley observed, as they passed the door of it. The bathroom, however, certainly yielded results. Its floor was covered with green and white linoleum, and Denis, observing a slight depression in it near the wall, began to take it up. Underneath was a hinged trapdoor – the hinges fairly new, but beginning to rust with the damp from water and steam. He pulled up the trapdoor – a very easy matter – and found himself peering down a long black shaft which seemed to have no bottom.

'Made in the thickness of an old wall. Interesting,' said Mrs Bradley. They both shone their torches down it, but black, straight and bottomless – so far as they could determine – it remained.

'Put the lid on, child, a moment,' said Mrs Bradley. 'Look out of the window and tell me exactly where we are.'

The bathroom window was not much more than a lancet. It was apparent that this side of the house was older than the rest of the building. Denis, on tip-toe, peered out.

'I'm looking north, I think. The church is to my left, but on a slant. This seems to be the north-west corner of the house.'

'It would be,' said Mrs Bradley. 'Then that shaft is in the angle of the wall, and goes right down to the ground, and under the ground, I expect. It isn't any use to us, Denis. Let's go and look next door.'

But the lumber room yielded nothing, so they went back again to the parlour to warm themselves by the fire.

'If there'd been a way out – but how did Linda get *in?*' thought Mrs Bradley. She went to the panelling and opened it. The priest's hole – if that was what it was – was as bare and as clear as ever. She went inside.

'Shut the panelling after me, Denis. I want to see whether I can possibly get out,' she said. 'Open it in ten minutes.'

'What an opportunity, Scab,' said Carey, entering as Denis closed the panel, and took out his watch – a Christmas present from his father. 'When Aunt Adela and you have finished your game of hide-and-seek, I want to speak to her.'

While he was waiting for the ten minutes to pass, Denis told Carey about the long deep shaft in the wall.

'Oh, yes. We found that last summer. It's a fourteenth century garde-robe, I believe. Don't tumble down it. I don't suppose we'd ever get you out unless we pulled the house down, and I couldn't undertake to do that. I hope the air in that hole is all right. Linda was certainly fainting when she fell out this morning.'

'Linda? Oh, that's what it's all about!'

'Yes, that's what it's all about. Keep your eye on that watch, old man. I'm nervous about the ventilation in there.'

Promptly at the termination of ten minutes, Denis opened the panelling and Mrs Bradley stepped out.

'The air remains fresh all right, then,' Carey said.

'I don't think I've been in there long enough to say, but I can't find another outlet,' Mrs Bradley replied.

'Oh? Well, come and look at Hereward for a minute. I don't think the poor chap feels too good this morning. I didn't much like the way he couldn't be bothered to come out and have a grunt at me when I made my rounds last night. We've never had disease on the farm. I hope he's not going to begin it. If he don't take his food I shall go and dig out the vet. I can't lose a valuable boar.'

'If he were a human being,' said Mrs Bradley, when she and Carey had stood by the solitary sty for about ten minutes and had steadfastly regarded the languid and snuffling occupant, 'I should say he had caught a cold. Is that a possibility with pigs?'

'Oh, yes, decidedly. They also get erysipelas, lung worms, large round-worm and swine fever. I suppose there's no way to prevent 'em catching cold, either. Same like us. It's silly. Although how on earth *you* managed it, you fathead,' he added, addressing the boar, 'is more than I can imagine. Look at that flooring,' he said to Mrs Bradley. 'The most modern type there is. And the loony has only got to remain doggo under cover if it rains or snows or anything. I don't see how he *can* catch cold, although, of course, these pedigree animals will do anything. What *have* you been up to, I wonder?' he asked the boar. 'One comfort. The sows are all right. I've a jolly good mind to bring this chap into the house for a day or two. I'd like to park him in the empty crib in the larger pighouse, but if I did, the sows would be made to go to him. They despise old Tom, I think, but this one drives them crazy.'

These sidelights on the contrasting degrees of sex appeal in boars interested Mrs Bradley, but not more so than the sudden appearance of Simith's pigman, Priest, who came hastening along the path to speak to Carey.

'Mester Tombley sent me over. I went up-along to feed they pigs this mornen, and it seem Mr Semeth never ben home all night, and Mester Tombley's rung up and he thenks they've took him to the Infirmary, and ef they 'ave, he's afeared they'll send him to Lettlemore, and he wants to know what he's to do.'

'Has he rung up the Infirmary itself, do you mean?' asked Carey.

'Ah. But they can't make out, it seems, ef et's Mester Semeth or not. They 'ave tooken en one or two oldesh men, over Chrestmas, they says, and he says, ef et esn't arsken too much of ee, like, would ee go over and gev an eye to our pegs, while he's see-en all about et? I'm getten married, myself, or I wouldn't be troublen ee, see?'

'Getting married?' said Carey. 'Congratulations! Er –'

'Lender Detch,' said Priest, grinning with acute embarrassment. ''Bout time, too an' all, poor foolish gal,' he added.

'Now what about this poor fellow?' said Mrs Bradley, looking at Hereward.

She chirruped sympathetically at the boar, who regarded her pitifully out of his little red eyes.

'If you don't mind, I'll have him indoors. He's quite sanitary, and all that. Not in the parlour, you know. He can stay in the outhouse. Mrs Ditch won't mind. She's used to pigs. I'll light the copper fire and put a guard up, and lay some old sacks on part of the floor, so that he'll have some comfort. Are you afraid of him?'

'No,' said Mrs Bradley, resolutely.

'All right. You open the gate, then, and I will conjure him forth.'

But the boar backed away, and would not have Carey come anywhere near him to touch him.

'Well, I'm dashed. You're mighty particular this morning,' said Carey, eyeing him with surprise. 'But please yourself. If you'd rather stay here, I can make you a bit more comfortable, I suppose.'

The boar, at the sound of his voice, became more tractable, and, in the end, permitted himself to be taken up to the house. The snow was melting rapidly in the sun, and the boar squelched along through the slush, and stuck in his toes and squealed when they came to a virgin patch of unmelted snow.

'He's got a complex, Aunt Adela,' said Carey, grinning. 'Do you mind treading over that patch, to make it look a bit brown? I believe it's the whiteness he hates. I say, I wonder what's happening to poor old Simith? Going off his onion, do you think?'

'I could not say, without seeing him. He didn't give that impression,' said Mrs Bradley cautiously. 'When are you going over to look at his pigs, for him?'

'Oh, not until later. Priest will have fed them once this morning. They'll do all right for a bit.'

'Well, will you come cruising round with me in my car, child, after lunch, for about an hour?'

'Yes. Come to that, Ditch and Young Walt can go over to Roman Ending.'

'They won't poison the pigs, child, will they?'

'Because of Linda, you mean? Oh, Linda's a bad lot, really, and they know it well enough. Anyway, pigs are sacred in this country. They wouldn't do pigs any harm. I'd love to come. What is it? Not a ghost-hunt, by any chance, I suppose?'

'That's just what it is. Bless you, my child, for your superior intelligence.'

'Superior to whose?'

'Hugh's.'

'Oh?'

'Yes, yes, yes!' said Mrs Bradley, with the nearest approach to peevishness her nephew had ever noticed in her. 'If you had gone over to Iffley on Christmas Eve, you'd have known a good deal about Mr Fossder's death. Hugh appears to know nothing. If the girl weren't prepared to swear him a solemn alibi, I should think he might have been the ghost himself!'

She cackled, loudly and harshly, and Hereward gave a sudden snort of fear. Carey headed him off from bolting, and wheedled him into the outhouse, whose interior he seemed to suspect.

'Hugh?' said Carey, kneeling down before the copper fire. 'Hugh? But why on earth *should* he, anyway?'

'Well, that I don't know,' Mrs Bradley answered absently, watching Hereward's close inspection of his new quarters. 'But I suppose there *isn't* any reason why he shouldn't have been, really, is there?'

'What are you getting at?' asked Carey.

'Hugh's sympathetic blindness, deafness and general idiocy,' said Mrs Bradley, regaining all her good-humour.

'But was he blind, deaf and silly? Excuse me a moment. I think this fire's all right, and the copper's three-quarters full, but I must just go and get some straw, and those sacks and things. Do you mind being left alone with him? If you do, come with me, and carry a sack or so, will you?'

After a glance at Hereward, who was now standing still, with his forefeet planted firmly and his snout almost on the ground, Mrs Bradley decided that she would accompany Carey.

'It's strange that Mr Fossder decided to keep the appointment in spite of the message that Tombley sent,' she went on, as they crossed the farmyard again.

'I suppose he heard what Hugh said, and understood it? He may not have done, you know.'

'I asked Jenny whether he was deaf. He wasn't deaf. Now, why did he still go to Sandford if Tombley wasn't going to meet him and go along too?'

'Reasons of his own that were nothing to do with Tombley, and one of the reasons turned nasty and chased him and killed him,' Carey suggested. 'Why not leave the thing alone? If the doctor signed the certificate without question, why worry, love? It ain't really our affair, is it?'

'I wish I thought it weren't.' To Carey's amusement, for once his aunt seemed irresolute. 'But I can't get over the feeling that Fossder was murdered, and, if he was, it's *everybody's* business, child, or so the law would tell us. I suppose Hugh *did* give him Tombley's message? You see, if he didn't –'

'Forgot it, you mean, and doesn't like to say so, seeing the old chap met his death by trying to keep the appointment? Yes, there's a lot in that. He's inclined to be weak, is Hugh, when it comes to facing up to things, although I says it as shouldn't.'

'You know,' said Mrs Bradley, eyeing him sternly, 'I think you're a fool about Jenny.'

Carey opened his mouth, and gazed at her in amazement.

'Oh, yes!' said Mrs Bradley, wagging her head. 'Talk about *Hugh* being weak!'

'Dash it,' protested her nephew, wiping the elf-lock artistically out of his eye, 'there's a certain delicacy attached to the process of trying to ingratiate yourself with a girl who's already engaged to another! Tell me, would you care to see my Academy picture? It's Sabrina, in all her elegant pink nakedness, lying belly-upwards in her sty. I'm calling it "Portrait of a Lady of Fashion, 1936". They won't hang it, but it's damned good, all the same.'

CHAPTER 6

Half-Hey on the River Thames

'Hereward took his food all right,' said Carey, 'so I shan't need to dig up the vet. At any rate, not today. What time with the car, my angel?' he enquired of his aunt affectionately.

'Young Walt took a message to George. He's to have the car ready at two.'

'Then I'd better be yodelling the next course in. Fried slices of Christmas pudding? I thought so. Here, Scab, have some honey on that. You'll need it.'

He poured himself out some more beer.

'I suppose you couldn't have George drive me over to Oxford Station in the morning? My leave is up tomorrow. It would save Carey turning out. The bike and sidecar, you know,' said Hugh apologetically.

'Yes, of course George can take you in. I'll tell him. What is the time of your train?'

'Well, seven-fifteen, I'm afraid. It's frightfully early. Otherwise I ought to go tonight.'

'On no account,' said Carey. 'Tonight will not be the binge that we had proposed, because of poor old Fossder, but we're running over for Jenny this afternoon. In fact, we shall bring her to tea.'

By a quarter to three Carey and Mrs Bradley were in Iffley, and had left the car near the church. They walked to the tollgate, and paid their money to walk across by the bridge and then by the lock.

'Pity it's the wrong time of year. We might have had a swim,' said Carey, gazing at the water as it flowed through over the lasher. 'What's the programme, love? We've only got about an hour and a half of daylight, I should say.'

'I'd like to walk to Sandford, along the towing path,' said Mrs Bradley.

'Blazing the trail?'

'The trail is already blazed, child. But after the snow on Boxing night, I doubt whether any tracks are to be seen.'

She looked across the lock to the flat fields which came almost to the lip of the bank. The towing path was very narrow here; it was no more than a muddy footpath beside the river. They crossed the lock, and turned left along the bank for Sandford. Pollard willows marked a narrow meandering water-course that trickled across the meadows from the low round Berkshire hills. Two of the trees grew close, with misshapen trunks almost touching.

'Marvellous fellow, Rackham,' said Carey suddenly. He pointed to the trees. Mrs Bradley nodded, but her sharp black eyes were fixed on the muddy ground. After about ten minutes she sighed and shook her head.

'No use, child, I'm afraid. Too many hoof marks altogether along here.'

'Oh, you're on to Hugh's suggestion that the ghost chap rode a horse?'

'I think there might be something in it somewhere,' said Mrs Bradley slowly. 'The police might be able to make something out of these hoof-marks, but I'm perfectly certain *I* can't,' she continued, still staring at the ground. 'It's possible, too, that the prints of the horse we are after may have been affected by the snow. Anyway, child, I don't see how the ghost could have ridden a horse.'

'Well, I thought myself it was rather a far-fetched idea. After all, if the chap intended to murder Fossder, he'd have been much less conspicuous without a horse than with one! Can't think what gave Hugh the idea.'

'Against that, one has to put the equally important argument that he would be likely to terrify Fossder far more completely if he were on a horse than if he had been on foot,' said Mrs Bradley.

'That's a good point,' said Carey. 'How do you think the ghost came? Over the lock, as we did?'

'Yes, I should think so, child. The way to the lock is left open, and no more tolls are collected after eleven at night, I have discovered.'

'I have an idea that if the chap was on horseback, he might not somehow have risked Iffley village, and leading the gee across the lock. Don't you think it more likely that he came here along the towing path from Folly Bridge, near Christchurch? Come and see what I mean.'

'I know what you mean,' said Mrs Bradley. 'A most feasible idea.'

'Came along in his riding clothes, you know, and got into the night gown, or whatever it was he wore, when he got past Iffley lock. That's what *I* should have done.'

They had continued walking towards Sandford, but now retraced their steps, passed Iffley lock again, and, walking north-wards and a point by west, passed the ferry, and, a little farther up, crossed the first of the Long Bridges, and passed the free bathing places provided by the Council for the townspeople. The river was full and looked dirty. It was a troubled dark grey, and a little wind whipped its surface and blew tiny eddies in under the bank. It made a wide bend near the boat house, and ran brownish over pebbles where in summer a shoal of small fish always lurked, looking, at first glance, part of the ripples and the stones, part of the flecked reflection of the sky.

Carey picked up a flat stone from the bank – the only place along there where the bank sloped gently to the water – and skimmed it across to the opposite side, where, to his great delight, it skipped suddenly out of the water and struck a willow tree in the half-flooded water-meadows opposite.

They passed the confluence of the Cherwell and the Isis, and looked at the rows of dark poplars, as beautiful in winter as in spring, which lined the banks of the Cherwell at its mouth; they passed the line of College houseboats which were moored by the opposite bank of the Isis, and came at last to the bridge. Here, to Mrs Bradley's delight, Carey's theory that a horseman had come on to the towing path at Folly Bridge received accidental confirmation. Finding a little shop, and desirous of proving his theory, Carey went in and bought some shag and half a pound of toffee. While he was being served he remarked,

'I suppose your back windows must look out on to the river?'

'Ah. They do.' The shopkeeper was friendly and talkative. 'Get quite a bit of fun, we do, in the summer, like, with the gentlemen and the boating and all.'

'But not much doing in the winter, I suppose?'

'Not much. Well, not so much. Though I'd dearly love to know what the fellow was doing with his horse on Christmas Eve.'

'Oh? Swimming it in the river?'

'Oh, no! No, not swimmen it in the river. No, he wasn't do-en that. He was riden it all right, but well after twelve o'clock at night. Ah, must a-been nearer one, now I come to remember, or, maybe, after one. Funniest thing, I shouldn't 'ave knowed nothen of it, but our Em, she had the toothache, and her mother, she had to get up to 'er in the night. Otherwise I don't suppose I'd have 'eard it.'

'Well, that's that,' said Carey, when they got outside again. 'What do you say? Sounds like the ghost of Napier, don't you think?'

'I think it most improbable,' Mrs Bradley observed. 'But what we have, so far, is this: the ghost knew that Mr Fossder was going to Sandford. It knew that he would cross the river at Iffley, and would follow the towing path, going towards Sandford lock. It knew how long it would take him, and it also knew that he would not trouble to be at the meeting-place by midnight, the time when the ghost is expected to appear. It also knew that he would be alone.'

'Of course, the main objection to the idea that this mysterious horseman was the ghost is the fact that Fossder was running *away* from Sandford and not towards it when he fell down dead,' said Carey.

'I know, child. The murderer could have turned the body round, though.'

'Wouldn't the police soon spot that had been done?'

'They would, perhaps, if there had been any case for them, but they were not called in, you see. And then there was that fall of snow. Goodness knows what difference it would have made, but I should think it must have made some!'

They walked back to Iffley to get the car, and were soon in Stanton St John.

'I'll just walk over to Simith's to have a look at his pigs and give them their dry-feed,' said Carey.

'Let us go in the car. It is quicker. And if Tombley is there, I can have a word with him,' said Mrs Bradley, signalling George to drive on.

But Tombley was not at the farm when they arrived, so, assisted by George, Carey made the round of the pigs and then came back to his aunt. It was just as they were getting into the car to drive away that Geraint Tombley returned to Roman Ending.

'I'm feeling worried,' he said. 'I can't trace my uncle anywhere. I've been to the Infirmary; I've even been to Littlemore; but there's nothing doing at all. It was queer enough, his going off on his own on Christmas Eve; but this is past a joke. I haven't seen him now for –'

'When did you last see Mr Fossder?' Mrs Bradley enquired. Tombley shrugged.

'Oh, weeks ago, must have been. But, all the same, it's terrible, that uncalled-for death, poor old fellow. But what's the good of worrying about it? Everyone knew about poor old Fossder's heart. I only wish now I'd been able to keep that appointment. I wonder,' he added, 'what Mrs Fossder is going to do with the money? Oh, yes!' he went on, in answer to an exclamation from Carey. 'She's still holding on to that two hundred pounds. I expect she's forgotten it wasn't really won!'

'Half of it belongs to Mrs Fossder, if her husband has left her his property, as I have no doubt he has,' said Carey, coldly. 'And the other half surely belongs to the man who made the wager, since you yourself did not go.'

'Now *I* should have said that the wager was won by the man who laid it,' said Mrs Bradley, judicially. 'Fossder *may* have died before he could keep the tryst. In my opinion, therefore, the whole of the money ought to be returned, as it is now improbable that we shall be able to prove whether Fossder reached Sandford at all that night.'

'It's a pity we don't know who laid the bet,' said Tombley. 'Whoever it was won't confess, now Fossder has died. Joke or not at the time, it's ended pretty seriously.'

'Mr Hugh Kingston, Old Farm, Oxfordshire, could tell us something about the bet,' said Mrs Bradley, with the grin of a demon with a pitchfork.

'Very awkward indeed for him,' said Tombley gravely, 'for somebody certainly took advantage of the bet to lay for old Fossder and kill him. I feel myself to blame. I made no secret of the bet, you know. Anybody could have found out all about it. I bet Hugh could kill himself now, for having had the idea at all.'

'I do rather think that if Hugh made the bet he might have said so. I said he didn't face up to things,' said Carey, as the car drove off and Mrs Bradley looked round and waved to Tombley through the glass of the small back window. Mrs Bradley cackled.

'Home, madam?' said George, as they turned into the narrow road that led back to Stanton St John.

'No, George. Back to Iffley. Mrs Fossder's house.'

'Iffley again?' said Carey. 'What's the idea now?'

'Jenny. We promised Hugh we'd bring her over for tea, and I'd forgotten about it.'

Mrs Fossder and Jenny had begun their tea when Mrs Bradley and Carey arrived.

'I'd love to come,' said Jenny, looking pleased.

'Hugh is going back, I suppose,' said Mrs Fossder. She got up and went to a large vase on the mantelpiece. 'These notes. I really don't know what to do with them. The money for that dreadful bet, you know.'

'Keep one hundred, and I will give you a receipt for the other hundred,' said Mrs Bradley, producing her pen.

'Oh, no!' said Mrs Fossder, horrified. 'I couldn't do that! It would seem like making money by my husband's death! Really, it's quite impossible.' She crammed the notes into Carey's hands. 'You two will know what to do with them. You'll see that they are returned! I'll be glad to be relieved of them.'

Mrs Bradley wrote a receipt for two hundred pounds. Carey counted the notes, and then folded them up and put them into his pockets.

'Mrs Fossder,' said Mrs Bradley, 'what grudge had Geraint Tombley against your husband?'

'None, that I know of. I tell you again, it was Simith who murdered my husband. They never got on, from boyhood.'

'Simith is missing. Cannot be traced,' said Carey.

'Yes, a guilty conscience,' Mrs Fossder remarked. She looked at Mrs Bradley. Mrs Bradley shook her head.

'I'd believe you,' she said, 'if Simith were Tombley's age, or even twenty years older. But Simith must be seventy.'

'He's sixty-eight – just ten years older than my husband,' said Mrs Fossder.

'The wrong age for inventing a murder that might possibly look like a practical joke,' said Mrs Bradley firmly.

'Something of the Roman matron about your aunt,' said Carey, strolling down to the gate with Jenny. 'Where are Fay and Pratt?'

'Out for a stroll. Maurice takes over the reins from tomorrow.'

'What sort of a fellow is Pratt?' Carey asked. 'Just seems a fool to me.' He visualised the tall, thin, sad-looking intellectual.

'Well, yes, he *is* silly,' Jenny confessed with a smile, 'although not in the business, you know. But I'm sure he's not weak and not wicked.'

'Hm! By the way, where's my aunt?'

'Having a last word with mine. It's all right. Here they come. And I can hear Fay and Maurice on the road, so I can leave the house with a clear conscience. What did you mean – Roman matron?'

'The stiff upper lip. You know. Grief in the heart but not on the handkerchief.'

'Well, she wasn't really terribly fond of uncle. Nothing serious, you know. Just incompatible. They used to have lots of rows, chiefly about Fay's marriage. Thank goodness nobody bothers about mine.'

'I say! I'm sure Hugh doesn't know they quarrelled! I say – forgive me if it's an awkward question, but – how's the money left? Do you happen to know?'

'Oh, yes, of course I do. It's equally divided. Auntie, Fay and I get one-third each. Maurice inherits the practice.'

'What a motive for Hugh, Pratt and Tombley!'

'Yes, but even if you proved to the letter it was Geraint Tombley, you'd never get aunt to believe you. Personally, I don't really think it was.'

'But what does Fay think?'

'She doesn't. It's a hard thing to say of one's girlhood companion, but Fay's a perfect fool! She dithered between Tombley and Maurice for ages and ages, and couldn't make up her mind. I think she was so thrilled at having two suitors at once that she liked to keep them dangling. She's always been rather a little mouse, you see, and the situation rather went to her head.'

'I wonder whether you're rather a little cat?' said Carey, laughing at her. 'But I'll put the point to Aunt Adela. You never know what may come in useful, do you? And Tombley?' he continued. 'How did he take the bird from Fay, when she finally decided to have Pratt?'

Jenny shrugged.

'Oh, to the manner born.'

'Like a perfect gent, do you mean?'

'Absolutely, according to Fay. It was in the garden. He raised his hat, said he never had any luck, kissed her hand, and departed, on foot, at six miles an hour. Aunt watched him from the window. She said that he looked noble. Fay cried for days, I know. Really, she *is* a fool!'

Jenny giggled at the recollection.

'It *must* have been Tombley,' said Carey to Mrs Bradley, after dinner. Hugh and Jenny were sitting side by side upon the settee, looking at a book and talking in undertones to one another on subjects unconnected with what they were supposed to be reading. Carey glanced across at them, and decided that they were more likely to be absorbed in their own conversation than in his. He told Mrs Bradley what he had learned from Jenny.

'It seems as though, with Fossder out of the way, there might be some chance of getting Fay to change her mind, and have Tombley instead of Pratt. Mrs Fossder was definitely in favour, and, according to J., young Fay was never certain which of 'em she wanted, and wept when, in the end, she decided to give the bird to poor old Tombley. It seems to me a cert that Tombley did it.'

'Interesting, child. I, too, learned a little more. According to Mrs Fossder, the two men who marry the girls are to inherit Mr Fossder's money. Mrs Fossder gets one-third, and the rest is to be divided equally between the girls' husbands.'

'Nothing at all to the girls, as such, so to speak?'

'Nothing. Mr Fossder seems to have thought his nieces feather-headed creatures incapable of managing money for themselves.'

'Rather a cheek. But he always was an old cuckoo in some

respects. I'd have married forgers or bank-robbers, if I'd been the girls, merely out of protest.'

'And quite right, too, I'm sure,' said Mrs Bradley. 'But, you see, whereas your tidings might help to exonerate Maurice Pratt and Hugh, mine bring them both back into the full strong light of suspicion. Neither could gain a thing until Mr Fossder's death. Then each could claim a third of all his property. How are Hugh's financial affairs? Do you happen to know?' She grinned and stretched her fingers.

Carey shook his head.

'He's poor, but solvent. That's all I know,' he said. 'Librarians are like schoolmasters. They have to be respectable, or else they get the sack.'

'We'll see,' said Mrs Bradley. 'Hugh!' she called. Hugh looked up.

'Hullo? Oh – yes, Mrs Bradley? Want me?'

'Are you able to write me a cheque for two hundred pounds?'

'Have to be a Post Office cheque, Mrs Bradley, I'm afraid. Don't have to owe it too long. It's saved up against my wedding.' He laughed and looked at Jenny.

'You don't really suspect Hugh, I know,' said Carey, 'but what makes you keep on talking about him in connection with the affair? Just a perverted sense of humour?'

'By no means, child. One can't exonerate him now that the business of the will has come to the fore, even though he *is* solvent, you know.'

'But you think it was Tombley, don't you?'

'Well, I might do so, child, except for one trifling fact.'

'Straws show which way the wind blows. Say on. Where's the snag?'

'Well, it was so very foolish to kill Mr Fossder at Iffley, especially as Tombley had brought himself to our notice so particularly that night by coming here to ask about his uncle. And I don't think Tombley is foolish.'

'But who damaged your car to prevent Hugh going to Iffley to pick up the girls and Pratt? That was Tombley, surely?'

'I hardly think so. Of course, it may have been Pratt. He was over here, too. And it may have been Linda Ditch.'

'Linda? But why on earth should she?'

'There are various reasons: to help Tombley, if she knew he was going to kill Fossder: to save Hugh if she thought that trouble would come of his going to Iffley that night: ill-will towards myself; to annoy my righteous chauffeur, who may have rejected her advances; devilment, of which she has plenty: to spite her father and brother, who might have to help put the car right –'

'Pax!' said Carey, laughing. 'It is possible, I agree, that Linda Ditch damaged the car.'

'But I think it was a man,' Mrs Bradley continued. 'A girl would have slashed the tyres.'

'Stuck a hatpin into 'em, you mean.'

'There are no such things as hatpins nowadays. At any rate, you will agree that she would have done something much less subtle than to produce a leak in the tank.'

'I thought women *were* the subtle sex,' said Carey.

'They haven't the brains to be subtle,' said Mrs Bradley, grinning. 'It was Eve who ate the apple, but all the subtlety, surely, was shown by the serpent.'

'I've never thought Tombley was subtle,' said Carey, meeting her eye. Mrs Bradley grimaced.

'Good heavens, child!' she said.

'Clever,' said Carey. 'Not subtle. Like Henry the Eighth. *You* know. "This weed cumbers the ground. I will uproot it." Or ain't that a reading of his character?'

'Tombley's, or Henry the Eighth's?' asked Mrs Bradley. 'By the way,' she continued, before Carey had time to answer, 'has it occurred to you that if Tombley did put the car out of action it might have been kindly meant?'

'I don't believe it. To save us from danger at Iffley, do you mean?'

'It's just an idea. I daresay there's nothing in it,' said Mrs Bradley pacifically. 'But it is better to admit every possibility.' She beamed at him affectionately.

'I wish I knew what you really think.'

'You do, child. At least, I mean, I've told you. I cannot help it if you haven't managed to take it all in!'

'Tombley murdered Fossder, because Fossder had prevented him from marrying Fay.'

'Does Tombley give the impression of a love-lorn swain, thirsting for vengeance on his lost love's guardian, child?'

'No. But with Fossder out of the way, it seems as though Tombley would marry her after all, and there's always the point that the ghost, or whatever it was that made Fossder run, may not have intended to kill him. That's been suggested, hasn't it?'

'I know.' She nodded. 'Ditch is going to teach me the stick-tapping in "Rigs o' Marlow". Come and watch my initiation into the mysteries of the Morris.'

'I'd love to. He's making me practise capers. We're all enthusiasts here. But it's Pratt you'll have to meet. He has the true fervour, I believe. A hopeless performer, though.'

'And does he come from Headington, too?'

'Oh, no. He's a Bampton man. Ditch won't have him dance in his side at present. Says he throws all the others out. He's a long, thin, weedy chap; stoops and peers; that type. Inferiority complex as big as Christian's burden, I should imagine. Not at all the man for the Morris. Oh, of course, you saw him on Christmas Eve. I'd forgotten that for the moment.'

'Ah, yes.' Mrs Bradley looked at her nephew sideways. Carey grinned.

'I want to borrow that two hundred pounds,' he said.

'Did *you* send the letters to Mr Fossder, child?'

'No. But I rather want to lead Tombley up the garden.'

'To what end, child?'

'As a matter of fact, only to about the middle. I want to frighten him into confessing that he was the ghost, because I'm quite certain he was.'

'Save your money and search the county, child.'

'What for?'

'To find the fancy dress the ghost wore on Christmas Eve. Have you never been to a fancy dress dance at which one of the gentlemen carried his head beneath his arm in a not particularly realistic, but, all the same, in an illogically terrifying manner?'

'You think the ghost really *did* look headless then, when poor old Fossder saw him?'

'I don't know, I'm sure,' said Mrs Bradley. 'Something frightened Mr Fossder, didn't it? Never mind, child. Come and see me do the stick-tapping.'

They left Hugh and Jenny in the parlour, and went along to the kitchen. Mrs Ditch and Linda were still washing up. Young Walt had a bicycle to pieces on the hearthrug, which was very gay with red, blue and grey strips of flannel. This rug was so dear to the heart of Mrs Ditch, whose mother had made it, that none but Young Walt would have been permitted to take a bicycle to pieces on or near it. Ditch was reading the paper, his stockinged feet on the fender.

'Arsenal's doen well,' he said to Young Walt. Young Walt, his hands brown with grease, a smear of black across his cheek, and his mouth full of small ball-bearings, said nothing, and took a spanner up from the rug.

'Hallo, Ditch. How's Hereward?' asked Carey.

'I took him back, like, and he seemed all right,' replied Ditch. 'Nervous-like, I don't say, but nothen wrong.' He nodded to Mrs Bradley. 'You stell got the same mind to learn the steck-tappen, mam? Tes easy. Look. I'll soon show ee.'

He picked up a concertina and a couple of Morris sticks from the top of the sewing machine, and handed one of the sticks to Mrs Bradley.

'I'll just give ee a turn of the toon, and then you'll hear when to tap. Er goes like this 'ere, now.' He laid his own stick aside and raised the instrument sideways. Then he pressed out the opening bars of the famous *Rigs o' Marlow*. Like a bird of prey flapping its wings, or a witch preparing for evil, Mrs Bradley, grinning with joy, accepted the stick, jigged up and down with a prancing motion which offended Ditch's expert eye, and listened to the strains of the music.

'Ah, yes,' she said, and Ditch raised his voice with his wife's to hum the tune. Then he laid down the concertina, fell in opposite the grinning Mrs Bradley, and admitted her to the secret of the stick-tapping.

'Now, sir,' said Ditch to Carey. '*Trunkles*, wasn't et? There ain't too much room in this ketchen, but maybe us could manage the corners with capers ef us don't cover too much ground.'

'Our mam, *Trunkles*!' shouted Young Walt from the floor. 'Seng up, my old duck!' He laughed and then laid the greasy chain of the bicycle on a piece of newspaper. He was a good boy to his mother, and knew how she valued her rug. Mrs Ditch came in again from the outhouse.

'Oh, ah, I knows en,' she said. 'Go on, our dad, dance up and gev Mester Carey the idea. See our dad do the capers, mam,' she said to Mrs Bradley. 'A fair treat to see 'em done proper. There, mam, what ded I tell ee?'

When the practice was over, the concertina laid aside on the dresser and the sticks put away in a drawer, Mrs Bradley drew Carey outside the kitchen again.

'Tombley hasn't confessed to the bet, but I'm going to ask him outright,' said Carey, before she had time to speak. 'I expect he'll deny it, and we shall have to take his word, but I want to see his face.'

'To see his fortune would be more interesting, child.'

'Yes. In a police case, they'd look at his bank-account, wouldn't they? Old Fossder was mad on money. Speculated and so forth.

Two hundred pounds would have tempted him into almost any nonsense. He wouldn't think of personal risk, especially as I'm pretty sure he knew where the money came from, in spite of the anonymous letter.'

'The second communication came in a separate envelope and by a later post, I believe, child, didn't it?'

'The drawings of the little shields? Why, yes. There's no proof the same person sent them and wrote the anonymous letter.'

'And no proof it was *not* the same person.'

'Quite.' He looked thoughtful, and then he added: 'If Tombley *does* confess, there'll be no need to drag Hugh into it.'

'I wonder whether Hugh gave that message, child?'

'Of course! Lord, yes! Jenny, you mean! To get old Fossder out of the way while he waited in the garden to get Jenny!'

Mrs Bradley looked pained.

'Hugh's pleasures seem rather selfish, child,' she said. 'No, I don't think *that* was the reason. Still, we'll go and tackle Tombley tomorrow.'

'I think I'll ask Hugh tonight, to make certain. Bless us, here he is! I say! Did *you* send old Fossder the two hundred pounds in notes?'

Hugh laughed, and, feeling in his pocket, produced a Post Office Savings book.

'I've got it handy to let Mrs Bradley have that two hundred pounds.' He handed it over for inspection. Carey glanced rapidly through it. The withdrawals for the whole of the past two years did not amount to more than fifty pounds. The last total (which had been entered two months previously) was two hundred and seventeen pounds two and threepence. Carey handed the book to Mrs Bradley.

'Aunt Adela thinks you sent the two hundred pounds to Mr Fossder,' he said. Hugh laughed again.

'I assure you I didn't,' he said. 'But even if I had –'

'Well, Tombley thinks that somebody who had a grudge against

Fossder found out about the bet, and took advantage of it to go to Sandford and kill him.'

'The things is,' said Hugh, '– not that I want to throw cold water on your romantic theories – it's yet to be proved that Fossder did not die naturally. There's nothing, at present, so far as I can see, to prove that anyone killed him, although for a time I thought so.'

He took his Savings Bank book again, and slipped it into his pocket.

'I was joking about the two hundred pounds,' said Mrs Bradley. 'At least –' She paused. Hugh's sombre face brightened. 'At least, I never thought it came out of that little book of yours.'

Hugh nodded, and left them, to put his book away.

'You know, I believe old Hugh is more affected by Fossder's death than anyone not knowing him well might think,' said Carey. 'By the way, love, have you heard of the scandal of Horsepath church?'

'Not more red paint, child, surely?'

'What makes you think of red paint?'

'Mr Fossder's gate with the Cross Patée painted on it.'

'Oh, yes, of course. No. According to Mrs Ditch, who's got relations living there, someone has stuck a paper arrow on the wall near the pulpit underneath a small stained glass window which has on it the rather unusual device of a man holding a boar's head on the point of a spear.'

'Really?' said Mrs Bradley. She felt uneasy. 'Is that all, child?'

'Except on the arrow there was a bit of Shakespeare – *Henry IV*, I think. "I have a gammon of bacon and two races of ginger to be delivered as far as Charing Cross."'

Second Figure

SHOTOVER SIMITH

The boar's head in hand bear I,
Bedecked with bays and rosemary,
And I pray you, my masters, be merry,
Quot estis in convivio.

Caput apri defero
Reddens laudes Domino.

THE BOAR'S HEAD CAROL

CHAPTER 7

Dib and Strike on Shotover Hill

George drove Hugh and Denis into Oxford to catch the London train, and Carey and Mrs Bradley decided to go with them and see them off at the station.

'And what would you like to do now?' enquired Carey, as they drove back to Stanton St John.

'Come with you to Simith's pig-farm and have another go at Tombley,' said Mrs Bradley. 'You can make the excuse that you came to look after the pigs.'

Tombley was not at home. Priest came out with a pig-bucket full of swill, announced that he was going to his wedding at noon, replied (to Mrs Bradley) that Mr Simith had not been at home all night; that the police had been informed; that Mr Tombley seemed upset and worried, and that Nero was more savage even than usual.

'Queer about these boars. Do hope there isn't an epidemic or something,' Carey said pessimistically. 'My boar Hereward isn't any too well. Let's have a look at Nero.'

Priest led the way to Nero's shelter. The boar was not housed in one of the movable shelters, but had a permanent sty of his own not far from the central feeding house. He was restless and uneasy. Carey stood looking at him a long time. Mrs Bradley, too, appeared to be interested in the boar. Nero resented their presence, yet seemed to be afraid of them. He backed away, his little eyes angry and watchful. His ears were cocked like those of a suspicious, unfriendly dog, and even his tufted tail lacked that air of roguery inseparable from the appendages of pigs in general.

'Sommat up with him,' said Priest. 'He looks to me like a sow what have eat her litter. What's more we dursent go nigh him. Never knew him so savage.'

'He *does* have a guilty expression. He's had a fright,' said Carey. Mrs Bradley, no pig-breeder, gazed at the boar and said nothing.

'Where's Mr Tombley this morning?' Carey enquired. Priest looked at him suspiciously.

'Tryen to get news of Mr Semeth.'

'Priest,' said Mrs Bradley suddenly, 'where does the old passage lead? Have you any idea?'

'What, her from Mr Lestrange's cellar, mam? I did hear as how her came out in that there barn near by, but I dunno as anyone have proved et.'

'Interesting,' said Mrs Bradley. 'Oh, here he comes!'

'Who? Mr Semeth?' said Priest, turning round. But it was Mr Tombley, accompanied by a plain clothes policeman – unmistakable even at a distance – who climbed the stile and advanced to meet them.

'I've put the police on the job. This is Sergeant Marcey. Can't think what has happened, unless the old boy's gone out of his mind. But, if he had, he'd be in the Infirmary, or at Littlemore, I should think. I just can't imagine what has happened.'

'Awkward for you,' said Mrs Bradley, with crocodile sympathy. Tombley stared at her resentfully.

'You look like Nero,' said Carey. 'Get it back, quick, while it's hot!'

Tombley smiled wryly.

'I'm worried to death,' he said. 'But what do you mean about Nero? I suppose you mean the boar?'

'Well, yes. But you could sit for the emperor's portrait just as easily! Cheer up, my good chap! The old man can't be dead! You'd have heard of *that* soon enough! Besides, now you have given the case to the police, they'll find him; you needn't worry.'

'Can't have got fur,' said the sergeant. 'You're the owner of the next place to this, Old Farm, sir, I onderstand,' he said to Carey. He moved away from the vicinity of Tombley, who had just been engaged in conversation by Mrs Bradley, and lowered his voice. 'Fact is, sir, I'd be glad of a word with ee, like. The Chief Constable is a friend of Sir Selby Villiers, who, seems like, is friends with your aunt, the old lady. Us know Mrs Bradley's work, sir, and Sir Selby as good as told the Chief to get her opinion. Et seems Mrs Bradley sent off to Sir Selby over that business at Effley on Christmas Eve –'course, we can't touch that at present, the doctor geven the sirsteficate, too and all, and no complaints from anyone, ee might say, but, to tell ee the truth, us takes an enterest in this old gentleman's disappearance. This Mr Tombley's the heir, and, ef he can persume his uncle's death, like, he won't be too sorry, do ee see. If ee can read between the lines of that, sir –. Well, you onderstand, I can't say in words what I mean, not just as thengs are at present, but a hent from your aunt might come in handy, if'er *ded* have ideas on the subject. As I tell ee, us knows her work, and if us didn't, Sir Selby do, too and all, don't him?'

'I know what you mean,' said Carey. 'I want you to let me tell you what we know of Fossder's death.'

From a hundred yards off, Tombley watched them anxiously, and all Mrs Bradley's questions about movable shelters failed to keep him from moving gradually towards them. But Carey managed to finish his report to the sergeant before Tombley came within earshot of what was being said, and when the party was reunited, the sergeant asked Tombley to take him over the house.

'We might as well take our leave,' said Carey to Mrs Bradley. They waved to Tombley and turned their backs on the house at Roman Ending.

'Child,' said Mrs Bradley suddenly, when they came within sight of Stanton St John and its church tower, 'I seem to be haunted by boars.'

'Boars? Oh, Hereward and Nero, you mean? Yes, so am I. I feel thoroughly nervous. Nero may have worms. That makes them irritable, naturally.'

'Yes,' said Mrs Bradley. 'Let's walk to Shotover, child.'

'Shotover? Right you are. It'll be muddy across the park of Shotover House, but it's much the prettiest way. Why Shotover, so particularly?'

'Boars,' replied Mrs Bradley.

'Oh? The Queen's College legend of the bloke and the volume of Aristotle? Rather a good idea, as we're both thinking about Hereward and Nero. Incidentally, I've been handing the sergeant our version of the Sandford ghost affair and the results of our researches. The police can't touch it, he thinks. The doctor's certificate was quite in order.'

'The doctor's certificate covers everything at present. There were no suspicious circumstances from the point of view of the police except the wager. I did mention that to the inspector.'

'The money, you think, was a decoy.'

'Oh, yes. But the point of interest is – did the dead man know who had sent it?'

'Do you think he did, Aunt Adela?'

'One might deduce it, child.'

'Oh, yes, I see. The chap who put up the money was someone Fossder thought he'd be able to trust, so that even if Tombley didn't show up at all, Fossder still knew – or thought he knew – that the chap would fork out the cash.'

'The "chap" had already done so,' Mrs Bradley pointed out.

'It's queer to think that Fossder trusted so well a bloke who was going to murder him,' Carey remarked, as they turned off the road and approached the entrance to what had once been the farmyard. 'By the way, what makes you so much interested in the passage and the priest's hole and so on?' he enquired, pushing open the gate.

'Protective colouring,' said Mrs Bradley vaguely. She stopped at Hereward's empty sty, and stood looking into it. Then she opened the door, stepped in, peered at the flooring, took an electric torch from her capacious skirt pocket and, by its light, looked into the sleeping quarters.

'Have pigs an acute sense of smell?' she enquired, coming out again, and shutting the door of the sty.

'Difficult to say.'

'I mean, child, suppose you went among Mr Simith's pigs after you'd been in Tom's house, would the pig react more or less favourably towards you than if you had gone among them with your Sunday clothes on?'

'Oh, it would make a difference. I don't know how much, of course.'

'Ah,' said Mrs Bradley. She did not press the point.

They decided to have a very early lunch, and to go to Shotover immediately afterwards. The snow had entirely disappeared. There were no traces of it in even the most sheltered crevices. Walking, even up the cart-track on to road for Stanton Great Wood, was muddy, and their shoes were clogged and heavy by the time they reached the gate. They turned left, climbed past the post office up to the church, then inclined to the left again to reach the main road through the village. Fields were on either side of them, Stanton St John was a huddle of roofs at their backs, and Forest Hill was ahead. Beyond the fields on their left, some of which were in plough, rose deep woods, massed with the gloomy leafless trees of late December. The woods were the colour of woodsmoke, and had almost the same dense obscurity; on the opposite side of the road, far off beyond fields and hedges, a line of trees, a thin straggle of windblown trunks and leafless arms, stood up on the crest of a ridge like ragged clouds in the wake of a windblown storm. The sky was grey behind them, and they were silhouetted against it, a scarecrow brood with menace in their very shapelessness.

'How are your shoes, Aunt Adela?' Carey asked when they had passed through the little old village of Forest Hill and had come upon the Headington–Wheatley road with its buses, cars and telegraph poles and the A.A. box at the crossways.

'Suitable for tramping through a bog,' replied Mrs Bradley cheerfully.

'Good. The footpath through the park, then, is the quickest and prettiest way. It will bring us out on to the turning to Horsepath, or near it, and we shall then be on top of Shotover.'

The stile they crossed was invitingly low, and from it the path sloped up past a lodge, and skirted a circular pond. Dark woods, squirrel and bird-haunted, but looking too thick and too grim for that friendly countryside (strongly fenced, moreover), climbed the slope with the travellers, and hid the view on the right. To the left were tended trees, an obelisk, and, further off, the house.

At the top of the slope – the path was as muddy as Carey had foreseen that it would be – another stile gave on to a made-up lane on the farther side of which a bank dipped steeply to a wattled sheepfold, beyond which a field was in plough. The lane was lined with tall trees. At the end of it was a hedge. Beyond the hedge was a way out on to a narrow sandy road bordered by bushes and promising autumn blackberries.

They turned to the right along it, and were soon on Shotover Plain. Ignoring the invitation of a sign-post which pointed the way to Horsepath, on they went, and stood at last on the top of Shotover Hill, looking down towards Oxford city.

'Ah, here we are!' said Mrs Bradley suddenly. She plunged forward down the slope, soon followed by Carey. Whatever she had seen escaped his eyes. A bird flew up from the bushes with a scream. Mrs Bradley stooped and parted wet fronds of the bracken that grew in an open space surrounded by stunted oaks. Carey, stopping short, gave a sudden exclamation and gripped Mrs Bradley's arm. Before them lay Simith, dead. Mrs Bradley knelt down.

'Good Lord!' said Carey unsteadily. 'He's been savaged by a boar!'

Mrs Bradley straightened herself, and glanced at him sharply.

'How do you know?' she said.

'Seen it before. Not to death, but pretty bad. Fellow I had as pigman. Dropped a pig-bucket on a boar I had, called Sam. Sam went for him. Got him down and savaged him. I had to kill the boar. Only way to save the man. They're terribly savage. Sam was of Nero's type – you know – that boar they've got at Roman Ending. Thick-headed and hated everybody. Good Lord, though! Poor old Simith! What on earth can we do?'

'Something which is against all the canons of correct procedure,' said Mrs Bradley briskly. Again she knelt on the ground, beside the body. 'You keep guard, child, will you? Nobody must come here until the police arrive. But I don't even want the police for a minute or two.'

To Carey's amazement she began, with strong, swift fingers, to take the clothes off the corpse. She was neat and deft, and handled the dead man with gentle dexterity; she carefully laid aside each blood-soaked garment, until the naked body, with its pitiful old-man's thinness, was lying on the bracken before her. Expertly she examined it. The wounds, which were chiefly on the abdomen, were savage and horrible, but they seemed to be of less interest to the long yellow fingers and rapidly darting black eyes than were a purple contusion near the base of the spine, the corpse's broken nose, and the extraordinary amount of blood on the clothing and on the brown bracken.

Having concluded her inspection, she dressed the body, laid it as she had found it, and nodded several times like a satisfied, Chinese mandarin.

'Murder, child,' she said.

'You can't hang a boar,' said Carey. His aunt wiped her hands on some snow-wet bracken twenty yards away from the corpse, and dried their resulting dampness on her handkerchief.

'What do you mean?' she enquired, as they walked to the path at the top.

'Simith was killed by a boar.'

113

'But a human being planned the murder, child. Otherwise, where is the boar?'

There were marks of a boar's hoofs, on the crumpled soil of the bank at the summit of the path, and wheel-marks, possibly of a car, possibly of a cart, had been roughly but sufficiently obliterated. Carey bent and examined them.

'You'd have a job to prove that the boar was taken into the vehicle,' he said, 'although, I grant, it looks just like it to me.'

'There don't appear to be other tracks made by the boar, and there is no sign of flattening of the bracken,' said Mrs Bradley. 'We'd better go back to that A.A. box, and get the scout to telephone, I suppose.'

'Did you really come to Shotover to find the body?' asked Carey.

'Well, *someone* takes great interest in the local legends, child,' was Mrs Bradley's oblique, unsatisfactory reply. She turned out the dead man's pockets. In one of them was an envelope, and inside it, on a rough piece of unlined paper similar to the one which had been sent to Fossder from Reading, were two little shields in pencil. One bore a horizontal embattled line, the other a crude but recognisable boar's head. On the back were the words 'B. H. T. Eastcheap.' The postmark on the envelope was Reading.

Sir Selby Villiers leaned back and grinned at Mrs Bradley.

'The Chief Constable doesn't like you a bit,' he said.

'Why ever not?' asked Mrs Bradley, stroking the sleeve of the orange and purple jumper she was wearing.

'You've put murder into his head. He doesn't want Simith to have been murdered. Spoils the county record or something, I think.'

'I thought that was Bucks,' said Carey. 'Besides, there's no doubt it was murder – or so Aunt Adela says, and I'd back her opinion against anybody else's, any day. Wouldn't you?'

'I realise, and so does the Chief Constable, that a contused back, and a broken nose are not usually the results of falling on bracken in Shotover Woods. I realise, too, that there is no evidence of a struggle with the animal. There is no animal, even, to be found on Shotover Hill. It is all perturbing, very perturbing, to a peace-loving man, you know.'

He looked pensive and slightly reproachful, and Mrs Bradley cackled.

'I suppose they'll arrest Geraint Tombley,' Carey said. 'He had the best motive, I suppose? And, added to the death of old Fossder, there doesn't seem very much doubt.'

'The police haven't made up their minds,' said Mrs Bradley.

'Now, how do you know that?' asked Sir Selby. 'You are not in their counsels, surely?'

'Oh, no. It stands to reason,' said Mrs Bradley. 'There is Priest to be considered. He married Linda Ditch. Linda Ditch is with child. Priest himself may be responsible, but it is possible that Simith is the father.'

'Or Tombley,' Carey observed.

'In which case, the motive of Priest for murdering Simith falls to the ground,' Sir Selby pointed out.

'Do you think Tombley's motive for the murder a strong one?' Mrs Bradley enquired.

'I don't know. It would be, if he wanted his inheritance in a hurry. But we don't know that he did. And, of course, they quarrelled, didn't they?'

'And fought,' said Carey. 'I expect that's how Simith got the broken nose.'

'And the badly-bruised back, I suppose?' said Mrs Bradley. She picked up her knitting. 'The bruised back, the broken nose, partial strangulation, then the savaging by the boar – it must have been a curious sort of fight. What does puzzle me, though,' she continued, 'is how the murderer managed to get the boar away from the body without being hurt himself. Priest, the pigman, might have been able to do it, I suppose?'

'Roman Ending aren't the only owners of boars, you know,' said Carey. 'I might be suspected myself.'

'You will be, later on,' said Mrs Bradley.

'The whole thing's very odd,' said Sir Selby slowly. He frowned. Mrs Bradley watched Carey.

'Go on,' she said encouragingly to him. Carey looked up with a sigh.

'It doesn't make sense,' he said. 'I mean people don't take boars about on leads, so to speak, as though they were dogs. For breeding, one takes the sow to the boar, not the boar to the sow. And if it had been with the idea of selling it –'

'I know,' said Mrs Bradley, pensively. 'But the death took place at Roman Ending, child. The Shotover setting is accounted for partly by the curious mentality of the murderer, and partly by the necessity for lending verisimilitude to an otherwise bald and improbable tale. The trouble is that the setting chosen happens to make this particular tale less bald, certainly, but even more improbable.'

Sir Selby looked at her sadly. 'You're a nuisance, you know. You shouldn't have examined the body. Nobody else would have bothered about that bruise, and the broken nose, and the partial strangulation, Adela.'

'Are you certain, child?'

'Pretty certain. And the broken nose, as your nephew suggested, may have had no connection with murder.'

'I know.' She still watched Carey. 'Go on, child,' she said, encouragingly.

'When do they think he died?' asked Carey, looking towards Sir Selby.

'Your aunt can tell you. She deduced it when she, very unpublic-spiritedly, decided to examine the body. The police doctor came to the same conclusion later. Simith died at between eleven p.m. and two a.m. In other words, probably at midnight.'

'Queer,' said Carey. 'Did you know that at one o'clock in the morning my pigs were disturbed and I had to go out to them? They're pedigree stuff and I don't take any risks, you know. One or two were restless, but my younger boar made no sign. I thought, at the time, that he must have been asleep, but since then he's developed a chill or a cold or something, and – well, I've a definite impression that, his sty being what it is, he caught the cold outside it.'

'You don't mean your boar got loose and killed Simith?' Sir Selby asked.

'I don't know what to think. I feel pretty sure that my boar was taken out of the sty that night, and that that accounted for the restlessness of the other animals and the fact which puzzled me at the time – that he didn't hear me when I halted outside his run.'

'You'll have to tell the police,' Sir Selby said.

'If I do, I incriminate either myself or my pigman.'

'Not yourself, surely? Someone can vouch for you.'

'Not after about eleven o'clock, I imagine. I know it was just turned eleven when I went up to bed, and I was the last left downstairs.'

'But surely other people in the neighbourhood besides yourself or your pigman are capable of taking an animal from his sty, and putting him back again later?'

'Well, I don't know,' said Carey. 'You see, a boar is a very suspicious customer. Hereward is young, I know, and not really savage, but to kick up the devil of a fuss and go for the nearest person is second nature to a boar. They're damned awkward brutes to handle if you haven't just the knack.'

'But that's my argument! It might easily have been someone with just the knack. In fact, if it had been someone *without* just the knack, surely he wouldn't have risked it?' Sir Selby put up his eyeglass and looked triumphant.

'But that's just the reason why he *might* have risked it,' Carey argued stolidly. 'Anybody who *realised* the risks wouldn't have taken them. As it happens, Hereward is a boar in a thousand. He's more like a dog than a boar. But very few people are aware of that. I should say the chap who took him out knew nothing at all about pigs.'

From this point of view Carey refused to be moved.

'Well, it isn't really my business, and, after I've condoled with the Chief Constable, and advised him to make Mrs Bradley responsible for tracking down the murderer (as a penance for raising the *accident* to Simith on to the plane of murder), I must get back to Town,' said Sir Selby, accepting the drink which Carey had just poured out.

Mrs Bradley waved a claw-like hand as his car was leaving Old Farm. Carey went over and stood just behind her left elbow.

'Well, are you going to jug your nearest and dearest?' he asked, with his arm round her shoulders. She cackled and jabbed a sharp elbow into his ribs.

'I want to go and look at boars again, child.'

'Which boars?'

'All the boars in the neighbourhood. Tomorrow you and I will make a circular tour, inspecting all the boars.'

'With the excuse that I want to purchase?'

'Except at Roman Ending. We don't need to make that excuse to the astute and suspicious Tombley. We will complain that Hereward does not seem to be better, and then we will enquire tenderly after Nero. Poor Nero! I wonder what they cleaned him with?' she added.

'You think Nero savaged Simith?'

'I think so, child. Don't you?'

'It *might* have been an accident, then?'

'With the body found on Shotover Common, child?'

'Why not? Simith may have been fearfully drunk, and have taken him out for a walk. People do do odd things when they're tight, you know, and, if you remember, Tombley told us that Simith was going a bit soft in the head.'

'No, no,' said Mrs Bradley. 'I think poor Simith was thrown to the boar as an early Christian might have been thrown to the lions – with malice aforethought, and with a very lively appreciation on the part of the murderer that the boar would certainly kill him.'

'That's all very well,' said Carey, lifting the elf-lock gracefully out of his eye with a sweep of his long brown hand, 'but I don't think you know too much about boars, you know, or you wouldn't be quite so certain. I mean, granted the chap let Nero loose on Simith, and granted that Nero is horribly savage and intractable: even so, how could the chap – the murderer, you know – be certain that the boar would go for Simith and maul him to death? It would have been equally boar-like to savage the person who egged him on, or even to go rooting off on a toot without bothering about savaging anybody. That's what's so odd to me about the whole affair, unless the wrong person got killed.' He glanced hopefully at his aunt. 'I suppose you'd considered that, had you? I mean, there's nothing particularly dependable about the behaviour of a boar. You couldn't possibly bet money on it; much less stake a murder on it, you know. *Simith* may have intended murder, and been the victim instead!'

'I see,' said Mrs Bradley, unconvinced.

'And, if you think Nero was the culprit, why did the murderer drag in my Hereward?'

'To make the tracks that Nero didn't make.'

'Riddle?'

'Sober fact. Hereward was the boar that went to Shotover Hill that night. Nero, I am certain, did not go.'

'Yes, but – you don't think Hereward would kill a man, Aunt Adela?'

'You mean that *you* don't think he would.'

'And, hang it, Nero is Simith's own boar, and, in spite of what I said about the uncertainty, a man ought to be able to handle his own boar, oughtn't he?'

'Tombley told me that no none but Priest could handle Nero, child.'

'If true, disgraceful – and frightfully awkward for Priest. If false' – he looked up and laughed – 'it might bring us back to Tombley, mightn't it? And all the Fossder business might be part of the very same plot. I've got a feeling, like you, that the two deaths hang together.'

'I know,' said Mrs Bradley. She seemed dejected. 'But, about the fact that Simith should have been able to handle Nero. Simith was in a semi-conscious state, I think, when Nero got at him.'

'The strangulation business? Oh, I see!'

The next day they breakfasted at seven, by the light of a yellow lamp that flung shadows under Mrs Bradley's bright black eyes, and painted her yellow skin the colour of old gold; she looked like an ancient, benevolent goddess, wrinkled but immortal. She ate a modest breakfast with appetite, and propped a book of very modern verse against the sugar bowl. Carey, distrait but handsome, the elf-lock well in evidence, his long mouth sentimentalised by the deceptive shadows, and his eyes dark pools, champed bacon, blackpudding, eggs, fried bread and pigs' liver with a serene, entirely masculine, disregard of his Byronic appearance and the well-being of his digestive organs.

'More coffee, Aunt Adela?'

Mrs Bradley passed her cup.

'Listen, child,' she said 'This is about pigs.' She peered at the book, and then read, in her deep and beautiful voice,

'Flattered,
As by significant form and Nature's bold
Subtraction,
Trompe l'œil to the stranded demi-gods,
Fat carcases et habeo B.B.C.! –
The fat-stock prices, Oxford-on-Cam pronounced.
(Stratford-atte-Bow, quoth Chaucer)
Fie, for shame!
Hoodoo, or Voodoo – same?

Shame, same; same shame as
Eve's.
Significant form? What else?
Squirms matter? *All* her dugs?'

Carey put his head on one side, and grinned.

'You know, it's rather good. The fellow's *seen* a sow. It reminds
me of Browning, rather! If you've finished your breakfast, let's go.
I've been thinking things over a bit. If we go to the village first
they'll think I'm mad. I think we should try a slightly wider
cast. What do you say to going to Wheatley first, and working
straight across country? I think I ought to tell you that this county
boasts three hundred and fifty-nine boars.'

'The first thing I want to do is to go to Garsington,' said Mrs
Bradley, producing an Ordnance map, and flipping it with her
finger.

'Garsington?'

'Garsington, child.'

'To see boars?'

'Well, not exactly. I, too, have been thinking things over, and
I fancy that, if Tombley was the ghost, he went on horseback
by way of Wheatley, Garsington, Toot Baldon and Nuneham
Courtenay.'

'Oh, bother Tombley and the ghost! You told me before that he
jolly well wasn't the ghost! And you said we were going to look at
boars!'

'So we are,' said Mrs Bradley, putting on a tweed coat and a hat.
'Come, child. The sun will be up very soon.'

Into the eerie half-darkness they sallied forth, and Carey was
very soon kicking the motor-cycle into a roar of life. Mrs Bradley,
with a veil tied under her chin to keep her hat on, and fur-lined
gloves on her hands, sat patiently in the sidecar. The sky light-
ened. The motor-cycle combination moved slowly towards the
gate, which young Walt obligingly held open.

'Garsington!' screamed Mrs Bradley, above the noise of the engine.

'Garsington ho!' bellowed Carey, as he turned the corner and slightly opened the throttle. Soon they were climbing past the post office, past the church; soon they were in top gear, rushing towards Forest Hill; soon they had opened up again on the other side of the village, slowing for the turning on to the main road, edging discreetly through a sleeping Wheatley, past the ancient lock-up and the silent public house, and at last they were rushing past Coombe Wood, which edged the road for about a quarter of a mile, and slowing to ten miles an hour past Garsington Kennels.

'Of course,' said Carey, pulling up at the cross-roads, 'if I'd been doing the journey, I believe I'd have cut out the main part of Garsington altogether and taken the lane that runs past Great Leys Farm and on past Sandford Brake. It isn't far, and you could lead the horse. See what I mean?'

He had dismounted and was standing beside Mrs Bradley, who had the map on her knee.

'He could have joined the main road by cutting through past the brick works, but the mystery is, if he *did* come round this way, what on earth possessed him to go back to Folly Bridge, and then come towards Sandford from Iffley?'

Mrs Bradley nodded.

'But you are assuming that the horseman came by night. I am assuming that he made the journey by daylight, and *led* the horse along the main road into Oxford. That wouldn't have attracted very much attention.'

'I see your point,' said Carey. 'Well, what's the next move, angel?' He assisted her out of the sidecar.

'I want to see Garsington Cross,' said Mrs Bradley, 'and I want to go by myself. You stay here, and, if I'm not back in twenty minutes or so, you can come along with the contraption and look for me.'

She walked briskly away, map in hand. A passing labourer, a stubble-faced man with broken, brown teeth, bade Carey good-morning cheerily, and asked him whether he had run out of petrol.

'Well, no,' said Carey, 'I'm trying to find some relations of mine who live about here, and whom I've never seen. Name of Season.'

'Season?' said the man. He shook his head. 'I don't know any-then about anybody named Season. Not in my time they wouldn't be. Why don't ee ask Mrs Tempson? Er'd know, ef anybody did, I should fancy. First turnen and second 'ouse. Ee can't miss er. Fuch-sias in the front window. Bloomen, too an' all. Wonderful ooman with flowers. Good-day to ee. Season? I'll try and recollect, but I don't some'ow thenk there's ben anybody o' that name in Garsen-ton. Not in my time, any'ow, and I've lived 'ere fifty-five year.'

He passed on, his workman's straw basket on his back, his blue can of tea in his hand. Carey followed his directions, and came upon old Mrs Tempson in the act of feeding the canary.

'Season?' She shook her head. 'Not en Garsenton. *That* I knows for sure.'

'It's odd,' said Carey. 'I could have sworn they said Garsington, and Tom, who came through here on Christmas Eve with his horse, would have said the same, I know.'

'Would that be the same white 'orse as cast a shoe?'

'I didn't know that, but a white horse, yes, that's right.'

'Very aggravated he was, I could tell, the way he was speaken,' said old Mrs Tempson.

'That wouldn't aggravate Tom. He's very mild-tempered,' said Carey.

'This un wasn't mild-tempered, but holden himself en, as ee might put it, like, tryen not to show all he felt.

' "Got to get the mare to Stadhampton, and late on the way as et is!" he said, very ell-tempered to 'Arry Brown, the smeth. Lost the shoe comen along Up Blenheim, er ded. But there! Esn't much us can't do for ee 'ere in Garsenton, so be us give a mind to et, you know, and us soon 'ad the 'orse upon his road again.'

Mrs Bradley returned with the same tidings. A grey mare had cast a shoe and the rider had given evidence of bad temper held in check with difficulty. She had learnt one other thing – the approximate age of the rider. 'Not short of sexty; older, maybe,' her informant had volunteered; 'a lettle, testy chap, and I'll back he were up to no good!'

'We'll have to go north through New Headington, and then past Headington Quarry,' Carey said. 'And now, what about these boars?'

'I want to see yours.'

'Yes, I know you do, but where?'

'I said *yours*, not *boars*! Your boars!'

'My boars? Oh, very well!'

'And now,' said Mrs Bradley, when at length they were back at Old Farm, and the motor-cycle combination was safely housed in the cartshed, 'be quiet, and let me think.'

Carey was silent. He accompanied her to the pigs. Hereward was feeding. He glanced up interrogatively at the sound of voices, and then went on with his meal. He ate with the steady concentration of a young boar who was not greedy but who enjoyed his food, and who had forgotten that he had once been in active competition with eleven brothers and sisters for it.

'That tusk,' said Mrs Bradley. She looked at it as closely as Hereward would permit. Occasionally he lifted his head to chew the food, and displayed it generously to her intent and interested scrutiny. When the boar had finished eating, she took her nephew into the house and they played at table-tennis in the room that Carey used as a studio. It was the one indoor pastime at which he could beat her. They played until it was too dark to see, and then abandoned the game and went in search of tea.

'Our Lender have to attend the enquest on Mr Semeth,' said Mrs Ditch, when she brought in the tray. 'And I s'pose you'll be goen, too an' all, won't ee? Dear, dear! What times we do live en, to be sure!'

'Yes, we are going,' said Carey, 'and I'll tell you all about it, Mrs Ditch.'

'Ah, do ee, then. Couldn't trust our Lender to tell the truth, less now she'm married than ever.'

'Is that really so?' asked Mrs Bradley.

'Can't gev evidence again her husband, can 'er?' Mrs Ditch enquired.

'So that's what you think? That Priest killed Simith,' said Carey, looking at her as she flicked the crumbs off the table.

'I don't thenk at all,' said Mrs Ditch, eyeing him calmly. ''Tes a bad 'abit, and shouldn't be encouraged en nobody. Ef us didn't thenk, us wouldn't make oursen miserable. That's what I ben sayen to our dad.'

'Where did Linda get to on Boxing Night? Have you found that out?' asked Carey. Mrs Ditch looked grim.

'Have I? You be asken somethen now! 'Er went over to Roman Enden, snow or no snow, shoes or no shoes, that I *do* know, say 'er what 'er well. Make what ee can of that, for I be sartain.'

'Shoes or no shoes,' said Mrs Bradley thoughtfully. 'That settles that, then, doesn't it?'

'You mean she went barefoot, and that's why her shoes weren't marked?'

'That's what I mean, child, yes.'

'But the ankle-length dress? Wouldn't that get bedraggled, and frightfully dirty?'

'I expect she changed it, child.'

'But – say it in words of one syllable. Do you mind?'

'Linda Ditch went up to bed as early as she could. She had an appointment with someone at Roman Ending. She slipped out at the front door, and neither we in here, nor her parents at the back, would have heard her go, because there was a fair amount of noise going on, and, in any case, the walls are almost sound-proof in this house. She had previously changed her frock for one which she had hidden in the hall. She risked very little in changing there.

125

Her parents would not come that way unless one of us summoned them, or somebody rang the front-door bell and brought them out of the kitchen. During the few moments it took her to slip out of one frock into the other, she had reason to hope that we would not come into the hall to go up the stairs. She may then have gone barefoot across the snow. Her outdoor shoes were probably in the kitchen, for the Ditch family very rarely keep their outdoor shoes in their bedrooms. They are almost invariably left downstairs under the dresser or somewhere. Linda kept her appointment, came back, dared not return to the bedroom, or, possibly, was too much upset to do so, and got into the priest's hole from another entrance – an entrance which Denis and I did not discover.'

'But why did she need to go back to Roman Ending? Priest wasn't there. He sleeps in the village, you know.'

'She may have gone at Simith's or Tombley's bidding. Somebody may have wanted to get her away from here while Hereward was taken out of his sty.'

'And why did she faint when we opened the panelling that morning?'

'I don't think she did faint. I think she was asleep, and fell out, and the shock made her feel faint. It might, quite easily.'

'I see. And what do you think we ought to do about her?'

'Nothing, child. I'll talk to Linda again some time, and see what she has to say. Meanwhile I'm going to see Tombley, and frighten him if I can.'

'You won't manage that. He's got guts.'

'All the more reason for supposing he isn't a murderer.'

'I bet he is, though,' said Carey. 'What's more, I'm coming with you. You don't visit Tombley alone. If he did murder Fossder and Simith, it wouldn't be healthy for you to go and ask him questions.'

'I don't think he is a murderer. But he must know something about the deaths, I should think. You noticed that the mysterious horseman, whose grey mare cast a shoe in Garsington, was Simith, I suppose?'

'That's fearfully odd, to my mind. Where on earth was he going?'

'To Folly Bridge, and along the towing path. He was the horseman the man in the little shop heard go by on Christmas Eve.'

CHAPTER 8

Half-Rounds on a Pig-Farm

Tombley was alone in the house. He explained this when he answered the door himself.

'I thought you were the police again,' he said.

'Dear me,' said Mrs Bradley, walking past him into the house. Carey followed her in, and Tombley shut the door.

'Come into the parlour,' he said. 'I've got a fire in there. I'm in a muddle, rather. I've got several letters to write.'

'Yes, I know you must be busy. We came to ask whether any of us at Old Farm could be useful,' Mrs Bradley said.

'That's nice of you.' He paused. His little piggish eyes looked them over carefully. 'You've heard the verdict at the inquest, I suppose? Murder by person or persons unknown. I'm going to be arrested, I may as well tell you. Very odd that you should be the two to find Uncle Simith's body, don't you think? He must have been drunk when he took out that animal, but no one will believe me when I say so.'

'So he *did* take out the boar?' said Mrs Bradley. She seated herself in the armchair which Tombley had drawn up to the fire.

'Oh, yes, he must have done. It makes the whole thing look so fearfully silly. He was tight when he came home, and must have been more so, I should imagine, when he took the poor brute for a walk on Shotover Common. It was hearing that broadcast from Queen's College on Christmas evening, that gave the old chap the idea, I'll bet a tenner. Did you switch on and hear it? Very interesting. Oh, yes, no doubt but that the boar turned savage, and did him in in a particularly nasty, but entirely boar-like manner. I haven't a doubt about it. It wasn't murder at all, whatever they say. It's a poor look-out for me. The police are hot on my track! As though I bore the poor old boy any malice!'

'Well, I'm very sorry to hear that the police are being a nuisance. It's their job, I suppose,' said Carey. Mrs Bradley nodded. Her sharp black eyes were roaming round the room; not so much roaming, as flitting from object to object. She even glanced under the table.

'Looking for bloodstains? There aren't any here,' said Tombley. 'I've had a lawyer down. He doesn't like the look of things a bit, but I tell him that even supposing I am arrested, I can't be convicted. To begin with, I didn't do it. To go on with, there's no evidence.'

'Has Nero been found? Is he in his sty?' asked Mrs Bradley, thus forestalling Carey, who was about to make a remark.

'Of course he's in his sty. I've lost nothing but a half-grown bacon pig – a mystery, but a mild one. But do you think that satisfies those busies? Oh, no! They make believe they think I've bought another boar. They seem to think I shot Nero after I'd let him kill Uncle Simith, or some such rubbish. The inspector has taken a bitter dislike to me. And then they talk of justice! It's all a lot of rot!'

He went to the door and opened it.

'Would you mind? I'm afraid I'm not in much of a mood for visitors. I'm being frightfully rude, but – would you go? If there's anything later on, and you wouldn't mind, I'll send Priest or somebody over. I'm so fearfully sorry to seem to be so rude, but – you do understand me, don't you?'

'So it wasn't Nero,' said Carey, as they walked across the fields towards the wood. Mrs Bradley cackled.

'And the half-grown pig, presumably, roves the wastes of Shotover Common still. And Tombley inherits the pigfarm, and all that therein is. That's his trouble, child. It makes such an obvious motive. Fossder dead – he gets the girl. Simith dead – he gets the farm and the money – everything, in fact.'

'Everything,' said Carey. 'Money, farm, bacon interests, all the lot. The motive, as you say, sticks out a mile.'

'But what a stupid murder! And Tombley is rather clever,' said Mrs Bradley.

'It's the clever ones who do the silliest things,' said Carey, helping her over the stile. Seated on the top of it, Mrs Bradley shook her head at him.

'It isn't safe to generalise. Tombley does odd things at times, but I really can't suspect him of this murder. He is altogether too chivalrous,' she said. 'Poor Tombley! It does look black, though.'

She sat back and began to murmur to herself. 'Boxing Day, and his own boar. With a motive that sticks out a mile, and a stone-flagged floor in the living-room of the house. With all that chasing over here on Christmas Eve to ask us whether we knew where his uncle was –'

'Alibi for himself, the last,' said Carey, 'to prove he wasn't the ghost, if anything came out about it later.'

'Possibly,' said Mrs Bradley. She gazed at him benignly. 'Very possibly, child. But, all the same, I think it was too foolish a thing for a man like Tombley to have done. I agree that he has something he wants to hide. There isn't any doubt about that. But it isn't murder, I'm sure.'

She took Carey's outstretched hand and finished surmounting the stile, and as they walked on up the road he said, 'I've been checking up a few facts and things, you know.'

Mrs Bradley nodded. She continued to nod for some time, rhythmically and slowly, and as though she had forgotten she was doing it. The road wound gradually uphill. Soon they could hear the running of the roadside brook.

'Proceed, moon,' she said encouragingly.

'It's about Tombley and his uncle.'

'Ah!' said Mrs Bradley.

'You see, there's every reason why Tombley should murder his uncle, and not much reason why anybody else should. You don't mind if I talk in words of one syllable, do you? Mine, unlike Tombley's, is not a powerful intellect. Now, you say that Simith was murdered at Roman Ending, but actually I agree with Tombley that there is very little proof that Simith was murdered at all. Why couldn't you have left the whole thing alone, and let it be thought an accidental death? It would have saved a whole heap of trouble!'

'And then –!'

'I don't know.' He laughed and put his arm round her bony shoulders. 'I know you had to point out the broken nose and the bruised back as evidences of murder, but, after all, they may not have been. Tombley and Simith used to fight like fiends. It was usually Simith's fault, but he might easily get the worst of it with a powerful chap like Tombley –'

'All this is well beside the point, dear child. You said you had facts. What are they?'

'First of all, there's that business of the ghost. I spotted the hand of Tombley in that from the very beginning, and so did you, I think. But I don't believe he meant anything more than a stupid –'

'Practical joke,' said Mrs Bradley. 'Do you remember,' she added, 'that when Tombley called here on Christmas Eve he mentioned his uncle's weak heart?'

'I know. I thought it very interesting.' He grinned. 'His uncle hadn't a weak heart, I think you are going to say. Well, I happen to *know* that he hadn't. And how do I know? Because, two days before you came to stay here, he was out trotting after the beagles or something, over on the other side of the village. You know those fields out there, opposite the pub? He went several miles, and came back without a sign of having run himself out. A very hearty old boy. Surprisingly spry. So you see that, unless he'd contracted a weak heart within the last week or ten days, Tombley was lying about him, which looks a bit suspicious, in the circumstances.'

'Interesting,' said Mrs Bradley, as they turned off towards Old Farm. She reversed the ash-plant she carried, addressed a rounded stone, and lifted it very neatly over the low stone wall. 'Go on, child.'

'On the other hand,' continued Carey, '*Fossder* really did have a weak heart, and Tombley (if the ghost *was* Tombley) chased him and upset it pretty badly – so badly that he died.'

'I know. It's certainly a coincidence, but it may be nothing more. But I had already given a certain amount of consideration to the point, and admit that it is significant. Tombley must have had Fossder on his mind.'

'That's what I think. I mean, unless he had weak hearts on the brain, why should he have mentioned them? He could just have said that his uncle's absence worried him.'

'I know,' said Mrs Bradley.

'Yes, well – Now, what about this business of the boar? You think that Nero killed Simith, and that my boar, Hereward, was taken to Shotover to make it look as though the death had taken place there instead of at Roman Ending.'

Mrs Bradley nodded. 'A mistake which Tombley would never have made,' she said. 'Does it not strike you as rather significant, child, that all that elaborate staging of the scene deceived nobody at all? And now I'm going back to Roman Ending. I'm going to drop in again on Tombley straight away.'

'When he's not expecting us, you mean?'

'When he's not expecting *me*. You, child, will remain outside the house and talk pig with Priest, and note carefully what he says. I have a shrewd notion that poor Tombley wants to confide in me, and he certainly won't do it while *you're* there, that I know.'

'*Confide* in you?'

'Well, yes, child. I expect he wants to find out whether I'll put him in touch with my son. He'll want somebody clever to defend him at the trial – if it comes to that, later on.'

'Ferdinand?'

'Ferdinand, child. A very clever boy.' She grinned reminiscently. 'A *very* clever boy.'

'I see. He really thinks he'll be arrested, then, for the murder?'

'Yes, child. But I am going to prevent it, if I can.'

'Oh?'

'They couldn't convict him on the present evidence.'

'Ah! Give him enough rope, you mean? But do you think you'll find some more evidence, then? I should have thought that, coupled with Fossder's death –'

'But, child, *nothing* can be coupled with Fossder's death. That's just the trouble. Fossder's death, so far as the police and the general public are concerned, was a most regrettable accident, but still – an accident. Hugh has made no statement to the police about the finding of Fossder's body. There has been no need, in view of the medical certificate.'

'You don't still think that Hugh – that there was anything – you know – *funny* about Hugh's behaviour that night?'

'I still think Hugh's behaviour that night was extremely odd, and that Jenny is to be pitied.'

'Being with him when the body was found, you mean? Still, they're in love.'

'Hm!' said Mrs Bradley. 'And, as we know, "*amor omnia vincit*" – even commonsense!'

Her tone was so unusually acid that Carey glanced at her in great surprise, and with a certain amount of disquiet, but she relieved his feelings by cackling harshly. In the quiet of the leafless little wood, she reverted to the subject of the boar.

'I'll tell you what happened,' she said. 'What I think happened,' she added. 'You, out of your technical knowledge, can correct me if I say something silly about the animals.'

'Go ahead.'

'Nero is so dangerous that nobody but Priest can approach him.'

'OK. I'm pretty sure that Tombley dare not, anyway.'

'Therefore, unless Priest is the murderer, Nero did not leave his sty.'

'So.'

'If Nero did not leave his sty, Simith was put into Nero's sty to be savaged to death. The only question is, who put him there?'

'Well, who did?'

'We have a fairly wide field of choice. There was no danger in putting him *in*. The danger lay in taking him *out*.'

'Priest, again, is the only person who could take him out.'

'Yes, I see. We may take it, then, that Priest did so. Tell me, child, how do boars react to cold water?'

'What, to drink?'

'No. Suppose I attacked a boar by swilling him with icy water from a hose, or even a bucket, what would be the result?'

'You might intimidate him for a time. Same with lions. Ah! I see what you're after! You think there was an accomplice!'

'Oh, I am sure there was an accomplice!'

'I thought I was getting warmer, but I ain't. Who was the accomplice? Linda Ditch? She isn't too keen on Priest, even though she's married him, you know.'

He laughed. A startled bird flew out of a tree with a screech. Mrs Bradley chuckled.

'Well, you do seem Linda Ditch-conscious,' Carey went on merrily.

'And rightly so, you will find,' said his aunt with a nod.

Carey thought this over, and shrugged his shoulders. Just then they emerged from the wood and followed an almost indecipherable path towards Stanton Great Wood. The path branched off into another wider one which led eastward to Roman Ending. Again they found themselves looking down on the farmhouse and barns and the movable pigpens scattered about the fields.

'Come along,' said Mrs Bradley. 'But, mind, you're to stay outside.'

She hurried down the long green slope, taking the shortest way across the grass. A gap in the stone wall had been rudely fenced, but beside it a couple of loosened stones stood out like steps, and, agile as a goat, she skipped over on to the other side, and set off towards the house. Priest was harnessing an old grey mare to one of the pighouses, preparatory to moving it to another part of the potato field where the pigs were rooting and feeding. Carey stopped to talk to the pigman. Mrs Bradley walked briskly up to the house, and, finding the back door open, walked in boldly.

'Anyone at home?' she called. Tombley, pen in hand, looked out from the parlour doorway, an ugly scowl on his face. It changed to a smile at the sight of Mrs Bradley.

'Lestrange with you?' he asked. Mrs Bradley nodded, her bright eyes on his face and her mouth pressed into a little birdlike beak as she looked him all over again.

'To make certain I don't get murdered,' she answered brightly.

'Come into the parlour,' said Tombley. 'No, wait a bit while I sign the last one of these letters, and then I'll come outside. Lestrange will have more confidence in me if he actually sees us together.' He finished his letter and sealed the envelope. 'I'm glad you've come back,' he said. 'You knew I wanted to talk to you, I think.' He led the way into the yard.

Mrs Bradley stared at a boarded hurdle which was leaning against the wall. 'What's that for, child?' she asked. Geraint Tombley eyed it without interest. His heavy face was dirty-looking with lack of sleep. His cheek showed incipient beard. His eyes – small and intelligent as those of the pigs themselves – were gazing at the sleeve of Mrs Bradley's winter coat, which she smoothed with an ungloved yellow claw as she stood there talking to him.

'You see,' he said, 'I've heard a lot about you, and I know you're very clever. That's not flattery. Of course, I could flatter you if I liked, and make you believe every word, but, honestly, Mrs Bradley, I'm not flattering you –'

'Oh, no. You're underestimating me,' said Mrs Bradley calmly.

Tombley raised his small eyes to hers, and shifted the chewing gum he was masticating to the other side of his mouth. Suddenly he turned his back on her and spat the gum at some pigs. One young porker snapped it as it fell. Tombley jerked his head towards the rooting animals.

'Now uncle's gone, I'm going in for Swedish methods, like Lestrange. That is, if you get me off. Look here: I'll tell you – what do you want me to tell you? I want you to be on my side. There are all sorts of awkward patches, and I want your advice very badly. And if I don't get a word with you very soon, they'll jug me, and then it'll be a darn sight more awkward for me to be able to get you on my side.'

Mrs Bradley cackled. It was an odd sound. Geraint Tombley had heard it several times. He could not persuade himself he liked it. Ghoulish was the word which best described it, he thought. To bring this terrible little old woman into the heart of his affairs was rather like asking a shark to defend one from cannibals. The shark might, and, he was certain, *could* eat the cannibals – in this case that particularly nosey inspector of police – but would it not turn upon him and engulf him also as a kind of relish to the meal? He shuddered.

'You see, I'm the old man's heir,' he continued. 'I don't know whether you knew? And if he *was* murdered and I get the benefit of his death, well, that is a motive straight away. Correct me if I'm wrong.'

'No, no. You're right. Indisputably,' said Mrs Bradley, grinning.

'Secondly, I haven't got an alibi.'

'Why should you have an alibi, dear child?'

'Well, if I had one, that would clear me, wouldn't it?'

'It might,' said Mrs Bradley cautiously.

'But of course it would. A man can't be in two places at the same time!' He bent and gently smacked a porker which was thrusting itself against Mrs Bradley's leg. 'Suppose I had been in – suppose I had been with a party of people, from ten o'clock until four in the morning. Wouldn't that clear me completely? One important point which did not emerge at the inquest was the exact time of my uncle's death. It was sworn to, to within three hours, but I should have thought – suppose, for instance, that I had been invited to Old Farm –'

'Yes,' said Mrs Bradley, gazing benignly at him. 'Well, suppose you *had* been invited to Old Farm?'

'Yes, well, supposing I had been, there would have been you to swear to me –'

'Not at midnight, child. I was in bed by eleven that night, and, after that, I could not swear positively to anything.'

'Carey, then. Carey would have been up.'

'I doubt it, child. We keep reasonable hours at Old Farm. Even Hugh, the hectic Londoner, reforms when he comes to the country.' She paused and eyed him. Tombley shuffled his feet. 'An alibi to cover the dead hours of the dark can often be established by one's *bedfellow*, though, if one *has* a bedfellow, child.'

Tombley leapt to his feet.

'Now, who the hell – ?' he shouted. His large face began to go purple and his little eyes gleamed red. His thick lips were drawn back, and his teeth showed yellowish. Suddenly his eyes began to water. 'Bit my tongue,' he said.

'I am not surprised,' said Mrs Bradley placidly. 'You *did* have a bedfellow, then. Was she in this house? Who was it, child? I think you'd better tell me.'

'It was Linda Ditch,' growled Tombley, 'but I dare not ask her to swear me an alibi. It wouldn't make any difference to me, anyway. She's got a bad reputation around these parts. The police would just say she was lying. She –' His voice tailed off. Then he began to bluster. 'Don't look at me like that! Call me a liar outright! Go on! But you'll have to prove it!'

'Yes, child. I'll have to prove it. Nevertheless, you are telling me lies, and, if you do that, I won't help you.'

'Oh, I expect Mrs Ditch has told you about Uncle Simith. Old Satyr! Old devil!' said Tombley, attempting, with a boldness which Mrs Bradley admired, to bluff his way out of embarrassment and dismay.

'Was he?' she said. 'And Linda Ditch was a victim, poor girl? Is that really so? Dear me! A pity that the lion should lie down with the lamb!' She grinned at him with fiendish, frightening amusement.

Tombley was moved to protest. 'I like her. She's not a good girl, as you say, but she suited me, Linda did. And I suited her. And I wish I could have married her. More suitable, really, I suppose, for her to have married Priest. But, anyway, you needn't sneer at her!'

'Splendid,' said Mrs Bradley, with apparent absentmindedness. 'Bless you, bless you, my child! But you're not a convincing liar. Why not tell me the truth? Go on about your alibi.'

'Well,' said Tombley, 'who'd believe her, anyway? They'd say she was out to help me because I saved her from uncle. And, besides, they'd say I was jealous of him, and in love with the girl myself. And they'd say I killed him for her sake as well as the money. Or else they'd say I bribed her to say she'd slept with me. No, no! I'm not bringing Linda into it, thank you very much!'

'I see,' said Mrs Bradley. She stepped back a couple of paces, avoiding a couple of pigs, and studied him, her black eyes bright with amusement.

He stared back, unresentfully.

'What's got to happen is this,' he said, when he had returned her gaze for a minute or two. 'I believe you're on my side, and it comes to this: the murderer has got to be found. Otherwise I'm for it.'

'I shouldn't be surprised if you were right. Very well, then, child. I will see what I can find out. Mind! *Whatever* I find out you will have to put up with! I'm not going to –'

'Soften the evidence,' said Tombley, with a grin. Mrs Bradley cackled. 'Come in,' he added, and led the way to the house.

'I don't propose to tell you again that you haven't been speaking the truth, dear child,' she said. 'I know your motive in lying. But some time or other I want you to tell me all you know about the Sandford ghost.' She seated herself beside the kitchen fire.

'The –' Tombley stared at her in genuine amazement.

'Including the why and wherefore,' said Mrs Bradley quietly.

'I thought I wouldn't keep that secret,' said Tombley. 'Yes, *I was the ghost*. I did it to give old What's-his-name a fright. It's lucky I haven't a motive for killing *him*, otherwise I suppose they'd say *that* was murder too.'

'You did have a motive,' said Mrs Bradley soothingly. 'But, all the same, child, it would be wiser far to tell me the truth about that. You haven't the same reason for secrecy this time, surely, have you?'

She had spoken gently and quietly, but Tombley suddenly growled, bent forward, and put his finger between the bars of the grate. He kept it there, whilst he counted aloud to five.

'See that?' he said. He held out the burnt finger for inspection.

'Clearly,' said Mrs Bradley.

'I trained myself to do that when I was ten. I wanted to be like Red Indians – impervious to pain.'

'But Red Indians are not impervious to pain; they merely know how to endure it,' Mrs Bradley pointed out, leaning forward and watching him closely.

'Yes, well, I'm impervious to it, see? But you're not!' said Tombley, seizing her skinny claw and dragging it near to the fire. 'If I held your finger on those bars, you'd scream!'

'Very probably,' said Mrs Bradley composedly. She lunged forward suddenly, poked her free hand out sharply, twisted her prisoned hand away, and sat back, staring unwinkingly at his watering, bloodshot eye.

'I only wanted to frighten you,' he said. 'I wouldn't have burnt you really.'

'Bless you, child, I know that. That's what I've been saying to Carey all along.'

Tombley held a handkerchief to his eye, and looked at her in perplexity.

'I suppose we're talking about the same thing?' he said doubtfully.

'Your chivalry,' said Mrs Bradley sweetly.

'You're too many for me,' said Tombley. 'Damn it, I see that you know! I thought at first you were bluffing. What are you going to do?'

'I'm not going to let you be hanged,' said Mrs Bradley. 'I suppose it's Fay who has a weak heart,' she added, 'and that's why you had weak hearts on the brain on Christmas Eve.'

CHAPTER 9

Back to Back in Kensington

'I want you to have a go at this,' said Mrs Bradley. Mr Derwent-water looked at the fish-paste jar full of soil.

'Analyse it, do you mean?' he asked. Mrs Bradley cackled and poked him in the ribs.

'Why not, dear child?' she enquired.

'And what do you suppose I shall find? Is this lunacy, murder or what?'

'Murder this time, child.'

'Oh? The Shotover Case? I heard you'd been pulled in on that. Old chap savaged by a boar. Very interesting.' He looked at the fish-paste jar again. 'And this, I presume, represents "Spot where the Body was Found." Am I right?'

'As always,' said Mrs Bradley. 'And my address, if you have to send on to me the result of your personal and, needless to say, private investigations, is Little House, Horsepath, Oxfordshire.'

'The private asylum?'

'Yes.'

'Aha!'

'Why so, child?'

'You think the murderer was a lunatic? Curious. So do I.'

Mrs Bradley looked startled.

'What makes you think that?' she asked.

'Oh, I don't know.' He began to take off his overall. 'Coming out for some lunch? I generally go out about now.'

'No. I have an appointment. Answer the question, child.'

'Well, it struck me that there might have been easier ways of killing the old fellow, if one felt one had to, than setting a savage animal on to him, that's all.'

'You disappoint me, child. I thought you were going to bestow on me one of your constructive ideas.'

'I don't construct. I'm an analyst – like you. I merely take to bits what other people have constructed.'

'Listen to me, then – or must you have your lunch?'

'No, no. Please! I've nothing special to do this afternoon. Our old friend arsenic turned up again in the Kerder case, by the way.'

'I thought it would. Well, now, these are the facts: two murders, not one, have been committed in Oxfordshire within the last two weeks. The first was on Christmas Eve, or rather, very early on Christmas morning, and there was not an inquest, because the doctor gave a certificate without any fuss, testifying that the man had died of heart failure.'

'Doctor a villain, do you think?' His grey eyes searched her face. Mrs Bradley shook her head and pursed her thin lips into a little beak.

'There is not the slightest reason to suppose so. The man, who had been his patient for a number of years, dropped dead on the towing path alongside the river between Iffley and Sandford. He had been running.'

'That isn't the whole of the story.'

'No, it isn't, child. The fact is, the man was running away from what he thought was a ghost.'

'I don't believe that. I should say that he knew the ghost was an enemy.'

'That is possible, too.'

'But what was the chap doing on the towing path at that hour? Tramp or something?'

'No. A respectable solicitor whose home was in Iffley, and who had gone out to keep an appointment.'

'Then he went to meet the man who had murdered him, I suppose? I can't see any other explanation.'

'Marvellous!' said Mrs Bradley. 'But not, I believe, quite true. I don't think, somehow, that he ever set eyes on the man he went out to meet.'

'Chap didn't turn up, do you mean? But, if it was murder, how did the doctor come to write the certificate?'

'Because the victim was not attacked, I tell you. He ran away and fell dead.'

'But –'

'And even *that* I have had to deduce. Well, goodbye, child, I must go.'

'Blood,' said the analyst, two days later. He had met Mrs Bradley, by appointment, at the Detection Club, of which she had been made an honorary member, and they sat in armchairs in the larger of the rooms which overlooked the street.

'Blood?' repeated Mrs Bradley.

'Not human blood.'

'Good. I thought it wouldn't be. No, I will be entirely frank with you. I *knew* it wouldn't be.'

'Quite. The soil is saturated with the blood of some animal.'

'Pigs' blood, possibly?'

'Very probably. That is to say, there is nothing to prove that it *isn't* pigs' blood, and, if there happened to be strong circumstantial evidence in favour of its being pigs' blood –'

'I see. Thank you, child.'

'Help you at all?'

'It confirms a theory of mine, and that is always pleasant. I like to be right.' She cackled and stood up. 'I want to see Sir Selby Villiers before I go back to Oxfordshire. Have you written a detailed report of your analysis?'

'Rather. I've got it with me. How does Sir Selby come into it? It isn't a Scotland Yard job, surely, is it? Or can't the local people tackle it?'

'Oh, yes, they can manage, child. The inspector in charge of the case came to a series of popular lectures I gave at the Oxford City YMCA a year or two ago, and we get on famously together. I teach him the art of knife throwing and explain Lombroso's theories, and tell him why most of them are discountenanced today, and he tells me how to prune trees and all about garden pests and how to combat them. He has also taught me the standard retail cuts of a Wiltshire side of bacon.'

They descended the dark and ancient staircase past the haunts of industry, pleasure and mystery which made up the remainder of the house and, turning into Shaftesbury Avenue, were soon at the entrance to Piccadilly Tube station, where they parted. Left alone, Mrs Bradley telephoned Sir Selby at his private address and was invited to come to dinner.

Sir Selby was delighted with her further account of the murders, and gave it as his opinion that either Tombley or Pratt was the murderer.

'Ah,' said Mrs Bradley, with evident satisfaction, 'so *you* think it might have been Pratt?'

'Decidedly I do. On the question of motive alone, he has as much to gain as Tombley.'

'But Tombley has confessed to being the ghost on Christmas Eve,' said Mrs Bradley, looking like a benevolent alligator and then suddenly screeching like a slightly demented macaw.

'Confessed, did he?'

'To being the perpetrator of a practical joke, that is all.'

'Oh, of course. One can understand that he wouldn't go further than that. Did he know that Fossder had a weak heart, I wonder?'

'He doesn't say so. But I have reason to think that he did know. He mentioned, on Christmas Eve, his uncle's weak heart, but I have evidence that Mr Simith's heart was perfectly sound.'

'Yes, I see the inference.'

'After confessing to the ghost business, he put his own finger in the fire, and then attempted to put one of mine in,' went on Mrs Bradley, with a reminiscent chuckle. 'I went back two days ago and had him taken to a private mental hospital for observation.'

'By his own consent?'

'Oh, yes. I told him it would save him from immediate arrest.' She grinned. Sir Selby looked at her reproachfully.

'Not right of you,' he said sadly.

'It was true,' said Mrs Bradley. 'I squared – is that the word? – my inspector purposely.'

'Now what about that business of the bet?'

'I know, child. It's very odd. I can't help thinking that something else besides the bet took Fossder along the towing path that night.'

'Don't you think he went to meet Tombley, then?'

'I think that Fossder had other fish to fry, and, possibly, so had Pratt. He came to Old Farm, you know, to find out why Hugh was delayed.'

'What kind of a fellow is Pratt? Of course, I am very much impressed by the fact that he, as I said before, had everything to gain, and nothing whatever to lose, by Fossder's death.'

'I have not formed any very definite opinion. It is a pleasure I have in store. As you point out, at Fossder's death Pratt, as Fossder's partner, would inherit the practice. I understand that he is fully qualified, in fact that, during the past two years, he handled most of the business.'

'Quite so. You know, I think you could put your Inspector on to Pratt, if only to find out, if possible, whether Fossder had any object in going out that night apart from the attempt to win the wager. Another point: you say that he was running along the towing path between Iffley and Sandford, when he fell and died. How did he get on to the towing path?'

'He crossed at Iffley Lock. Since someone broke through and was drowned, the tollkeepers leave the way open after eleven at night.'

'It all looks fishy,' Sir Selby said decidedly. 'And what's fishy is always instructive, in our profession. I should get the Inspector to stampede Pratt into telling all he knows. But now for the Simith affair. I should certainly say that the evidence points to Tombley there.'

'In a way it does. But there are some interesting doubts. To begin with, it seems assured, from the medical evidence, and from what I saw for myself when we found the body, that the savaging of Simith by the boar was not necessarily the most direct cause of his death. He had fallen heavily backwards – the result, I surmise, of having had his chair snatched away as he went to sit down – and, also, his nose was broken. I think he was dragged out in an unconscious or semiconscious condition, heaved up by the murderer and pitched over into the sty. The boar, possibly, had been teased to work him up to the requisite state of savagery. He thereupon tackled Simith, who must have been lying full length, and ripped him up with his tusks.'

'Nasty,' said Sir Selby, 'but I haven't seen the hitch. It looks all Lombard Street to a china orange like Tombley's work to me. The fall, we'll say, took place in a stone-floored farmhouse kitchen, and the boar was his own boar. You said they were pig farmers, didn't you?'

'But somebody took the body out again, and then, you see, it was conveyed to Shotover.'

'Well, Tombley's idea would be to get it as far from Roman Ending as he could.'

'I know,' said Mrs Bradley. 'I don't know how much experience you have of boars,' she added pensively, 'but I can assure you that it is one thing to shoot something over into a savage boar's sty, and quite another to go in after it and drag it out again.'

'I see your point. But a good dousing with water from a powerful hosepipe will keep most animals at bay. Men, too, for the matter of that. Depend upon it, that's how it was done. But it means there was an accomplice.'

'Yes,' said Mrs Bradley. 'If we could only find the hosepipe. *Or* the accomplice,' she added.

'Has the inspector looked for such a thing?'

'As a hose? Oh, yes. It was one of the first things he himself suggested he should look for. The only difficulty is that he has not found it, and he's a very thorough searcher, I can tell you. The police really *do* know how to look for things.'

'Buried.'

'I don't think so. I expect it's eaten. That is, if it ever existed.'

'Eaten?'

'Chopped up and mixed with the pig food,' Mrs Bradley explained. 'From what I've seen of pigs during the last two weeks, I don't believe they'd notice, if the hosepipe was chopped up small.'

'It's a very ingenious theory,' Sir Selby admitted, knitting his brows and turning round the signet ring on his finger. 'It isn't always easy to do away with a material clue like that, but still – as you say. Eaten by the pigs! Yes, most ingenious.'

'An effective method, as you say, of doing away with it,' said Mrs Bradley. 'And now for the pigman, Priest.'

'I don't think I've heard of him, have I?'

'He was Simith's pigman, and, according to Tombley, who may not be telling the truth, is the only person capable of handling the boar Nero.'

'Simith's boar? The one who savaged the body?'

'Yes. But, you see, it may not have been Nero who savaged the body. Simith *may* not have been killed at Roman Ending.'

'I see that. Please go on.'

'Priest had a grudge against Simith, who seems to have seduced a certain Linda Ditch, now Linda Priest, who used to be a servant at Roman Ending.'

'Oho! So the pigman married the victimised Linda, did he? That looks bad. I assume you are going to tell me that the marriage took place after the murder.'

'Very shortly after; and we are keeping a careful check on Priest's movements. To him, the disgraceful seduction of his sweetheart may have been a sufficient motive for the murder, don't you think?'

'I certainly do. But this is really interesting! What kind of a girl is Linda?'

'A hussy,' said Mrs Bradley with great firmness. 'I make all allowance for girls being girls, as you know, but when everything has been said in her favour, the fact remains that Linda is a bad lot. But I like her, you know,' she added, with a chuckle. Sir Selby nodded and laughed.

'All the same, there does remain the fact that a wife cannot be compelled to give evidence against her husband, doesn't there?' he said, becoming serious again.

'That's the whole point,' said Mrs Bradley. 'Then,' she went on, 'there is the other fact, of which the inspector has made nothing up to the present, that Linda left the house on the night of Simith's murder, and fell into the parlour out of the priest's hole early on the following morning.'

'Pray go on,' said Sir Selby, as she paused.

'But I can't,' said Mrs Bradley comically. 'That is the fact, and that is all I know.'

'But not all that you surmise?'

'Well, no. My first impression was that she went out so that she could give either Tombley or Priest an alibi for the murder.'

'By saying that she slept with one of them?'

'Yes. But Tombley told me later on that Linda would not swear him an alibi, although she was his bedfellow.'

'Well, if she's now married Priest, it is reasonable to suppose that he is right!'

'You don't know Linda Ditch. My own impression is that she did *not* sleep with Tombley.'

'Oh?'

'But that somebody else did, and that Tombley is prepared to risk being hanged rather than compromise this other woman, whoever she may be.'

'That means that he's in love with her.'

'Precisely.' Mrs Bradley beamed on him. 'It's that that makes the thing so very difficult. You see, I don't really think they slept at Roman Ending.'

'But who *is* the girl? She ought to be easy to find.'

'I have found her. She is Fossder's niece.'

'I thought – No matter.'

'You thought that Fossder's niece was engaged to Carey's friend Hugh.'

'Well, yes. But, I suppose –'

'Mr Fossder had two nieces,' said Mrs Bradley. 'Or rather, one niece and one niece-by-courtesy, to put it tactfully. Jenny is engaged to Hugh; Fay is engaged to Maurice Pratt; but Tombley was in love with Fay. Fossder, however, preferred Pratt's suit to Tombley's, and Fay appears to have been guided by her uncle in the matter.'

'You think, then, that she is in love with Tombley?'

'I don't know, child. But I do know that if Tombley wants her name kept out of this affair of the murder, he is going a very foolish way to work in giving out that he spent the night with Linda.'

'I don't altogether see that.'

'My dear Selby, have you ever tried spending a night with a woman when it seemed necessary to keep the whole affair a dead secret?'

'Heaven forbid!' said Sir Selby, his mind recoiling almost visibly from the suggestion.

'Well, if you had,' said Mrs Bradley, unperturbed, 'you would very soon realise that merely to talk of *walls having ears* is absurd. They have eyes, ears, tongues and logical minds. They know exactly what happened, and when, and why, and how. In the end, you might just as well have advertised your intentions in the *Morning Post*.'

'Oh! Private detective stuff!'

'Not private detective anything! Merely speculative theories advanced by your friends and casual acquaintances. *That* is in London. When it comes to a small and fairly remote village –'

'I see what you mean. You mean it ought to be easy enough to find out whether he spent the night with Fay or with Linda. Well, I should put your inspector on to it. It's quite a good point, and might lead you almost anywhere.'

'Including up the garden,' said Mrs Bradley sadly. 'You know, Selby, Fossder was a greedy, grasping and rather foolish old man, and Simith was a nasty, bad tempered old man. Why should we bother who killed them?'

'Morbid curiosity on your part; a sense of civic duty on mine,' said Sir Selby, grinning. 'Come and play Bridge for a bit. It'll do you good.'

'What would *really* do me good,' said Mrs Bradley, 'is to know whether the deaths of Fossder and Simith are separate and unrelated, or whether they are two pieces of the same pattern. If the latter is the truth, then the pattern will have to be completed, and I find the thought of that a little trying, you know.'

'What on earth do you mean?' asked Sir Selby.

'Well, if they are part of a pattern, it seems to me that the pattern, to be completed, requires the death of still another person. Doesn't it strike you that way?'

'Well, it hadn't. I see your point. Prevention is better than cure. And you haven't got Tombley in your private mousetrap to save him from being arrested, but to save him from murdering, or from being murdered by, Pratt.'

'Marvellous!' said Mrs Bradley, poking him in the ribs. 'You see further to the side than anyone else I know,' she added with a cackle. Sir Selby, straightening his tie, hoped that this was a compliment.

'Of course, there's still that pigman, Priest,' he added.

*

The inspector in charge of the Simith case returned to his tall narrow house at the foot of Headington Hill and sat there with pencil and notebook working out details of the deaths of Fossder and Simith. The first problem to be solved, he decided, was the identity of the person whom Fossder had set out to meet after midnight on Christmas Eve – really on Christmas morning. Mrs Bradley, he remembered, had said she thought that the probabilities were in favour of its having been Simith, but he considered her evidence, which rested on the fact that the mysterious horseman in Garsington might have been Simith, rather unreliable and slender. Still, if Simith had really been absent from Roman Ending that night, it was possible that he had had an appointment with Fossder. If this was the truth, he wondered what Simith had done when he found that Fossder did not turn up. He supposed that the old man had cursed Fossder, and then had returned to Roman Ending. Another point the inspector wanted to solve was the problem of the meeting place. Where had they agreed to meet, he wondered. It could not have been arranged that they should meet at Sandford, he thought, for, if so, there would have been the chance of running into Tombley, unless the uncle and nephew were in league together against Fossder. It was possible that they had been fellow conspirators. He knew that, frequently though the uncle and nephew had quarrelled between themselves, it was more than likely that they had made common cause against Fossder – Simith because of an ancient enmity, and Tombley because Fossder had prevented his marriage with Fay.

'So, if Simith and Tombley were in league on Christmas Eve,' thought the inspector, staring at the coal fire, 'the death of Fossder was prearranged.' Furthermore, he decided the uncle and nephew had given each other a very clever alibi. Simith could have declared, with truth, that he had not so much as set eyes on Fossder that night (and probably had witnesses to prove it), whereas Tombley – if he had been detected as the ghost of Napier – would have been able to declare that Fossder's death was an accident; the result of a stupid joke. This was still an assertion which it was very difficult to contradict. There still was not anything to prove that Tombley had intended to murder Fossder. In fact, had Tombley decided to declare that his had *not* been the white figure that had frightened Fossder to death, the inspector could not have proved satisfactorily (to a coroner's jury, for example) the contrary. Then, again, if Tombley and Simith had conspired to murder Fossder, who could have murdered Simith? Incidentally, had there been a ghost?

If a combination of Simith and Tombley would account for the luring of Fossder from his house, it still did not explain how Fossder could have made separate appointments with them for approximately the same hour. A second theory, more startling in its implication than the one which made Simith and Tombley joint murderers of Fossder, shaped itself in his mind. What, he wondered, if the boot were on the other foot? What if *Fossder* had intended to murder *Simith*, and had been prevented fortuitously by Tombley, who had told the truth when he declared that the ghost had been intended for a joke?

Neither theory, however, successfully accounted for the subsequent murder of Simith. Fossder might have had a second try – if he had not been dead already! Tombley might have intended to murder Fossder first, and then his uncle, but this idea did not square with Mrs Bradley's theory that Fossder might have gone out on Christmas Eve to meet somebody other than Tombley. He wondered whether to discard this inconvenient idea. A third argument would be that a fourth person was involved, and that this mythical character – 'Maurice Pratt?' he wrote in his notebook – had been prepared to assist Fossder in the murder of Simith, and, when the plan miscarried through Fossder's own sudden death on the way to the trysting place, had carried out the murder of Simith single handed on Boxing Night. The difficulty presented by this theory was that the fourth person could not be called 'Pratt' without some motive being shown for Pratt's having desired the removal of Simith.

Pratt had expectations of taking Fossder's place, and of marrying his niece Fay. That would account for the murder of Fossder, perhaps, but Simith, so far as the inspector could determine, simply did not come into it. 'Unless,' he thought, striking his knee, 'old Simith was killed *in mistake for Tombley, or summat!*'

He went to bed, but lay for some time pondering on theories two and three. Both were attractive. Both had a certain amount both of psychological and circumstantial evidence to recommend them.

'I must get into touch with that there Maurice Pratt,' he thought. Curiously enough, Mrs Bradley, in her own bed at Horsepath, to which she had returned, was thinking the very same thing. 'Young men are apt and intelligent in sizing up other young men,' she said to herself. 'The only difficulty lies in wresting their conclusions from them. Still, Carey will tell me what I want to know.'

She chuckled, turned over, and was soon enviably asleep. Next day Carey arrived in the early afternoon, kissed his aunt, and announced that he was going to stay to tea.

'All the pigs quite safe?' enquired Mrs Bradley.

'Oh, yes. I have left them with Ditch.'

'I've told the inspector that Fossder may have had an appointment with someone at Sandford on Christmas Eve, child. I thought at first it was merely the money which attracted him, but later I wondered whether he went to meet someone else – not Tombley at all.'

'A country solicitor like Fossder would see most of his clients at his own home, wouldn't he? Or at *their* own homes,' suggested Carey.

'Exactly,' said Mrs Bradley. 'What does your trained mind make of that, dear child?'

'Well,' said Carey, pushing the rug with his shoe, 'it sounds to me like two old enemies getting together like two old buddies. What do you make of it yourself? Unless it was somebody Mrs

Fossder disliked, and so Fossder had to do business with him elsewhere.'

Mrs Bradley extended a yellow claw.

'Child,' she said solemnly, 'you show intelligence. I think we both know that – Never mind! Pray proceed, naming the names where necessary.'

'Well,' said Carey, 'so far as I have ever been able to make out, Fossder and Simith have had rows for years. Mind you, there's nothing shady about Fossder's affairs. I'm pretty sure of that. Pratt is a fathead over some things, but he's got a pretty good head for business, and is perfectly honest. I think that Simith decided to make Fossder his executor, and didn't want Tombley to know; and I think Fossder wanted to get Simith on to the books without letting Mrs Fossder know.'

'Why shouldn't she know, child?' asked Mrs Bradley, who was making rapid hieroglyphics in her notebook.

'You know why not.'

'Never mind. Say on.'

'Well, Mrs Fossder would have used it as a handle to get Fossder to consent to an engagement between Fay and Tombley, I imagine. Mrs Fossder has always been on Tombley's side, and against Pratt, in the matter, and old Fossder, who was always a bit afraid of her, you know, might have found it hard to stick it out. Naturally he wanted Pratt to marry young Fay, and to carry on the business. As a matter of fact, Jenny told me once that old Fossder had inserted a clause in his will saying that the firm was to be called Fossder, Pratt and Pratt, if Pratt and Fay ever had a son. He was fearfully keen on the marriage. Jenny always used to say that he didn't care two hoots about *her* marriage, and would probably end by cutting her out of his will.'

'Apart from the fact that Tombley is heir to Simith's property, had Mrs Fossder any special reason for preferring Tombley as a husband for Fay?' asked Mrs Bradley. Carey stared out of the window, which was opposite him as he sat.

'I couldn't say,' he answered. 'She thought him more of a man, if you know what I mean.'

'I think I had better see Jenny,' said Mrs Bradley. 'There are a number of small points I'd like to have clear. Could you ask her over to Old Farm to meet me, child? I don't care to ask her here.'

Carey nodded.

'This evening? Yes, very well. I'll run over there at once.'

'First, tell me more about Pratt,' said Mrs Bradley.

'Pratt?' said Carey. 'I don't know any more about him. Keen on folk lore and comparative religion. You know the sort of bird. Must exist by the hundred in the suburbs and Bloomsbury – well, no, not quite Bloomsbury. No, upon reflection, not a bit Bloomsbury. Oh, well, *I* don't know. Just not my sort at all, if you know what I mean. Besides, I've come to the conclusion that he may be a bit deceptive.'

'Not such a fool as he looks?' said Mrs Bradley. 'I think you may be right. We shall wait and see.'

CHAPTER 10

Corners to Places at Stanton St John

'Of course you may talk to me while I have my bath,' said Jenny, looking across at Carey, and laughing. So, escorted by Mrs Bradley, she undressed in one of the bedrooms, answering Mrs Bradley's questions as she slid out of her garments at the maximum possible speed, thrust her bare arms into the sleeves of a gaily coloured bathrobe and her bare feet into slippers, picked up sponge bag and towel and pattered along to the bathroom with Mrs Bradley still in attendance and both their tongues wagging hard.

'As a matter of fact,' said Jenny, in response to a request for a description of Maurice Pratt, 'he's really rather deceptive. You get the impression that he's spineless and brainless, but actually he can be rather determined, and, of course, he's awfully clever. Uncle relied on him for everything, and was always saying to auntie that he must think about taking Maurice as his partner. Auntie wasn't very sympathetic. She doesn't like Maurice a bit. She wanted Fay to marry Geraint Tombley, and Fay will do it now, I suppose.'

'Fay will marry Tombley?' Mrs Bradley demanded. 'But isn't she engaged to be married to Maurice Pratt?'

'Oh, Fay will break that off, if I know anything,' said Jenny. 'She never really cared for Maurice, you know. It was uncle she was afraid of, and, now he's dead, she's rather afraid of auntie. Fay is ineffective, rather, I think. Wants other people to make up her mind for her, and then wants to quarrel with them over their decisions. You've met the type, I expect.'

Mrs Bradley said she had.

'Yes, well, she encouraged Tombley at first, until she found that he was Simith's nephew, and that Simith was Uncle Fossder's bitterest enemy. Then she gave him up, or pretended to, and got engaged to Maurice.'

'One point,' said Mrs Bradley. 'What caused the enmity between your uncle and Simith?'

'It happened when I was a little girl of four, so I don't know anything about it except by hearsay – chiefly hints that auntie has let fall from time to time. Uncle and Mr Simith both came from the other side of Oxford – from Bampton, just south of Witney – and as boys they were very friendly. Then uncle went to a small public school on a scholarship, or something, and Simith went to Canada, and came back fairly rich and knowing all about the marketing of pork. Well, he soon made uncle his lawyer over here, and almost immediately got into trouble with the University authorities for building a causeway across a brook from his land on to theirs. He tried to prove that the land for thirty feet on the other side of the brook was a public right of way – I don't understand all about it – but the University proved it wasn't, and Simith had to take down his causeway and pay the most fearful costs and fees and things. He always declared that uncle had let him down over it, and had told him he was safe in building the causeway, but uncle swore that he had done his level best to point out to him that the law was not on his side.

'Anyway, Simith took his business out of uncle's hands, and bought Roman Ending, and uncle sustained a considerable loss, I should think, and was always very bitter about Mr Simith, and called him a fool and all kinds of names. But when the nephew, Tombley, came from Cowley to live with his uncle at Roman Ending, which happened about eight years ago, he, Tombley, put his personal affairs into uncle's hands, and became uncle's client. Of course, Tombley wasn't really worth very much, but he let uncle know that he was Simith's heir, and once or twice, I know, uncle advanced him money on the strength of that.'

'Was it repaid, do you know?' asked Mrs Bradley.

'Oh, no. I know it wasn't. Uncle didn't mind, although he didn't like Tombley. He used to say there was plenty of time for repayment when Simith was dead. He said he knew Tombley was honest, although he refused to have him hanging round Fay. He was very fond of Fay. I think he was fond of me, too, but, well – ! He was always saying that if Fay got engaged to Maurice he should take Maurice into partnership and leave him everything, except for auntie's share. That was so that Fay could have it. He didn't promise *me* anything – I couldn't expect him to – I'm not really his brother's daughter – but in the end he left the money to all three of us. I say, I hope I'm not boring you with all this.'

She was ready to get into the bath by this time. Mrs Bradley hung the bathrobe behind the door, and seated herself on the cork topped bathroom chair.

'Of course not, child,' she said. 'It is most enlightening, most. So, at one time, you did not expect to inherit anything under your uncle's will?'

'Well,' said Jenny, with a little shiver of rapture, as the warm water closed over her rosy body, 'I wouldn't say *that*, altogether. He changed his mind a good bit. At one point, a few months ago, I think he did have some idea of leaving it all to Fay and Maurice, with a bit of money and the furniture, but not the house, to auntie, but I don't know a terrible lot about it. He used to talk things over with Maurice, but hardly ever with Fay and me. He always thought girls were silly. I think that's all I know, except something which I found out quite by accident, and ought to keep to myself.'

'If I told you what it was, I wonder whether you would feel able to let me know whether I had guessed correctly?' said Mrs Bradley musingly.

'Glad of getting it off my chest so easily,' said Jenny eagerly. 'Go on. What do you think it is? I shouldn't have thought anyone could guess. Of course, I realise you're not quite exactly "anyone",' she added, with naive sweetness, retrieving the soap from the bottom of the bath and taking her sponge from the rack.

'Your sister meets Mr Tombley, and spends the night with him when opportunity offers,' said Mrs Bradley concisely.

'Good Lord!' said Jenny, awed. 'How on earth did you find that out?'

'I didn't, child. I deduced it. Thank you. That helps. In fact, it makes all my conclusions come right first time!'

Jenny looked rather alarmed. 'You won't give her away, Mrs Bradley, will you? Auntie would probably die, and I don't know what Maurice would do. I've often told her what a fool she is, but she's completely crazy at present over Tombley. I believe that Maurice suspects she doesn't care about her engagement very much, but he can't do anything about it. In any case, I should think the engagement will soon be broken, anyway, now that uncle is dead. I'm sorry for Maurice. He isn't a bad sort really.'

There was silence for a while, except for pleasant splashing sounds from the bath. Then Mrs Bradley said, 'Carey's friend, Hugh, your fiancé, was telling me that Mr Pratt is interested in folklore.'

'Is he?' said Jenny indifferently. 'He's a jolly rotten Morris dancer, but that's all I know about it.'

Jenny, a youthful, shrimp-coloured Venus, rose from the waves and commenced to dry herself. When she was dressed, and when the two of them were seated before the fire in the parlour, which was empty except for themselves, Mrs Bradley said suddenly, 'Some time I think I must get Carey, Tombley and the Ditch family to dance for me again.'

'By the way,' said Jenny, a trifle diffidently, 'did you know that Geraint Tombley had left Roman Ending?'

'I did, child. In fact, I suggested that he should.'

'But it isn't true that he's in a mental hospital, Mrs Bradley, is it?'

'A private one. Yes.'

'But –'

'Don't worry about it, child. A precautionary measure.'

'Do you mean that he is being kept under observation?'

'No, child. He is merely being kept from arrest.'

'Arrest! But you don't believe *he* murdered his uncle, surely!'

'Don't you believe it, child?'

'No, of course I don't. Oh, I know he's a fool about Fay, and, of course, I believe he has it in him to be a very selfish, violent kind of person. And I know he would go to a lot of trouble, and even get into danger, and so on, to get his own way. But I don't believe he'd have murdered Mr Simith. Besides, why should he?'

'He happens to be Mr Simith's heir.'

'But – Oh, I see! He wants to marry Fay, and he has to have something worth while to offer her – for them to live on – Yes. That does sound feasible.'

'But you reserve the right of disbelief in Tombley's guilt,' said Mrs Bradley, cackling. Jenny held out her fingers to the blaze.

'Well, I don't want to think he's a murderer. I'd sooner Fay married him than Maurice, and she can't if he's convicted of murder.'

'Or proved to be insane,' said Mrs Bradley. Jenny looked reproachful.

'You said just now –'

'I know, child, I know.' She cackled.

'And why would you rather Fay married Tombley than Pratt?' she asked, as Jenny looked up.

'Oh, I don't know,' said Jenny. 'You see – Oh, *I* don't know,' she concluded.

'You think she'd make Pratt unhappy,' said Mrs Bradley, and took no notice of Jenny's half hearted denial.

'Now then, be off with you,' said Mrs Bradley, when dinner was over. She looked at Carey, who was taking Jenny to Iffley in his sidecar. Jenny bent and kissed her. 'Don't make too much noise coming in. I happen to know that Ditch takes a pistol to bed with him, and that Mrs Ditch sleeps with the poker at her side. Be good children.' She smiled at them kindly, the smile of a satiated snake.

She herself went to bed soon after tea, and did not hear Carey come in at half-past four. He appeared fresh and rested at breakfast, which was at nine, and came in for lunch at twelve.

'Jenny cried on me last night,' he said. 'What's the matter with the girl? Haven't accused her of murder or anything, have you? And by the way, I do wish Tombley would return the little pig book he borrowed a fortnight ago.'

'No. But I've found out something rather interesting,' said Mrs Bradley slowly. 'I know why Tombley confessed to being the ghost.'

'Oh? Why is that interesting? I mean, I thought you knew he was, whether he confessed it or not.'

'You see,' said his aunt, 'I always thought that the poor child's confession was either a stupid mistake or an absolute, utter lie. Consider, Carey! *Why* should he confess that he was the ghost? Nobody could prove he was!'

'Yes, but why *shouldn't* he confess? Nobody could say that Fossder's death was anything but an unfortunate accident.'

'I know. But what about Fay, with whom he is in love? She wouldn't care to think that Tombley had been the cause of her uncle's death.'

'We don't know she wouldn't,' said Carey, looking directly at his aunt. 'She may have been jolly glad to see the end of old Fossder.'

'I happen to be fairly sure that she was. But, *if* she was, it might be because he had opposed her engagement to Tombley, whom, apparently, she loves, and had forced her into becoming engaged to Maurice Pratt, who occupies, let us say, the second place in her affections.'

'All very well,' said Carey. 'But if Tombley was not the ghost, *who was*? And, in any case, how do you know he wasn't?'

'Because I think he was with Fay on Christmas Eve.'

'But if Tombley wasn't the ghost –'

'Pratt may have been,' said Mrs Bradley, nodding. 'Quite right, child. Or Hugh, as I said before.'

'But that doesn't seem to make sense.'

'I think it does. And, incidentally, which of the three was the most likely to know that Fossder had a weak heart?'

'Pratt, of course. But you couldn't prove anything from that. You might, with as much reason, say that Mrs Fossder or one of the girls was the ghost. Mrs Fossder certainly knew that her husband had a weak heart.'

Mrs Bradley nodded.

'True, child. Very true.'

'Another thing,' said Carey, swinging his feet to the ground and waiting until Mrs Ditch, who was laying the cloth, had gone out again. 'If you are right in what you say, and Fay really loves Tombley, surely for Pratt to kill off Fossder was playing into Fay's and Tombley's hands! Isn't it well known that the old chap pressed for the Fay–Pratt engagement, and wouldn't have Tombley at any price because of a years-old row with old Simith? Whereas Mrs Fossder, still alive and in command, so to speak, is all in favour of Tombley and his suit.'

'I know,' said Mrs Bradley; but there was a gleam in her bright black eyes. 'I'm going into Oxford after lunch to talk to the inspector again,' she added. 'Don't you see, child, that what Tombley is worried about is not so much an alibi for murder as an alibi for the nights he slept with Fay!'

Carey laughed, and at that moment Mrs Ditch, respectably staid and apparently placid as ever, came in with the first course and drew out their chairs from the table.

'Our Lender been took as Superintendent's parlour maid at the Little House, mam, you'll be pleased to hear, see-en ee recommended her, like,' she said.

'That's good,' said Mrs Bradley. 'She'll be company for Mr Tombley, won't she?'

'Ah, ef such as him warnts company,' Mrs Ditch responded.

'That last remark was a bit two-edged or something, don't you think?' asked Carey, pouring out the beer. Mrs Bradley nodded.

'I thought so, child. By the way, I want her again. It will do when she clears away.'

'Mrs Ditch,' she said, when lunch was over and, yodelled for by Carey, the woman came in again, 'I wish your husband and sons would dance again some time.'

'They couldn't make a side, mam, not without Mr Carey would stand up with 'em again.'

'Of course I will, if Ditch will shout the directions,' Carey said.

'Detch was sayen he hoped ee'd practise with 'em this Easter, to dance at Whetsun, but I told him it wasn't in nature to expect a gentleman wouldn't have somethen else to do. Every week from Easter tell Whetsun they'll practise, and –'

'Why don't you get Mr Pratt from Iffley, Mrs Ditch?' asked Mrs Bradley suddenly.

'I don't know of Mr Pratt,' said Mrs Ditch.

'I don't think he's much of a dancer,' said Mrs Bradley, 'but I'll give you his address, if you think your husband would care to get into touch with him.'

'Tes kind of ee to trouble, but I reckon Ditch have his eye on two or three young fellows en the village,' Mrs Ditch responded, shaking her head. 'Don't do to learn strangers everythen, do et, now?' Mrs Bradley nodded. 'There be young Billy Watts and John Greenaway,' Mrs Ditch continued, as though in excuse for her churlishness. 'Detch thenk well of both on 'em, so he says. And they be hereabouts a'ready, mam, don't ee see.'

'Yes, yes, I see,' said Mrs Bradley, waving a skinny claw. 'I shall be going to see Mr Tombley tomorrow, I expect. Have you any message for Linda, if I see her?'

'Not as I'd ask ee to gev by word of mouth,' said Mrs Ditch, glowering darkly. 'Thank ee again,' she added, with an effort.

'I can't help thinking that Mrs Ditch doesn't exactly dote on you,' said Carey. 'I wonder why it is?'

Mrs Bradley cackled. She got up and went to the window. They had had their tea very early. It was not yet dusk. Faintly upon the air came the sounds of hungry pigs – of pigs, moreover, expecting to be fed. She listened to their squealing, an indignant reminder to Ditch that he was nearly ten minutes overdue.

'The enspector was over at Roman Enden this mornen,' said Mrs Ditch in a conspiratorial whisper just behind her.

'Yes?' said Mrs Bradley, without even turning her head.

'He don't be finden nothen. Scoured al over the kitchen floor, he ded, so Priest was sayen to Detch this afternoon. I thought ee'd be glad to know as he hadn't found nothen.'

'Thank you,' said Mrs Bradley. 'I'm very glad to know.'

'It looken suspicious for Mr Carey, like,' said Mrs Ditch with a sigh, as she picked up a plate and departed.

'Good gracious!' said Mrs Bradley. 'She thinks you murdered Simith.'

'Unlikelier things have happened,' said Carey, grinning. 'What do you want to do now?'

'I think I'll leave the inspector until tomorrow, and go and talk to Priest,' said Mrs Bradley. 'Some time or other I must get into Roman Ending. Into the house, I mean.'

'But Priest was telling me, when I was over there yesterday, that the inspector has turned the house upside down, and hasn't found a thing.'

'He didn't know what to look for,' said Mrs Bradley.

'Do you, then?'

'Yes. And the beauty of it is, that it doesn't matter whether I find it or not. I now know enough to be able to get a part of the truth out of Tombley. And I think I ought to see Fay. I wonder whether she knows anything about Maurice Pratt's movements on Christmas Eve? Probably she doesn't, except that he came over here, but I might be able to get at something, I think. Goodbye, child. Do you think Priest will let Nero loose on me?'

'You'll be telling me next that Priest is the murderer, and that I should never believe, you know,' said Carey. 'Do you really want Ditch and his sons to dance for you?'

'Some time soon, yes, I do.'

Priest was mixing feed. He touched his cap to Mrs Bradley, and went on stirring toppings and cut up potatoes as though she no longer existed. She recalled him to the realisation of her presence.

'How is Nero, after his bath?' she asked. Priest left the copper-stick, with which he was doing the mixing, standing upright in the wooden tub, and stared at her as though he were taking her measure. Mrs Bradley, small, thin, black-eyed, clad in a dark purple coat trimmed with silver fox, and a mustard-yellow felt hat, was a not unimpressive sight. She fixed her eyes on his face, and clasped her brown gloved hands on the top of a tall and beautifully rolled umbrella. Priest dropped his eyes and muttered, and began to rub green mildew off the top of a dilapidated, unused, brick floored, broken fenced sty.

'I don't know what ee be at, mam, asken me that,' he observed with dignified simplicity.

'Look here, Priest, my man,' said Mrs Bradley briskly, 'did, or did not, Mr Tombley wash down the boar Nero on the morning after Boxing Day? You *must* know, and I want you to tell me.'

'I don't know anythen about et,' said Priest sullenly. Like most countrymen, he hated being bullied because he mistrusted the sharpness of his wits compared with those of town bred people. He scorned townspeople, but did not want to be made to look a fool by them. 'All I know is the boar was not so well. The poor fellow had cotched a cold.'

'Where were you on Boxing Night, when Mr Simith was murdered?' asked Mrs Bradley. The pigman looked at her and suddenly grinned, and replied, 'Mam, I'll tell ee, so long as ee don't tell that there old woman Detch, Lender's mam. I thought to myself to be a married man on Boxen Night, only that never come orf, parson not be-en willen, so I conduct myself like a married man, all the same. Small blame to me! What says *you*?'

'You slept with Linda Ditch, who is now Mrs Priest? I see. Where, child, did you sleep? Not in this house, I suppose?'

'Well, mam, as to that —' He hesitated.

'You *did* sleep here. Tell me more.'

'I can't, mam. Never slept alongside a maid before, and gev my wholly attention to et, like.'

The mixture of devilment and solemnity in his atrociously ugly face made Mrs Bradley laugh again, and she said, 'But Linda was not a maid.'

'Well, no.'

'Now look here, Priest,' said Mrs Bradley seriously, 'I want to know who borrowed Mr Lestrange's boar on Boxing Night and put him back next morning.'

She watched, with great satisfaction, Priest's face assume an expression of cunning and fear.

'Mr Lestrange's boar, mam?'

'Mr Lestrange's boar. To make the tracks on Shotover Common, you know.'

'Well, mam, it was me.'

'You, was it? Have you told the police it was you?'

'No, I 'aven't, mam. What be more, I ain't a goen to tell 'em, neither, too and all. Have me up for the murder an' all they ud, and 'twudden be fair, that wouldn't.'

'I see,' said Mrs Bradley. They eyed one another.

'Ow did ee tumble to et, anyway?' asked the pigman. He had picked the copperstick out of the pig food and was handling it in a highly suggestive manner. Mrs Bradley grinned.

'The boar caught a cold,' she said.

'Ah. So did Nero, though, and he never went out that night.'

'No. Poor Nero!' Mrs Bradley sighed. 'It was the cold water, poor beast, with him.'

Priest took a step nearer, and flourished the stick. Mrs Bradley suddenly gave a flick. A dart, of the kind that is used in the public house game, flew like a bird from her hand, and, striking Priest's cap, picked it swiftly from off his head and carried it just behind him. He picked it up, and looked at the dart in perplexity.

'What be playen at, then?' he demanded indignantly, taking the dart from the cap and staring from one to the other.

'Jael and Sisera,' said Mrs Bradley, giving a hoot of laughter. 'Thank you, child.' Dexterously she regained possession of the dart. 'Put the stick down,' she said. 'You have nothing to gain by hitting me over the head. Be reasonable, and tell me what you know. You need not worry. I assure you that I don't suspect Linda Ditch of having killed Mr Simith.'

'Lender?' He pondered. 'Don't ee, now? That's good.' He thought again, while Mrs Bradley watched him. 'I dunno what to tell ee. Guessed et, I ded, that be all. Lender can 'andle pigs as well as 'er father or me. I knowed she was ripe to do Mr Semeth a mischief. 'Twas 'er took the boar to Shotover, I reckon.'

'She couldn't have done,' said Mrs Bradley. 'It wouldn't make sense, Priest, would it?'

'I dunno as to that. Seem as ef the gal thenks I done et myself, and she was for coveren the tracks. I reckon as Nero done the killen of Semeth, and somebody doused him down to wash off the blood. Look bad, that would, again anybody who had done et. Ah, very bad that 'ud look.' He shook his head, eyeing her solemnly.

'But don't you know who did it? Come, now, Priest!'

'I couldn't tell ee, not ef ee asked tell Doomsday. Sleepen t'other side of the 'ouse, we was, Lender Detch and me. Never seed nor heared nothen as I remember. Have to take my word for et, ee well. Tell ee as soon as spet, I would, ef I could, now I knows ee don't thenk it was Lender.'

'Linda wasn't with you all night long, then?' Mrs Bradley said.

'How do ee make that out?' His eyes were suspicious again. Mrs Bradley shrugged.

'Didn't you tell me you thought it must be Linda who had taken Mr Lestrange's boar to Shotover? Look here, Priest, be truthful! Did you sleep with Linda Ditch at all?'

'Ah, that I ded, tell mednight, or thereabouts, her haven dodged away from Old Farm to do et. Then the light went up en the ketchen, and us thought I'd better clear off.'

'What light?'

'Ah, that I dunno. Candles, or something of that. Flickeren, a shadder behind the winder moven about and two men quarrellen.'

'What time was this, do you say?'

'Et would a-ben just about mednight, I should reckon. Ah. Twould a-ben about then. Us heard the ketchen clock strike twalve a bet before, I remember.'

'Go on. What happened next?'

'Ah, that's what I dunno. It were all quiet, do ee see, when I slethered my way past the winder over the snow. The light was still flickeren, but I kept well away, so as I shudden be seen.'

'Where did you go, after that?'

'I went to the new shed on wheels, and bedded meself on the straw. Us hadn't put no pegs in 'er up to then.'

'And after that?'

'I reckon I went to sleep.'

'And Linda?'

'Ah, I dunno. I somehow reckon she run orf home to Old Farm. I couldn't account for she, without she kelled old Semeth and heaved him in with old Nero, but don't seem likely, now I comes to thenk.'

'But how could you think that she got him away again, and then went over to Shotover with the body, and with Mr Lestrange's boar?'

'Ah, I dunno. Her had said to me time and again her thought her should kell old Semeth one of these here days, he was always a-pesteren and worryen, wicked old stag that he were!'

'You know, you're a fool,' said Mrs Bradley dispassionately. Priest looked sheepish, and gave the pig food a couple of half hearted stirs.

'Pray ee be right, mam. Foolish I may be, but truly wicked I ent.'

'I am certainly right. Now think again, and tell me about the quarrel. Did you recognise either of the voices?'

'Ah, that I ded! But neither of 'em wasn't old Semeth, that I'll back!'

'I see, Priest, and whose was the other?'

'I dunno as I oughter say. Ee won't like et, I'll back ee won't, then!'

'Come along, now. What's the matter?'

'I thought et sounded like Mr Lestrange hisself. Couldn't-a ben, I suppose.'

'Why not?' asked Mrs Bradley. Priest stood gaping at her, as she began to nod her head slowly and rhythmically, whilst her saurian smile grew wider. '*Why not?*' she repeated. She cackled in the astonished pigman's face, then turned and walked rapidly away. Priest stood gazing after her. Then he tilted his cap forward, the better to scratch the back of his head, sucked at his bottom teeth audibly, and, giving up the struggle of attempting to understand what she meant, walked back to the feed and stirred it, whistling irritably.

'For a mixture of cunning and obstinacy, give me a countryman,' said Mrs Bradley, later, to Carey.

CHAPTER 11

Corners – Good Fellowship – from Iffley to Waterperry

'Priest?' said the inspector in disgust. 'I can't get any sense out of Priest, mam. One thing I ded get out of him, though not too easy, and that was to the effect he had suggested putten off his wedden tell the spring, but Miss Detch was all for bringen of et about. Wanted to be wed on Boxen Day, and Priest tried to fex up with the parson, but had to wait tell the followen mornen, it seems.'

'Ah,' said Mrs Bradley thoughtfully. 'Well, now, inspector, it is easy to see where that leads, don't you think?'

'Ah, I reckon you're right, mam. Priest thought Miss Detch would get into trouble, and, appears to me, she thought the same about him.' He chuckled, a hearty sound. Mrs Bradley shook her head reproachfully.

'You're getting your dates mixed up, inspector,' she said. 'If they wanted to be married on Boxing Day, they wanted to be married *before the murder was committed*.'

'That was my meanen, mam. Looks black, I says, for both. One o' them two might be the murderer, I says, or else they might, either one or both, be accessories, seems to me. They *might*. Don't say they *are*.'

'Quite,' said Mrs Bradley. 'I agree with you that there must have been a helper in Simith's murder.'

'That don't get us any *nearer* the murderer, though,' said the inspector, 'except et was one of them two.'

'There *is* one other point,' said Mrs Bradley. 'The most important clue we've had, I think, if it is the truth! Priest says he slept with Linda Ditch at Roman Ending on Boxing Night, and that he left her just after midnight, because he heard quarrelling going on in the kitchen, and saw a light in the window.'

'Where were they, then?'

'I should think they were in the woodshed. I can't think where else they could have been.'

'There's the pigpens.'

'He said he went to one of those when he left Linda.'

'Oh, ah! Well, I'll back the best I can do is to go back to Roman Enden and talk to the chap again. A rare old dance, this case.'

'And the death of Mr Fossder is part of it,' Mrs Bradley added, looking at the inspector to see how he proposed to take this view. He accepted it with a nod.

'Oh, ah! I shouldn't wonder. Though I can't see my way through the wood. And then there's this letter I had from Mester Tombley. It makes me thenk ee ought to let him go, safe or not, like. Something of Habeas Corpus, somehow, about the theng, somewhere, mam, if ee'll excuse me.'

The letter was an impassioned plea for liberty.

'Let us go to Little House and talk to him again,' said Mrs Bradley. 'Perhaps he'll tell us where he spent Boxing Night. I confess I should like to know. It was almost certainly not at Roman Ending.'

'We could talk to Linda Detch some time,' amended the inspector. 'Better talk to her first. Can *you* persuade her, mam, do ee thenk?'

'I may be able to frighten her,' said Mrs Bradley slowly, 'but I don't think it will be necessary. I fancy that she may have thought things over. I can always report my conversation with Priest if she proves recalcitrant.'

'Oh, ah,' agreed the inspector. He took up his cap. 'Well, I'm off. Shall I meet ee outside Little House, or where, mam?'

'Let's go together. Both Linda and Tombley know that we hunt in couples.'

Tombley was indignant when he saw them. 'I can't think why you don't have me arrested at once! This beastly place! These ghastly meals! The rules! The hours! The beds! My God! It's enough to *turn* anyone into a lunatic, that's what I say!'

'And rightly, child, I feel sure,' said Mrs Bradley soothingly. Tombley snorted.

'And sending Linda Ditch along to spy on me! What do you mean? She won't find out anything here! You needn't worry! I'm not left alone five minutes! There's even a mealy-mouthed fool of a barber told off to shave me each morning! With a safety razor! You've got to let me out! I'm not staying here any longer! I'll write to my lawyer!'

'Pratt?' asked the inspector suddenly. Tombley glared and gritted his teeth.

'Yes, Pratt! Or are you going to have him arrested, too?'

'Some time, perhaps, some time,' said the inspector soothingly. 'This es a very nice place, you know, sir. You might do worse than stop here for another few days.' He looked round the Visitors' Room approvingly. 'A very nice place indeed. I don't see what ee've got to grumble at, blowed ef I do! Stell, if ee want to go back to Roman Enden, no objection on Mrs Bradley's part, she tells me, so long as you behave yourself, and none at all on mine.' He winked at Mrs Bradley.

'It'll be your own fault if any harm comes to you, child,' said Mrs Bradley sadly. She eyed him with pensive benevolence. 'I thought perhaps you'd stay here just a little longer, whilst I completed my investigations, and the inspector concluded his case. But I understand your impatience. The worst of it is, I still can't persuade the inspector that you are not guilty. I shall have to ask Fay for that alibi.'

Tombley leapt up. The inspector leaned forward, and, with a huge hand like a forehock, pushed him back into the armchair from which he had risen.

'Now, then; now, then,' he said gently. Tombley glared at Mrs Bradley, who was toying with the clasp of her handbag.

'Don't you talk about Fay! Don't you dare to ask her anything!' he muttered. 'I don't see why you want to bring her into it! It's nothing to do with her!'

'Where were you both on Christmas Eve, and again on Boxing Night? Were you together?' asked Mrs Bradley gently.

'No, of course not! Why should we be? You can't prove anything!' said Tombley with agitation. 'I've told you already what I did on Christmas Eve! I was the ghost, I tell you. I frightened old Fossder to death. You'd better jug me for it! Oh, it was murder, right enough. No, it wasn't! You couldn't call it murder!'

'Be quiet, child! Your noise confuses me,' said Mrs Bradley placidly. 'If you were the ghost, why was Mrs Ditch agitated? If you were the ghost, why did you send a message to Mrs Fossder to say you couldn't keep the appointment with him? If you were the ghost, why did somebody damage my car? If you were the ghost, why were you so anxious to find out whether your uncle was at Old Farm that night?'

She stopped, and beamed at him. Tombley, breathing almost as stertorously as a man in apoplexy, stared at her, his small eyes round marbles of horrified amazement. He began to gurgle desperately, and made feeble passes with his hands.

'And now,' she said, leaning forward and speaking briskly, 'I want to spend a day at Bampton when the weather gets a bit better. Tell me all about it – where to go, what to do, how to see the church, which public house to patronise, the nicest walks, the most admirable views, the address of the oldest inhabitant – will you?'

'Bampton?' said Tombley. He licked his lower lip, trying to recover his poise. 'But – are you serious?'

'Of course, child. I must certainly visit Bampton, and I thought that, as an inhabitant of the place –'

Tombley stared at her.

'Is this a catch? You're trying to trip me up again,' he said. Mrs Bradley remained silent, watching him. 'You know I was never in

173

Bampton in my life!' he burst out at last. 'I was born and brought up in Cowley. As you seem to know so much, I wonder you didn't know that! It was Uncle Simith who lived at Bampton, not me!'

'Cowley?' said Mrs Bradley. She nodded, as though well satisfied. 'Very well, child. I believe you.'

'You can prove it, you know,' said Tombley, a glint of irritation returning to his eyes. 'Old Fossder came from Bampton, too,' he added. 'And that's where Jenny was born. You, who think you know so much, had better find out who Jenny's father was!'

Mrs Bradley rose.

'I'll see the matron and get you your order of release, Geraint, if you really want it,' she said. Tombley blinked at her use of his Christian name. 'But I warn you, you'd better stay here,' Mrs Bradley continued, eyeing him with the maternal anxiety of a boa-constrictor which watches its young attempting to devour their first donkey.

'I believe you mean well,' said Tombley. She waited. He swallowed. Suddenly there came a tap at the door.

'Damn!' said the inspector under his breath. The interruption, he was certain, had nipped a confession in the bud; not necessarily a confession of murder, he thought, but certainly a confession of something. He growled, and stood up awkwardly as the matron came in with a doctor.

'What do ee thenk he was goen to say, mam?' enquired the inspector presently, when they were driving back through Headington. Mrs Bradley cackled.

'You know,' she said, 'I'm rather fond of that child. I shall always remember his chivalrous defence of himself with the pig bucket when his late uncle was attacking him that afternoon.'

'What afternoon would that have been, mam? Just lately?'

'I suppose it would have been a couple of days before Christmas,' Mrs Bradley replied. The inspector looked thoughtful.

'Old Mr Semeth attacked him, did he? Meanen that ef Tombley

had made up his mind to the job of murderen him, it would have come en handy to have pleaded self-defence? Is that what you're getten at, mam? There was plenty of evidence at the inquest about how they used to fight.'

Mrs Bradley shrugged.

'My chauffeur and I would have made two respectable and creditable witnesses,' she observed. The inspector continued to look thoughtful.

'We ought to check up the young lady, mam, Miss Fay, chance what Mr Tombley says. I do thenk that.'

'Yes, so do I. If we turned off here, through Cowley, I fancy we should arrive at the house before Geraint can get a conveyance. I expect he'll make straight for Iffley to see the girl.'

Fay was in. Confronted with the suggestion that she could give Tombley an alibi for the nights of Christmas Eve and Boxing Day, she nodded. She was a slight, pale, fair-haired creature, anaemically pretty and with a trick of clasping her hands and holding her head on one side. She obliged them with a repetition of it, but the inspector remained respectful, stolid and businesslike and Mrs Bradley, fixing the most piercing glance upon the trickster, continued briskly, 'Then do so, child, so that the inspector can take something down for you to sign.'

'But I'm not going to sign it! I never sign anything!' bleated Fay. 'And Geraint will be so angry! And Maurice, my fiancé, won't speak to me again.'

'Very well, miss,' said the inspector, replacing his notebook. 'I know what to do about you, then.'

'You're not going to arrest me!' cried Fay. 'I – he did – we did! But please don't tell Maurice, or my aunt! I'll sign it if you like, but it won't come up in evidence or anything, will it? Perhaps I ought to tell you that Jenny was to switch my light on, to look as though I was still at Iffley that night!'

'I can't promise that,' said the inspector. 'Where did you spend the nights in question, miss?'

'At Old Farm in Stanton St John.'

'Ah,' said the inspector. Mrs Bradley nodded. Neither showed the slightest sign of surprise at the meeting place chosen by the lovers.

'Have you broken your engagement, child?' Mrs Bradley asked. Fay's blue eyes opened wide.

'How did you know I was going to?'

'There are signs and portents everywhere,' said Mrs Bradley, in deep tones of extraordinary relish, 'and one of them foretold a broken engagement!' Her voice altered. 'Don't break it yet! You might be very sorry later on.'

Fay's little nose looked pinched, and the staring pillarbox red of the rouge on her lips was as incongruous and artificial as the paint on a clown.

'What do you mean? What do you mean! Geraint – you can't prove he killed his uncle! And I *know* he wasn't the ghost that killed Uncle Fossder! You don't know! You can't prove anything!'

'Can't I?' asked Mrs Bradley, gently. 'Listen, child. It is better to tell me the truth. Did Geraint Tombley leave you on Christmas Eve?'

'No.'

'Did he leave you on Boxing Night?' She watched the agonised working of the characterless, thin little face.

'Yes,' said Fay, very low, after searching Mrs Bradley's eyes with her own.

'Ah,' said Mrs Bradley. Her black eyes bored a little deeper. 'When was that?'

Fay drew a breath and let it out again in the ghost of a sigh.

'When the pigs made such a noise. But he came back later.'

Mrs Bradley nodded.

'Now I know you're telling the truth,' she said. 'How long was he away?'

'I don't know,' said Fay. She blushed and suddenly giggled. 'I went to sleep. I was tired. It was one o'clock in the morning, just about, and I hadn't been asleep up to then. He was there when I woke up, but that was not until five o'clock by my watch.'

'He didn't wake you?'

'Not until five. Then he woke me and said we'd better sneak down to the kitchen, and Mrs Ditch would give us a bit of breakfast, and then we'd better be off. So we lay there for half an hour, and then we got up.' She paused, and then said firmly, 'That's all I know, and if Geraint gets into any sort of trouble because of me, I think I shall kill myself. When are you going to let him out of that beastly asylum? He isn't ill!'

'No. But he might be dangerous,' Mrs Bradley responded. Fay looked incredulous.

'You don't know Geraint. He looks awful – just like Henry VIII – but he wouldn't hurt a fly, and, somehow, I think you know it.'

Mrs Bradley tapped the white face with a thin yellow finger – a kindly touch and a reassuring one. 'Bless you, my child,' she said and suddenly cackled.

'Now Mrs Ditch,' said Mrs Bradley briskly, 'cast your mind back (a) to Christmas Eve and (b) to Boxing Night.'

'A pleasure, mam,' said Mrs Ditch with dignity. Mrs Bradley chuckled.

'You and your Linda!' she exclaimed. Mrs Ditch looked down an aggressive nose.

'Somebody 'ad to be helpen on the course of true love,' she observed.

'Yes, well, that's what I'm trying to do myself, Mrs Ditch,' said Mrs Bradley complacently. 'That is, if either of us knows, or remembers, what true love is,' she added, her black eyes narrowing in laughter. Mrs Ditch responded with a deep hoarse crow of amusement, and wagged her head admonishingly.

'To thenk on et!' she said. 'Well, mam, do ee take a seat –' she dusted one of the Windsor chairs by the fire – 'and I'll tell ee all I can, ay, so I well, I prarmise ee. Our Walt, do ee get outside, and do ee be feeden they pegs. Them's squealen.' She waited until Young Walt had shut the door behind his long thin form, and had gone whistling across the yard, before she resumed her remarks. Then she settled herself on the opposite side of the hearth, rested a surprisingly well shod foot on the iron fender, pushed a bag of bullseyes towards her visitor, and observed, without noticeable regret, 'Our Lender, she'm a betch.'

Mrs Bradley nodded.

'A not uncommon occurrence, when one girl has to hold her own in a large family otherwise composed of boys,' she pointed out.

'Ah, I knows all that there argyment,' said Mrs Ditch, uncontroversially. 'But when all's ben said, mam, she do be'ave somethen terrible. Old Semeth, he were the last she flarted about at. That Tombley, well, I don't know. Somehow I don't believe it, say our Bob what he may. That Tombley's too tooken up with his own young lady, and purty and sweet she is.'

'I'd sooner have Linda any day,' said Mrs Bradley, taking a bullseye and sucking it. ('Tes low, I submet, but I orfen envies the gippo women with their pipes,' observed Mrs Ditch in parenthesis.) Mrs Bradley, incapacitated for speech at the moment, nodded, and readjusted the bullseye, which was a large one. Then she said, 'So you had the two of them here? Does my nephew know?'

'That lamb?' said Mrs Ditch with an indulgent smile. 'Bless ee, Mr Carey wouldn't mind. But I never thought to worry him, that were all. What eye don't see, belly don't yearn after,' she added, with a sly and malicious chuckle. 'But, ah, they come here sex or seven times altogether. I gev that there Tombley my advice, and the young lady, too an' all, not wishen harm to come of et, but, bless you, mam, no harm never come of true love, as ever I knows on, so I makes 'em up a bed in the room next yourn, and calls 'em en the mornen, time for 'em both to get back to where they belong, and nothen else to et at all!'

She sat back, sucking a bullseye, and regarded with the blinded eye of charity the Rabelaisian order of her world. Mrs Bradley sat on, and waited patiently. The kitchen was cosy and bright. A warming pan winked and shone; the fender gleamed in the firelight; the piece rug was freshly shaken up and looked gay; the glass of a picture portraying the Infant Samuel reflected a deep red comfortable glow from the grate.

'Christmas Eve I was all en a fever,' Mrs Ditch continued, 'what with our Lender comen away from Semeth's the way she ded, and the motorcar all goen wrong at the very last menute, and me afraid for my life – not knowen ee then so well as I do at the present – as ee'd ferret out Tombley's doens and make a virago, and our dad as innocent as the day he was shortened, and knowen nothen at all, and me not liken to tell him, and *certainly* not wanten him to be finden all out on his own – and old Semeth roamen goodness alone knows where, and fetchen up and asken after his nevvy, maybe! See how I was fexed, I reckon, and why I was all of a flether!'

Mrs Bradley nodded, and crunched the remainder of the bullseye.

'Help yourself. Wholesome on the stomach, pepperment is,' said Mrs Ditch, pushing the bag towards her. Mrs Bradley took another bullseye. 'Course, Chrestmas Eve, there wasn't no trouble en the end, but get Mr Hugh off never I thought us should, and perhaps the Old Neck to pay at t'other end! I was en a fever, thinken he might be enquiren after Miss Fay, and her bedded here a'ready with Mr Tombley! But all went well, it seems, and nothen to say how Fossder came by his death. But Boxen Night! Oh, dear! Oh, dear! What weth all the upset about our Lender – thank goodness, I do, she'm married and out of my hands! – trapesen and trollopsen over the country to sleep in them there pegpens and woodsheds and the dear knows what an' all – and then they pegs, and Mr Tombley see-en after 'en as well as Mr Carey, and me with the heart en me mouth for fear they'd meet! Oh dear, oh dear, oh dear!'

She paused for breath.

'What I really want to know,' said Mrs Bradley, 'is the name of the person, man or woman, who took Hereward to Shotover that night.'

'Ah, I couldn't tell ee that, I'm sure. I do know as that there Tombley came sneaken down they stairs just after Mr Carey, because I 'eard him, and I nepped down after Mr Carey came back, and took the front door off the chain and put back the catch, so as the foolesh feller could get enside the house and up to Mess Fay again.' She took a second bullseye, and the two women sat and stared at the bright red fire. 'But *when* he come back, the dear knows, for I don't, and so I tell ee.'

'You're not shielding Tombley, are you?' asked Mrs Bradley at last.

'I may be shielden him for ought I know,' said Mrs Ditch with obvious sincerity. 'I never heared Tombley come back, as I'm bound to tell ee, but then, I mightn't you know, ef he laid low a bet before comen. Went orf to sleep I ded, not thenken nothen. He swere he'd take all the blame ef et ever come out he'd slept en this 'ouse weth Mess Fay. Thought nothen tell I heard old Semeth had ben murdered. Terrible news, that were, as you may guess, and Tombley weth nothen to say for 'isself, nor nothen.'

Mrs Bradley nodded, and Mrs Ditch sighed.

'Terrible,' she repeated, shaking her head. 'Wecked he were, I'll back, but dreadful to thenk of him passen out like that there, so sudden and all, en his sens. Like a judgment on him, it were.' She sighed again and reached for another bullseye.

'Well, child, we progress,' said Mrs Bradley. Carey stood in the doorway of the parlour and smiled at her.

'First,' she said, 'although Geraint Tombley doesn't know it, he is going over to Denmark for six weeks. He is going to see Danish pigs.'

'Lucky devil,' said Carey. 'Who's arranging it? You?'

'In collaboration with friends,' said Mrs Bradley. 'You don't think he'll refuse the invitation?'

'Good heavens, no! He means to run Roman Ending on a different system now that Simith's dead. The old boy left him everything, of course.'

'So for about a fortnight we do nothing in particular. If we could get rid of Priest for a few hours, once Tombley is out of the way, I'd like to make a thorough exploration of Roman Ending. I know the police have searched the house and found nothing, but I don't feel perfectly satisfied. The trouble with this case is that it looks like Tombley, it feels like Tombley, Tombley had the means and the motive, and yet it isn't Tombley. But I'm having the most terrible difficulty in holding off the inspector.'

'You *don't* think Tombley did it?'

'I *can't* think Tombley did it. It's all too foolish and too theatrical for Tombley. He isn't like this murder. He isn't this kind of a fool.'

'Yet the evidence, what there is of it, seems to point to him. I still think he has much the strongest motive.'

'I'm not too sure about that. But he wouldn't have risen from Fay's side, gone out and killed his uncle, taken the body to Shotover, come back and climbed in again beside Fay. It's unbelievable. Besides, I *know* the deaths of Fossder and Simith are connected.'

'How? Those bits of heraldry, you mean?'

'The local legends, too. It's rather too much of a coincidence, surely, for one man to be killed by the Sandford ghost, and another by the Shotover boar, if there's no connection at all between the deaths. And then the arrow on the wall of Temple Farm, and the arrow in the nave of Horsepath Church –'

'I understand you. You think Maurice Pratt did the murders, don't you, Aunt Adela?'

'I don't feel I know Maurice Pratt. I shall have to make his acquaintance. But there's nothing at present to connect him with the deaths except much the same motive as Tombley's – the desire to win a position which will enable him to marry and maintain that poor little wretched Fay.'

'M-yes,' said Carey. 'But the motive is thinner in Pratt's case than in Tombley's, surely, isn't it? Seems to me that having Fossder's consent to the engagement was a big step in the right direction. Can't see why he should hound his future wife's uncle to death, said uncle being entirely on his side. It was Tombley, I still say, who wanted Fossder dead. Gives him a chance to establish himself with the aunt. Then he kills his own uncle, Simith, to get the property, then he –'

'Kills Maurice Pratt to get Fay, and then he lives happy ever after, if the hangman doesn't lay him by the heels,' said Mrs Bradley with a hoot of laughter, poking her nephew in the ribs. Carey got away from the yellow forefinger.

'I don't care what you say, love. It all hangs together very well,' he argued determinedly. Mrs Bradley nodded.

'I know it does, child. And I know it is what my nice inspector thinks. But at present, thank goodness, he can't prove it. He's a very conscientious man, and he has searched Roman Ending and Shotover Plain and Hill, and every yard between them, I imagine, and hasn't found a single material clue, except the blood of the pig. And as nobody at Roman Ending has chosen to report that the herd is one pig short –'

'My boar ought to be a clue. I say, Aunt Adela, suppose you had not examined Simith's body and found those bruises and drawn attention to them and to the broken nose, do you think a verdict of "death by misadventure" might have been brought in?'

'With a rider from the jury advising pig farmers to keep their boars under better control?' said Mrs Bradley ironically. 'No, child. That's what I mean when I say that the murderer cannot have been Tombley.'

'I don't understand.'

'Well, we will assume, for the purpose of my argument, that Simith was killed at Roman Ending.'

'I thought that had been established.'

'No, child, only surmised. If once it were established, my inspector would certainly apply for a warrant for Geraint Tombley's arrest.'

'But Fay, you said, would swear to him. I thought that was your reason for getting Fay to declare she had spent the night with Tombley – to give him an alibi.'

'That alibi would fare very badly in court. It would probably be regarded as perjury on the girl's part. It would be assumed that she was providing it to save her lover. I wanted a theory of my own confirmed, and Fay confirmed it, but I shouldn't dream of advising Tombley to take that alibi into court, my dear, even if he decided to do so – a point which seems very doubtful.'

'Oh,' said Carey, blankly. 'But Mrs Ditch could support it, couldn't she?'

'She could support the Christmas Eve alibi, perhaps. But neither she, nor, as a matter of fact, Fay, can give him an alibi for Boxing Night after your pigs began to complain so bitterly. You remember?'

'Oh, yes, I remember. The snow. And so beastly cold. So Tombley left Fay, and came down to see to the pigs?'

'It seems so. As a pigkeeper, child, how does that strike you? Was it reasonable, would you say?'

'Oh, quite. Absolutely natural. Like teachers with kids, you know. I taught in a boys' prep school for a couple of years, and I couldn't, for ages afterwards, see a kid doing something he ought not to without feeling that unholy zeal for interference which one acquires as part of the system. Same now about pigs. If I heard pigs in trouble, I should hasten pigwards without a second thought. The whole thing is unhealthy and morbid, and strictly on the lines of the so called maternal instinct – but there it is.'

'You relieve my mind. Let us assume, then, that Tombley obeyed a deep-seated pigkeeping urge, and went to the pigs' assistance. What do you think happened next?'

'He heard Ditch and me, and remembered they weren't his pigs, and went back to bed like a sensible fellow,' said Carey.

'Ah,' said Mrs Bradley, waving a yellow forefinger and speaking with unholy relish, 'but that's just what he *didn't* do, child. At least, it doesn't appear that that's what he did.'

'Oh?'

'No. Mrs Ditch says she didn't hear him return, so that does away with her as a witness, doesn't it? And, more curious still, Fay says she fell asleep before Tombley returned to the bed, and the next thing she knew was that he woke her at five o'clock next morning.'

'And was he dressed or undressed?'

'Dear me,' said Mrs Bradley. 'I didn't ask her that.'

'Why ever not?'

'Because I didn't think it important.'

'But if he'd only just returned – from Shotover, say – he'd be dressed.'

'And if he were the murderer of his uncle, he would probably have had the forethought to undress and so give the girl the impression that he had been back a much longer time than was really the case. Don't you think so?'

'I suppose so, yes,' said Carey. 'So he hasn't got an alibi for the most important hours of Boxing Night?'

'Not a smell of one,' said Mrs Bradley. 'But I attach some importance to the fact that he has one for Christmas Eve.'

'Not that Fossder's death can ever be classed as murder now, Aunt Adela.'

'No. But –'

'I know. What you said before. The deaths are connected. I see. Well, how do we go from here?'

'Well, the fact that Tombley came here on Boxing Night to sleep with Fay helps him to this extent: that Simith was left alone during some of the hours of darkness; that, therefore, people other than Tombley could have got at him to kill him, and that, according to Priest, quarrelling was going on in the kitchen at Roman Ending and became so noisy that he thought he would make himself scarce and leave Linda Ditch to slip off home.'

'Linda? Oh, the priest's hole! It *has* got an outlet at Roman Ending, then?'

'Difficult to say. She certainly got back here dry shod, but, as I said before, I expect she went bare foot. Besides, I don't really suppose she lay in a woodshed with Priest in her best party frock, you know. It's a nuisance she's such a liar. That passage from your cellar doesn't go any further than the barn. It certainly doesn't go to Roman Ending. She tried to persuade me it did.'

'She's a daisy!' And Carey laughed. 'Some people know how to keep Christmas, at all events,' he said. 'I suppose I ought to sack Mrs Ditch for loaning out my premises to Tombley and young Fay! Where did they sleep, by the way?'

'Next door to me,' said Mrs Bradley, chuckling. 'But, bless you, I didn't hear them, and, if I had, I should never have thought it was Fay. I should have plumped for Tombley and Linda Ditch. Oh, and by the way, child, it's a good thing for you that you got up and went to see your pigs.'

'Oh?'

'Yes. Pressed hard by me about the voices that he heard quarrelling in the kitchen at Roman Ending, Priest indicated that one was Simith's, and the other, he thought, was yours!'

'Hm!' said Carey. He looked at her expectantly. 'Ever heard Maurice Pratt talk? Yes, of course you have! Well, don't you agree with me, a born and bread Oxfordshire bloke like Priest might easily mix us up? We don't really talk the same language, but – that give you anything to go on?'

'I had thought of it for myself,' said Mrs Bradley. 'Of course, it means little or nothing. There must be hundreds of semi-educated people who speak in much the same way.' She poked him in the ribs. 'But I'm glad you're safely accounted for,' she added.

'But *I've* no call to murder old Simith,' said Carey.

'One never knows,' said Mrs Bradley calmly. 'Motives for murder are extraordinary things. What kind of a place is Cowley, child? Could we go and walk about there at some time, do you think?'

'Half a minute,' said Carey. 'Cowley? Oh, yes, any time you like. Tombley spent most of his young life there, I believe.'

'That is important, you know,' said Mrs Bradley, 'because it seems fairly certain that he was not connected with the Bampton quarrels of Fossder and Simith. But what were you going to say to me, my dear?'

'Reconstruction of the crime, love. Go ahead. Simith was killed at Roman Ending. Somebody snatched his chair away as he went to sit down, fell on him and half throttled him, perhaps banged his head on the floor to knock him out, lugged the body to old Nero's sty, bunged it in, watched the boar savage Simith, and then –'

'And then kept the boar off with a hosepipe (which, incidentally, cleaned the blood off the boar and out of the sty), fished Simith's body out when the boar had backed into his sleeping shed, carried the body over here, stole Hereward, took Hereward and the body to Shotover, planted the body, loosed the boar to make tracks where they would be seen, brought the boar back, and went home to bed.'

Carey looked at her reproachfully.

'Golly,' he said. Then, after a pause, 'Is that the inspector's version, or your own?'

'Both, child,' said Mrs Bradley innocently. 'I invented it, the inspector tested it, and we both swear that we swear by it. If you know of a better reconstruction, tell it me.'

'But the fellow must have been mad!'

'Why so?'

'Just think of the risk!'

'Very slight.'

'Well, it still sounds to me like Tombley.'

'I don't think so. In any case, Tombley would not have brought Hereward back to Old Farm. He'd have let him stray over Horse-path Common and into the village and on to the railway line – anything to get the boar noticed. He'd even have plastered him with blood – and human blood at that –'

'Local colour?' said Carey. 'But you're wrong, you know, about Tombley. The same psychological factor that caused him to leave Fay and risk his alibi – if it *was* one – and creep down to see to my pigs when he heard them crying, would have made him bring the boar back to its home and its warmth and its food. You can't have it both ways, love!'

'Oh, dear,' said Mrs Bradley.

'Furthermore,' said Carey earnestly, his eyes alight with amusement, 'you can't prove that the pigs began crying before he came down to see to them. Mrs Ditch may be a prize liar. He may have been the person who took out Hereward and disturbed the other animals. In any case, love, you know enough about boars to be certain that if *anybody* handled Nero and, later, Hereward, that person is much more likely to have been Tombley than Pratt. Ask yourself! Tombley the pig farmer: Pratt the solicitor. Which one handled two boars in one night without being hurt by either?'

'Oh, dear, oh, dear,' said Mrs Bradley again.

'Well?' said Carey triumphantly.

'You stagger me, child.' She grinned. 'I wonder where Tombley is now?'

'Let's both stroll over to Roman Ending and see.'

'No, child. I'm going to wait until Tombley has gone to Denmark. Then, when the coast is clear, I'll go over to Roman Ending and turn it inside out. There must be evidence somewhere.'

'Why *won't* you believe that Tombley did it?'

'It isn't that I won't believe it. At present I *can't* believe it.'

'God bless the girl,' said Carey. He gave her a swift kiss on her yellow cheek. 'Never mind. Let's have some grub.'

He yodelled cheerfully, and Mrs Ditch came hastening.

'You see,' said Mrs Bradley, when the meal was on the table and Mrs Ditch had gone, 'the flaw in your reasoning about Tombley is this: if he heard the pigs crying because they had been disturbed, he was not the person who had disturbed them. From that we may infer, I submit, that he was not the murderer. But, if he *was* the murderer, he disturbed the pigs and that is why they cried, and therefore your point with regard to his kind hearted feelings towards pigs becomes void.'

Carey, who had a drink halfway to his lips, replaced it on the table and shook his head at her.

'You know, you'll come to a very bad end,' he said, 'and, what is more, your specious arguments don't outweigh my other, considerably more important, point that *Tombley* would have been able to handle the boars and *Pratt* almost certainly would not.'

' "Almost certainly" is good,' said Mrs Bradley. 'But suppose I could prove that *Priest* had handled the boars? Would you then believe in Tombley's innocence?'

Carey looked at her sideways. 'You will see that I have nothing up my sleeve,' he said, with a wink and a chuckle.

CHAPTER 12

Dib and Strike at Roman Ending

'You must entice Priest from Roman Ending, child,' said Mrs Bradley, just over a fortnight later, 'whilst I have a look round by myself. Can you get him away for a couple of hours, do you think?'

'I'll try,' said Carey. He wondered. 'I can. I'll tell him I'm going over to Garsington. I know there's a man there that he wants to see. I'll offer to take him over in the sidecar.'

'Won't he be suspicious at being got out of the way?'

'I shouldn't think so. In any case, I'm doubtful whether you'll find any evidence worth having after all this time at Roman Ending.'

'I can but try,' said Mrs Bradley, grinning. 'I'll give you twenty minutes' start. That ought to be sufficient. Which way shall you go to Garsington from there?'

'Oh, I shall come round by the road and go through Wheatley. If you take the path through the wood we shouldn't run any risk of meeting you on the way.'

Mrs Bradley stood at the farmhouse door and watched him drive down the lane. Then she went inside the house, sat down and looked at her watch, her notebook and, later, again at her watch. Then she put on her hat and coat, took a stout ash stick from an umbrella stand near the front door, and set out through the wood and across the fields towards Roman Ending.

The afternoon was cloudy and rather cold. A nagging little wind was blowing north-eastwards, and the sky gave promise of snow. It was quiet and a little warmer in the wood, for the trees kept off the wind. The path wound serpentwise round the boles of trees, and a robin hopped in Mrs Bradley's path, so tame that she could almost come up to it before it flew along. Beyond the wood the fields were desolate. A hawk hovered, fairly high, over a long and gradually sloping landscape. A quarter of a mile away loomed Stanton Great Wood, dark blue with its wintry sea of branches, stark with its great bare limbs.

Mrs Bradley screwed up her keen black eyes and looked to where the house at Roman Ending shouldered off a couple of barns and a little farmyard hayrick, and presented a blank early ninteenth-century respectability to the eyes of a curious world; for even to the quiet village of Stanton St John there had come sensation seekers anxious to see the home of a murdered man. When Mrs Bradley arrived, however, the house and its environs were deserted, except for the pigs. She glanced about her, and then explored the immediate surroundings of the house. One of the barns was in use as a storehouse for the various kinds of pig foods from which extra diet was mixed. The woodshed bore out Priest's assertion that he and Linda had slept in it. There was a rough couch of sacking on the floor, with bolster, pillows and blankets. Beside the bed was a table, old, and precariously balanced on three legs instead of four. A candle in a saucer, a workman's billy, a labourer's leather belt and a couple of dubiously-clean large handkerchiefs were upon the table. In the floor, in a corner of the shed, was a slab with an iron ring. Mrs Bradley examined it. The slab had been lifted not very long before; so much was obvious. She herself tried to lift it, but her slight weight was not sufficient to raise it even an inch. She stamped about over the floor, and banged her stick down, to locate the hollow sounds which should indicate some sort of cellar. The cellar was not as large as the shed, it seemed. To the north and northwest it did not ring hollow at all.

'It might be a passage,' she thought. 'It might even go up to the secret room Denis found in Carey's house. Interesting, but readily deduced. Linda might have come that way from Old Farm on Boxing Night.' She emerged from the woodshed and walked towards the back door of the house. Her first cursory tour of inspection revealed no means of entrance, but closer scrutiny proved that a pantry window was very slightly ajar. 'Queer of Priest to lock up the house. Oh – morbid sightseers, of course,' she added to herself, as she climbed in through the window.

The pantry door was locked. Mrs Bradley produced a thin pair of pliers especially made for the purpose, and turned the key from inside. She opened the door and came out into the stone passage opposite the kitchen door. The kitchen was the only room in the house to which she had ever been admitted, and she made it the first object of her researches.

It had the usual two doors; one into the passage and another into a kind of scullery or outhouse at the back. The scullery, to which she immediately turned her attention, was a long narrow enclosure containing a pump, a copper and a collection of ancient harness, somewhat mildewed and obviously out of use. Below the pump stood a large zinc bath, and the copper fireplace was clean swept and gave no indication of having been lighted for months. Wherever the domestic washing of clothes had been done, it was apparent that it was not usually done on the premises at Roman Ending. A small strip of matting lay on the floor by the pump, and a couple of pig buckets stood just inside the doorway.

Mrs Bradley inspected the pig buckets and shifted them, explored the recesses of the copper, tentatively pumped a little water, ran a yellow forefinger over the decayed looking harness, sighed, and went back to the kitchen.

She looked at the Windsor chairs, and searched the floor. There was nothing in the kitchen to reward her patient scrutiny, not even a suspicious scratch on floor or chair. After about a quarter of an hour's exhaustive inspection of the sparely-furnished room, she relocked the pantry door, and went out by the scullery door, which she closed behind her. She did not wonder that the inspector had found no clue at Roman Ending. Before going over the rest of the house she went off to look at the boar.

Nero was restless and troublesome. He was a wicked looking old beast with one great yellow curling tusk, and little savage red eyes.

'I wonder?' said Mrs Bradley thoughtfully. She returned to the outhouse and pumped water into one of the empty pig buckets. She carried the heavy bucket to the primitive sty in which Nero was housed, and, exerting an amount of strength unsuspected of her frail-looking body and skinny arms, she raised it on to the top of the fencing which surrounded the sty and tilted it so that some of the water splashed down near the boar.

At the flicking of the small cold drops, the old boar looked up suspiciously and hastily backed away.

'I wonder?' said Mrs Bradley again. Carefully, taking care not to spill water over herself on the one side nor the boar on the other, she lowered the bucket and swilled the water over the ill-smelling yard. 'Your manoeuvres are not proof positive that you've been annoyed by being doused to get Simith's blood off you, Nero, poor old thing,' she continued. 'But –' She put the pig bucket into the outhouse and went back into the house. Only two of the bedrooms were furnished with beds, and none of the rooms in the house possessed either bolt or lock. She knew that Priest lodged with an old woman in the village. She wondered whether Linda Ditch had been in the habit of going home to Old Farm each night. In the face of all she knew about the girl and her mother, it seemed unlikely, else why had there been such disturbance when she turned up on Christmas Eve? Mrs Bradley was sufficiently puzzled to be interested. She continued to search the house.

'It's really rather odd,' she said to herself. Then another solution struck her. 'Perhaps the murderer has had to get rid of Simith's bed. Awkward, that. I must present the idea to my inspector. It isn't very easy to burn a bed. Perhaps he buried it. But when? And where? Oh, dear, it looks more and more like poor Geraint, and yet I can't believe it. I'll go and see Priest's landlady. I expect George will be able to tell me where she lives. She can confirm whether he slept in her cottage on Boxing Night. That will clear up a bit of the muddle, anyway.'

She left the house and was about to return by the field path and the wood, the way she had come, when she saw her nephew Carey come striding across the stile which gave on to the road. She waited for him.

'Why, child! Where's Priest?' she said.

'Staying the night with those friends. He's vetting a sow for them. She's supposed to farrow tonight. Lot of rubbish really. Sows shouldn't want any help if they've always been properly cared for. These cottagers' pigs make me sick. Anyway, here I am, to see that you don't get into too much mischief. I don't like this business of your poking about alone.'

'So we have the place to ourselves. Come into the woodshed, dear child,' said Mrs Bradley. She pointed out the ring in the floor.

'"Oh, the days when I was young!"' sang Carey softly. He bent and tried to lift the slab.

'We want a lever,' he said. 'Now, what have they got, I wonder, that will do?'

He went outside, and came back with a long iron staple.

'I must put it back when we've finished. It closes the cartshed door. They used to keep a bull in that cartshed once, and had to secure him sometimes, wherefore the staple. Now, Aunt Adela! What ho! for the smugglers' cave!'

Between them they moved the stone slab away and disclosed a short wooden ladder. Carey began to descend.

'Wait a minute. Take the candle,' said Mrs Bradley. She lighted it and handed it down to him. 'If it goes out, child, come back. I think the passage goes to Old Farm,' she said. 'If it does, you – Look here, I'll come with you, I think.' She had remembered that Carey, as a little boy, had hated narrow passages and the dark.

'Better not, in case somebody closes the slab,' said Carey. 'Nice fools we should look, lying dead in each other's arms, like the woman in the *Mistletoe Bough*. You stay where you are, love. Cheer-oh.'

He disappeared under the flooring.

Mrs Bradley listened for some time and then went back to the door and stood there, looking out. She had been there twenty minutes, and was feeling cold and forlorn, when she saw a car coming up the lane to the house. Her first thought was, 'So it does come out at Old Farm, and Carey has come to fetch me in the car, or else he's sent George along.' Her second, as soon as she saw the car more clearly, was, 'No, that isn't my car! Now who on earth is coming here at this time in the evening? *More* people who want to see where poor Simith lived?'

It was rapidly growing dark. The woods were a blur of shadow; the lines of the furrows of the half ploughed field she had crossed were lost in the dusk. A pale streak in the western sky was all that was left of the day, and an owl called, and suddenly flew, as it heard the sound of the car.

Mrs Bradley determined to hide. She could not very easily explain her presence and the next best thing was to conceal it. She went back into the woodshed and shut the door. A very small, cobwebbed window, beneath which stood a rainwater butt green with slime, gave on to the north of the yard. She planted herself by this, and, clearing some of the cobwebs with a yellow forefinger, she peered out cautiously at the strangers, who proved to be two young women.

'Good heavens! Fay and Jenny,' thought Mrs Bradley. 'Now, what on earth do they want?'

They tried the outhouse door and seemed surprised to find it open. After a whispered consultation they entered the house. In less than five minutes they emerged, and, shutting the door behind them, glanced hastily round, and then ran away as fast as ever they could, making pretty going, vaulting the stile, one after the other, in spite of the clinging mud on their heavy shoes.

Mrs Bradley waited until the car drove off, and then she also emerged, and quickly went into the house. They had come to the house for a definite reason; they had come with a purpose; that was evident. If they had come to make a search they must have stayed longer, she thought. She concluded that they had come to take away something, and that they knew where it was to be found. She wondered what it could be.

The darkness was now setting in, but she had an electric torch. She did not want to use it for fear of attracting attention, but had no choice. Her memory was remarkable. At 'Kim's Game' she had few equals. She thought she could remember the inventory of the house sufficiently well to notice whether anything was changed, so, beginning with the kitchen, she made her second inspection of Roman Ending. In the bedroom over the parlour a drawer which had been partly open was now shut tight. She noticed this at once, and opened it. It was empty except for a copy of the bulletin published by the Ministry of Agriculture and Fisheries on the subject of pig keeping.

'Queer,' said Mrs Bradley. 'I wonder what they took? Some letters, I suppose.'

The thin little yellowish book had its interest for her, since a similar copy had been found near the body of Simith, and had been impounded by the police. She picked this one up and carried it down the stairs. At the kitchen door she heard voices. Quick as thought she whipped the key from the pantry door, slipped in, and locked the door upon herself, keeping well away from the window, which she had fastened.

'But there wasn't anything else,' said Jenny's voice.

'Wasn't there a paper-covered book? Perhaps he means that,' said Fay.

'I believe there was, now you say it. We had better go up and see.'

'It's horribly dark. I hate to go in there again. I'm sure Mr Simith was murdered here.'

'Well, the police think so too. But come on. Don't let's be soft. There's nothing to be afraid of, and you promised!'

'Yes, I know, but – Very well. Come on. Let's go.'

Mrs Bradley could hear their feet on the stairs, and again as they tramped overhead. Then the footsteps ceased, as the girls went further away to the bedroom over the parlour.

'But the book's not here, and I – and I thought I left the drawer shut!' said Fay, in a terrified voice which Mrs Bradley heard clearly in the quiet of the old stone house. There was clattering overhead and a rush of feet on the stairs.

'Oh, oh, I'm so frightened!' said Fay, as they shot past the pantry door. Mrs Bradley counted one hundred, standing there in the dark, before she followed them out. She soon saw the lights of the car and a little later she heard the moan of the engine across the silent fields. She went back into the woodshed and stared at the black hole down which Carey had gone. She shone her torch on to her watch. He had been absent for forty-five minutes. She began to feel worried about him. She shone her torch into the hole and leaned over and called his name. Then she went into the yard and at the sound of her footsteps the pigs gave shrill squeals of welcome, and came up to the gate of the yard and poked their snouts through the bars.

She scanned the unlighted countryside for any sign of her car, then went back into the woodshed up to the hole. Suddenly she pursed up her lips into a little birdlike beak and softly whistled. When she shone her torch this time she was met by the fact that the flagstone had been lowered into place. As she stood there, from under the floor of the barn came a muffled knocking. Mrs Bradley called Carey by name, then flew for the iron staple, but, inserting it, wrestled in vain.

Carey had gone blithely down the ladder into the underground passage, carefully carrying the candle, and having, beside the matches on the saucer, another box of his own.

For a little while he found he could make slow progress whilst keeping his feet, although he had to bend his back a good deal, because the passage was low. Soon he had to put out the candle because it singed his front hair. It was pitch dark, clammy and cold down there under ground, and Carey, who still suffered from slight claustrophobia, began to feel a considerable amount of mental and physical discomfort. To add to the horrors, the passage grew lower and lower, and soon he had to break the candle away from the saucer, abandon the latter, stuff the now cold candle into his pocket, and crawl on his hands and knees. He began to wonder whether he would come out alive, and only the utter impossibility of turning round in the passage prevented him from giving up exploring it and returning to the comforting presence of his aunt, a Freudian reaction at which, he reflected ruefully, she would probably cackle with joy. He comforted himself a little by reminding himself that the passage had certainly been constructed by human agency, and that therefore the probabilities were strongly in favour of the supposition that it led somewhere and certainly had a second outlet.

He struggled on until he was sweating and panting. The going was rough. His hands and knees were sore. He had gone through the knees of his trousers and fancied that the palms of his hands were bleeding. The passage seemed to specialise in what seemed to be elongated S-bends. He began to count them, but soon was in too pitiable a state to trouble about the number of them he traversed. Sometimes he fancied that the supply of air in the passage was giving out. It was truly a dreadful experience. He began to wish he had never embarked upon it. If Linda had chosen this means of reaching the bed of the pigman she deserved every possible pleasure the night had bestowed on her, Carey decided grimly. His courage sank lower and lower. He wanted to burst into tears of panic and despair. He had not the slightest idea how long he had been in the tunnel. It seemed like hours upon hours. Actually, at the end of fifty minutes – the most dreadful he ever remembered – the passage widened again, and he was once more able to stand almost completely upright. Instead of doing so, he seated himself on the ground, drew a breath of the fresher air which now surrounded him, fished out the candle and lighted it again, and began to survey his environment.

As the candle flame burnt steadily and gave a more certain light, he saw a flight of steps in the form of a short and almost upright ladder . . . Something about the ladder seemed familiar.

'Good God!' said Carey aloud. The truth dawned quickly on him. 'All that sweat, and I've come back again to the beginning! That beastly passage is circular!'

Soon he explored, and found the two entrances opposite one another and narrowing off very quickly into tunnels.

Too much relieved to be irritated, he began to ascend the ladder. He held the candle aloft and then received a shock. The aperture above his head was gone. The slab was in place again. He began to hammer on the underside with a tobacco tin he had in his pocket. Mrs Bradley, who had just come back to the barn, sank down on her knees, put her lips almost on to the ground, and shouted loudly, 'Carey! Carey!'

'It's me! It's me!' yelled Carey, in answer to the thin tones which reached him through the thickness of the slab. He heard her steps overhead, and knew she was fighting to release him.

'Don't! Don't! You'll kill yourself!' he cried. Mrs Bradley realised that, at any rate, she was not, of her own strength, going to be able to lift the heavy slab. She gave up the reckless attempt, and, panting from over-exertion, knelt down and bellowed, 'Hold on. I'm going for help!'

She took off her heavy coat, her hat and her skirt, and tucked her silk petticoat into the top of her knickers. Then she set off, across country and through the wood, running as hard as she could in her quite outrageous garb, and fell in on Mrs Ditch in Old Farm kitchen and gasped with relief to find George and Ditch there as well.

She gave the two men instructions and shoved them off. Then she went up to her room. Mrs Ditch appeared at the door with a cup of wine.

'My gracious, mam, you never run all that way from Roman Enden? Well, there, I never ded!'

Mrs Bradley, lying on the bed, done, but indomitable, cackled.

Later, after dinner, she and Carey exchanged experiences. Carey told his first.

'But fancy the wretched passage being circular!' Carey concluded. 'Who on earth do you think would perpetrate such a joke? I mean, apart from the senselessness of the thing, it must have been damned hard work to make a passage that length, I should have thought.'

'I fancy it's part of some old foundations. I'm going to explore it myself,' said Mrs Bradley.

'Oh, don't! It's pretty beastly!' Carey said. 'I was jolly glad to get out, that's all I can tell you.'

'Which brings us to the second mystery,' Mrs Bradley observed.

'Says which?'

'Who put on the lid again, child, in the woodshed? Fay and Jenny didn't, that I declare.'

'Fay and Jenny? What on earth has it got to do with them?' asked Carey. Mrs Bradley explained.

'*Fay and Jenny?*' Carey seemed astounded.

'I've got what they came for, I think,' continued Mrs Bradley. She produced from beneath a cushion on the sofa the thin, yellow publication she had secured from the parlour bedroom.

'But what's the good of that? It's only the government publication on pig keeping,' Carey said. He took it and began to turn the pages. 'There's a lot of stuff underlined, but people do annotate books, especially practical stuff –'

'And poetry,' said Mrs Bradley sadly.

'Yes, but – Hallo! Look here! This is something different, I should say. And, dash it, it's my copy!'

Just over halfway down the sixty-first page was an English Sale entry, dated the thirtieth of November, 1930. Under the heading it began as follows:

'Lot 60. – Gilt No. 4, born January 19, 1930: sire – Edmonton King David 74th, 64783, by Bourne King David 145. 52353.'

The next line ran:

'Dam – Westacre Surprise 104th, Vol. 47, by Histon King David 17th. 61115.'

Under that again was:

'G.d. – Westacre Surprise 31st, 173612, by Bourne Baron 137. 47429, etc.'

The fourth line stated:

'Served September 13, 1930, by Westacre King David 96. Vol. 47.'

Mrs Bradley took the book, and, seating herself on the sofa, patted the place beside her. Carey crossed the room, and seated himself.

'Aha!' said Mrs Bradley. The entries had been altered as under:

'Lot 60. – Gilt edged, not until January 193?. Spouse – Bampton foot up by 166.'

The second line was altered to:

'Dam – no matter go West Surprise Heston would do.'

The third read:

'D.v. bMGP surprised 31st 1836 by Bold Baron Round Table.'

The fourth line was nearly all crossed out, and consisted of the first word, 'Served.'

'It doesn't make sense,' said Carey, who had read it through six times.

'I'm afraid it must,' said Mrs Bradley placidly, 'if somebody was so anxious to get hold of it.'

'What makes you think of Tombley this time? Fay?'

'Yes, child, and the description in line three.'

'Can't see any description in line three.'

'Or it might be a signature, of course,' said Mrs Bradley, pursing her beaky little mouth and stubbing her finger towards the end of the line. Carey shook his head.

'I think I ought to get hold of Fay again,' said Mrs Bradley briskly. 'Meanwhile, I badly want to know who closed the hole in the floor, and where the underground passage really goes, if it does branch off at all. I also want to talk to Priest's landlady. But all must wait until tomorrow.' She sighed with pleasure at the prospect.

'You don't think the passage really comes out here, into the priest's hole Denis found?'

'We'll see. But next time you will stay on guard, and I shall take George as henchman. And, by the way, I think we should hide this book. Can you suggest a good place?'

'There's my safe. You could put it in there.'

'The chance that Fay and Jenny are able to force a safe is sufficiently remote to encourage me to accept your offer, child. Take the book and put it away for me, then.'

Third Figure

PARSON'S PLEASURE

The Side-step is, perhaps, the most graceful, as it is indubitably the most troublesome of all the steps of the Morris dance. The difficulty lies in adapting the step to the character of the dance, or of the music.

Cecil J. Sharp and Herbert C. Macilwaine,
THE MORRIS BOOK

CHAPTER 13

Stick-tapping at Old Farm

'Buried Simith's bed, ee thenk, or burnt et,' said the inspector, eyeing Mrs Bradley with interest. 'Right you are, mam. I'll be putten a couple of fellers on the job right away, I reckon. Happen et won't help us; happen et well. Can't tell, as the sayen is. Obliged to ee, all the same. Ought to 'ave sen et myself.'

'And now for this wretched passage,' said Carey, when the inspector had gone. 'Where are you going to start – this end or at Roman Ending?'

'Roman Ending!' said Mrs Bradley thoughtfully. 'I wonder where the name comes from? Was there a villa hereabouts, do you know?'

'I don't. I only know that a bit of the Roman road runs identically with the highway on the fork from Headington Quarry which comes this way on the west side of the village about two miles from here. It runs south from Headington Quarry in a footpath, skirting Shotover Hill and Brasenose Wood and meeting the road that joins Horsepath and Temple Cowley just south of Bullingdon Green.'

'Ah yes,' said Mrs Bradley. 'Well, child, I don't want to disappoint you, but, before we explore the possibilities that Old Farm and Roman Ending are connected by a passage – a matter of secondary importance in the case, I rather suspect – I want to see the widow with whom Priest used to lodge.'

'He still lodges there, madam,' said George, outside the door. He had been sent for to show Mrs Bradley the way to the cottage.

'Mrs Priest lodges there too, and shares his bed and board, when she gets time off from her situation, I believe.'

'Very nicely and modestly expressed, George,' said Mrs Bradley, with an eldritch shriek of mirth which started up a collection of sparrows outside who were busily picking up grain which Ditch had dropped when he carried the pig food out. 'Lead on. What's the name of the widow? Is she respectable?'

'Her name is Mrs Templeton, and she's perfectly respectable, madam, although somewhat hard of hearing,' George replied.

'I'll go the round of the pig sheds whilst you're gone. I want to see how my Tamworths are settling in,' called Carey, after her. Mrs Bradley waved a skinny claw. She went through the gate politely held open by George, and walked up the cart track to the road. Side by side she and George climbed the slope, walked past fields and the rushing brook, then past cottages and the post office, until they reached the church.

'To the left here, madam. Mrs Templeton lives along this arm of the village. Here we are, madam. Yes, this one, thatched with straw.'

Mrs Templeton was at home, and seemed suspicious.

'I hope ee ent brought them there police, you-young-I-say,' she observed, staring hard at George. George indicated his employer.

'Madam and I are here in a private capacity, Mrs Templeton,' he said, disarmingly.

'Oh, ah,' said the woman. She looked older than her age because she wore a grey woollen shawl. Her voice was drawling and peevish and rather high pitched. It gave the effect of a whine. Whether she was really hard of hearing it was not easy to say. She seemed to hear Mrs Bradley. 'Come in, mam, ef ee must. The vicar was here this marnen.'

'Really?' said Mrs Bradley. George remained outside. 'You can go home, George. I can find my own way back,' she added. George saluted and went. 'And did you enjoy the murder?' Mrs Bradley proceeded, as Mrs Templeton, apparently most unwillingly, dusted a chair for her.

'Et's desgraceful,' said Mrs Templeton, straightening an antimacassar on the back of a red plush armchair, and a photograph frame on the what-not. 'I don't know what the country's comen to! What's that there League of Nations doen? That's what *I'd* like to know.'

'Quite,' said Mrs Bradley. 'So you thought it very odd?'

'Well, *ain't* it odd? A respectable man as has lived on his farm for years, and Oxfordshire born, though not in these parts, tes true, to be found on Shotover Common like the poor young feller in the story?'

'But I thought the poor young fellow remained alive? I thought he pushed a volume of Aristotle's philosophy down the boar's throat, and so escaped safely back to Queen's College,' said Mrs Bradley.

'Let them as likes believe et,' said Mrs Templeton, darkly. 'Ave ee ever been chased by a boar? I'll back ee 'aven't, or ee wouldn't be talken so gleb.'

'Well, no,' said Mrs Bradley, 'but I must say I thought it strange that your lodger, Priest, did not sleep here on Boxing Night.'

'Strange? Ongrateful, I calls et. And now to wed with that there Lender Detch, who, everyone know, esn't any then better then er shud be, no matter who er mother were, ner how respectable neether. Nice goen's on, I should thenk! I says to Jem Priest the very first theng next mornen, I says, "that ee should be layen with gals, sted of comen 'ome nice to your supper," I says to him straight, "that esn't 'uman." Supper first, and gals come later. That's the way o' the world! But there! He only laughs! What can you do with 'em, I ask ee? All as bad as one another. Crook their lettle fenger and up come all they gals. Thenk *they'd* know better, wouldn't ee? But there! Mother's teachen, parson's preachen – tes all one to them! En at one ear 'ole and out at t'other, and whestlen up they boys the way we'd a' thought ourselves trollopsen 'ussies ef ever we'd dared to do likewise! But them! They're bold as brass, and that there Lender the boldest!'

*

'So he *was* out all night, but went back to his lodgings for an early breakfast,' said Carey, when Mrs Bradley, returning for lunch, had told him of the conversation. Mrs Bradley nodded.

'But nothing else could I gather. That's all the woman knows, I'm perfectly certain. So after lunch we'll try the passage, child, and then I want to see Maurice Pratt, if you can think of a way in which that can be managed.'

'Easy enough. Go over to Iffley for a talk with Fay and Jenny. Tell them you saw them yesterday at Roman Ending, confront them with the book on pig keeping, and extort a full confession.'

'Hm!' said Mrs Bradley. 'We'll try the passage first.' They went into the priest's hole and subjected it to another careful search, but the little chamber seemed as bare and innocent as before.

'Bother you!' said Carey, looking all round the tiny room. 'Come along, Aunt Adela. Don't let us waste more time. What ho! for Iffley. We'll give those girls a shock.'

'I don't think I want to,' said Mrs Bradley, betraying, for once, a hint of indecision in her tone. 'I don't think it would do much good, dear child. There's Maurice Pratt to consider ...' They paused and considered him. Then Carey said, 'Going back to Priest –'

'I have, child. Ever so many times. But the same objection, in an even stronger form, applies to him as to Tombley.'

'The folk-lore part of the business?'

'Exactly. Now, Maurice Pratt is interested in folk-lore. Jenny told Hugh that, long enough ago. I wish I could devise some way of finding out to what *extent* he's interested, and what particular aspect of the subject takes his fancy.'

'Probably a dilettante, you know. I vote we go into the kitchen and have another go at Mrs Ditch.'

Maurice Pratt himself was in the kitchen, a thin young man with long, untidy hair, the colour of half ripe corn if the corn were dirty, elegant hands, very large, and proving clearly what might otherwise have remained theoretical only, that their owner was actually male. His face was pallid and soulful, his eyes were large and blue. He was executing, unnecessarily badly, Carey thought, some Morris steps, under the slightly sardonic eye of the second youngest Ditch.

'Ee gotter bring each foot forward, not peck 'em up,' Our Bob repeated firmly. 'And ee doesn't dance up on them toes, but on to the broad o' the shoe. And sweng that there leg from the joint. Keep the knee straight, not so steff as all that there; and now ee must 'old up your 'ead.'

'Heavens!' said the pupil, in a high, rather throaty voice. 'And one wanted to go to classes at Cecil Sharp House when one took one's summer vacation!'

'Ee'll be able to go to classes, ah, and show 'em all 'ow to do et, too and all,' said Mrs Ditch encouragingly, as she stood with arms akimbo and watched his emasculate prancings. 'Can't expect to peck all up in a menute, ee can't, sir, can ee? Do ee gev Mr Pratt a bet of a rest, Our Bob, and show him sommat fresh, for to comfort him with 'emself, now, there's a good boy.'

At this moment she observed that Mrs Bradley and Carey had entered the kitchen. She introduced the pupil.

''Open as ee 'aven't no objection, I'm sure, Mr Carey, but tes for the Whetsun dancen, by special request. Ee knows Mr Pratt from Effley way. Our Bob be learnen him 'ow to dance Trunkles, seemenly, but he don't make much of a show, not so far, like.'

Pratt bowed, and Mrs Bradley beamed.

'One desires to learn the Morris, Mrs Bradley, the more particularly since one is advised by one's medical man to reorientate the lumber region with skipping, jogging, leaping and the like. And finding oneself in the very cradle of the dance –'

'Headington?' said Mrs Bradley brightly.

'One was impressed – but naturally impressed –' crooned Mr Pratt, dropping his voice to a low caressing note, and gazing at Mrs Bradley soulfully – 'by the uniquely aesthetic nature of one's opportunities.'

'I believe you'd do,' said Mrs Bradley briskly, as though she had sized him up. 'Put on a coat, dear child, and then cool off a little, and then come along with me. Tell me, are you a claustrophobe, do you know?'

Pratt, making mild bleating noises, put on a black velvet jacket, and arranged a cerise silk handkerchief round his neck.

'One has reason to believe oneself perfectly normal,' he chanted. He looked doubtfully at his black suède shoes, then added abruptly and nervously, 'One isn't going out to see pigs!'

'Of course not,' said Mrs Bradley, bustling him along the passage. 'As one is not a claustrophobe, one is going to explore a priest's hole behind some panelling.' She grinned ironically.

'Is one indeed. Most jolly!' said Pratt, politely, but with faint enthusiasm. Mrs Bradley hustled him into the parlour and left him standing just inside the doorway whilst she lighted all the candles in the room. Then she opened the door in the woodwork and beckoned him forward.

'One leaves the door open, of course?' said Pratt, advancing as though he were hypnotised. Mrs Bradley gave him a candle and a box of matches.

'Well, no,' she said, urging him onward. 'Seventeenth century. Really exceedingly interesting.' Raising a yellow hand, she pushed him in and shut the door with some firmness. She listened. The wood was thick. Although Pratt, on the other side of the panelling, was beating with both his fists and wailing shrilly, not a sound could be heard in the parlour.

'Nothing like putting in a rabbit to find the way out of a rabbit hole,' said Carey cheerfully, coming up close behind her. 'Now, what do you want us to do?'

'I want George and Ditch and a couple of the young Ditches to go over to Roman Ending. Two of them, legally or illegally, are to get Priest out of the way, and then explore the passage at that end. I've told George where it is, and all about it. You and I, child, will watch the rabbit hole, as you call it, and see where the rabbit comes out!'

'But what about that poor fish in there if the priest's hole hasn't an outlet?'

'In a quarter of an hour,' said Mrs Bradley calmly, 'we will open the door and let him out. That is, unless he's found another opening.'

They waited in silence. At the end of fifteen minutes Carey stood by, and Mrs Bradley pressed the knob of the panelling. No one was in the priest's hole. Maurice Pratt had gone.

'So far, so good,' said Mrs Bradley cheerfully.

The parlour door opened and Maurice Pratt walked in.

'May one intrude?' he asked, advancing towards the candle-light.

'Good heavens, Pratt!' exclaimed Carey. 'You haven't walked from Roman Ending, have you?'

'Roman Ending?' said Pratt. 'An enticing name. One feels one has heard it before. A village, one supposes. One knew that the Roman Road called Akeman Street passed this side of Marsh Baldon on its way to Wallingford, but one has not heard of the hamlet of Roman End.'

'Ending,' said Carey. 'It's not a village; it's a farm. Simith's place. You must have heard of it.'

'Simith? Oh, yes. Very sad. Really most odd, one felt. First Mr Fossder, one's late partner, and then Mr Simith, at one time his greatest friend. One almost felt a connection somewhere. Impossible, one supposes, but the feeling persisted, believe one or not, for a week.'

'And now has gone?' said Mrs Bradley, eyeing him with foxy, female, sycophantic admiration. Carey picked up a book and removed himself to his favourite chair to read. Mrs Bradley patted the settee, and Pratt sat down beside her. 'What did you think of the story of Napier's ghost?' she asked him in a whisper. Pratt looked pained.

'One regarded it as a not-too-brilliant camouflage of what really happened,' he said.

'And what was that?' asked Mrs Bradley sweetly.

'One reconstructs as follows: one's sister-in-law-to-be has a wild ebullient nature. What more feasible than that she should play a jest on her uncle and guardian? The result she has not foreseen. The overtaxed heart fails; one's uncle falls dead. One is, from the girl's point of view, naturally and deeply agitated. What is one to do? Ah, fortunately one is accompanied by one's lover, Hugh, Carey's own capable young friend.' He inclined his head in homage towards Carey. 'One's lover knows the story of the Sandford ghost. Voilà! Nobody else was there. The story passes the critics. Nothing can save one's uncle. One did not intend his death. One can trust one's lover not to talk in his cups.'

He paused dramatically. Mrs Bradley clapped her hands. The rings on her yellow fingers flashed in the light of the fire.

'Or, of course, it might have been one's young acquaintance Hugh, who killed Mrs Fossder,' she said. Pratt brushed aside the idea.

'Improbable. The whole story, to the trained mind, is an obvious fabrication invented to stay the remorse of a terrified, hysterical girl. One has met such girls. One has lived in the house with this one. Modern life is lived too fast to suit such persons. Would it interest you to know –' he put his lips to Mrs Bradley's ear – 'that already she is repenting of her engagement? The little room, by the way,' he added, in his ordinary tones, 'had an outlet in another part of the house. In one of the privies, as a matter of actual fact. Very ingenious. One leapt up to open the window, and as one struck the wall a panel crept open and in one went. A short passage led to steps. At the top one found a trap door. One pushed it up without meeting much resistance. Such as was offered came from a small rectangular mat which effectively concealed all trace of the trap door from the top.'

'Indeed!' said Mrs Bradley. 'Exceedingly diverting! Are you interested in the architecture of old houses, Mr Pratt?'

'One vaguely likes them. One cannot pretend to knowledge.

One recognises salient features, of course. Actually, one confesses to a preference for ecclesiastical architecture. The domestic is not sufficiently impersonal.'

'Well, since I've been living in Oxfordshire,' said Mrs Bradley, nodding, 'I've visited more churches than in all the rest of my life.' (This was by no means true). 'Horsepath Church, for example, I liked very much. And this one here at Stanton St John is delightful. Transition. Early English to Decorated. Reign of Edward the First. The chancel is particularly fine. The chancel arch is transitional Norman. The poppy head pews, carved in the likeness of curious human heads, are most distinctive. Don't tell me you haven't been in! Then, of course, there is Bampton. Do you know Bampton at all?'

'One was – yes, one spent some years of one's early life in Bampton. One fears –' he giggled shrilly – 'that one forgets the church. One probably disliked the Litany.'

'Then,' proceeded Mrs Bradley, 'I went to Forest Hill. The gabled bell cote, with its supporting buttresses, is, in my experience, unique. Of course, I suppose one could class a certain gabled building having a large blocked east window, the flanking buttresses and the late Perpendicular doorway –'

'You are not now referring to Forest Hill, but, of course, to Sandford. One believes there was a chapel belonging to the Knights Templars,' said Pratt. 'It is part of a farmhouse now.' He rose and languidly smiled. 'I wonder whether you would think one very discourteous? One did rather desire to learn to caper correctly.'

'By all means, child, but don't become overheated. Those Morris dances are strenuous,' Mrs Bradley observed.

'Thank God that's gone,' said Carey, with a yawn. 'There's one thing. Now you've seen it in its entirety, what about it as a murderer?'

Mrs Bradley shrugged and suddenly cackled.

'But consider,' persisted Carey, laying aside his book. 'Do you really see that object snatching chairs from underneath old Simith, and dragging him out, half dead, to Nero's sty? And can you, by any flight of fancy, imagine him having the guts to get the body out of the sty when Nero had done with it? Ask yourself, love! It's impossible!'

Mrs Bradley sighed.

'Put like that, child, in your own inimitable way –'

'Put it how you like! You've seen the silly fathead, and talked to him. What's the matter with you? I tell you, again and again, that Tombley's your man!'

'Tombley?' said Mrs Bradley. 'If Maurice Pratt couldn't have tackled the boar, Tombley couldn't have tackled the legends and their funny little trimmings. In these cases, child, you know, a physical disability may be no great handicap; but a psychological one is insurmountable. But supposing we allow your fairly reasonable objection. Pratt couldn't: that's what you say. Tombley wouldn't: that's what I say. What, then, is the explanation?'

'Another murderer,' said Carey.

'Good heavens, child!' said Mrs Bradley, gazing in admiration. 'But where on earth shall I find one?'

'What's the matter with Priest?' asked Carey, picking up his book and going on reading. 'Oh, same like Tombley, of course. Oh, dash it, *I* don't know!'

Priest was washing down the back house, and accepted with alacrity Ditch's suggestion that he should accompany him to the 'Star,' for beer and a gossip.

'Got some good reason to get me away from here, I reckon,' he said with a wink. Ditch laughed, and they walked away. From behind the little haystack, George, Young Walt and Our Bob watched them cross the second stile, and then went into the woodshed. George and Young Walt, armed with electric torches, undertook the task of exploring the passage, and Bob remained on guard. He was to allow them an hour, and then return to Old Farm if they had not reappeared.

Down they went, and pursued the path by which Carey had travelled before, but with exactly the same result. They moved a little more slowly than he had done, and scrutinised the walls as they went.

'Happen we're down in some old foundations,' said Young Walt, who was the leader. George thought it likely, too. Just before the hour was up, they rejoined Bob at the top of the wooden ladder.

Mrs Bradley frowned thoughtfully when they brought her their report. It seemed as though her first theory about Linda Ditch had been the correct one – she had changed her shoes and her frock, and had gone out of doors across the snow to Roman Ending. Except as a witness of suspicious occurrences on Boxing Night – and it seemed as though she had been some time in the woodshed at Roman Ending before Simith's death – the girl was not important unless – Mrs Bradley shook her head slightly, but the suspicion would not allow itself to be completely dismissed – unless Priest were the murderer, instead of the murderer's accomplice.

'I shall certainly have to tackle Linda again,' she told herself. The inspector had tackled Linda twice, but had not shaken her story – what there was of it. Nevertheless, the sudden marriage with Priest was most suspicious, and she might know a great deal more than she had told, Mrs Bradley decided.

Next day she thought again of the slab. It was not easy to know whether it had been put back deliberately or innocently, or to decide whether the person who had covered the hole had known that Mrs Bradley was on the premises. She shook her head again. One might speculate with a certain amount of profit about Linda Ditch, but the identity and the object of the unknown prowler were insoluble mysteries for the moment. She wondered whether another interview with Mrs Fossder would be of any assistance.

'So you're going to bounce something more out of Fay and Jenny?' Carey said, when he heard her order the car.

'Possibly, child; and possibly not,' said Mrs Bradley urbanely. She declined his offer to accompany her to Iffley, and arrived there to discover that Mrs Fossder had gone to Oxford, and that Jenny, except for the servant, was alone in the house.

'Fay went off to Denmark to see Geraint Tombley, with some money she borrowed from me. Maurice Pratt doesn't know. He thinks she's with friends in Devonshire, getting her nerves to rights. He isn't to write to her. She *is* a little tike,' said Jenny, dispassionate but sincere in her criticism of Fay's conduct.

'Oh?' said Mrs Bradley, wondering when Fay had gone.

'And how goes the sleuthing?' Jenny enquired, when Mrs Bradley was comfortably settled by the fire.

'Jenny,' said Mrs Bradley, 'I've come to an impasse. What time is it? Nearly six? When do you expect your aunt?'

'Not before eight o'clock.'

'Then I want you to listen to me. I'm going to be frank with you. Where I think your family are implicated, I'm going to say so fearlessly. You don't mind plain dealing, do you?'

'This means that at least you don't suspect *me*,' said Jenny.

'Maurice Pratt suggests that you murdered your uncle, and that Hugh concocted the story of the ghost,' said Mrs Bradley, cackling.

'That's not too bad,' said Jenny, considering it on its merits. 'Hugh *is* chivalrous, and he'd never give me away. But the fact is that I simply did not go out of the house before uncle's death that night.'

'But still,' said Mrs Bradley, 'who am I, to declare that you did not bear your uncle some grudge?'

'Well, of course, I *did*!' said Jenny. She laughed, a little self-consciously. 'There is all that old stuff about my purple past. I'm illegitimate, I think you know. Not Uncle Fossder's real niece. It used to come all over him at times. More than once he has cut me out of his will. I believe I told you that. Lately – just before his death – there was another spasm of it, but apparently it didn't come off! I'm rather glad, I must say, now that it appears that those shares he bought have done so particularly well.'

'Yes,' said Mrs Bradley, who seemed to have become depressed. She looked full at the girl. 'Do you think that if your Uncle had cut you out of his will once more, it might have been for good and all?'

'I don't know, I'm sure,' said Jenny. 'You see, I don't know much about those other times, because it happened when I was small. This present will – the one that's just been proved – has stood for years, I believe. It was just a sudden idea to cut me out again.'

'Then, don't you see, child, that if you knew of the idea – ?'

'Heavens!' cried Jenny. 'Quite right! So definitely I am suspected. Go on. This is terribly thrilling!'

'Well, to take the death of your uncle, without reference, for the moment, to Simith's death –'

'Oh! Are you still investigating the murder of Mr Simith? I say! You *are* going it!' said Jenny.

'Listen, child. I want to know more about your aunt, Mrs Fossder. She expected to gain by your uncle's death –'

'Oh, no, she didn't!' said Jenny. 'By the time Maurice Pratt and Fay and I had been provided for under the terms of the will – or rather, when our *husbands* had been! – aunt must have known that she would have been rather worse off than in uncle's lifetime.'

'That's interesting,' said Mrs Bradley, noting it down in her book. 'And now, child, can you help me to eliminate anybody else? I've taken out you and Mrs Fossder for the moment. What about Maurice Pratt?'

'I couldn't tell you. I know he went up to bed, because he went before I did. I was waiting for Hugh, and, of course, Hugh didn't come until ever so late, as you know, because of the car. I knew that Fay had gone off to meet Geraint. (Silly name for a man of the present day!) Maurice went up to bed at ten o'clock. He often does. He detests late hours. I've never known him stay up of his own free will.'

'Is he abnormally sensitive to cold?'

'No, I don't think so. He wears all those pullovers and mufflers and things that men always put on, but he never complains of the cold. He doesn't have chilblains, either.'

'Does he drink?'

'Oh, yes. He drinks beer. And he drinks the kind of thing that is mentioned in ballads and old songs. You know "the blood red wine," and "the good Rhine wine" and all that kind of business. He's an awful ass! I don't wonder Fay doesn't like him! It was like her, little fathead, to allow herself to be frightened into getting engaged to him!'

'Which is his bedroom?'

'It's in the front of the house.'

'Hm!' said Mrs Bradley. 'When Maurice Pratt goes to bed, does he read, or keep a diary, or anything of that kind, do you know?'

'I'm certain he doesn't. He's always boasting how that the minute he gets into bed he falls asleep, and then he burbles all that rot about "mens sana" – you know that fearful chestnut?'

'I suppose,' said Mrs Bradley, looking at her closely, 'you haven't any definite suspicions?'

'Suspicions?' Jenny looked embarrassed. 'Whatever makes you ask that?'

'Curiosity,' said Mrs Bradley. 'I beg your pardon for it. I should have said, I suppose you know quite well who murdered your uncle? That is what I meant.'

Jenny got up.

'I – you mustn't think that it has anything to do with the murder, but I do know Maurice didn't go to bed. I know he went out of the house. He *said* he was going to find out whether Hugh was coming to fetch us in the car.'

'Really!' said Mrs Bradley, non-committally.

'Don't let anybody know I told you. I'm not trying to get Maurice into trouble. And – and it was I who promised to switch his bedroom light on, to make it look as though he was still in the house! Fay's as well.'

'Never mind that for the moment,' said Mrs Bradley kindly. 'Is there anybody we can *exonerate*?'

Jenny shook her head, and said she did not know.

'And now,' said Mrs Bradley more briskly, 'what about the murder of Simith on Boxing Night? Whom have we here?' She began to read from her notebook.

'*Linda Ditch.* It seems that Simith seduced her.

'*Priest.* His motive would be revenge for what was done to Linda, who is now his wife. These two can give one another an alibi until about one o'clock – roughly the time of the murder – but not after that, which doesn't look too good.

'*Geraint Tombley.* Thought he would inherit the property. He does, too. He and his uncle are known to have indulged in violent quarrels. His alibi is supplied by Fay, but only until about 1 a.m. – roughly the time of the murder. His reason for leaving Fay at that hour is, however, so absurdly true to the kind of person he is that I feel disposed to accept it. He went to see what was up with Carey's pigs.

'*Fay.* Thought Tombley would inherit the property if his uncle were dead. This would dispose of the second obstacle to her marriage – the first, Mr Fossder, being already disposed of.'

'It sounds horrid and logical, the way you put it,' said Jenny with a shudder.

'Merely scientific,' said Mrs Bradley. 'To continue:

'*Mrs Fossder.* Revenge for her husband's death. However, as I am strongly of opinion that the deaths –'

'But that *would* connect them,' Jenny said. 'Not,' she added hastily, 'that I want to accuse poor auntie. In fact, I don't see how she could have *thought* of such a way of killing anybody.'

'That's true, ' said Mrs Bradley. 'One rather feels about both the crimes that the method is masculine, somehow.'

Jenny looked relieved.

'I'm glad you think that,' she said. 'What about Maurice *this* time? Poor old Maurice!'

'I've got him down,' said Mrs Bradley doubtfully, 'but the motive seems obscure. Why should he murder Simith?'

'Of course, Linda Ditch is her father's daughter,' said Carey a little later.

'Meaning what, exactly, child? Oh, Jenny sent her love and did not commit the murders.'

'Well, Ditch is my pigman, isn't he? So Linda ought to know how to handle a boar.'

'And Priest and Linda supply one another with an alibi up to the time of the murder,' said Mrs Bradley. 'We've had all that before.'

Carey began to hum an air from the *Mikado*.

'Speak up clearly, child. There's something on your mind,' said Mrs Bradley. Carey stopped humming and grinned. Then he sang softly, rolling his eyes at her,

> 'The flowers that bloom in the Spring, tra la,
> Have nothing to do with the case.'

'But they have, of course,' admitted Mrs Bradley. She sighed. 'That's what makes me feel so depressed all the time. All that decorative rubbish – heraldry, defaced church walls, two-hundred-pound bets and the dragging in of the local legends – the two that happen to get themselves into books moreover – could not possibly emanate from the minds of Priest and Linda Ditch.'

CHAPTER 14

Corners with Capers at Stanton St John

'It comes to this, mam,' said the inspector stolidly. He was in the smaller pig-house, gazing at Carey's young Tamworths. Regardless of him, the reddish brown, long snouted pigs snuffled contentedly, lay down and slept, explored the empty feeding trough or rubbed side against side with their brothers. 'Myself, I fancy the Berkshire,' he added, leaning over and slapping the deep, flat ribs, 'but these are good bacon pigs, mam. Well, I was sayen, about Mr Semeth's death, accorden to you yourself, there's more than one could a done et, and would a ben glad to, most like. The death of Mr Fossder I don't entend to consider.' His quiet eyes met her sharp black ones. He raised his hand from the pig he was caressing, and waved aside Mr Fossder's death with a magnificent, Jove-like gesture. 'Et don't consarn me and was brought in onder Natural Causes. Not murder, any'ow. Now, as to the death of Mr Semeth, we 'ave various comby-nations. There's the nevvy and his young lady, notably loose thenking and amorous.'

He looked questioningly at Mrs Bradley, who nodded.

'Now, there's them as'll tell ee that that's a far cry from murder. But, mam, I was brought up en chapel, and one theng *do* lead to another, for that's my experience, man and boy, and seventeen years in the Force.'

Mrs Bradley nodded again.

'You think that Fay and Tombley killed Simith, so that Tombley could inherit the pigs?'

The inspector leaned over again and scratched a pig on the top of the head.

'Well, mam, you knows et's likely enough um ded. Such thengs 'ave been done afore, and – and well be again, we fears. Besides –' he straightened up. There was a twinkle in his eyes this time – 'this 'ere connection between the deaths of Mr Fossder and Mr Semeth that you be so ready to see, et bears ee out ef Tombley and the young lady are the colprets, don't et, now? Mr Fossder stands atween them and their wedden, preferren t'other feller, and Mr Semeth stands atween them and their liven, ee might as well say.'

'I know,' said Mrs Bradley gloomily. 'But, you know, that's all wrong, inspector.'

'Well, mam, ee'll agree I've waited on ee several weeks over this 'ere case. Now, I ought to tell ee, the time 'as come when I can't ondertake for to do et no more. As soon as Mr Tombley gets back from Denmark, I arrest him for the murder of his uncle, and the young lady as his accom*plyce*. I can't 'old me 'and no longer. I be sorry ef et 'urts your feelens, like, but I thenk this time ee're mestaken.'

He cleared his throat apologetically.

'Ah, well,' said Mrs Bradley philosophically. 'But, inspector, think of the others in the case!'

'I 'ave. Ad enfy-ny-tum, mam, as the young gents says en the colleges. And I can't see nothen to 'em. Pratt, ee says. Well, what of him? I've talked to un. Seems fair selly, what I can make out about him. Then them there signs and wonders in the churches. All them lettle shields. Everythen ee can tell me, I've drawn my attention to 'em, and stell I comes back to Tombley. Et wasn't natural as a young lady brought up proper should want to sleep with young fellers onless there was somethen else en et. I know the world, mam. No desrespect entended. Young ladies may *warnt* to misbehave themselves. I don't say nothen about that. But the plain fact is, um don't *do* et.'

He began to walk towards the door. Mrs Bradley remained

where she was, staring down at the Tamworths. She heard the door close. She smiled, and passed the tip of her tongue very gently over her lips. Suddenly her smile widened. She hastened after the inspector, and caught him up at Tom's sty.

'Don't forget to ask who killed a pig on Christmas afternoon,' she said, 'dear child.'

The inspector gazed after her as she walked briskly on towards the house. Then he took off his cap and scratched his head and took out the warrant for Tombley's arrest and read it.

'Well, *I* dunno,' he said. 'Ef et weren't for what I've had said to me down en Headenton –' He replaced the warrant. 'Who *would* kell a pig on Christmas Day? That's what I want to know.' His thick back stiffened. 'And et's what I'll find out, too an' all,' he said.

'Linda,' said Mrs Bradley, who was visiting the private mental home ostensibly in her professional capacity. She had gone the rounds and had been given tea by the matron. Linda, who had been sent to talk to Mrs Bradley alone, stood stiff and looked defiant. 'Who taught you the Bampton words of *Constant Billy*?' Mrs Bradley enquired.

'Mester Semeth,' Linda replied with a sniff. But her pose was somewhat relaxed, Mrs Bradley noticed.

'Not a young man called Maurice Pratt, by any chance?' she suggested.

'Don't know un,' said Linda shortly, avoiding Mrs Bradley's eye.

'He's engaged to the young woman whom Mr Tombley would like to marry,' said Mrs Bradley, watching her.

'Oh, ah?' said Linda, with elaborate lack of interest. 'Nothen to do wi' me. Respectable *I* be, these days.'

'Linda, how did you get into the priest's hole at Old Farm on Boxing Night?'

'From the upstairs WC.'

'How did you find out about it?'

'See the lettle trap-door once when I was a cleanen, and opened er up, to see where er led, that's all.'

'But what made you do it on Boxing Night? What had you to hide?'

'I went wi' Jem Priest en the woodshed at Roman Enden.'

'Whose idea was that?'

'I dunno. Et came to us. I couldn't 'ave un to Old Farm cos of our mam. Skenned me, she would, ef er'd took a sneff o' Jem there.'

'But you had a bed of your own at Roman Ending. Why didn't you use that, child? Why go and sleep in the wood shed?'

'I deddun 'ave no bed. Allus slept en the woodshed cos ee can bolt the door. Couldn't lock nor bolt any doors en Roman Enden. Petty ee didn't find that out, like, while ee was about et.'

Mrs Bradley nodded, unruffled.

'You came back across the snow, I presume?' she said.

'Ah. Left me best dress and me shoes en the secret lettle room, and came back to 'em later on when I run away.'

'You ran away because you heard quarrelling, didn't you?'

'Ah. Jem made for a peg shelter, and me, I run 'ome, like, for fear.'

'Fear of what?'

'I don't know. Meddle o' the night, and whatall, makes ee narvous.'

'I see. But, Linda, what made you put your best dress on again when you came back to Old Farm?'

'Never 'ad me dress on to go to Roman Enden. Never 'ad no shoes. What else do ee warnt to know? I got to get back to my work.'

'I suppose *your husband* didn't by any chance kill Mr Simith, Linda?'

'What, Jem!' Linda shrieked with laughter. 'That beg cart 'orse! Should a liked un to; felt fine, I should, to be 'aven old Semeth kelled for the sake of I!' Her amusement was clearly hysterical.

'Yes, but, even supposing *you* were scared and ran home, I can't imagine that Priest was frightened by the sound of people quarrelling,' Mrs Bradley said.

'Twas on account of the peg he kelled,' said Linda.

'What pig, child?'

'Kelled a peg a Christmas Day, ded Jem, and run the blood ento buckets. And buckets of blood they talked about. That's what. And he says "I'm done ef I'm found!" And with that he made off, and I very soon up and follered. All en a lather he've ben ever sence, poor fool, on account of the peg's blood drenched over Mester Semeth when they found him. As soon as he read en the papers about that old there dirt ee had anerised up en London, he've ben en a sweat and a twetch. Took this 'ere jarb, I ded, cos I couldn't a bear to be weth him.'

'I'm not your enemy, Linda,' said Mrs Bradley, with a sudden, startling smile. Linda stared at her.

'No more ee ent, mam. Don't need as ee shud be, neether. Too many for me, ee be.' She nodded, acknowledging defeat. 'But kellen anythen begger nor a peg – that udn't be Jem Priest!'

'And now, my man,' said Mrs Bradley to Priest, 'no more of your nonsense! What did you overhear, whilst the quarrel was going on in this kitchen on Boxing Night?'

Priest slopped a bucket of potatoes irritably into the copper in the outhouse.

'What's Lender told ee, mam, I'd like to know?'

'The truth, I believe.'

'Well, happen *I* well, then, too an' all. Be et known to ee as I kelled a peg for a chap on Chrestmas Day?'

'The question is – what man?'

'Ah, there ee goes too far, because I can't tell ee. A chap brengs a peg over here and asks me to kell et.'

'A curious proceeding, surely?'

'Ah, 'twas. But I dedn't thenk much about that. He offers to pay me my price, and I says two barb. The peg was a rare lettle young 'un, and so I tells him, but he says he can't help that. Et's got to be done. So I kells the peg, and runs off the blood, like he told me, ento a bucket, and he leaves that there bucket en the old sty us don't use – that un all tumblen down – and takes the carcase away with him en 'is car.'

'Did he give any reason for all this? It seems extremely odd,' said Mrs Bradley.

'Ah, said they'd done him down about his duck. He paid me the two barb, and slipped a ten-barb note en me hand as well, and weshed me a Merry Chrestmas, and off he druv. Don't know 'im. Never sen 'im. But when that there yellen about buckets of blood come en at the woodshed door, I took a fright, I don't really know for why, and off I went, and Lender, she went home.'

'You deserted her rather suddenly, Priest, did you not?'

'I ded, I be sorry to say. Took by surprise be them and their "Buckets o' blood" and sprung off over the snow to that there old shelter, and laid meself down en the straw, and sweated, too an' all.'

'I see,' said Mrs Bradley. 'Where were Mr Tombley and Mr Simith whilst you were killing the pig for this kindly stranger?' Priest looked at her suspiciously, but her gaze, although reminiscent of a serpent's unwinking watchfulness, was urbane.

'They went to church,' he announced unwillingly.

'Ah, yes,' said Mrs Bradley, trying in vain to envisage such a proceeding on the part of Tombley and Simith. 'Ah, yes, of course. On Christmas morning. Naturally. They would. How many times did you feed the pigs, by the way, on Christmas Day?'

'Three times, mam, as usual.'

'Ah, yes. Of course. Three times. I should hardly have thought,' she added reflectively, 'that one of these times would have come within the hour of Divine Worship, but, of course, I don't know. I am not an expert on pigs.'

'No. No, ee ent, be ee?' said Priest. He did not seem very happy.

'When is Linda coming back to live with you?' asked Mrs Bradley suddenly.

'Arst me another,' said Priest. He spat into an old zinc bowl half filled with foul looking rain water.

'I'm sorry,' said Mrs Bradley, taking her leave by stepping over two small heaps of pig muck and a couple of empty tins. Priest looked after her with a puzzled frown. He could not understand why she was sorry.

'I've found the pig killer, child,' she said to the inspector. 'I doubt, though, whether you'll manage to get him to say very much about it. And if I assured you that he must be the accessory after the fact, I suppose you'd still decide to arrest Geraint Tombley?'

'Mam,' said the inspector, regarding her squarely, 'what would *you* do en my place?'

'The same as you are doing. But I want you to have a successful case to your credit, child, you know,' said Mrs Bradley.

'Ah, I know.' He went away, looking worried.

'And now,' said Mrs Bradley to Carey, 'it's time I got back to work. Keep your ears open, child, for rumours and such-like, won't you? And let me know immediately Geraint Tombley comes home. He's probably keen to get back, and I imagine that he'll marry Fay as soon as they can get the banns business over. Good-bye, dear child, and thank you so much for putting up with me.'

'Come back for Easter,' said Carey. 'Hugh and Denis are coming again for a long weekend. I'd love to have you as well. We'll have Jenny, too, for Hugh. Perhaps we'll have better luck than we did at Christmas!'

The weeks went by. Easter time arrived. Primroses and violets in the shade, cowslips in the fields, and the snakeshead fritillery on the water meadows at Iffley might have persuaded Mrs Bradley to go to Oxfordshire for a second visit to Stanton St John, even without the excitement of the case. Tombley was back at Roman Ending, but Priest had taken a job on a farm not far from Marsh

Baldon, and Tombley had taken on, not only another pigman, but half-a-dozen workmen to construct long pig rearing sheds on the Scandinavian plan. He had brought back plenty of ideas, but they did not appear to include his marriage to Fay. He had received a letter from Mrs Bradley the day after his return.

'Let Fay remain nominally engaged to Pratt. Lives may depend on this. Be good, child. It won't hurt you to wait a month or two.' Tombley, snorting with annoyance, took the unpalatable advice. 'And keep me in touch with developments, especially if any more armorial bearings appear,' the letter had gone on commandingly.

Mrs Bradley returned to Old Farm on Maundy Thursday. That day and Good Friday passed quietly. On the Saturday Mrs Bradley, accompanied by Denis, walked over to Roman Ending. There were dandelions everywhere. The villagers gathered them for wine. Elms were in their small leaf, and even the oaks showed signs of the sun and the spring. A couple of pear trees on Roman Ending were white, and a gnarled apple was in bud.

Tombley was leaning against a finished pig-house. Another four were in course of construction, but a friendly rush of young porkers, still being reared on the open air system, nearly carried Denis off his feet. Mrs Bradley advanced.

'Have you checked the stock, child, since you've been back from Denmark?'

'Had a rotten crossing,' said Tombley, who did not look pleased to see her. 'Yes. I'm the same Middle White short that I was on Boxing Day. Priest, I'll bet.'

'Right and wrong,' said Mrs Bradley. 'Priest killed it, but at somebody else's instigation, child. You remember the pigs' blood that someone poured over and round your uncle's body?'

Tombley continued to scowl. Mrs Bradley walked round and admired the finished pig-house and watched the men at work.

'All day yesterday, and all day Sunday and Monday,' groused Tombley, following her, 'these lazy blackguards are going to sneak for a holiday.' He was wearing a pair of dilapidated riding breeches, hedge torn in the seat and plastered with pig muck almost up to the waist. His gaiters were thick with mud and his shirt was abnormally dirty.

'It's certainly time that Linda Ditch came back to do for you,' said Mrs Bradley, eyeing him offensively. Tombley laughed loudly and harshly.

'That slut of Priest's! I wouldn't have her in the place! I'm all right as I am, until I get married, and when *that'll* be, apparently no one knows but you, you interfering old busybody! Why can't you leave me alone?'

Mrs Bradley shook her head at him.

'I shall leave you to be hanged. You're a nasty, ungrateful child,' she said admonishingly.

'I want Fay,' said Tombley thickly.

'Child, you must wait. You *must*. I'm not talking idly. You don't want anyone else to be murdered, do you?'

'It's all a lot of rot,' said Tombley gloomily.

'So was your uncle's death, and Mr Fossder's. Don't be foolish, child,' said Mrs Bradley. 'What were you doing on Christmas morning, at the time other people were at church?'

'I was at church myself. I told you when you came over. Special message from the vicar.'

'Did your uncle go, too?'

'No. He was fast asleep. Hadn't had much sleep the night before. Don't know why I went. Turned out to be a mistake. Somebody playing a silly joke, or something. Still, it wasn't too bad. Used to go regularly at one time, when I was younger. Not here, though. That was at Cowley.'

'Temple Cowley? There's some connection with Sandford, isn't there?'

'I haven't the slightest idea. Maurice Pratt would know.'

'Ah, yes,' said Mrs Bradley. 'Yes, of course he would.' Tombley looked at her. His sullenness had gone.

'You think that handful of chickweed did in Uncle Simith?'

'And Mr Fossder? And you, if you be not very careful?' said Mrs Bradley. Tombley laughed.

'I don't believe it,' he said.

'I'm not sure that I do, either, now I've seen Mr Pratt again,' said Mrs Bradley, 'but don't forget that you've stolen Fay from him! By this time he probably knows it! At any rate, the police have not arrested you, thanks to me.'

When she got back to Old Farm she took from her notebook the little heraldic badges, and placed them side by side upon the table. She drew up a chair, sat down, rested her elbows on the table and stared at them as though she were playing Patience. Carey, coming in, stood behind her chair and looked at them over her shoulder.

'I wish you'd copy these, making them larger,' she said, without looking up at her nephew. 'I think they'd look pretty in red.'

'So that you can compare my efforts with those of the original artist?' said Carey, grinning. 'Very well, love. Give 'em 'ere.' He bent over them more closely for a moment.

'They must mean something, mustn't they?' he said.

'I know what they mean,' said Mrs Bradley mildly. 'I've got them arranged in order. The top pair represent (a) the heraldic symbol known as the Fret, and (b) the Cross Patée or Formée. The middle pair, reading from left to right, represent the Chief Embattled and the English version of the Boar's Head Erased. The third pair are, first, the Chief Dancetté, and, second, the Batôn Sinister. Last comes a "signature" symbol, the Hand Sinister.'

Carey frowned.

'I can see that the Boar's Head might have some connection with the murder of Simith,' he said, 'but why should there be a second paper with that battlements sign on it? The other symbols don't seem to connect at all.'

'On the contrary,' said Mrs Bradley, 'the third set ought to help us to prevent a murder. The obvious connection is dancing (given by the warning word). The batôn strongly suggests a Morris stick, don't you think?'

'Possibly,' said Carey. 'But what do you mean – the warning word – exactly?'

'The first warning word, the Fret, indicates that the murderer of Fossder has lost his temper. The Cross Patée puzzled me for a bit, until I went cruising about in the car on Christmas Day, and had a good look at Sandford, where Tombley, you remember, was to have met Fossder to keep the terms of the bet. The gabled building with the large east window, blocked up now, is at present used as a barn, but I find it was once a chapel. Over a gateway dated 1614, some pieces of ornamentation in stone are still to be seen, and among them is a shield bearing the badge of the Cross Patée. That fact connected pleasingly with the rest of the story, as I knew it. Whilst I was in London I obtained a little information on the subject of Armorial Bearings, and discovered that the badge was that of the Knights Templars, whose headquarters, after they had been driven from Temple Cowley, were on the site of the present Temple Farm in Sandford.'

'Go on,' said Carey. 'What's the meaning of the Chief Embattled? The murderer's blood was up, or something of that kind?'

'That is the way I read it, child. The Boar's Head, as you pointed out, has a very obvious connection with the murder.'

'And the Sinister Hand, you think, is the fellow's trademark? Something a bit undeveloped about that, somehow.'

'Yes, child, I know.' She cackled.

'But you won't agree with me that it's just the sort of thing a half-baked savage like Tombley would think of, and like?'

Mrs Bradley pursed her lips, gathered up the papers carefully and put them into his hands.

'A nice bright red, child, if you please,' she said.

'If you're so sure of Pratt,' said Carey, after a pause, 'why don't you get the inspector to arrest him?'

'For a weighty reason. I am convinced that the two deaths,

Fossder's and Simith's, are part of the same plan, child. And yet, if you remember, it had been arranged that Hugh should call for Pratt, Fay and Jenny, on Christmas Eve and bring them over here. If Pratt had thought that he was going to be called for, he would not have arranged to murder Fossder on that particular night. You see, he must have heard, later on, that Hugh was coming, and I suppose he would have decided, on that, to abandon the attempt, but my point is that he wouldn't have *planned* the murder –'

'Yes, he would,' said Carey. 'I didn't go over until Sunday, the 20th. Fossder had the warning on Saturday, the 19th. So, if Pratt is the murderer, the thing was all planned out before I went to see them.'

Mrs Bradley nodded.

'In that case, he would have refused the invitation, or abandoned the plan,' she said.

'I'll bet,' said Carey, thoughtfully, 'that that little ass Jenny never said a word about it until too late!'

'Jenny?'

'It was Jenny I saw on the Sunday. She, as you can imagine, was the only one who hadn't gone to church.'

'Of course,' said Mrs Bradley. 'So you think Pratt had made all his plans before he knew that Hugh was coming over on Christmas Eve. By the time he *did* know, he realised that it was too late to alter anything. He must just give in to Fate and wait for Hugh. There wasn't much harm done. Mr Fossder would keep the engagement he had at Sandford, and come safe home again.'

'Then, when Hugh didn't turn up at the proper time –'

'He thought, after all, he would risk it. He left word with Jenny to keep his bedroom light burning, to give any passers-by the impression that he was in the house at the time of the murder, and off he went. He knew that to make Fossder run was the simplest way of finishing him off – both the murders are simple in essence, you see. The warning heraldic signs and other devices – yes, they'd fit in pretty well with what we know about Pratt.'

'His vanity?' said Carey.

'Well, yes, I think so, child. The murderer is proud of his knowledge of local legends and customs. He considers himself erudite and clever. He likes it to be known that he takes an interest in heraldry, and –'

'A thought strikes me,' said Carey. 'The third set of shields – the Batôn Sinister and the Chief Dancetté. Where did you get those from? *There hasn't been a third set of warnings issued!*'

'Not yet,' said Mrs Bradley, ghoulishly. 'But if the murderer's mind works as I think it does, he will not be able to resist the implication of those messages. For this purpose they are perfect – better than the first two, and even more complete than the second. Scotland Yard are even now checking up the Public Libraries in London and the suburbs. When they have found the library reference room which can recognise a description of Pratt, and when that description checks up with his signature in the book – all readers in such reference rooms fortunately have to sign their names and give an address before they can use the books – we shall know better where we are.'

'So Scotland Yard has come into it,' said Carey.

'To check up the London end, child.'

'But how did you know there *was* a London end?'

'I guessed. First, from the letters with the Reading postmark. One doesn't need to change trains to get from Oxford to London, but most of the trains stop at Reading, and one could post a letter there without any trouble. Secondly, there was the reference to the Boar's Head tavern. Now, the only Boar's Head tavern which would be likely to interest our dilettante littérateur and murderer, would be the original Boar's Head tavern which used to stand in Eastcheap, and is famous because of Shakespeare. Dame Quickly kept the inn, and Falstaff drank sherry there.'

'Sherry? Boar's Head tavern?'

'Sack, child. And the initials B. H. T.'

Carey grinned.

'Bit of a dilettante littérateuse yourself, love, ain't you?'

'The connecting link with the case, of course, is the name "Boar's Head",' said Mrs Bradley, ignoring the graceless gibe.

'Odd that you should have brought us one for Christmas,' said Carey, remembering the heavy package they had shifted into the kitchen. Mrs Bradley nodded. 'So you think Pratt's number is up?' he went on, reverting to the main subject.

'I wouldn't say that. He may not have obtained his information from a library reference room. But we can safely leave all that side to the police, I'm thankful to say.'

'But I thought you said that if you could square off the business of the murder of Fossder – you remember you said that he wouldn't have planned it for Christmas Eve because of coming over here? – you could have him arrested.'

'Well, I *could*, although the inspector still suspects poor Geraint Tombley.'

'Suppose Scotland Yard don't discover the murderer's signature in a public library? What will happen then?'

'The handwriting experts would have to be called in. I expect he's written it on these –' she indicated the messages – 'but by now it would be indecipherable, I think, because the pencil has rubbed so.'

'You don't think he'd sign a *false* name in the library, do you?'

'I don't think he would. The thing is,' said Mrs Bradley, 'that I am loth to arrest him. It seems such a pity. He hasn't done much harm.'

'You don't hold human life sacred?'

'Well, not more so than other life,' said Mrs Bradley. 'Why should I? Besides, at present his guilt would not be too easy to prove. Juries like something tangible. They don't want mere theorising about the Oedipus complex.'

'That doesn't come into this case, surely?' said Carey.

'I expect so, if we delved deeply enough,' said Mrs Bradley, with her mocking, saurian grin.

'Be reasonable! When do you expect to have the inspector arrest him?'

'When? After he has made a murderous attack on his third victim, child, I think.'

'But suppose – I mean, it's a terrible responsibility to take upon yourself.'

'No. Forewarned is forearmed. The only thing I'm afraid of is that the victim, being forewarned, might turn the tables.'

'And murder the murderer?'

'There's such a thing as self-defence, you know.'

'That would be rather awkward!'

'No. A very neat solution, I should call it.'

'You've got a ghoulish mind.'

'No, child, I haven't.'

'I suppose you're right about Pratt?' said Carey gloomily. 'He doesn't strike *me* as a bird who is capable of pulling off two murders, and attempting a third.'

'The inspector sees him like that,' said Mrs Bradley. 'As for you, child, your intelligence does you credit!'

Carey looked suspicious.

'Whose leg are you pulling?' he said.

CHAPTER 15

Corners – Reconciliation – at Garsington

'Well,' said Carey, on Easter Sunday morning, 'we've got our Morris side fixed up at last, and we begin serious rehearsals tomorrow. Ditch, Young Walt, Our Bob, Pratt (if he improves sufficiently in the time), Priest and me. Every Monday evening with extra practices for Pratt. Oh, Fay has broken off the engagement.'

'Has she, indeed?' said Hugh. 'So I'm to have Tombley as a brother-in-law instead of Pratt, I suppose.'

'Unless he's hanged before the wedding day,' said Mrs Bradley with unwonted pessimism.

Hugh looked perturbed.

'Good Lord! The police aren't still on that old trail? Why on earth don't they let it drop? They'll never find anything now.'

'It doesn't seem as though they will,' said Carey, 'but they've horrid suspicions of poor old Tombley still. You see, he's blossomed out into quite a wealthy man. Old Simith's fortune proved to be bigger than anyone had supposed, and Tombley, although by no means a millionaire, is very comfortably off. He's just bought a pedigree sow – a Middle White – that I'd give my eyes for. My word, she is a beauty. Face like a pug dog, sweetest temper in the world, and averages eleven point seven nine pigs per litter with an average total weight at three weeks old of a hundred and thirty-five point four pounds.'

'Marvellous!' said Mrs Bradley, to whom, from careful perusal of the Government publication on pig keeping which she had filched from Roman Ending, these figures meant a good deal.

'One of a litter of thirteen, twelve of whom were reared. Her sire's sire was the famous Kesteven Hamilcar the Third, and her dam's sire was Kerriston Blueboar the Seventeenth; her sire's dam was Compton Old Rose the Fourth, and her dam's dam was Bericastle Bathsheba the Tenth. As nice a bit of pedigree stock as you'd see in twelve counties, bless her heart! She took a first at Tring last year, and a second at Peterborough, and got a place at the RASE show.'

Hugh looked at Mrs Bradley and lifted his eyebrows. Denis said, 'I'd sooner have a decent Alsatian puppy. Young Walt knows a man at Garsington who's got one for sale, he thinks, but I don't know how much he wants for it. He said he'd take me over, one day next week.'

'I'll come too,' said Mrs Bradley, 'to see fair play, as they say. But, Denis, will your mother let you keep a dog?'

'We can have them at school now. I should take him back with me. You can get out of joining the Bug Society if you've got a dog. It counts as Natural History, and you have to pass an examination in him. We've got a vet on the staff, and an RSPCA permit, and we're going to run a show, on the day after the sports. Nothing's barred, except monkeys. Old Spewdie's got a leopard cub, but it's got to go to the Zoo when it's six months old. It bites you pretty hard as it is, he says. Old Spewd is always sticking iodine and things all over himself because of tetanus.'

'Good gracious!' said Mrs Bradley, immensely impressed.

'Don't know what schools are coming to, nowadays,' said Hugh.

'Oh, I don't know,' said Carey. 'All these compulsory games are rather unfair, I think. All right when you're older, but I can remember getting most fearfully mauled, and then being hauled up afterwards and whacked for slacking.'

'Serve you right,' said Hugh. 'You *did* slack, I remember.'

'I never shammed sick to get out of playing against the masters, anyway,' said Carey.

'Good Lord! Did Hugh do that?' asked Denis disapprovingly. Hugh slung a book at him, and another at Carey, and continued his occupation of taking a fishing rod to pieces.

The other three went to church, and sat at the back, Denis choosing to sit next to the carving of a grotesque head on the end of the pew. About four hundred people lived in Stanton St John, and the church could seat two hundred and fifty of them. On that Easter Sunday morning it was full. Village girls in their Easter Sunday finery sat in rows by themselves, and a number of fresh faced lads, uncomfortable in collars, sat on the opposite side. Mrs Bradley, between Carey and Denis, contemplated the pointed arches of the nave, and knelt and stood and sat automatically as the service proceeded. Sometimes she looked at the East window, and sometimes traced with her eye the span of the chancel arch or the carved wooden dark brown heads on the ends of the pew in front of her. Her thoughts were not on the service. She had to make a decision, and she made it, finally, just before the conclusion of the sermon. She had nothing to say as they walked down the steps to the road, crossed over, and took their way to Old Farm. Hawthorn was green, bright and tender, and its new leaves aspired like young green flames on blackish branches and little thorny twigs. The hazel catkins were heavy with yellow pollen, late because the winter had been so long and spring was so late that year. The oaks were not even green; their tiny unfurling leaves were reddish, and the great boughs kept their winter outline still. The elms stood up like giants in the fields. A group of young people passed by, chaffing each other in the broad Oxfordshire speech so pleasant and homely to hear; a man went by with a horse – the man in his Sunday clothes, the horse all glossy like a chestnut newly out of the husk, and its mane plaited up with fresh straw and little bows of red ribbon.

'Good mornen,' he said. 'Nice mornen.'

'It looks well for the Bank Holiday tomorrow,' said Mrs Bradley, courteously.

'I like the way they all speak to us on the road,' said Denis suddenly.

'Yes,' she answered. 'When would you like to go to Garsington?'

'Tuesday, please. I'm going to play for the Morris men tomorrow, and I want to go with Mrs Ditch on a steamer from Oxford to Henley. The Village Woman are going, and Linda booked a seat, but she doesn't want to go, so she said she'd like to take me. The carrier's going to take us to Folly Bridge in his car. There are eleven of us, and the car won't hold more than five, so I don't know how we shall all squash in. I say –' he paused and blushed – 'you don't think I'll have to sit on Mrs Ditch's lap, or any rot of that sort?'

'George shall take the overflow in *my* car,' said Mrs Bradley.

Easter Sunday lunch was roast fowl, hot ham and greens, and creamed potatoes. Tombley came over by invitation, and stayed until after tea. Since his uncle's death he had become far more cheerful and sociable. He practised airgun shooting with Denis between lunch and three o'clock, and then practised Morris capers with Carey and Ditch until tea-time.

'We ought to have a very good side,' he said. 'Of course we shall have to find another Fool, because when Ditch takes over the playing, Priest will have to dance. It does seem a pity. Priest makes quite a good Fool although he's such a deadhead, and Ditch is our very best dancer. Still, there's no help, I'm afraid.'

'Couldn't you do without a Fool?' asked Hugh.

'Well, the Headington men always have one – or *did*,' responded Carey, 'and at Bampton, of course –'

> 'With rare head-dress and painted face he looks
> Just like the Bogey man you read about in books.'

said Hugh, with considerable aptness. He looked at Mrs Bradley.

'You read modern poetry, but I bet you won't place that one,' he observed.

'I accept the challenge. How long do you allow me?' she enquired.

'How long do you want?'

'Until Tuesday midnight, I expect.'

Hugh laughed and agreed, and Tombley went home to feed pigs.

'Funny if Fay and Mrs Fossder had inherited the money between them, and Jenny had been left out,' said Carey, later, 'especially as the speculations turned out so jolly well.'

Denis had gone to confer with George about the car for the morrow, and Hugh had taken his leave and had gone over to see Jenny in a pony cart driven by Priest. Priest had returned on Easter Sunday morning to Roman Ending.

'He could have had my bike and sidecar,' Carey had remarked, when he heard what Hugh was going to do.

'I think he wants to spend the weekend at the Isis hotel for fishing,' said Mrs Bradley. 'But, child, the girls have not received a penny under Mr Fossder's will. It is their husbands, you remember, who are to benefit.'

'Anyway, I'm very glad that Jenny is to be able to provide her own dowry. Put it like that, if you like.'

'Yes, of course, so am I.' She picked up her knitting and walked across to the casement. A cherry tree and a pear were in blossom outside, and wallflowers, dark and heavily scented, filled the narrow flower bed underneath the window. Carey came up and stood beside his aunt.

'Love, you're brooding,' he said.

'Yes, child, I think I am. What do you make of Priest?'

'Make of him? Well, he's ugly, and, I should say, ignorant, but, of course, he's a good pigman.'

'Do you think one would be justified in allowing him to be killed?'

Carey whistled.

'So that's how the land lies, is it? Well, he hated old Simith pretty badly, I should think. Still, I'd hardly have thought he'd have killed him. But I thought you were fixed on Pratt?'

'And the inspector is fixed on Tombley. It's very depressing,' said Mrs Bradley suddenly. '"That I were out of prison and kept sheep",' she added with gloom.

'Cheer up, love! Bank Holiday tomorrow.'

At nine o'clock the next morning, George took Mrs Bradley's car to three of the cottages in turn and presented himself and his cargo of village women outside the gate of Old Farm. Mrs Bradley and Denis added themselves to the passengers, and, proceeding slowly, George took the car round to the White Horse public house from which the start was to be made.

At Carfax Mrs Bradley left the party, and, waving a skinny claw as the traffic signals allowed the drivers to turn down St Aldates for Folly Bridge, she walked swiftly towards the station and by noon was in a taxi on her way to her Kensington house. Her servants, Henri and Celestine, were out, so she rummaged in the kitchen and assembled the materials for a passable lunch, finished up with a cup of tea, and then rang up Sir Selby Villers.

'Difficult,' said Sir Selby, over the telephone. 'Don't suppose we could locate him, you know, today.'

'But surely somebody else has got a key?'

'Oh, yes, the cleaner, but you'll have to get permission.'

'I'm getting it, child, from you. It's very important to me to have the place to myself, and today offers an opportunity that won't occur again until next Sunday, and then it may be too late.'

'Very well. I'll send you a man in uniform. It'll be all over the suburb by tomorrow, you know. There's that.'

'Yes, I know. That won't matter. Thank you very much.'

'Confide in me when you see me.'

'Of course I will. Goodbye.'

*

Denis enjoyed his day. It was his first experience of being the only male in a party, and his sedulous care of the village women, his anxiety for their comfort and happiness, and his pleasure at being permitted to navigate the launch for nearly fifty yards of her course, would have made his great-aunt cackle with sympathy and delight. The village women enjoyed themselves, and the weather remained fine, although there was no brilliant sunshine. George and the other driver had spent the day at Reading, where they had picked up two girls at a fête, and had finished up at the pictures. They were back in time to meet the steamer party, and, oddly enough, Mrs Bradley, who walked out of the Mitre as George pulled in to the kerb.

'Well done, George,' she said.

'Thank you, madam,' George replied, as he opened the door for her.

'Where've you been, Aunt Bradley?' Denis enquired.

'To London, child, and then to Tanners Walk.'

'What did you do there?'

'Caught a mouse,' said Mrs Bradley. She grimaced, not very pleasantly, and quoted, half to herself,

> 'Pussy-cat, pussy-cat, where have you been?
> I've been to London to look at the Queen.
> Pussy-cat, pussy-cat, what did you there?
> Captured a little mouse under a chair.'

Denis giggled.

'And have you had a good time, child?' she enquired.

'Lovely. Fell in once, steered the launch once, we ran aground once, got two coconuts (they stood me at the half-way line, rather a swindle, but I told them my age, and they didn't seem to mind). Mrs Barton rolled down a bank, and we all yelled, and Mrs Peel paddled and her feet slipped and she sat in the water, and we all yelled again, and I've had seven bottles of ginger beer and thirteen ices. Do you think it matters, being an unlucky number?'

'Ices *this* weather, child?'

'Good for you, Aunt Bradley. Ice-cream's a food, and they were all so jolly decent, and kept buying them for me, I didn't like to refuse. Oh, and we all had our photos taken in a sort of amusement place.'

He played for the dancers for an hour that evening, and then went up to bed.

'I hope he won't be ill,' said Mrs Bradley. Denis was not ill.

'I say,' he said next morning, 'that bet you had with old Hugh.'

'What bet was that, child?' Mrs Bradley enquired. Denis helped himself to fried potato, and Mrs Ditch put another piece of black-pudding on his plate.

'You know about the quotation you said you'd place. Got any ideas?'

'Oh, yes,' said Mrs Bradley. She spoke dispiritedly. 'Oh, yes, I've plenty of ideas. Too many for comfort and safety, more's the pity. But it wasn't a bet, child, was it? When do we go to Garsington to see this puppy of yours?'

Denis hesitated.

'Spent all his money yesterday,' said Carey. 'Treated the Mothers' Meeting. Poor old Scab! See what it is to behave like a perfect gent!'

'Well, they all kept buying me things. It seemed so frightful,' said Denis, over the top of his cup of coffee.

'It doesn't matter much,' said his great-aunt cheerfully. 'Surely your birthday comes very soon, child, doesn't it? I think I might anticipate it, just for once in a way.'

'Good egg!' said Denis. 'Good frightfully egg! That would be frightfully decent! It's frightfully decent of you, Aunt Bradley. I say, could we go straight away?'

'Why not?' said Mrs Bradley. 'Come along.'

They went by car through Forest Hill and Wheatley and then

by Coombe Wood, and, passing the turning to Horsepath, were soon in Garsington.

'It's Mr West's house,' said Denis, 'but I don't know where it is. We shall have to ask.' They left the car by the old brick kiln, and walked round the straggling village. It lay at the foot of a hill, and was set among trees and market gardens – a quiet little backwater of a place, off all the main roads from Oxford. It had both thatched cottages and tiled, old houses and new, and sandy roads with banked green grass for a pavement. From one end it was approached by a forked road, so that, once at the village cross, it did not matter which way of the street they walked. They came out upon the same road in the end.

They stopped at the ancient monument which stood on its pedestal of steps, made way for a horse and cart, and then crossed the road to the public house to enquire for Mr West.

'Ah, ee warnts Up Blenheim,' the innkeeper said, and sent his son to direct them. Mr West proved to be a smallholder who grew vegetables and flowers for his stall in Oxford market. He had four of the puppies for sale. It took Denis twenty minutes to make up his mind, but at last the bargain was concluded, and the lively, handsome puppy was taken back to the car.

'When *are* you going to settle your bet with Hugh? I suppose he's back at work today,' said Denis. They got out at Roman Ending, so that Mrs Bradley could have a word with Tombley.

'It wasn't exactly a bet,' said Mrs Bradley, again. She sighed. Then she took out her notebook, wrote the date and a few lines with her fountain pen, waved the book in the air to dry the ink, and then tore out the leaf.

'Take this, and keep it safely. It's the answer to Hugh's challenge,' she said.

'May I read it, Aunt Bradley?'

'Yes, if you can read my writing, child.' Denis deciphered the very small, neat caligraphy fairly easily.

'The quotation comes from a ballad entitled "The Morris

Fool," composed by William Wells, of Bampton-in-the Bush, Oxfordshire. This ballad was first printed in the *EFDS News* for the month of April 1936,' he read aloud. He looked at his great-aunt, puzzled.

'But that must be this month's issue! Where did you get it, Aunt Bradley? You haven't got a copy with you, have you?'

'No child. I found it in a library.'

'Yes, but, Aunt Bradley, the libraries aren't open! And he only told you yesterday.'

Mrs Bradley chuckled.

'I have my methods,' she quoted, digging him in the ribs. 'There's Geraint Tombley, child. Run, before he gets off to those pig rearing houses of his, or we shan't get any sense out of him at all.'

Denis ran after Tombley, who turned and waved. Then they waited for Mrs Bradley to come up.

'What is it now?' asked Tombley.

'Child, I must enter your woodshed.'

'Very well. I'm not stopping you. What do you want in there?'

'Buried treasure,' said Mrs Bradley solemnly.

'It belongs to me if it's on my land, you know.'

'Be cheerful. You won't want it if I find it. Indeed, you may be glad to have it buried again,' said Mrs Bradley mysteriously. 'Denis, go and feed pigs, or something, with Geraint.'

Denis and Tombley sauntered off together.

'That inspector from Headington was hanging round here again,' Tombley said to the boy. 'Had the cheek to hint that, if it weren't for Mrs Bradley, I'd be in jug by now!'

'Well, so you would, wouldn't you?' said Denis. Tombley scowled, and then laughed.

'Well, yes, I expect I would,' he admitted ruefully. 'Oh, never mind! But it gets on my nerves! I wish they could find out who did it!'

'I expect Aunt Bradley knows.'

'Maurice Pratt,' said Tombley.

'No. I believe it's Hugh.'

'*Hugh*? I'd grab at anybody who'd get between me and the gallows, but I think it'll have to be someone who knows the neighbourhood,' said Tombley. 'Besides, there's the question of motive, old lad, you know.'

'Oh, yes, of course there is. Well, who, then, hated your uncle?'

'Well, *I* used to quarrel with him. And old Fossder at Iffley, of course. But Fossder was dead before uncle died, so it couldn't be anything to do with him, you see, could it? It's because we're known to have had a good many rows that the inspector has got the goods on me – or thinks he has! – and, of course, I got all the money.'

'I suppose you *didn't* do it?' Denis suggested politely. 'Not that you'd tell me, of course!'

They arrived at the first of the brand new pig rearing houses. Tombley went in without replying, and Denis followed him.

Mrs Bradley went into the woodshed and looked at the floor. Dust was thick round the slab. It was evident that several weeks had passed since last it had been disturbed. She stood by it and addressed it in dulcet tones.

'You must have been used for *something*, you know,' she said. 'If you don't lead back to Old Farm – and it's plain you *don't* – what *are* you for, I wonder?'

'Smugglen, I reckon,' said a rough male voice at the door.

'Ah, come in, Priest,' said Mrs Bradley sweetly. 'You're just the man I want. You might get an iron staple, or something handy, and help me prise up that lid.'

Priest slouched away, and returned with the long iron rod which Carey had used before, and in a few moments the slab was up and Priest and Mrs Bradley were peering down the hole.

'Old foundations, ben hollered out a bet more,' said Priest in explanation, placing a hand on either knee, and leaning further forward.

'Priest,' said Mrs Bradley, 'is blackmail a paying game?'

The countryman stared at her as she straightened up.

'What's that, mam, ded ee say?'

'Does blackmail pay?'

'Well, I dunno, I'm sure. Depends on the party, and 'ow much money they got.' Regarding her suspiciously, he departed. Mrs Bradley stepped to the woodshed door, and watched him until he had reached the nearest pig house, which was quite two hundred yards off, then she went back to the hole, took out her electric torch, and began to descend the steps. She made a careful search, completing the circular tour of the passage, as Carey had done, without finding what she wanted.

Priest was standing beside the hole again, when, after about three-quarters of an hour, she emerged, and dusted her skirt.

'Ah, you haven't closed the trapdoor, I see,' she said, with a fiendish grin. Priest stretched out a hand to help her up. Mrs Bradley ignored it.

'It's dirty, Priest,' she said. He stared at his huge palm critically.

'Ah, so et be. Tes clean muck, though,' he said.

'Rubbish, man! It's blood guilt if you've been blackmailing him,' said Mrs Bradley, staring him in the face.

'Yes, but, mam, I ain't blackmailed no one. That's a town game, that is! I don't know no one to blackmail.'

'I'm very glad to hear that,' said Mrs Bradley calmly, and, leering up at the astonished pigman, she walked coolly out of the shed.

She was just in time to encounter Tombley and Denis.

'By the way, child, what have you done with it?' she asked.

'Done with it?' said Tombley.

'The fancy dress.'

'The – gosh. You haven't traced that here?'

'Traced it? Well –' she paused, and her bright black eyes took in his perspiring face.

'I mean, what made you think – ? I mean, does the inspector know?'

Mrs Bradley laughed, and Denis said, 'You silly ass, Tombley! You're giving yourself away!'

'Yes – well, no,' said Tombley.

'Now, come along, Geraint. No nonsense,' said Mrs Bradley.

'But why do you want it?'

'I don't, child. It was in the hole beneath the woodshed floor.'

'That's where Uncle Simith put it.'

'Why?'

'He wanted to keep it, I think. Then, when he was found dead on Shotover, it looked pretty bad for me, so I thought I'd better hide it.'

'Rather foolish, child.'

'Well, I don't know so much. It would have clinched that damned inspector.'

'Where did your uncle find it?'

'Well, I don't really know.'

'Nonsense!' said Mrs Bradley. He looked at her, and she looked back at him. Then he shrugged his shoulders resignedly.

'Very well, I'll give it you, and I'll tell you all I know.'

'That's a good boy, Geraint.' She walked beside him to the house.

'I took it out of the passage under the woodshed as soon as I knew the police were on my track, and hid it under the bricks of the floor of Nero's sty.'

'So you *can* go into Nero's sty?'

'Well, yes, I suppose so. Yes. Risky, of course, but in a case of necessity –'

'But I understood,' said Mrs Bradley distinctly, 'that nobody but Priest dared go into Nero's sty.'

'Well, one didn't like the job – Oh, Lord! that sounds like Pratt!'

'But one *could*, on occasion, nerve oneself to tackle it,' said Mrs Bradley sternly.

'Well, yes, I suppose so. Yes.'

'Geraint,' said Mrs Bradley sorrowfully, 'you have been very foolish.'

'But –'

'Go and get that fancy dress at once! The sty is empty now. Oh, that's another thing! Who helped you to move Nero to the pig house?'

'Eh? – Oh, Priest, of course.'

'Of course,' said Mrs Bradley. She stopped and looked at him. 'Don't lie to me any more.'

'No. Very well,' said Tombley. He cleared his throat. 'The fact is, I've killed old Nero. The boar in the pig house isn't Nero at all. It's a new Large White called Potiphar – Hamptonwick Potiphar the Seventh.'

'Why did you kill old Nero?' Denis asked.

'For an obvious reason. Think it out, Denis,' said Mrs Bradley quietly. 'Did Priest see you kill him, I wonder?'

'No. I did it one night with a shotgun after he'd gone home to bed. That inspector had a good look at Potiphar when he came over last time, but he didn't say anything about him.'

He left Mrs Bradley and Denis in the kitchen. A village woman came in each day to cook and clean, so that everything was tidy and the room looked far more homely than it had done in Simith's time. They sat there, with the puppy. George had been minding it in the car, but Denis had gone to fetch it in order to show it to Tombley whilst Mrs Bradley was busy under the woodshed. Presently Tombley returned with a crumpled, dirty garment, and a mildewed brown paper parcel.

'Here are the doings,' he said. He seemed sheepish and half defiant. Denis undid the parcel.

'Golly!' he said. 'The ghost!'

'Oh, yes! It's the ghost, all right. Head under arm – that's the bit in the parcel – and all.'

Mrs Bradley spread out a long garment rather like a woman's nightgown.

'Uncle saw where the "ghost" stowed the bundle after Fossder fell dead,' said Tombley in explanation. 'I don't know what he was going to do with these things. I don't know, really, why he brought them home. *He* may have been the ghost, for all I know! I shouldn't be surprised. After all, he was away from home that night.'

'Yes, we know that. You told us,' said Mrs Bradley. 'Another person who was abroad that night was Maurice Pratt,' she added, as though to herself.

'And me,' said Tombley with a groan. 'But, in spite of all that I've said, I wasn't the ghost!'

'You're to come to Iffley with me,' said Mrs Bradley. 'I want you to show me the spot where your uncle declared that he had found these clothes.'

So she, Denis and the puppy, accompanied by Tombley, got into the car and drove to Old Farm, where Denis and the puppy were dropped.

'Iffley, George,' said Mrs Bradley, and in twenty minutes they were outside Iffley Church.

'We shan't be very long, George,' said Mrs Bradley.

'Very good, madam.'

'Come along, Geraint.' Tombley found a penny for the toll, and they crossed the river by the lock.

CHAPTER 16

Whole Hey at Roman Ending

'Now, child,' said Mrs Bradley. Behind Iffley Mill – or where the mill had stood before it was burnt – the tall poplars were in leaf and were golden green. The water flowed, broken surfaced, blue grey and silver, flashing in the sunshine, furtive under the bank. Lines of pollard willows meandering over the broad flat fields beside the towing path, showed the courses of little streams, and on the horizon were hills, low crowned and rounded, and oddly capped with mushroom shaped clumps of trees.

'Well, along here a bit,' said Tombley, 'was where he *said* he'd found it.' They walked beside the river towards Sandford, rounding its curve, and came upon a couple of pollard willows whose trunks were almost touching.

'Shoved down between these trees, he *said*,' said Tombley. Instead of looking at the trees, Mrs Bradley turned her back on them and looked back along the towing path. Then she looked at her watch.

'Listen, child,' she said. 'I want you to compare your wristwatch with mine. Then, when I give the word, I want you to run. Run your hardest; don't stop at the toll house. Throw them your half-penny and then run on until you are within about sixty yards of the turning to Mrs Fossder's house. Drop into a brisk but not a hurried walk, and as soon as you get to Mrs Fossder's hedge – not the gate – not quite as far as the gate – look at your watch and carefully note the time. Then walk back here towards me. We meet –'

'At Philippi?' asked Tombley, half serious, half ironical. She shook her head.

'Oh, no, child. Not at Philippi. I don't believe that *you* killed Mr Fossder, and I *know* you weren't the ghost.'

'How do you know that for certain?'

'You'd have burnt the clothes, I imagine.'

'Well, why didn't the – well, weren't they burnt?'

'The murderer didn't find them when he came for them. Your uncle had already taken them away.'

'But Uncle Simith may have been the murderer.'

Mrs Bradley held her watch in her hand as though it might have been a stop watch, and synchronised it with Tombley's. She did not reply to his remark.

'Ready? Go!' she said; and had the great satisfaction of seeing him pound along before her, the soft earth flying in little damp blackish clods from his boot heels, and his elbows sawing the air in businesslike, although unorthodox, manner. She sighed with gratification, and began to walk briskly after him. They met by the great old elm outside the public house. Tombley was sweating, but seemed to have plenty of breath.

'Much puffed, child, when you arrived?'

'No, not at all. The sixty yards steadied me nicely. Bit hot, of course, but that's all.'

'Ah, but that would hardly be noticed at midnight,' said Mrs Bradley contentedly. 'How long, child, did it take?'

'Three minutes thirty-three seconds, as near as I can judge without a stop watch.'

'Ah,' said Mrs Bradley. 'Then, child, we can go home. Now tell me: what was your uncle doing in Iffley on Christmas Eve at midnight?'

'Trying to spy on me, I rather think. I let out that I had an appointment with Mr Fossder, and he hated old Fossder, so that I suppose it intrigued him to try and find out what on earth we were up to together.'

'What kind of a man was Fossder?'

'Honest as the day. It was Uncle Simith who kept the breach

open, you know. Fossder would have come round. In fact, he *did*, to the extent of getting Uncle to witness his will.'

'Honest? That's what I'd heard. Frank and honourable – for these two qualities, child, I believe he was murdered.'

'So you know who the murderer is!' said Tombley, suddenly enlightened. He said nothing more until the car was passing Bayswater Brook.

'But how did you hit on it, Mrs Bradley?' he asked.

'I didn't, at first. Well, no, that isn't true. I did hit on it straight away, but I couldn't believe it. I turned my attention in various other directions, and, at one point, I almost convinced myself that my first surmise had been wrong. But always there were definite indications – notably that of the temperament of the murderer, and, later on, when the will was read, the motive – which I could not overlook. But, child, why didn't you tell me that your uncle had discovered the "ghost" stuffed in between those trees?'

'I didn't think it important. Besides, I knew you'd tell that inspector. He would have arrested me at once as Fossder's murderer.'

Mrs Bradley chuckled.

'The inspector doesn't really believe that Fossder *had* a murderer,' she said.

The car drew up outside the Star public house.

'Not here, George. Drive to Roman Ending,' said Mrs Bradley hastily.

'What for?' said Tombley. 'I've got the pigs to feed.'

'Yes, child, I know. But when we get to your house I want you to put on the ghost clothes and let me see how you look in them.'

'Me?'

'You.'

'But why?'

'For purposes of comparison. I want to know how tall you are in comparison with Mr Fossder's murderer.'

'But probably the nightgown thing didn't come down to his feet.'

'I know, child.'

'You're not going to get me all togged up in it and then pull that inspector out of some hole or corner, and tell him to arrest me, or anything, are you? No rotten games like that!'

'Not a single rotten game, child. Don't be so nervous and suspicious.'

'I *feel* suspicious. I don't really trust you at all.'

'That's very ungrateful of you, then. I've told you I don't suspect you.'

'There's no one but Fay to give me an alibi, and I won't take it from her.'

'Yes, but there will be many more people than Fay to give you an alibi for the next murder, child.'

'The next murder? When's that going to be?'

'I don't know. At Whitsun, I should think. However, the murderer may not wait as long as that. I don't know how hardly pressed he thinks he is at present.'

'Yes, but who is he going to murder? You don't mean he'll murder *me*?'

'I don't know, child, I'm sure. I'm pretty certain that one of the people he is after is your pigman, Priest. Whether it will occur to him to murder anyone else, I really don't know at present. It will be interesting to see. There's always the chance of Carey, except that the murderer doesn't know something that *I* know.'

'Yes, but it won't be very interesting to *feel*! I think you might have given the fellow the tip.'

'What fellow?'

'The murderer, of course.'

'Oh, the murderer? Well, he knows that I suspect him, but he doesn't know what I can prove.'

'Then doesn't that put you in danger?'

'Oh, yes,' said Mrs Bradley. 'But not in terrible danger.' She cackled harshly. 'He knows that I haven't persuaded the inspector to arrest him.'

'Have you tried, then?'

'No, not yet.'

The car drew up in the lane that led to Roman Ending. Mrs Bradley and Tombley got out and climbed the stile.

'There's a little point about which I confess to feeling a certain amount of curiosity,' she said. 'I was over here with Carey one evening whilst you were away in Denmark, and somebody shut the trapdoor to that hole in the woodshed floor. Carey was down under the floor exploring the circular passage, and I was in the house. Fay and Jenny came over, but it was not either of them.'

'One of them pinched a Government book on pigs,' said Tombley.

'*I* took that. I think it was what the girls had come there for.'

'Who put them up to that, I wonder? That's a bit odd, you know.'

'I am going to ask you a direct question,' said Mrs Bradley. 'Don't answer it unless you mean to tell me the truth. Do you know who killed your uncle, child?'

'No, I don't. What's more – though I'm hanged if I'd care to have the inspector hear me say it – I don't particularly want to know. Old Uncle Simith had begun putting the screw on someone – that's all I know – and I shouldn't care to have been whoever it was. He was more than a bit of an old devil when he liked, you know. His idea of a joke, more than anything else, I think. He wouldn't go in for blackmail.'

'But who could have shut the trapdoor?' said Mrs Bradley, looking keenly at him.

'Priest,' suggested Tombley.

'Priest was over at Garsington helping with a farrowing sow.'

'Lot of rot,' said Tombley. 'Sows shouldn't want any help. They ain't like cows and horses.'

Mrs Bradley looked at him.

'Curious,' she said. She remembered that Carey, the other pig breeder of her acquaintance, had said very much the same thing.

'You mean he may have followed Carey back from Garsington? I certainly did not see him, but that proves nothing.'

'It couldn't have been Linda Ditch – Linda Priest, I mean, I suppose?'

'Hardly. Apart from the fact that I couldn't prove she was anywhere near the premises at that time, I don't think a woman could have lifted that lid by herself.'

'At any rate, it couldn't have been me.'

'No, child, it couldn't have been you, if you were in Denmark, could it?' Her black eyes were ironic.

'Was Pratt anywhere on the scene?'

'I didn't see him. He may have come in the car with Fay and Jenny, but somehow I don't think he did. In fact, I think he might be avoiding their society at present.'

'Another thing,' said Tombley. 'If Linda couldn't lift that lid to shove it back on the hole, I shouldn't think Pratt could, either. Chap looks an awful weed.'

'I know he does. But you can't always go by looks, especially in younger men.'

'I suppose it wasn't Hugh What's-his-name – Carey's friend – having a game with him?'

'I'm afraid not. Hugh was in London. He's got a job in a library, you know. They don't give him many holidays, poor boy.'

'Oh, yes, of course, I remember. I should say it must have been Priest. Looks rather suspicious to me. Priest ain't cleared by a long way of being suspected of murdering Uncle Simith. Bad feeling over Linda Ditch, you know.'

'I know,' said Mrs Bradley.

'This lid business – had it any connection with the murder, do you suppose?'

'I haven't the least idea. If it had, it failed in its object.'

'Done from annoyance? Somebody got a grudge against Carey? Done to distract your attention while the person got busy somewhere else?'

'The last might prove a valuable suggestion. I'll certainly bear it in mind.' She still eyed him closely.

'The whole thing's queer though,' said Tombley, knitting his brows. 'After all, if the person who did it knew that Carey was underneath, he'd also have known that you were on the spot and could release him.'

'Just what I couldn't do,' remarked Mrs Bradley, grinning at the remembrance of her frantic dash across country in her knickers to get assistance. 'It must have been Priest,' she said aloud. 'Mustn't it, child?' she added, still looking narrowly at him.

'I should think so, yes,' agreed Tombley. They had reached the outermost of the new pig houses, five in number, which Tombley had had erected. He nodded his head towards them. 'Look better than the old stuff, don't they?' he said proudly. 'I shall have the whole place looking quite ship-shape come next August, and then I shall get married. I shall be awfully glad to get Fay away from Mrs Fossder. She'll be better and happier away.'

'Jenny, too, perhaps,' said Mrs Bradley. 'Has it ever struck you, child, that, if Hugh were out of the running, Jenny and Carey might make a match of it?'

'Good Lord, no! Carey was born to be a bachelor,' said Tombley, looking amused. They passed the other four pig houses, came to the farmyard gate and crossed to the house. Here, after some demur on the plea that the pigs were past their feeding time already, Tombley put on his thickest overcoat and then got into the night-dress of the ghost. It came down past his knees and – they had fixed the 'head-under-arm' part of the costume firmly into place before he began to dress up – soon he stood before her, a grim and horrible spectacle. The whole performance, exclusive of the fixing, had taken less than two minutes.

'And it was certainly all in one when Uncle Simith brought it home,' said Tombley, when Mrs Bradley had given him permission to take it off again. 'I myself took it to bits and hid the pieces separately.'

'Put it on again, child, and walk about. I want to see the effect.'

Obediently Tombley, in the semblance of a very tall, headless man with his horribly grinning head beneath his arm, paraded up and down. It was a sight Mrs Bradley had seen before at fancy dress parties aboard ship. She said, when at last she allowed him to take the costume off again, 'You'd make a very good ghost, child. Where did your uncle get a grey horse to ride on?'

'Oh, he'd have ridden old Neddy, the plough horse, I expect. You've seen the creature I mean. Why do you want to know?'

'Somebody rode over Folly Bridge on the night of Mr Fossder's death on a grey horse, child. Somebody rode one through Garsington on the same day, too.'

'You don't mean Uncle Simith was the ghost?'

'The person I mean certainly rode along the towing path towards Iffley. I cannot say how far along the towing path he went. At least –' She hesitated.

'Go on,' said Tombley. 'You can't think how much you interest me!'

'Tell me about your uncle and the horse.'

'How can I? I can safely say that if uncle had the choice between riding a horse and driving a car he'd plump for the horse every time. I can also say that if he didn't want to meet the people he knew about here, he would possibly go to Oxford by way of Garsington. But how is it you're so sure of him?'

'They grey horse cast a shoe.'

'Oh? Well, do you mind if I go and feed my pigs?'

'I thought you wanted to hear more about your uncle.'

Tombley hesitated. 'Well, yes, but the pigs come first.'

'Very well, child. But I want you to give me the ghost.'

'But what about the inspector?'

'Leave him to me. Goodbye for the present. Give Priest a message, will you?'

'Yes, if you want me to.'

'Tell him,' said Mrs Bradley very earnestly, 'to make himself scarce. Tell him I won't be held answerable if he remains in this neighbourhood any longer.'

'You want *me* to tell him this?'

'Why, yes, child, if you don't mind.'

'You really want me to tell the best pigman in Europe – perhaps in the world – to make himself scarce? To take himself off my land and out of my sight because you won't be answerable for the consequences if he stays? Is Priest the murderer? Don't you want him arrested?'

She did not give him an answer to his question.

'I want you to tell him what I say,' she said.

'But suppose the murderer is *never* arrested? What then?' demanded Tombley. Mrs Bradley looked at him and then looked away. He heard her sigh.

'Tell me, child,' she said casually, 'why *did* you shut the trap-door on top of Carey?' She began to fold up the fancy dress of the ghost. Tombley groaned.

'So you *knew* it was me! What *don't* you know, I wonder?'

When she had been given a piece of brown paper and string, she walked out with the parcel to her car. She handed the parcel to George.

'What hateful things leading questions are,' she said. 'But does that parcel remind you of anything, George?'

George took the parcel out again, and weighed it in his hands. His eyes met his employer's.

'Yes, madam, I'm afraid it does,' he said.

'Ah,' said Mrs Bradley. 'But we couldn't prove it, George. Stow it away again, child, and drive me back to Old Farm.'

Tombley followed her out.

'But how did you know it was me? Of course, I need hardly tell you that I didn't know Carey was down there until later.'

'I know that, child. I also knew that Fay did not go to Denmark with the money she borrowed from Jenny.'

'No, I went there for a fortnight and then I came back and we lived in a furnished flat not far from Hove.'

Mrs Bradley shuddered.

'But it was fine. I enjoyed it,' remonstrated Tombley. 'As a matter of fact, it seemed a palace to me after being used to the way this hole is furnished. Anyway, it struck me I ought to sneak over here just now and again to keep an eye on the pigs and so on. I've never been able to account for that pig we lost over Christmas. I can't really think Priest had it.'

'When I saw Fay that evening I had a suspicion that you were not far away.'

'You must have second sight. Well, when I saw that trapdoor open in the woodshed, I didn't stop to think. It occurred to me that if anybody found the fancy dress of the ghost down there I should soon get into trouble.'

'That, too, I deduced,' said Mrs Bradley. 'In fact, that was how I knew for certain that the ghost outfit was here at Roman Ending. As I knew the identity of the ghost, and that he was neither your uncle nor you, I could be pretty certain that I knew the reason for some at least of the curious deeds which have taken place in the neighbourhood since Christmas Eve.'

'Now off us goes,' said Ditch. He was in his proper place, top left, in the Morris side, and opposite him was Young Walt. Our Bob stood next to his father, and Pratt was next to Walt. The last pair were Carey and Tombley. Priest stood by and watched.

The dance was *Blue-eyed Stranger*. As the handkerchiefs were lowered to the dancers' sides, and Pratt wiped his face with his shirt-sleeve, Ditch fell out, and, laying aside his handkerchiefs, picked up his concertina.

'Now, Mester Priest,' he said. 'You take my place, will ee, and I'll gev ee all the toon with this 'ere.' So far, they had been humming as they danced. Priest took the top place, and Ditch, looking up at the north-east corner of the ceiling, began to play the air.

'It's like training a boat race crew,' said Carey to Tombley as they seated themselves on the table. 'What wouldn't I give for a drink!'

'Now peck up your stecks, and us'll do *Regs o'Marlow*,' Ditch commanded, picking up his own stick from the table. He took his place again at the top of the side and Priest took from a poacher's pocket in his coat a long reed instrument whose mouthpiece he wiped on his sleeve.

'Ull I gev ee the toon on this 'ere?'

'Ah, go on, Mester Priest, play er through again to see as ee've got er right, and never ee mind that there fancy fingeren. Just see as ee keps us moven.'

'Oh, ah. But I'll back I can manage the fingeren, too an' all. Like sweet'earts us be, this lettle whestle and me. Played er en Kirtlenton at the lamb-ale I ded, ah, long enough ago, afore Young Walt was born.'

'Oh, ah! Tell us another!' grinned Young Walt. Priest smiled, and, setting the oboe to his lips, he raised his eyes like a man who drinks good ale, and began to play the tune. It was lively, blood stirring music that set the feet moving involuntarily and brought all the dancers tapping their sticks very softly to the chorus.

'Now then, all,' said Ditch, and the dancers formed into line. Ditch crossed his stick on Young Walt's, and, standing straight legged and on the balls of his feet like the well made fellow he was, he held his well knit body easily and well, ready to begin the dance. As he looked in front of him with mild and level gaze, he seemed no unworthy keeper of a Mystery centuries old, a tradition venerated and honourable. Several times he stopped the dance to remonstrate with the dancers.

'Ee be coveren too much ground. Come up to et more sprightly, like, and not so grass-'opper flighty, Mester Pratt. And our Bob, do ee mind that there back-to-back. Ee knocked Mester Pratt on his shoulder when ee passed him a menute ago.'

'OK, our dad,' said Walt. He was really a very fine dancer, as became his father's son, but it was understood that Pratt must not be blamed for every mistake that was made.

'Tes too discouragen, poor chap,' said Mrs Ditch, in the bosom of the family, after the third or fourth practice, and Mrs Ditch's word was law.

'Now all of ee can rest off a bit,' said the trainer, sinking into a chair, 'and then us'll do the hey. Now ee recollects that the second man follers the first man round. No fancy trecks. Just foller, Mester Pratt, do ee see, and ee can't go wrong. Ah, and just you mind them there elbows o' yourn, Young Walt. You tweddles them hankerchers too bold, at times, for my liken.'

'Oh, ah,' said Young Walt pacifically, laying aside the ritual handerchiefs in order to find a secular one with which to mop his brow and wipe behind his ears.

'Now another rest for five menutes, and then I warnts ee all to put on the bells,' said Ditch. 'The dances don't seem like nothen without the bells.'

Out came the leather pads with their latten bells and the men took a pair each from the cloth in which they were wrapped, wiped the grease off the bells, gave the pads a shake and tied them on to their shins between knee and ankle, pulling the knees of their trousers up a little to give the knee joint full play.

'Now then, up, lads,' said Ditch, when the side were rested. 'Mester Priest, go ee en dancen this time and I'll strike up the toon. Start with the back-to-back, and on from there. Us needn't do the first two figures again, so long as Mester Pratt remembers right shoulders.'

'Oh, yes, I'm sorry,' said Pratt.

'Ef ee *don't* remember, ee'll have to stand down,' said Ditch, with unwonted sternness. 'Can't have ee messen all up. Tesn't en reason, that ben't, and let our mam say what her well. Ee'll 'ave to stand down en favour of Mester Carey's friend from London. He dances not too bad, and remembers what I tells him, too an' all. He'll be over again to these parts, come Whetsun, I reckon.'

Carey grinned, and confirmed this supposition. Pratt meekly bowed his head beneath the threat, and got through the dance very creditably.

'That'll do for tonight,' Ditch observed. 'Us'll do *Trunkles*, and *Bean-Setten*, and maybe *Country Gardens*, next time we meets, and all knows when that es. Now ee onderstands, Mester Priest, that ef lettle Mester Denis turns up with his lettle feddle, ee'll be the Morris Fool. But ef he *don't* show up come Whet-Sunday, like, ee dances where ee be now, and I plays the concertina, excepten for *Bean-Setten* and *Regs o' Marlow*, where we got the stecks to help out that there whestle ee be so fond of.'

'I onderstands,' said Priest, 'and I warnts to be the Fool. I ent no Apollinaris, as well I knows!'

'Well, *I'd* sooner dance like ner play,' Ditch remarked. 'My dancen days beant over yet, be a long chalk, or so I do pray.'

'Who's for a drink?' suggested Carey hospitably. He yodelled loudly and clearly, and Mrs Ditch came in with bottles of beer. They had turned her out of her kitchen whilst the dancing was being practised.

'And how do Mester Pratt be shapen now?' she enquired, as she studied his streaming brow with a mixture of Spartan calm and motherly interest.

'One will get it right if one *dies*! There is time to master it *yet*!' said Pratt, with enthusiasm.

'Well, of course, ee ent Headenton yet, and I doubt ef Bampton ud take ee,' said Ditch, deliberately, but not with unkind intent. 'Ee means well, Mester Pratt, us knows ee do, and that's the best us can say about ee at present, but ee're parseveren wonderful, I *well* say that.'

'One hoped one was improving,' ventured Pratt.

'Oh, ah, ee're emproven proper,' Ditch granted him magnanimously. 'Emproven famous, ee are. I don't say nothen about that. And come to Whetsun, ee'll do as well as us others, I make no doubt of et, like.'

'There now,' said Mrs Ditch. 'Ee mustn't lose heart, then, Mester Pratt, do ee see? Tesn't everybardy can dance the Morris, is et now, our dad?'

'Tes a Mestery,' said Ditch, 'a prarper Mestery, and very, very old. Tesn't right that nobody should be larnen of er too easy.'

Denis came down to Stanton St John in his Uncle Ferdinand's car on the Saturday before Whitsun, and spent two hours in the kitchen with Mrs Ditch, playing the Morris tunes on his violin. Mrs Bradley had a twenty minutes' interview with her son, and at the end of it Ferdinand returned to London. Carey and Ditch were superintending the storing of bottled beer, and Young Walt was feeding pigs. Our Bob was plucking and singeing a couple of fowls destined for Whit-Sunday dinner, and was listening with a critical, well informed ear to the notes of the violin.

'How's that, Bob?' Denis would ask, having played a tune six times.

'Ah, that's all right, Mester Denis.'

Mrs Ditch was ironing the Morris shirts, and pressing the dancers' white trousers. The shirts were of linen with beautifully pleated fronts and sleeves. The Morris costumes had been worn by the men on the last Monday evening practise, and since then Mrs Ditch had washed the clothes with proud and loving hands. When she had ironed the shirts, and pressed the white flannel trousers under damp cloths, she was to press out the ribbons and ribbon rosettes with which the dancers' costumes were always decorated. Denis laid down his violin.

'And how's the murder going, Mrs Ditch?'

'Now, now, Mester Denis!' Mrs Ditch began.

'Oh, rot! I *know* there has been a murder and it doesn't do me any harm to ask about it, does it? They haven't caught anybody yet.'

'The old lady, your great-auntie, is expecten to capture him on Monday,' said Mrs Ditch unwillingly. 'She seems to think he might interfere with that Priest while he's a-dancen, and then she can nab him up queck.'

'I say!' said Denis. 'How frightfully decent that would be! I say, I should like to see that! I say! I bet I stick to Aunt Bradley like a leech! I say, I shan't *need* to, shall I? I mean if I play for the dancing, I'll see it all happen, I suppose! I say! That's most *frightfully* decent! Thanks awfully for telling me, Mrs Ditch.'

'Now, none of your nonsense, Mester Denis! Ef anythen was to happen, why, what en the world should us do?'

'Did Aunt Bradley say *when* it would happen? Which dance, I mean, or anything definite, or anything?'

'Her ded not. Her can't tell, I reckon. And I, for one, don't like the sound of et. There's that there Mester Pratt. He've emproved quite wonderful these last two weeks, he 'ave, but 'twouldn't take much, I reckon, to throw him out, and then our dad'll be vexed, and so I tell ee.'

'I expect it will buck him up. The excitement, I mean. I jolly well know it will me! I bet I'll play better than ever on Monday, Mrs Ditch! Who's taking round the hat?'

'Et ought to be our dad, as trainer. The Fool is often the trainer,' said Mrs Ditch. 'But dad, he loves the dancen, and don't care so much for the foolen, and he've passed et on to that Priest, as done very well last year. But it seems as though the old lady have warned him of danger. He don't seem too happy, I don't thenk, some'ow, lately. Brooden and spiteful, he is, and got somethen on his conscience, I shouldn't wonder. And our Lender playen up, and never comen 'ome to him at all. Oh, dear! Now I dedn't ought to 'ave telled ee that!'

'It's quite all right,' said Denis. 'I won't tell anyone else.'

Mrs Ditch laughed and blessed his innocent heart. Denis looked grieved, and decided to change the subject.

'Have you found out any more about the priest's hole, Mrs Ditch?'

'Speaken for myself, I have not. But your great-auntie, the old lady, had a try to get back 'ere from underneath the woodshed at Roman Enden, but nothen come of et. Goes round and round, that passage do, or so our Lender telled me long enough ago. Used to be a very old 'ouse there, I ded 'ear, one time and another, and they'd be part of the foundations, likely as not, I reckon. Ef ee warnts to know how to get out of that there priest hole, or whatever ee likes to call et, go up to the lettle old double-u – I expect ee knows where I mean – and take up the oilcloth on the floor. Mind how ee goes, and be careful down they steps, else ee'll break your neck afore Monday, and then et'll be who'd a-thought et!'

'I can hear someone calling,' said Denis suddenly. He put down his violin, and opened the kitchen door.

'It's Hugh,' he said. 'He's shouting to know if there's anybody at home. I suppose the carrier has just brought him over from the Plain.'

'That means lunch time, then. Go ee and get Mester Carey,' commanded Mrs Ditch.

They all went the round of the pig houses after lunch, and then Hugh and Mrs Bradley became audience, and Mrs Ditch critic-in-chief, whilst the Morris side performed for the very last time before the great annual display during Whitsun week. The side wore their working trousers and tennis shoes, and were in their shirt sleeves, except for Maurice Pratt, who was dressed in shorts and a singlet. His long thin body looked longer and thinner than ever, and drooped, in the picturesque phrase of Young Walt, 'like a daffy-delly as have er 'ead too 'eavy for her stalk.'

He commended this simile to Carey, who laughed and smacked his head, and it was in light-hearted fashion that the rehearsal proceeded. Even Ditch, dancing as well as ever, forbore to stop the music, or offer any criticism, and Pratt, to the surprise of his companions and to his own relief, made not a single mistake.

On Whit-Sunday morning, Mrs Bradley rose very early, and, having made herself a cup of tea, walked through the little wood and across the fields to Roman Ending. Priest was in the entrance to one of the pig houses, mixing pig food. His face brightened when he saw her.

'I got they pictures, mam, ee was arsken me about. Here em be. Mester Lestrange brought em over, all coloured pretty like this ere, last night.'

He produced the two little shields. On one was the Chief Dancetté, on the other the Bâton Sinister.

'Interesting,' said Mrs Bradley, taking them away and putting them into her pocket. 'But you haven't received any others, drawn in pencil? Just these from Mr Lestrange?'

'That's all, mam. Gev me last night.'

'Well, now, I think you had better get away at once. You say you've got relations living in Berkshire. I should go to them today. I'll get George to drive you over. Keep hidden until after tomorrow night. Then you can come back here.'

'But I can't be away all day tomorrow, mam! What about that there dancen?' Priest protested.

'I can't help the dancing. They'll have to find somebody else.'

'Damned ef they do,' said Priest. 'No, mam, et ent no good. I be goen to dance the Morris Fool tomorrow. I don't know why ee've pecked on me to be the next one murdered, and I don't take et very kind. Suppose I *'ave* behaved like a fool over Mester Semeth when I found him in wi' Nero, what's that got to do with me be-en murdered? That's what I'd like to know. I en't goen to be murdered! Bless ee, I ent done nothen to be murdered *for*!'

'You know, you're a stupid fellow,' said Mrs Bradley severely, 'and if you're going to be obstinate – still more, if you tell me all these silly lies – I'll leave you to your fate, whatever it is!' She drew near to him and looked him in the eyes. 'You killed a pig on Christmas morning. You took the body of Simith out of Nero's sty on Boxing Night. You went to fetch Mr Lestrange's boar at one o'clock the next morning. You helped to take Simith's body over to Shotover Common. You helped to drench it in pig's blood to mislead the public into thinking that the killing was done at Sho-tover instead of at Roman Ending. You –'

'Killen o' the peg, or killen o' the man?' enquired Priest with an expression of childlike innocence upon his ugly face.

'You've been a living menace to the murderer ever since. On top of all that, do you *really* think he'll spare you?' demanded Mrs Bradley, without answering his question.

She waited a moment for an answer to her own, but none, it seemed, was forthcoming. Priest went on stirring the pig mixture, his repulsively ugly countenance now in complete repose.

'Why don't ee 'ave me arrested, and 'ave done with et?' he enquired.

'Because I can't frighten the murderer yet, with advantage. You ought to see that.'

'Meanen ee can't get him 'anged, cos ee ent got et black enough again him? Meanen too and all, as ee can't prove nothen agen me?'

'Meaning just that, my good fellow.'

'Who know ee've come over 'ere s'mornen?'

'Nobody, so far as I am aware. You could murder me with confidence – I don't say with impunity, although that, too, might be true.'

'Then I'm damned ef I don't have a try! Ee've pestered me these seven or eight weeks good.' He lifted the stick with which he was stirring the pig food.

'Tes iron!' he yelled, as he brought it down with a swing. Mrs Bradley leapt nimbly aside, and the descending bar struck the top of the copper, in front of which she was standing, with so much force that a sharp pain flew up Priest's arm almost to the elbow and he dropped the weapon in order to hold his wrist. Mrs Bradley picked up the iron bar, and handled it as though it had been a rapier.

'Quick march, outside,' she said, as she gave him a vicious poke. He swung on her, but a smart push in the diaphragm settled

268

his hash. He doubled up. Mrs Bradley poked him upright. He turned, and, cursing her, began to walk to the door. Half-way up the centre gangway, he essayed a surprise attack, and received another jab.

'Ee'll enjure me for life, that's what ee'll do!'

'So would the hangman, if you had killed me,' said Mrs Bradley, laughing.

Her tone, however, was so implacable, and her behaviour so much at variance with that which he had always expected from her sex, that he thought it might be as well to comply with her wishes. She marched him up to the house and suddenly electrified him at the very door by blowing shrilly three times upon her fingers, and bringing Tombley out in protest.

Tombley was sketchily dressed in pyjamas and a blazer, and had not shaved.

'Good morning, Geraint,' said Mrs Bradley, grinning. 'Has there been any post this morning?'

'Well, no. It's Sunday. What are you doing with Priest?'

'Teaching him the art of self-defence. You can go back and feed the pigs now, Priest, if you want to.'

'Half a minute, Priest,' said Tombley. 'A letter came for you last night. Your speaking about the post reminded me,' he said to Mrs Bradley.

'I thought it might,' said Mrs Bradley, with her disquieting grin.

'Here you are,' said Tombley, handing it over.

'Ent got a stamp on,' said Priest, turning the envelope over in his hand. He seemed to be very uneasy, and was obviously in no hurry to open it.

'Open it, man,' cried Tombley, who seemed to be equally uneasy, 'or give it here to me! Anyone would think it would bite you!'

'Ee better 'ave et, then. My readen ent all that flowent.' And Priest, apparently glad to be relieved of the responsibility of opening the missive, hastily pushed it into his employer's hand. Tombley tore it open. Inside was a sheet of rough unlined paper, and on it were drawn two little shields. The first bore the device of the Chief Dancetté, as Mrs Bradley herself had sketched it out for Carey to copy, and the second showed the Bâton Sinister, also according to her prophecy.

'Why, what on earth is this!' exclaimed Tombley, holding the paper at arm's length as though it had the power to do him harm. He looked at Mrs Bradley. 'It's like the paper Uncle had on him when he died.'

'Oh, you knew about that, Geraint, did you?' said Mrs Bradley. Priest looked at her, and muttered uneasily something she did not catch. Then he went slouching off, leaving the paper still in Tombley's hand.

'Oh, dear! He'll want this stick thing,' said Mrs Bradley. She aimed it high in the air. It turned over once like a caber and came to rest about twenty paces in front of the astonished pigman. He walked forward and picked it up, and then turned round to look back in the direction from which it had come. Mrs Bradley waved her hand and went into the house with Tombley.

At tea-time the inspector and a constable appeared at the door of Old Farm.

'What now?' enquired Mrs Bradley, taking the inspector into the garden to look at the early roses.

'Outrage in the church of St Peter ad Vincula at South Newington, mam.'

'Where is South Newington, inspector?'

'It's on the River Oke, mam, and also lays between Chipping Norton and Banbury.'

'Don't tell me there's some connection between the outrage, whatever it is, and the murder of Becket, inspector.'

The inspector gaped at her.

'Then ee've 'eard about the similar outrage en the Cathedral, mam?'

'No. But if you are going to mention the Becket window –'

'Well, I be jiggered, mam! Ee *do* know all about et, say what ee well contrary.' He gazed at her in honest admiration. Mrs Bradley grinned and shook her head.

'I assure you I have heard nothing, dear child,' she said. 'Recapitulate, if you please. Charlie won't mind hearing it all again.'

The fresh-faced constable smiled, and strolled away out of earshot.

'The report come en last night about South Newington, and in view of them earlier outrages which ee always thought had some connection with this 'ere case, I 'opped over there meself en the car with Charlie, to see into et like, on the spot. Nothen to find out really, any more than there was at Sandford and Horsepath. Just a bet of paper – that adhesive stuff they sells in rolls all ready gummed to use – ee've seen the tack, I suppose? – pasted on the wall en the shape of an arrow, and the point of the arrow pointing to the wall painting they oncovered there some while back, showen the murder of Becket. I never should a-knowed that that was what et was, ef I hadn't asked the parson.'

'And the Cathedral outrage?' Mrs Bradley enquired.

'Nothen much. Pretty much the same as t'other. Another paper arrow stuck on the wall, pointen to the window that shows the murder of Becket. Here's the arrow. We couldn't get et off whole.'

'A comfort the murderer doesn't do much damage in the churches,' said Mrs Bradley. 'In fact, he seems to be a person of sensibility and refinement. Well, look here, child. Tomorrow you shall make your arrest. And there won't be any difficulty about it. In fact, you may even have the extreme felicity of seeing the murder committed, since I cannot persuade the victim to stay away from the revels.'

'And who be the victim, mam?' enquired the inspector.

'The pigman, Priest, of course,' replied Mrs Bradley. 'You really ought to offer him police protection.'

'Just as you say, mam,' replied the inspector doubtfully. ''Ere, Charlie, I warnts ee,' he called. The youthful constable came up.

'Get on your bike and run over to Lettlemore, well ee, and bring back young Billy Middlen on your step. I be goen to put the two on ee on to Priest, and see ef ee can stop him be-en murdered! Be good practice for ee! Bet of Scotland Yard work for a change!'

When the inspector had gone, Mrs Bradley walked into the house. The first person she met was Denis. He was looking very solemn and excited, and was obviously bursting with news.

'I say, Aunt Bradley!'

'Say on, dear child.'

'I *say*, you know, old Hugh has had one of those papers!'

'What papers, child, do you mean?'

'You know – those little shields. Or, rather, just one little shield. He's in a frightful stew. He thinks he's going to be killed, like those two old men who got them.'

'And what is on the shield this time?'

'Well, it's really only a hand, but what seems to scare him is that this hand is the left one. Is the left hand worse than the right, Aunt Bradley, or something?'

'It depends upon the meaning one attaches to the word "sinister," child, you see. I think Hugh does very well to be alarmed. There is still Whit-Monday to come, however, and the Morris men . . . "their pypers pyping, their drummers thundering, their stumpes dauncing, their belles jyngling, their handkerchiefs fluttering about their heads like madde men, their hobbie horses . . ." how does it go on?'

Carey came in, laughing.

' ". . . and other monsters skirmishing amongst the throng," ' he said.

Mrs Bradley looked at him and sighed.

CHAPTER 17

All In and Call at Stanton St John

Whit-Monday morning was brilliant. Ditch was up at half-past four, and Mrs Ditch was taking early morning tea to Mrs Bradley less than half an hour later.

'Be ee comen to see they lads of ourn a-dancen round the may-pole afore em do begin the Morris prarper?' she enquired, as Mrs Bradley, drawing a magenta wrapper round her thin old shoulders, took the tea and commenced to sip it delicately. Mrs Bradley raised her bright black eyes. She looked more like a witch than ever, Mrs Ditch decided, and, superstition triumphant for once in her usually practical mind, she crossed her fingers, averted her gaze and looked towards the window. A rose, stirred gently by an early morning breeze, knocked gently against the open casement, and a bird on the sill flew suddenly and noisily away towards the heavy, summer trees.

'I shall get up immediately,' Mrs Bradley said.

'Very good, mam. Ef ee 'earkens en a menute, ee'll be 'earen the Morris tune. That be to call the dancers, and when ee 'ears et, ee might as well be getten up, like, see?'

'Perfectly,' said Mrs Bradley. She finished her tea and Mrs Ditch took the cup and went away. Sure enough, in a little while, the sound of a thin tune liltingly played on a violin came in at the open window. She got out of bed, a thin little yellow faced woman, upright, and curiously vivacious even in her quietest movements, and walked across the room to look out on to the farmyard. Near the gate stood Denis in flannels and school blazer, his violin under his chin, his bow in his thin brown hand, a silk scarf about his neck with the ends dangling down in front, and – shades of the public school to which he was going in the autumn! – a wreath of artificial roses placed sideways on his thick, fair hair. Mrs Bradley put her head out and screamed at him like a macaw.

'Come down!' bellowed Denis. 'It's glorious out here this morning! Carey says I'm the Queen of the May!' He gave the ridiculous wreath a further shove to the side.

'You look Bacchanalian, child! *I* want a wreath!' cried his great-aunt, withdrawing her head. Very soon she was dressed and downstairs. Carey met her as she got to the front door of the house.

'Scab is playing the Morris tune to get the dancers together. Hugh's idea,' he said. 'Hugh and Tombley are mowing the grass in front of Roman Ending. That's where the dancers finish up. They'll dance in the village first, then we shall have the sit-down lunch in our yard – we're borrowing tables from every house in the village, I should think! – then they're going to dance here, and again outside the church, and last of all we're going to Roman Ending, where Tombley's giving a tea. It's going to be marvellous weather! Come and have breakfast. Scab will be in in a minute. He's got to play that tune once more outside the vicarage, that's all. We won't wait breakfast for Hugh, as he isn't a dancer. I've got to get into my whites when I've fed the pigs, and then we're all set until lunch time.'

'Delightful!' said Mrs Bradley. 'And here is our friend the inspector!'

'Ask him to breakfast, then.' Carey lifted his head and yodelled for Mrs Ditch. She appeared with a large blue pinafore completely covering the front of her very best bodice and skirt. Her face shone, polished as an apple, and her hair was drawn so tightly back from her temples, that it seemed as though the combs that held it in place must surely burst from their moorings and drift her grey hairs to the breeze.

'Delightful,' said Mrs Bradley. She herself was wearing a costume of pale purple cloth. In lieu of the wreath she had craved, she wore on her head a small toque completely covered with yellow velvet pansies. Her shooting stick stood in the corner, and in the capacious pocket of her skirt was a life preserver of handy weight and size.

'Aha!' she said. 'Inspector!'

The inspector put his head in, over a window box of yellow calceolaria.

'Present, mam, and Charlie is en the lane.'

'Fetch him along,' said Carey. 'Come and have breakfast, both of you.'

Hugh returned to find them at the last-cup-of-coffee stage. Mrs Ditch brought him ham and eggs and blackpudding. Denis, who had returned to the house soon after the commencement of the meal, had gone again, his wreath still stuck on his head. Carey looked at the clock.

'Time I fed those pigs and got changed,' he said, getting up and leaving the table. Mrs Bradley got up and followed him.

'I suppose you haven't seen Priest this morning?' she said.

'Well, no, I haven't. But he's due over here in half an hour or so. We begin outside the "George," go on to the "Star" and then the "White Horse," then we dance in the road by the gate of the church before we come back here. We have to have rests in between, and it's Priest's job, as Fool, you know, to keep the crowds back to give us room to dance, and then when we *have* danced, to collect the money. He's not a bit a good man for the job, I'm afraid. The Fool is supposed to make jokes and keep the crowd jolly, so that they'll part with their cash, but you know what a taciturn devil he is – never has a word to say unless it's in answer to a question.'

'Does he paint his face?'

'Yes, I think so. Perhaps he'll black it this year. Hugh wanted a hobby-horse, but we've never had one, and Ditch didn't want innovations. Not that the hobby-horse is really an innovation. It's as old as the hills – well, as old as the Morris, anyway, I should think. What are you going to do? Coming with me to feed the pigs?'

'Yes, I'll come with you while you're still fond of me,' Mrs Bradley said, grinning. Her grin was not mirthful. It was a grimace of distaste and anxiety. Carey looked at her.

'What's up, love? Sickening for something?'

'No, child, I don't think so.'

'Cheer up, then! All's well and the weather fine!'

'All isn't well, and I think it's going to thunder before midnight.'

'One confesses,' said Pratt to Mrs Bradley, who, with Jenny, Fay and Hugh, was walking from Old Farm to the rendezvous of the dancers for the commencement of the display, 'to a feeling of nervousness to which one can only compare one's emotions on the occasion of one's first cricket match.'

'Oh, do you play cricket?' Mrs Bradley enquired. Jenny broke in on the question before Pratt could frame a reply.

'Play cricket? I should think he does! He's a jolly good deep field, and is one of the reserves for the county.'

'The county,' said Pratt, with modesty, 'is weak this season, one fears.'

Mrs Bradley regarded his weedy form with new respect.

'Have you got your Morris stick, Maurice?' Fay asked suddenly.

'One believes that the leader, Ditch, is responsible for the properties.'

'It's a big responsibility for Ditch,' Mrs Bradley observed. 'I do hope he's going to feel that the day is worth it.'

'It's a bigger responsibility for me,' said Carey, as he dropped behind for a moment to tie up a trailing boot lace. 'I've got to feed the village.' The others began to linger, but Mrs Bradley made a sign to Jenny, and she walked on ahead, with her half-sister and Hugh in tow.

'Very nicely done, child. Now I must say it quickly. Look out for yourself. Don't worry, but, if in doubt, hit out with your Morris stick as if you were hitting a six. Be no respecter of persons. Don't stop to think, "It can't be". Hit your hardest!'

'But whom am I to look out for?'

'If I told you that, you would give the game away.'

'One hopes that one is discreet, as Pratt would say.'

'Yes, yes, I know. But, child, be guided by me. The police *must* catch this man! I can't have another murder. I couldn't prevent the first two, but I can and will prevent this. I'm warning you because your nerves will stand it.'

'I'm a long sight less certain of that than you appear to be.'

'You had better pull yourself together, then, and take heart of grace, dear child. And just look after Jenny when the Morris dancing is finished. That girl is in love with you, Carey. Now forget all this, and dance your very best. Nothing will happen until after lunch, I promise!'

They caught up the others, who were loitering.

'Maurice Pratt has been telling us that he no longer knows his right hand from his left,' said Jenny, giggling.

'Rotten to get the needle,' said Hugh sympathetically. 'Never mind, Pratt. It'll be over long before tomorrow.'

'One realises that. One finds peculiarly little comfort in the thought. However, one is grateful for all kind words and good wishes.' He looked at Jenny. Jenny kindly took his hand in hers and gave it a heartening squeeze.

'Cheer up, duckie,' she said. 'Look, here we are.'

A sizable crowd of villagers had gathered, and augmenting them were dozens of people who had come in cars and on bicycles, in pony carts, wagons and tradesmen's vehicles, to see the dancing and join in all the fun. Prominent in the throng, and keeping them back with sweeps of a calf's tail tied on to the end of a stick, was the pigman Priest. The bladder which dangled at the opposite end of the stick he disdained to use, but whacked out

277

with grim pleasure with the tail to clear a space for the dancers. He was unrecognisable, even apart from the tradition that the Morris men are unrecognisable by the rest of the villagers, for he had blacked his face except for two vermilion streaks on his cheek-bones, and was wearing a low crowned hat from which numbers of coloured streamers covered not only his shoulders but most of his face as well.

'Looks pretty grim,' said Hugh, with a laugh, as they came to the outskirts of the crowd and began to manoeuvre for a good position from which to see the dancing. Seeing them, Priest suddenly raised a shout, and clove his way through to Mrs Bradley, whom he ushered into the centre of the circle he had cleared.

'Come on, my gal,' he said to her, in ringing tones and with a kind of savage good humour. 'Look, neighbours! 'Ere er be! Old Mrs Moll, the wetch!'

Mrs Bradley smiled her saurian smile, snatched his ribboned hat, and substituted for it her toque of yellow pansies. The low crowned beaver with its myriad streamers she perched on her own black hair, and then, picking up her skirts, she danced a wild pas seul to the music of *Bean-Setting* which Denis, nearly doubled up with laughter, was playing on his violin at twice the usual pace. This by-play was well received by the crowd, and the Morris men took their places to begin the dance as soon as Mrs Bradley had taken back her own hat and Priest had dashed into the public house to rearrange his on his head in front of a mirror.

Mrs Bradley slipped out of the ring again, and rejoined Hugh, Fay and Jenny, and, with them, moved on behind the dancers to the next public house outside which the dancing was to be continued. Pratt was dancing well. She saw Ditch pat his shoulder as the Morris men moved off along the road, Priest still keeping order with his wand of ceremonies.

Lunch was a happy affair. Priest counted out the money and handed it over to Ditch, who took it into Old Farm kitchen where Mrs Ditch deposited it before going out with the food. Linda had come home to help, having got the day off from service, and seven or eight girls from the village also served at the tables. It was open house to the villagers, and nearly two hundred people sat down in the open air, having brought their own chairs or stools to sit on, and their own mugs and plates for the food and drink. A barrel of beer was on tap, and another of cider. Jokes were cracked, songs sung, Tombley's gramophone was playing part of the time, and Carey's health was drunk.

'And now, friends,' said Carey, 'we're going to dance again as soon as we've had time to get our dinner down.'

So they danced again, and Mrs Bradley, pleading a fatigue which in fact she did not feel, went into the house and up to her room. She threw herself on to the bed and bounced up and down until the springs protested loudly, a sound that could be heard in the courtyard below. Then she rose without a sound, and tip-toed along the landing and, entering the privy in which the passage from the priest hole came out, she drew aside the floor covering, raised the hatch, and descended the steps. Gaining the priest's hole, she observed that the door in the panelling had been left ajar in accordance with her instructions, and, scarcely drawing breath, she pushed it open and entered the sunny parlour. Keeping below the lower level of the window, she seated herself on a very low stool which she herself had placed there in the early morning, and waited patiently.

Outside the window Denis struck up the tune of *Constant Billy*, and in a minute the dancers were off, the sound of bells coming clearly and loudly into the room where she sat. She strained her ears, listening for another sound, and very soon she heard it. It was the sound of footsteps ascending the stone stairs. She waited until she was certain that the person ascending had reached the landing above, then, life preserver in hand, she sallied forth, a small, indomitable woman, watchful eyed, and armed with a grimness which her friends would not have recognised. She crept to her bedroom door, and turned the key which she had left on the outside. Then she went downstairs again and back into the parlour.

'Now I wonder whether I've treed the right person, or caged some unfortunate innocent,' she said to Mrs Ditch, when the latter came in to ask about getting the tea.

'That was Mr Hugh went upstairs, mam,' said Mrs Ditch, having learned that all the people from Old Farm proposed to go over to Roman Ending for tea.

'Mr Hugh? Oh dear, oh dear! I wonder whether you'd mind going up and letting him out, Mrs Ditch?' said Mrs Bradley with a chuckle. 'Tell him I left my handbag up there, and thought I'd better return and lock the door. Don't tell him I thought I was locking a would-be murderer in!'

'Ee don't mean ee thought someone was after ee, like, to murder ee, mam?' said Mrs Ditch in mild surprise. Mrs Bradley cackled, and went outside to see some more of the dancing. Priest seemed quite to have shed his boisterous mood of the morning, and was sitting on an upturned bucket, his head in his hands, a prey to morbid thoughts. His low crowned hat was on the ground beside him.

'Cheer up, Priest! It won't be very long now,' she murmured as she passed him. Priest looked up with the ghost of a grin on his ugly visage.

''Taint that so much. But thes 'ere 'at weighs about ten ton I'll back.'

'Never mind. Put it on,' said Mrs Bradley briefly. Priest took up the hat, and then, avoiding her eye, he slunk away, trailing his calf's tail and bladder dejectedly in the dust, until he reached a group of boys who were clustered round the entrance to the little tent which housed the barrel of ale. He flicked them away and went in. Carey had pitched this tent in the paddock adjoining the farmyard, and Priest was followed, not only by the shouts of the boys he had driven away, but also by the envious eyes of the dancers, who, having finished their dance, were resting before commencing upon the next one.

Mrs Bradley looked up at her bedroom window, but there was no sign of an imprisoned and gesticulating Hugh, so she concluded that Mrs Ditch had obeyed instructions and released him. She put a stool on top of a trestle table, and mounted aloft, like the umpire at a tennis match, to watch the Morris men in the dance called *Laudnum Bunches*.

As the dance proceeded, out came the Morris Fool from the beer tent. It seemed as though a drink had done him good, for he began to dance and flick at the dancers playfully with the bladder which was tied on to one end of his stick. He seemed to be making a special butt of Pratt. Again and again the bladder flicked round Pratt's head, confusing him, and once or twice causing mistakes in the dance. Pratt grew annoyed, and the villagers who were watching began to laugh, rather enjoying the clowning. The dance concluded, the Fool leapt away, to be out of the way of reprisals.

'Ee'd needn't overdo et, Priest,' called Ditch. 'Us all knows ee've ben en that there tent, you know!'

This sally provoked a roar from the good humoured crowd, and the Fool waved a mocking hand in reply, and, to the obvious irritation of the dancers, went into the tent again. Mrs Bradley scrambled down from her perch, and, amid roars of laughter, darted after him and pulled him out by the tail of his shirt, which had somehow come out of his trousers, and, to the almost hysterical joy of the onlookers, was flapping briskly as he ran back towards the Morris side which was forming up for *Blue-Eyed Stranger*.

Blue-Eyed Stranger was a handkerchief dance, and Mrs Bradley had asked, as a special favour to her, that Carey and Tombley might be allowed to take the top place in it. The Fool again began his antics, although twice Ditch shouted angrily at him. In one of the figures the dancers had to cross over, and as this happened the Fool struck out at Carey. Carey dodged aside and tripped him up. Down he sprawled, amid laughter, and quick as lightning Mrs Bradley was in the dance as well, her life preserver in her hand. Amid shouts of dismay, and to the general consternation, she struck at the writhing figure on the ground until it lay there motionless.

'Into the beer tent, some of you!' she called. There was a general rush. The foremost entered. The others waited round the entrance. Suddenly there was a shout. Two men came out, carrying between them a third who hung, a dead weight, in their hands. His face was black, streaked with red. Otherwise he was fair skinned and naked. Somebody took off a jacket and put it over him.

'Bring him here to the dancers,' called Mrs Bradley. 'We'll finish this as it began.' They brought him over and laid him beside the other prostrate Fool.

'Gather round, dancers,' said Mrs Bradley authoritatively. 'Magic killed, and magic can cure. Make wide lines, and dance *Bean-Setting*, Morris men, please.' While they danced, she knelt beside the men, and appeared to be bathing their faces. Denis, round-eyed with amazement, struck up the tune. The men, obedient to their Mystery, commenced the dance, and dibbing and striking, tapped out the rhythm, and watched, amazed, as the naked man apparently rose from the dead with the pigment all removed from his face – Mrs Bradley's handkerchief was covered with butter! – and, wrapping the jacket modestly about him, picked up the calf's tail and bladder and gave the stick into Mrs Bradley's hand. The fully clad Fool took longer to recover, but when he did sit up, Denis raised a shout.

'I say! Oh, look! It's Hugh!'

Hugh Kingston struggled to his feet. But, almost before he could gain them, two men stepped forward, and one laid a hand on his shoulder.

'It was foolish of him to persist in his intention. I even warned him. I sent him the Sinister Hand,' said Mrs Bradley. She picked up the Fool's stick, which was heavily weighted, and handed it to Tombley. 'Feel it,' she said.

Tea was over and the excited villagers had all been persuaded to go home. 'Luckily the steel hat which Priest was wearing was more than equal to the strain. He was hit on the head the minute he entered that tent where the murderer, who had blacked his face in the house, was lying in wait for him. He was going back to make sure he had finished the job when I ran after him and pulled him out again.'

'I think you're a marvel,' said Tombley, handing the stick to Pratt. 'This is the Batôn Sinister, I suppose?'

'One finds it difficult, if not impossible,' said Pratt, 'to imagine how you finally discovered the identity of the murderer. Are we really to believe that Mr Kingston – one cannot bring oneself, somehow, to refer to him by his baptismal name – murdered Mr Fossder and Mr Simith, and attempted to murder Priest?'

'It was easy enough to discover the identity of the murderer. The difficulty has been to prove it to the satisfaction of others.' She looked at Carey, who was sitting, glum and unhappy, at the opposite end of the table. 'To begin with, there was Hugh's character. He was timid; he loved to kill things; and he was conceited.'

'But how do you know he was? You never saw him like that when he was here,' said Carey, surprised. Mrs Bradley wagged her head.

'I didn't see it all at once, of course, child. But do you remember telling Denis one day that Hugh was afraid to play games against the masters when you were both at school?'

'But you couldn't go by that! To begin with, I meant it in joke. To go on with, plenty of chaps bar playing against the masters.'

'Then plenty of chaps are timid,' said his aunt, with her sea-serpent grin. 'At any rate, you agree he loved to kill things.'

'But once again –'

'Very well, child. Once again, plenty of chaps are murderers in embryo or by proxy. You won't deny he was conceited.'

'Conceit is a relative term.'

'I know. Do you remember his saying that one of your sows was the only female who had ever taken a dislike to him except for the lady who gave out the prizes at school one year?'

'But, hang it all, Aunt Adela –'

'Have it your own way, child. Now, as to the murders themselves, the first thing that intrigued me in connection with the death of Mr Fossder was that Hugh had taken Jenny for that walk along the towing path in the course of which she stumbled over the body.'

'They went in chase of old Fossder to get him to go home because Tombley wouldn't keep the appointment, and the night was so beastly cold,' protested Carey.

'It was Hugh's suggestion, child, not Jenny's. I took care to find out. I should have thought that a young man's instinct would have been to return with the girl to Old Farm without delay. The time was then past midnight.

'Well, as we know, they found Fossder. Jenny tumbled over him. Now I found out from George that Hugh had already gone after Fossder once to warn him that Tombley did not intend to keep the appointment. There seemed singularly little object in going again unless – an idea which came to me fairly early in the case – Hugh wanted a witness to the finding of the body, a witness who was – forgive me, Jenny! – both innocent and fairly ignorant.

'Later, when I heard about the will, it struck me that of all the beneficiaries Hugh stood to lose the most if Jenny were to be disinherited. The money, you remember, was to go, not to the girls themselves, but to their husbands. Hugh was a poor man. He was employed as librarian in a London suburb. He was solvent, I know, and apparently had no debts; nevertheless the money he would inherit if he married Jenny would make a tremendous difference in his life. Fossder, he knew, was inclined to speculate, and was inclined to be lucky. The chances were that by marrying Jenny he would gain several thousand pounds.

'The point about Fossder's death that made the police suspicious, and upon which they undoubtedly would have acted had there been the slightest suspicion of foul play, was the ridiculous wager. A bet of two hundred pounds made in such circumstances made me think that the person who laid such a bet must have a very strong reason for wanting to get Fossder to Sandford that night. It was not easy to trace this bet to Hugh, but, as his Post Office savings were suspiciously small for a young man contemplating marriage, I concluded that he had a banking account to draw on, and that the two hundred pounds came out of it.'

'But the bet took not only Fossder to Sandford, but Tombley, too,' said Carey.

'Tombley, too.' She nodded. 'Well, it seemed to me – this all came later, of course – that Fossder must have told Hugh, in a frank and honourable way, that he proposed to disinherit Jenny. Before that could be done, Hugh decided to kill Fossder. He knew that for Fossder to get a shock, or to have to run very fast, was enough to cause his death, and he thought he saw a way to kill him without the slightest risk to himself. The mistake was his choice of a locality in which to carry out the deed. Instead of the utterly deserted landscape he had anticipated, the whole performance was seen and heard – more heard than seen, as the night was dark – by a very cruel old man.'

'Simith,' said Pratt. 'But what was he doing there at that time of night? He was the horseman who went through Garsington in the daytime. That was never in doubt, but how did he – ?'

'I thought at first that he went to spy upon his nephew, for he probably knew about the bet. Later I decided it might have been for another reason. He might have been going to meet Fossder at some house or other, to witness Fossder's new will.'

'What, the one disinheriting Jenny?'

'Exactly. Mind, we shall never know for certain which it was. No will was found on the body, but Hugh would have searched the pockets. I imagine that the will was one of the subjects brought up by Simith when he sent for Hugh to go to Roman Ending. You remember the gramophone, Carey? That was an excuse to get Hugh over there, so that he could torture him by describing the ghost and its activities on the towing path on Christmas Eve. Simith also described in detail, I have no doubt, the fancy dress the ghost had worn, and which he himself had impounded.'

'Why didn't Kingston chuck the clothes into the river?' Carey enquired. 'That's what I should have done.'

'I don't know whether he heard suspicious sounds – Simith coming along on his horse, perhaps – or whether he hoped, if anything ever came up later on, to try to incriminate Tombley, whose reason for failing to keep the appointment he probably knew. Well, that accounts for the murder of Simith. It was the direct result of the murder of Fossder, you see.'

'Uncle Simith got what he asked for,' said Tombley. 'And Priest has behaved like a fool. What do you think?'

'Priest knows!' said Mrs Bradley. 'Of course, the attack on you, Carey, was due to the fact that today Hugh has seen for the first time something which his vanity has not permitted him to see sooner – Jenny's obvious preference for you. There was also some attempt to put *me* out of the way. He discovered, too late, that I was more dangerous to his safety than he had thought.'

'Did you get anything from those little shields?' asked Carey.

'Not at first, except that they helped to eliminate from my list of suspected persons people like Priest and Linda Ditch. Hugh, as I realised very early in the enquiry, was in the most favourable position of anybody to obtain all the necessary oddments of information which kept cropping up in the case. I was able to verify all my suspicions in this direction on Easter Monday, when I obtained special permission to visit the library in which Hugh worked. From a book on Heraldry which I saw there he could have obtained the models for those little shields, and the library also contained a county directory of Berkshire, Buckinghamshire and Oxfordshire which gave notes on the churches in addition to other information. There was a book describing some of the villages round here, and there were also the Morris Book, and, in the Reading Room, the current number of the *EFDS News*. Denis will remember the challenge, that I accepted, to place a quotation from it. In the Reference Library, there was even a little book about the Boar's Head tavern in Eastcheap – the one referred to in Shakespeare's *Henry IV* from which Hugh quoted.'

'So Priest did help Hugh Kingston in the murder of Simith?' said Carey, later on, when he was alone with Mrs Bradley.

'He helped to get Simith's body out of Nero's sty, he took your boar Hereward out and carted him over to Shotover, and he killed the pig for Hugh and poured the blood on the body as it lay on Shotover Common.'

'Didn't Simith hear the pig being killed?'

'I expect Priest took it to the other side of the little wood. Tombley, of course, was at church. Simith had already seen Hugh Kingston that morning, and the pig was killed on Christmas Day, you remember. There was no doubt in my mind that Priest was willing to help *anyone* to be revenged on Simith. He owed him something for Linda.'

'Yes, I see that. What I can't understand is that Kingston should have turned on him like that.'

'Hugh was timid. Too timid to trust Priest. I thought at first that Priest might be blackmailing him, but that was not the case. That was why I found it almost impossible to convince Priest of his danger. He could not believe that Hugh had turned against him, and wanted him out of the way. Hugh, for his part, did not see that by incriminating him – if it ever came to that! – Priest would have incriminated himself as well.

'Hugh had to square his conscience all the time. That is another point we must not altogether lose sight of. He tried to do this by sending the warning messages – the little shields, and the arrows in the churches, for example. His guilty conscience may have given him an additional reason for wanting Priest out of the way.

The presence of the pigman reminded him all the time of his own dreadful deeds.'

'But how could he reconcile with his conscience the murder of Priest, if that had come off?' asked Carey. He was already looking a little less strained and ill, Mrs Bradley noticed with satisfaction. It was good that he was willing to have the whole matter discussed, and fully explained. And there was Jenny to comfort him, and be comforted.

'On the principle that to the average European the slaughter of coloured people is not a matter of conscience in the same way that the slaughter of whites would be. Abyssinia is a classic example, of course!'

'I say, that sounds rather terrible! You mean that just because Priest was poor, and a countryman, and uneducated –' His voice trailed off. He shook his head.

'Of course the warnings were rather obscure,' went on Mrs Bradley cheerfully, 'and, for the most part, he sent them when it was too late for them to fulfil their office, even if they could have been understood by the victims. Even after Fossder had been killed, it took me some time to find that the Cross Patée of the Knights Templars on the gateway of Temple Farm was the same as the cross on the pencilled shield, and the red paint decoration on Fossder's gate. When I did, it connected, not precisely with the ghost of Napier, but at least with the ghost's venue. You noticed the flaw in time, of course! Later than midnight at Sandford! That made me suspicious. A genuine practical joker would certainly have made it midnight, the proper time for the ghost.

'Then there was the warning of Simith's death – the boar's head in the window of Horsepath Church. It was depicted on the end of a spear, you remember. The murderer of Fossder also reminded us of the boar's head by making reference in conversation to "a little Bartholomew boar-pig". That was in this very house. Perhaps you don't remember the quotation? *Henry IV* again.'

'Yes, I remember. Of course he used to spend hours of his time in that library with very little work to do, and I suppose he read most of the books. He had a mind stocked with odds and ends of information that he had picked up simply by browsing.'

'So I imagine. Well, then came two more shields. In Simith's case I did not see those until after his death, but they were particularly interesting ones, particularly the Chief Embattled, giving, as you pointed out, the impression that the murderer's blood was up. Poor Hugh! His trouble was that he had no knowledge of human nature. When it came to the point, I think that a man of Fossder's type would have altered his will again in Jenny's favour. Simith would not, and, in fact, *could* not have exposed him as Fossder's murderer in the face of the doctor's certificate and the fact that there was no mark of violence on the body. As for Priest, I explained before that the pigman hated Simith so much that he was prepared to regard as his benefactor the man who put Simith to death.'

'That was pretty obvious to you, then, about the Chief Dancetté and the Batôn Sinister?' said Carey. 'But you couldn't have gathered from those that he intended to murder Priest. I mean, you could connect the Sandford stuff with Fossder because he had taken the bet to meet the ghost, and you could, by a bit of a stretch, see the point of the boar's head in the case of Simith, as he was a pig farmer on such a large scale. But Priest was not even a dancer. It was well known to Kingston that Scab was going to play for the Morris men, and that therefore Ditch would dance, and Priest would be the Fool.'

'I had deduced that Priest was in danger as soon as I had proved to my own satisfaction that he had helped in the murder of Simith. Instructed by me, the inspector pressed him hard for a confession, but Priest is brave and obstinate. As to the intention to murder him, the murderer gave us, boldly – he was vain, as I said before, and really thought that I was quite at sea over the other deaths – an absolutely unmistakable clue to the identity of the proposed third victim. His attack on *you* was sheer overmastering jealousy, and was unpremeditated. By the way –' She broke off and grinned at him. 'Do you remember the pig farming book that Fay and Jenny came for that time at Roman Ending when Geraint Tombley shut you into the old foundations by mistake?'

'Yes. Something cryptic or something.'

'The murderer's time-table, child. Worked out in idle sport one day, I fancy, and suddenly remembered. I thought at the time that Fay had come to get something for Geraint Tombley, but it was equally possible that it was Jenny who had come in search of something for Hugh. Then when I realised that the pig book had been borrowed from Old Farm – !'

She produced the copy of the Government publication on pig keeping.

'Lot 60. Gilt edged, not until January 193?' she read. 'That was Fossder and his money, child. "Bampton foot-up" refers, without doubt, to Simith, who was a Bampton man and had taught Linda Ditch, when first she took his fancy, the Bampton version of the words of "Constant Billy"! Next in the time-table comes the desire to go to America by air, and start a new life and so forth. The line which begins "d.v. bMGP." is a caustic reference to the fact that Hugh was aware that Tombley (referred to as Bold Baron Round Table – his name is Geraint, you see) had usurped the affections of Fay, and indicates that the murderer had no great love for either Tombley or Pratt – the small "b" in front of Pratt's initials gives us the state of Hugh's feelings towards him, I fancy!'

'And you think it was all written out in fun?'

'Oh, yes. It was the occupation of an idle hour, that's all, but the murderer thought it was dangerous, and wrote to Jenny asking her to get it.

'As I say, it was your copy, really, and Hugh did the scribbling in it here, not realising that the book belonged to you. Then when the Roman Ending copy was found near Simith's body and impounded by the police, Tombley, I expect you remember, borrowed yours. Hugh wrote to Jenny asking her to go over and get it for him, I think, but I have not asked Jenny anything about it, because it's of little importance.'

'Interesting, though,' said Carey. 'But to go back to where we left off – I still can't see how you got the definite warning that Priest would be a victim.'

'Oh, the Becket window, and the wall painting in South Newington church,' said Mrs Bradley. She smiled and stroked the sleeve of her orange jumper. 'None of the chroniclers seem to be in complete agreement as to the actual words used by King Henry II on the historic occasion of his having desired to be rid of the Archbishop of Canterbury.' She looked at Carey appraisingly. 'Of course, there was the business of my car on Christmas Eve,' she broke off, suddenly. 'I soon decided that Hugh himself had put it out of action, hoping to be relieved of George's company and to go to Iffley alone with the motor-cycle combination.'

'Lord!' said Carey.

'Pratt's coming over to Old Farm like that, on Christmas Eve, simply convinced me that Fay was somewhere in the neighbourhood, and that he suspected it,' she added. 'And when Tombley fell against the parlour door I knew I was right.'

'Gosh!' said Carey devoutly. 'But what was that about the identity of poor old Hugh's third victim?'

'Well, in one of the books in that library, the words of Henry II with reference to Becket's murder were as follows:

' "What a parcel of fools have I in my Court, that not one of them will avenge me of this one upstart Priest!" '

Also available from Vintage

GLADYS MITCHELL

Murder in the Snow

Mrs Bradley, sharp-eyed detective and celebrated psychiatrist, has decided to spend Christmas with her nephew at his beautiful house in the Cotswolds.

It isn't long before a mystery unfolds. There are strange events occurring in the nearby wood and local villagers are receiving anonymous threatening letters. Then the snow begins to fall – and a body is discovered.

Mrs Bradley is on the case, but she'll have to hatch an ingenious plan to reveal the truth and find the culprit . . .

'Take yourself back to a time in which people say "Dash it" and mixed-up telegrams land you in the wrong place at the wrong time. *Murder in the Snow* is a chocolate-box delight of a book'
The Times

VINTAGE MURDER MYSTERIES

dead good

*For all of you who find
a crime story irresistible.*

Discover the very best crime and thriller books on our
dedicated website – hand-picked by our editorial team
so you have tailored recommendations to help you
choose what to read next.

We'll introduce you to our favourite authors and the
brightest new talent. Read exclusive interviews and
specially commissioned features on everything from the
best classic crime to our top ten TV detectives, join live
webchats and speak to authors directly.

Plus our monthly book competition offers you the
chance to win the latest crime fiction, and there are
DVD box sets and digital devices to be won too.

Sign up for our newsletter at
www.deadgoodbooks.co.uk/signup

Join the conversation on:

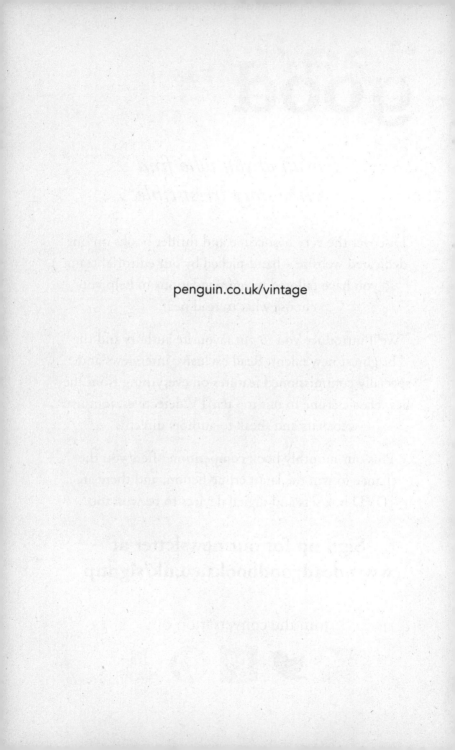

penguin.co.uk/vintage